PRAISE FOR
WHILE THE MUSIC PLAYED

"Throughout, the powers of music and Nathaniel Lande's beautifully written words provide evidence that, even in the darkest times, man's creativity shines through. *While the Music Played* is a compelling novel, with brilliant characters never to be forgotten and long remembered."

—DR. ANDREA TANNER, SENIOR FELLOW, INSTITUTE OF HISTORICAL RESEARCH, UNIVERSITY OF LONDON

"Through an epic WWII landscape following the footsteps and footfalls of young Max Mueller and David Grunewald, master storyteller Nathaniel Lande has unleashed a moving novel for a new generation of readers."

—VÁLCAV AND ZDENA FLEGL, SENIOR CORRESPONDENTS, ČESKÝ ROZHLAS, CZECH RADIO PRAGUE

WHILE THE MUSIC PLAYED

BOOKS by NATHANIEL LANDE

Cricket: A Novel

Mindstyles, Lifestyles: A Compressive Overview of Today's Life Changing Philosophies

Stages: Understanding How You Make Moral Decisions

Self-Health: The Life-long Fitness Book

The Emotional Maintenance Manual

The Moral Responsibility of the Press: A Graphic Folio

Blueprinting: Rebuilding Your Relationships and Career

The Cigar Connoisseur: An Illustrated History and Guide to the World's Finest Cigars

Dispatches from the Front: A History of the American War Correspondent

The 10 Best of Everything: An Ultimate Guide for Travelers

The Life and Times of Homer Sincere, Whose Amazing Adventures are Documented by his True and Trusted Friend Rigby Canfield: An American Novel

Spinning History: Politics and Propaganda in World War II

WHILE THE MUSIC PLAYED

A Remarkable Story of Courage and Friendship in WWII

NATHANIEL LANDE

Published in 2022 by Blackstone Publishing
Cover and book design by Sean M. Thomas

Printed in the United States of America
Originally published in hardcover by Blackstone Publishing in 2020

First paperback edition: 2020
ISBN 978-1-7999-5643-3
Fiction / Historical / World War II

Version 1

CIP data for this book is available
from the Library of Congress

Blackstone Publishing
31 Mistletoe Rd.
Ashland, OR 97520

www.BlackstonePublishing.com

They were the dreamers of dreams, the singers of songs. They were the music makers. They would not hear nor play nor love without each other. This is a prelude to their experience, an overture to who they were and how they arrived on the shores of friendship.

It is twelve o'clock. The hands on my watch have come together, the watch that is my prized possession, given to me by my father to always make sure "you keep your appointments." It is a timepiece that has gone through everything with me—the worst, the darkest times—a constant companion. It is a very personal thing, part of me, a vintage silver army wristwatch from the First World War, with slender Breguet hands, hands whose points extend out into tiny circles at their extremities. The second hand arrives at six o'clock. It's a twilight number, marking out that period between day and night, and this hand moves with delicate, musical rhythm, taking small jumps, one at a time, keeping a perfect beat. It has black Arabic numerals and the number twelve was once a deep, rich crimson, but is a slightly faded red by now.

In my pocket are strips of red felt. I have always carried them. Like the watch, these are signatures of who I was and who I am, a reminder of the perfect pitch I inherited from my father, the Great Viktor Mueller, a reminder of how things were. A reminder of the music I always heard. On my lap is a red notebook, the most recent of the many I've kept since childhood, in which I am writing these memories.

Prague 1955

The church outside Prague was full. Those who had somehow made it through everything, had survived that terrible time, that terrible place, that grotesque camp that I still visited every night in my dreams—had come to commemorate the tenth anniversary of the end of the war. I was just one of them and had come back with the rest, the few, and like them I had to face my past. One way or another, we all, those who had come through, faced it every day. But this was different, being there, going back, not knowing how much and how vividly it would return.

When it was all over in 1945 and the camps closed, only a few had survived the place where I had been. The world we had known then and before the war, all that had been taken away. There was almost nothing, almost nobody left. Most of us moved on alone, traveled alone to wherever we were going, wherever fate or choice—if we were lucky enough to have any choice left—would take us. I'm still here, and now I am back where it all started, where it all unfolded. I am here, somehow I survived. Back then, so long ago, when I was so much younger and still untainted by seeing what I would see, I used to think of strength and courage, of heroism and kindness and resilience and God or the gods, all the curious, unknowable forces, whatever and whoever they were, that save and condemn us, that shape our lives. Now I just call it luck. Nothing more. Plain, dumb, ugly, stupid luck. Destiny is a concept that means nothing to me now.

I survived because of luck and because of a community that took me in, that withstood, until—

THE BELLS TOLLED MIDNIGHT

I sat waiting for the service to begin in the ornate baroque church. I thought of how my father had once marveled at the familiar biblical scenes, fading but still there, enduring on that impossibly lofty ceiling, and a choir sounding like angels singing Giuseppe Verdi's *Messa da Requiem*. Gazing at me from behind the altar was a stunning painting created by a gifted artist I had come to know so well—Norbert Troller, who had also been at Terezín. It was a very large painting of redbrick fortress walls. At the fortress's entrance, where the gates once stood, Troller had painted a landscape of fruit trees, clouds, and mountains, inviting a notion of freedom in a quiet distance.

Stirring rhythms came from an orchestra consisting of flutes, piccolos, oboes, clarinets, horns, trumpets, trombones, strings, timpani, and bass drums. I listened to the quiet notes; the last time I had heard the *Requiem,* I was a boy. I remembered when I would lie awake at night and hear music rising through my soul, and I would feel warm and secure. I would think that no one had a better father than mine; no one could have a better, more charmed life. And I would think of myself growing up, what I might become, when I wasn't a child anymore, when I stepped into manhood, when I became somebody, some perfect fusion of my parents with the elegance of my mother and the talent of my father. That was and would continue to be such a fine time to be alive, I thought then. I would always be happy and loved, I would always hear beautiful music, immeasurable, almost touchable but always out of reach in its invisible dimensions. There was always music, the sweet dialogue between piano and strings and the deep-throated horns, before the Germans swept across the continent and occupied Prague.

The memories came unbidden, unwelcome, assaulting me as I sat there in that church, these bold visions with their vivid colors and jarring sounds. I closed my eyes and the past unfolded before me. I remembered that early morning in September with those new dissonant chords: the screaming sirens, the throttling motorcycles, rumbling and smoking tanks, the minatory clacking of footsteps, the sharp rhythm and relentless pace of unstoppable platoons invading our landscape. Prague's passing parade had a new song.

The *Requiem* sung that night was a refrain in honor of all who had died—it overpowered me and overwhelmed me, its beauty somehow wrapped in horror. I could take no more, not a moment more of the sound or thoughts and images, all those memories pressing in against me from all sides. I left my pew quietly and sought respite, refuge in the cold air outside. In the bitter chill of night, I walked down to a railway track below the stone steps, past a wreath of green and red holiday lights hanging from paneled church doors whose brass hardware seemed to be washed in pewter and was as old as the republic itself. There, as far as I could see, were rows of scintillant flickering candles, lights of hope and life, their flames bouncing around inside glasses along the tracks, just below a rising silver mist. I followed their procession, the lights leading me on, leading me back, leading to my childhood, returning to a time standing still, frozen in the past.

TEREZÍN

Through this fog that seemed to me the natural habitat of ghosts, some compulsion drew me onward, and I walked inside the gates. Beyond grass-covered slopes was the church's bell tower, housing a blue clock—long broken and itself frozen in time and never repaired. The church was supposed to be a protector of the weak, the guardian of children, a place for prayer and hope, but it was here, within these walls that I saw the worst of things; it was here where humanity paused. I wondered then as I had wondered countless times before why God had abandoned that church, that place, and so many of us through those times.

In front of the church, on the many squares, were patches of gray-green fields where children had walked and played in their strange uniforms, wearing stars on their jackets, stars over their hearts. The children played in barrack yards, went beyond the walls to work in gardens, went to improvised schools. Secretly they drew pictures and wrote poems, for a year or two, depending upon their luck, as the trains to the east continually came and went. They did what we couldn't and somehow saw past the endless lines of those arriving, leaving, of those queuing for meager rations, saw past the famine and fear, the beatings, the funeral carts and infirmaries, the summary executions. They heard it all: the tears, the screams, the shouts of SS men, the roll calls, and the faint mumblings of prayer at curfew. They witnessed it all, yet still they saw or somehow made themselves see that thing that Norbert Troller was trying to capture—that sense of hope, the beauty beyond the village gates, past the ribbons of highways—and they imagined road markers heading toward Prague, toward freedom. They acted out fairy tales and sang in an opera called *Brundibár.* Did they ever imagine death?

There were still rusty railroad tracks near the small town with tree-lined streets, tracks leading to Terezín and another to Auschwitz, where the last doors were thrown open with a breath of fresh air falling upon the bleary-eyed, tired, unwashed, stumbling, terrified human cargo. The passengers filed in single columns to the deceptive strains of a quartet playing a sweet tune. Then the musicians stopped playing when an officer selected who would go one way and who the other. Then the music started up again.

An approaching winter wind carried some of the strains of the *Requiem* from the church, and with the music came memories that seemed like a lifetime ago, of my friends. David was my best friend. And a picture of Sophie was conjured up from somewhere within, because we had first heard this mass together. I remember how Poppy, my father, used to say that friends are treasures that come our way only occasionally and we must be sure to spot them when they do. A peculiar sense of inner peace enveloped me, amazed me as it did so, along with an awareness of a time and of people, this company of heroes there beside me who, like me, clung on to some ineradicable hope bolstered by the awareness that there really were things to live for, and that someday we, or some of us, would be able to reclaim the shattered pieces of our lives and compose new beginnings for us all. That is what we hoped for, the dream that we all shared. Sophie, David, and the others, they were my friends, they were with me, they saved me. We had vowed to save one another, to make it together. They changed my life forever. This is how it was. This is how it all began.

PART I
PRAGUE

THE TOPPER

Prague 1938

"Let's face it, Max; you need to open up. I'm incredibly smart and charming, of course, but"—David snapped his fingers—"you need a girlfriend!"

I rolled my eyes. I should try to be more like David. As usual, his black hair desperately needed cutting. But he pulled it off, managing to look like a young reporter should, always breathless, always in search of the next story. Right now, the next story was my romantic life.

David laughed. "I'm all you need in terms of a friend, but have you ever thought about having an actual girlfriend?"

"I'm perfectly okay with Poppy and Hans," I said. Even as I said it, I realized I sounded stupid. I was just reaching twelve years old, racing to become fourteen, skipping over as many years as possible. But was I okay with just David and my father and his best friend as my social circle? Brilliant musicians they might be, but David was right. I should want a girlfriend. But I dreaded the sweaty palms and stammering that overcame me whenever I tried to talk to a girl.

David snapped his fingers again. "The written word, Max. That's your answer. It so often is."

David acknowledged that I was, as usual, not quite as quick as him: "Letters, my friend, letters! That's it! Boys our age have pen pals, Max. At least consider it. I may not always be around, and I can't teach you everything. Well, most things, but not everything. And she'll never know you're nervous." He paused and grinned. "As long as you're not actually shaking while you write. You'll be fine. You'll be a hit."

"Really?"

"Really."

"Promise?"

"I promise."

I sighed. I was still struggling to make sense of the world. David was always a step ahead to know things, to understand. Unlike me, David was always sure of himself. His powers of persuasion were impossible to resist. He could even convince himself of anything. I remember the first time he told me about it all on the way to school a few months earlier. We were crossing a square and he stopped me in my tracks. "Look around you, Max. What do you see?" I shrugged. He pointed from person to person. "Stories, my friend. Everyone has a story, and I am curious to know them all. Max, it's perfectly clear. I'm going to be a writer, a journalist. I'm going to tell people the truth. And you know how I know? Because I looked at myself in the mirror last night and told myself that I am going to make it, I am going to find out the truth and tell people." I shook my head and he smiled, but I guess you had to be like that if you had ambitions to be a world-famous journalist. He planned to start with becoming the most famous one in Prague, then Czechoslovakia, then the world.

Right then, I knew resistance was futile. "Fine, I'll do it. I'll write a letter to a girl. It will improve my writing at least. After all, I'm going to be your next ace reporter."

"Let's not get ahead of ourselves, Max," David said. "As editor of the school paper, it's my job to keep out the riffraff."

"*Riffraff?*" David used phrases I wasn't too sure of.

"Riffraff. Undesirables."

"Now, why would I need another friend when I have you?" I asked.

David Grunewald was my best friend. He was a *topper*, a word I made up. He was tops—in friendship, in school, in music. In persuasion. He was a musician, a writer, a footballer—a topper. He had been with me from my earliest memories, he'd helped me through the very sad days when my mother's illness was terminal, and I imagined he'd be with me always.

"So since you know everything, who will be receiving my letters?"

"Sophie, that's who. She's the daughter of a friend of my family. She lives in Austria. She's perfect for you. She's musical, she's pretty, she's a girl. Perfect. Write about things you like, what you want to know, about yourself. With every word, you'll be making a new friend."

The thing about David was that he really made you believe everything he said.

That evening I sat at the desk in my room, laid out a crisp sheet of writing paper, dipped my pen in the ink, and set out to write my first letter. I wasn't sure what to write at first. I was nervous, beginning with a rough draft, just the way all writers do, David said. Gradually I began expressing myself, even better than I thought I could.

May 14, 1938

Dear Sophie,

I'm happy that David suggested I write to you and that you like music.

Music is part of me, too, a great part of my life. I came by it naturally. My father is the conductor Viktor Mueller.

We live in an apartment in Malá Strana, the old

quarter, near the castle. Nearby there are parks where I play, and concert halls I love, and classic boulevards where I walk, usually with my father.

In Old Town, there's a telegraph building, where messages are received and sent. Sometimes I pass by, hearing the keys clattering away, hoping that I will receive a message from my mother. It's just a silly thought, I know, because she died when I was little, but somehow, I still hope. I often go to Prague Castle. It's in a beautiful place across the river, where there are a million steps. It's like a castle in a dream or a fairy story.

This is a city of red-tiled roofs and flowers, and a tram that introduces her bells as she swings around the corner. Even the trams have a musical rhythm.

But something is happening now, and I see my father and others whispering about the flags that are appearing everywhere, red flags with their black swastikas on white circles, and I wonder what it all means.

Maybe I've not written enough in my first letter to you.

I hope you'll write me.
Max Mueller

For days that turned into a week, and more, I wondered if she'd got the letter, if she'd read it—but at last, a lilac envelope appeared in my mailbox, and I just knew. I ran up to the music room, grabbed my father's silver letter opener, almost panting as I slit open the envelope. It was like a gift.

May 28, 1938

Dear Max,

Thank you for your letter. I'm pleased to learn about you, to meet you through your words. Well now, I love music too. I don't like to brag, but my great-uncle was Gustav Mahler.

You make your city sound so appealing. I would love to see Prague. Things in Vienna are not easy these days. There are a lot of new ideas in the air—ideas that seem to be dangerous to people like us. We have those same flags flying too. Mama tries to protect me, and I let her think that I see nothing, but sometimes at night I hear her weeping. She cries, asking, "Why do they hate us?"

Well, where to continue? I guess, at least my friends say, that I'm a daring and curious girl. I'm learning Hebrew, and it's not the easiest language to learn. It has a lot of symbols, and you must read backward. Someday, I hope to go to Palestine.

I've never written to anyone with so many of the secrets that I carry, and I'm not sure why I'm writing and telling you so much, Max, but there must be a reason, mustn't there?

Sometimes I go to Sacher's. The hotel has the best bakery in the world. Someday I'd like to treat you to a torte. They are arranged in perfect rows protected by a polished glass case, and they are as colorful and as beautiful as the flowers in the market. Yellow, red, pink, white, and of course, chocolate.

You wrote to me about your father and mentioned your mother. Can you tell me more about her? I will tell you about mine. Mama works every night, and when she was not here, my father was always nearby. He was a professor of history by day, and in the evening, wrote beautiful poetry. He read all kinds of poetry to me—not just Austrian poets but anything that has been translated into German. But things have changed and he's not around to read to me anymore. He was taken away by the soldiers who have invaded our country. He sold our silver settings and our paintings so Mama and I would have money to leave for a better place. He promised to join us.

Suddenly, in the middle of the night, he was taken away by men in black. They smashed up the house and just dragged him off in their car. I don't know why, except maybe because he knew too much history, and maybe because he is Jewish. It's an awful feeling when someone knocks at your door and tells you that you don't live there anymore. I hope it's a feeling that you will never know.

"Don't worry," he said to us. "I'll be all right. You and Mama must go. For my sake." Those were the last words he said to me.

Every day, I play my piano more than ever and I play for her. Music has its own language and I strive every moment to learn its meaning. I want to find the music to soothe her. I think we might be leaving Vienna soon, and I shall miss it. After all, it's a city built with music.

I'd love to see you. I hope that this may be soon.

Yours affectionately,
Sophie

I finished the letter and then read it again slowly. I was moved and a little stunned by her honesty. It struck a chord with me. I had never spoken about my mother to anyone, and it was hard to express my feelings, but I took a chance. I'd never really tried to say these things, but as soon as I began, I knew what to write without even thinking, as if my pen were moving on its own, and I started to express words and feelings that I didn't know I had. The words started to flow, they seemed to be writing themselves onto the page.

I remember one time I asked Hans, my father's best friend, how it felt to compose music, and he told me that sometimes, most times, it was hard work, but other times something seemed to take over, almost like magic, and he wouldn't even be thinking, he would be existing in some space removed from the world and afterward he would look at the sheet and the notes would be there as if they had always been there, or had been waiting to appear. That's how it felt writing to Sophie that day.

June 14, 1938

Dear Sophie,

It's strange, isn't it, but I think we get along, looking for ways to make our lives better when things are bad. I don't talk about my mother really and remember only a little about her, but I do know she was an actress. From her clippings, I can imagine why she was admired by many, and I can see why my father adored her. I remember her like a fading photograph but one that sometimes becomes sharp again just for a moment and then she goes away again. Sometimes I can't believe she ever really existed, but a lot of the time I feel as though she's still here. To me she was always a summertime lady, because she always wore a large sweeping hat with a huge bow, and underneath its brim was a smile that was brighter than any footlight onstage. But then I think she can't always have been like that—not in the snow, not in the rain. But that's how I see her. No matter whether she was onstage, at home, or by my side, my father tells me that she was as gentle as a whisper, and it is that whisper that I can still hear, can still feel sometimes, when I need it most.

My father and mother met here in Prague. He was on tour and once he met her, he never wanted to leave.

I was born soon after they married. Then she became ill. Nobody could do anything for her. I didn't know how to save her. I didn't even know how to manage, how to get through the day. But Poppy, my father, said that he would help me, and I would help him, and we'd do that every day from then on. We'd be there for each other. They met here, and Poppy said that, in many ways, Prague was her city and we both feel closer to her here. It seems she's just out of reach, just around the corner, just out of sight, looking down on us, checking that we're doing all right.

I think you'd like Poppy. He has a low, steady voice, and I can see, when he doesn't know that I am looking at him, a hint of sadness in his soft brown eyes. I know he doesn't want me to know it, to see it, so I never let on.

After my mother died, my father threw himself into his work. I think maybe he was hoping to dim her memory, to keep the sadness away, but it doesn't work. I always know he is thinking of her from the way he looks after me, the way he does everything. He lives his life with a lot of courage. I know that, and I try to be like him. And he tells me often that life's like a seesaw. Up and down, back and forth. Hurt and happiness. And I want to be on the side of happiness. Do you think we can choose which side we get to be on?

My world revolves around music almost as much as yours does. I think we need all kinds of music—from when we are born to the moment we die. After all, we all live with the rhythm of our own heartbeats, and Poppy says: "Music reminds us of the mysterious beauty that is in each of us and connects everyone to everyone else." But he reminds me so often that it's not easy, "You must work to master it, and you may never master it, but you will improve, you will learn to understand it, and to express yourself, but you must practice," and I'm getting more comfortable with the piano every day. I take lessons with Hans Krása, who also writes operas.

We will meet one day. I know this.

Yours,

Max

We exchanged letters more and more regularly, sharing our memories and experiences, in every letter revealing more about ourselves, more of our lives, and every word made a difference. I was learning about her and sharing feelings and memories I scarcely knew I had. The letters from Sophie were the things I looked forward to most in my life. In one of her letters Sophie enclosed a photograph. *I thought you'd enjoy one of me at the piano. I must follow who I am, after all.*

The snapshot brought my movie to life. She was smiling, wearing a jacket with ruffles. I looked carefully at the photograph and my heart skipped a beat. The photo was shaded in sepia. It appeared like a picture out of an old photo book, as though Sophie were stepping through time to smile at me. Her hair was a light brown, I imagined, and her eyes were blue. It didn't make any difference. It was Sophie, sitting at her favorite place in the world, at her piano, her fingers about to touch the keys. I knew that feeling, that the music was about to begin. That moment before you create the first note, when it seems that anything is possible. It is a special kind of silence, that moment before. A magical silence. Sophie knew that magic as well as I did.

I knew I wouldn't show the photo to anyone except David. I slipped it into a secret place in my pocket to have it with me always. Close to my heart. I felt it belonged there more than anywhere else.

I had to return her sentiment. I sent Sophie a picture of myself in my father's study, surrounded by his musical scores, showing I was a musician too. The local photographer who took it told me that I looked tall and handsome. I guessed he was just being polite, but *tall and handsome* was an ambition of mine. When I stared in the mirror, all I saw was that I had brown eyes and brown hair. I hoped Sophie would like how I looked. Every day I raced to the mailbox, hoping for a letter. The world seemed to be getting darker, but these letters cast light into my life, Sophie's words on the page electric and thrilling. Her words were the closest I could get to hearing her play music. And music was how I made sense of the world.

Soon I received another letter, in which she talked about a group she belonged to called Aliyah. She didn't tell me much beyond that, and when I asked my father about it that night, he just shrugged and looked puzzled. I asked her in my next letter and waited anxiously for an answer.

July 2, 1938

Dear Max,

Aliyah means that we will make a return to our homeland, Palestine, after being away for two thousand years. It's a faith that we will be restored to who we are and what we want to be, that we will fulfill the wish of every Jewish person, this never-ending dream of my people.

And after all, Max, we all dream, don't we?

People in our country don't want us here, but there's a village near Prague where we can live in the meantime. We hope to build a new community there. Since Mama is a nurse, she'll be needed.

But all of this means that we will be coming to visit Prague for the day, in a few weeks.

Love,
Sophie

My heart skipped a beat as I read these words and I wrote back at once saying I'd be pleased to come to the station and show her around my city. *She's coming my way!*

Saturday couldn't arrive fast enough.

ANNA

Oxford 1938

Anna Kingsley had the markings of privilege and success, and the virtues bestowed upon her came from the confidence gained mostly from her family and her education at Oxford's Lady Margaret Hall. Founded in 1879, it was one of the newer and more progressive colleges, a neo-Georgian, white-trimmed, redbrick building standing alone along the River Cherwell. A spot on the river's edge was a favorite hiding place, where she often picnicked. She took a first in politics, philosophy, and economics.

Fiercely independent, she grew up respecting her mother but never intending to follow her into fashionable society. If the truth be told, Anna's mother was more concerned with the way things looked than the way they were. Her grandmother, by contrast, was Danish and far less concerned with appearances. A noted novelist, Madeline Kingsley's historical romances had a loyal following of devotees. She was a fringe member of the Bloomsbury Group, a pack of nonconformists whose novels and essays were widely considered controversial in tone and thought. When these artists and poets met, often in the salon of Virginia Woolf, they discussed everything of the moment in literature and politics, with E. M. Forster and Lytton Strachey taking the lead. Occasionally, Madeline's group welcomed a guest who had started his career as a journalist and was deeply interested in history. His name was Winston Churchill. The group promoted sexual equality and sexual liberation, among other things, attempting to establish a new order liberated from established norms. Liberalism, pacifism, and socialism united them. Her husband, Sir William Kingsley, had been a respected member of Parliament, awarded a knighthood for his service to the nation.

Most English fathers looked to their sons, rather than their daughters, in a bond that carried more admiration than emotional currency. There were few outward displays of affection, but, taking in to account their wealth, whatever affection had accumulated over the years was secure in the family bank vault. Anna's father never showed any disappointment as she reached for what were uncommon goals, leading the way for young women of her generation, and his distance was never taken for a lack of love or loyalty.

At Oxford, she began attracting notice with editorials published in the *Oxford Mail* warning of the rising political tide in Europe; upon graduation, she received an enthusiastic invitation from *The Observer,* whose editor asked her to join their ranks at the European desk. Anna seized this opportunity.

She would forever recall the exchange with her father and the sacred promise she'd made to him when her first piece had appeared in the *Mail* in her second year at Oxford: "Whatever I write, it must mean something. I want, perhaps even need, to make a difference through my writing. I will do just that. I will make a difference." Her father had looked at her earnestly and said: "But what about when writing alone isn't enough?"

Her humanity was clearly evident; her interest was clearly history, as was Sandy MacPherson's, Anna's forward-looking managing editor, who enlisted writers with a voice of their own and a respect for research. Her first editorial for *The Observer* soon appeared:

June 27, 1938

THE END OF ILLUSION

Indeed, the destruction of Germany began on May 10, 1933. On that occasion, great bonfires were lit on the Opernplatz, an open square in Berlin next to the opera house where Mendelssohn had conducted. Nazi loyalty rituals scripted for the event called for high Nazi officials, professors, university rectors, and student leaders to address the participants and spectators. The Sturmabteilung (a paramilitary group under the Nazi party), wearing their familiar brown shirts, threw tons of great literature into the flames. Propaganda Minster Goebbels was on hand to address the crowd and the newsreel cameras. The burning of books, he said, was a symbolic action to "show the world that a new Germany will ascend from the flames in our own hearts." In Berlin alone, more than thirty thousand books were burned, part of a calculated effort to redefine German culture and world history. Like many propaganda events, such as those at Nuremberg, the book burnings were designed as spectacle, and, as in Nuremberg, featured torchlight parades and a show of extravagant German nationalism. The fires burned pages by great German thinkers such as Albert Einstein and Sigmund Freud to ash. Books by Thomas Mann were also thrown into the flames, and to add a bit more literary fuel, so were works of American novelists Jack

London, Ernest Hemingway, Theodore Dreiser, John Dos Passos, and the Nobel prize–winning Sinclair Lewis. Writings of German philosopher and political theorist Karl Marx and Marxist revolutionary Vladimir Lenin were tossed and torched, and most egregiously, the works of Helen Keller, born deaf and blind, who had triumphed over hardship and documented her inspiring story. "Tyranny cannot defeat the power of ideas," Heinrich Heine, the great German poet, wrote a century before. "Where one burns books, one will, in the end, burn people."

Germany appears a country in a film running backward, with two ideologies, both profane, both about political doctrine and performance. One is the war against liberal democracies and communism; the other, at its core, is ruthless and brutal. It is a war against European Jewry, blatantly clear since Hitler's manifesto, *Mein Kampf.* In it, the leader of the Nazi party advocates for lebensraum ("living space") and purification. He wrote, "I believe I am acting in the spirit of the Almighty. By warding off the Jews, I am doing God's work."

All through Eastern Europe, police and troops are herding Jews into newly designated ghettos where they wait for a solution not yet clear. The Nazis have a problem: What are they going to do with so many decorated Jewish veterans of the First World War—the wounded, the honored? How will they treat the children? How will the vaunted German army treat its citizens who fought valiantly for their Fatherland? And the writers, composers, conductors, scientists, philosophers, actors, directors, respected throughout the world? How will Hitler avoid international embarrassment and moral outrage?

Now comes Anschluss. That's what the Germans call it. What does it mean? It means inexorable expansion. It means the fate of Austrian Jews is in peril. Jewish people across the continent are doomed to places where they are not wanted; for them the world is divided into places where they cannot live and countries they cannot enter. In March the Germans annexed Austria. Its 190,000 Jews came under the control of the Nazis. They are being humiliated and deprived of their citizenship and subjected to the infamous Nuremberg laws. A favorite new sport in Vienna is residents looking on and cheering as Jewish women are forced to scrub sidewalks on their knees and in their lingerie. Isolation and persecution continue with the same torrent of anti-Semitism unleashed in Germany over the last five years. Their property and homes confiscated, those who cannot leave are isolated and rounded up for slave labor and sent to a holding camp called Mauthausen, a small village in upper Austria. It is the end of illusion. The Germans are looking to expand their systematic march of tyranny into Czechoslovakia.

THE CZECH ALL STARS

Prague 1938

Aside from my father, my friends, and Hans, I had three great passions in life. I had music, I had football, and I had my job. I loved each one, and somehow, they defined me. David was my best pal on and off the field, and we'd been friends ever since I'd gotten sick with polio. I was housebound for more than a year, but nearly every day, David was at the door of my house, with a book or a newspaper article to read me, or a chocolate, and true to his endlessly positive personality, he breezily assured me I would get better. I finally did but was left with a limp. I hated the looks I got from strangers. David just ignored all of it and treated me no differently than he had before I got sick. It was a real handicap in its way, though. My right leg was a little shorter than the left, and I wore a special shoe to make up the difference. I did my best to walk straight—I didn't want a limp—and that special shoe was part of me, the thing that made me instantly recognizable on the streets of Prague.

In the real world, I didn't walk so well, but I had my imagination, and in my dreams, I danced and danced . . . I had seen an American movie with Fred Astaire and Ginger Rogers, and they seemed to float. All I had to do was close my eyes and the limp was gone. "Take it, kid," Fred shouted and, defying my disability, I did a turn or two while the orchestra played. Even in my dreams there was a musical score to my life.

When I got back to school, some of my classmates made fun of me, always the same ringleaders with others behind them laughing. David would always be there, and he took me aside one day and whispered: "Remember, Max, they're just looking for a victim, someone to make them feel better. But you're better than this and you're better than them. They don't do it because they're stronger than you but because they're weaker." Those words stuck and became a prayer to me, and I tried to ignore the teasing and the taunts, but there were days that I practically longed to be sick again, so I wouldn't have to go to school. David changed that. David was a star and he told me, "Okay, let's show them something." He was already in charge of the school paper, and he was the smartest, fastest-talking student in the place. But he was also an athlete. The Czech All Stars was David's team, and he invited me to join. The "Topper" could control the ball with as much skill as he had when crafting words. The coach said he was poetry on the field, a perfect description. We developed a strategy. With daring footwork, a couple of shimmies, and a frenzied dash down the field, David would cross the ball to me. I wore a brace with a special boot which gave my right leg greater weight, allowing me to kick the ball with astonishing power. It was our secret weapon. Time and again, with that one unexpected kick, I would score. We beat the team known as the German League, who were bigger and stronger, wearing armbands with *HJ* written on them. That *HJ* would haunt me later. It was a symbol of who they were, of what they would become, though we didn't know it at the time. All I knew was that it was special to beat these kids who looked down on me and couldn't bear to lose to some handicapped Czech. Scoring a goal with an assist from David created a special bond between us. With David's help, I could do just about anything.

And when I needed a little boost, I would reread one of Sophie's letters, picturing her sitting down at her desk by candlelight, smiling or deeply thoughtful, thinking about what to write, thinking about me. So often I held that photograph and tried to imagine her actually playing the piano at which she was sitting, to imagine how she would move, how she would talk. Soon I would no longer have to rely on my imagination.

SOPHIE COMES TO PRAGUE

"I'll be part of your welcoming committee," David announced.

When we arrived at Praha *hlavní nádraží*, Prague's spectacular Art Nouveau train station, David bought the largest bunch of flowers I had ever seen. This wasn't helping me to deal with the strange, stirring, churning feeling inside, or the marked difficulty I was experiencing in regulating my breathing.

"Give them to Sophie," he said.

"I'll look silly with all of them. I'll look like a walking florist."

"It's a custom, Max. Always present a bunch of flowers."

"Some bunch."

I nervously tapped one foot, and then the other.

We heard a train chugging into the station.

My foot-tapping continued. I began humming Mozart.

"Are you nervous?"

I couldn't even look sideways at David. "Of course not."

"You are."

"I'm not," I said, still tapping my foot.

"You a tap dancer? You seem a little jittery to me. Got the butterflies?"

"You're here to introduce us, but you are not helping so far. Please don't make me nervous."

David grinned. "You mean more nervous than you already are? Will you remember her name?"

A sleek overnight train stopped in front of us with bursts of billowing steam. A porter jumped to the platform, followed by a few well-dressed passengers. I saw a girl who could only be Sophie. The first thing I noticed were her eyes. They were sky-blue. I must have said it out loud, because David whispered in my ear: "Cerulean." Of course, I didn't know the word, so I just nodded in agreement. Her hair was straw-blond, and she seemed to glow. I stepped forward, concentrating hard on walking straight. I handed over the bouquet. Sophie accepted them with a dazzling smile.

"I'm Max. Um, obviously. I'm Max." David appeared at my elbow, a trouble-making genie.

"He's Max," he said helpfully. I glared at him. "She's Sophie," he said, his eyes dancing. "My work is done."

Sophie had come all the way to Prague from her home near Vienna to spend the day with me, and I couldn't get a word out other than "I'm Max." I was searching for something to say, but nothing else was coming. Sophie didn't seem to care and was beaming. She stood beside her mother, Edith, who was dressed in a padded blue coat and a beaver collar with a parade of brown buttons. I noticed how her coat hung from her sagging shoulders, and how pale her face was. She had put on some makeup, and even through fractured powder, I could see the lines of worry crisscrossing her face. But I also saw a lady whose loveliness explained why Sophie was so pretty.

David nudged me in my side. I cleared my throat to try to speak, but Sophie stopped me by flinging herself into my arms.

I was self-conscious about my brace, but it didn't seem to make any difference to her.

"Oh, Max! It is really you. You're as handsome as your photo!"

I hugged Sophie back, and for a moment, everything disappeared. The train, the station, David, Edith—everything. Who needed words?

"Hello, Max," said Edith, breaking into a smile almost as perfect as her daughter's as she set down her luggage. "What a gentleman you are to meet us."

"Thank you . . . of course," I stuttered, picking up the bags. I hoped Sophie realized from all the letters I had written her that I could use words. Based on these few moments, she would think I was practically mute.

Sophie laughed and gave me a little pat on the shoulder. "Come on, Max, don't be shy. It's just me."

With complete confidence, she hooked her arm through mine and we set off down the platform. Her long flowing hair bounced in rhythm with her every step. In a periwinkle cotton dress that brought out her eyes, she wore matching blue socks, and polished black Mary Janes. I could smell the fresh scent of her hair. Sophie was springtime.

Out front, David hailed a taxi and helped us into the backseat.

"Have a great afternoon," David trilled with a mischievous grin as he closed the door to the taxi. I was going to have to fend for myself without any more of whatever help David could offer. I began silently practicing my next lines to say, wanting to sound smooth and comfortable. The flowers had been embarrassing enough.

"So, Sophie, what brings you to Prague?"

Well, that didn't come out as planned, I thought.

"Well, as I said in my letters, we're relocating to a glorious place called Terezín. I wrote you about it. Don't you remember? You do read my letters, yes?"

"I . . . um . . . I mean . . ."

It wasn't going well. I wanted to tell her I'd read every one until I could recite them to myself at night. I wanted to tell her that I kept her picture with me always, that I had dreamed of this moment, that I had so often conjured up her face and her words to make good times better still but also to help me through some bad times at school; I felt that I had known her forever. But now I couldn't speak because she was even prettier in person, and my heart was beating so fast I was sure that she could hear it pounding away in my chest.

"I'm kidding. I know you read them." Her smile settled my nerves and slowed down my racing heart and mind.

I looked from Sophie to Edith as the cab wove its way through the city streets. "I thought you would like to rest awhile with a visit to Hans's."

She turned to Edith. "Mother, I know you'll just love Hans. Max tells me he's a musical genius!"

Edith quietly nodded and returned her gaze to the window. We drove past parks and through squares and in fifteen minutes reached Hans's place. He lived near us in what Poppy called a "French provincial house," and, judging by the movies I had seen, I always felt it was a film set.

SOPHIE IN PRAGUE

I knocked, and Hans threw open the door with his arms outstretched in a theatrical gesture, which served as a kind of counterpoint to his soft-spoken patrician ease. Hans's gestures were often grand, yet as gentle as a Chopin prelude, sweet and symmetrical, punctuating his conversations with a lot of hand waving—the better to show off his long dexterous fingers, Poppy said. He had true pianist's hands, strong and nimble. He also had the look of a movie star, someone who could happily exchange quips with other movie stars in a nightclub or in an elegant Parisian restaurant, and I always saw him either dressed in tweeds or with his favorite paisley silk bathrobe draped over him. The gown had two large square pockets, envelopes to warm his hands. It was the bathrobe today.

"Max!" Hans said, beaming. "And who are these delightful people you've brought with you?"

Sophie gave a small curtsy, which Hans appreciated, and he answered it with an elegant bow. His drawing room was filled with peonies in vases and leather-bound books lining the walls. I loved to sit on the white linen sofa near the carved-stone fireplace. I sank into its voluminous, plump cushions, and Sophie carefully took a seat beside me. She sat looking straight ahead, a bit primly.

Edith admired the paperweights Hans kept on his mantel. I had often wondered about them. They were exquisite clear crystal and together they appeared as if they were precious jewels, each reflecting light, each telling a story.

"My mother collected them. They were made by Clichy and Baccarat in France," Hans said, "and they are among the most famous glassmakers in the world."

Edith held up a particularly beautiful piece to the light.

"From the turn of the century," Hans explained. "I buy one whenever I can find them. They're rare these days."

"Stunning," Edith said, rubbing the smooth crystal with her hand.

"That one was made just outside Paris in 1830."

I spotted a small house with falling snow inside a faceted miniature universe.

"I bet you'll be living in a place like that," I said to Sophie, giving her a nudge.

"That would be nice." Sophie gazed at the crystal in her mother's hand.

Lucie, Hans's cook, politely entered the room with tea and cakes.

"Thank you, Lucie," said Hans. She had been with Hans for as long as I had been alive and had always made me feel as though this was my second home. She set the tray down on a side table, winked at me, and then gave a polite, not altogether customary nod, and left the room. I had never known Lucie to be so formal. Sophie had that effect on people. I'd certainly been stunned into silence . . . again.

Edith cleared her throat. "Mr. Krása, I'm sure you're curious as to why we've come."

I was. I still couldn't imagine leaving my home without a good reason. What could it be? I suppose Poppy and I could have left after my mother died. Losing her was a reason to leave, people said, but for me, it was also a reason to stay. I could remember her here in Prague. I was afraid that if we moved to another city, we would be leaving her in some way. Perhaps I would forget her. As much as it hurt to think of her, not to think of her, no longer to be able to bring her to mind, would be worse, and leaving Prague, our city, her city, would be unbearable. Would it not be the same for Sophie and Edith?

Edith held Hans's eyes for a while and then glanced briefly out of the window. "It was no longer safe after my family opposed the reunification of Austria with Germany, the Anschluss."

Anschluss? What was that? I was embarrassed not knowing. It was exactly the kind of thing David would know. It was all so strange, so confusing. Just as it seemed my life was getting lighter with my friendship with Sophie, it was also getting darker and less understandable with everything else that was happening all around, all these flags and these changes, these things like Anschluss. Well, I was growing up; I had to learn more. Apart from anything else, I had a reporter's curiosity.

"When the Germans marched in, they made our country their own. We've been looking for a country where we'll be safe until we can be reunited with my husband. He was detained and taken away."

My mother and Sophie's father—we had already agreed that this was another connection between us, another sign that our friendship was meant to be. I stole a look at Sophie. She had gone very pale and was gripping her hands together in her lap. I used to think that with my mother gone the worst had already happened, that it couldn't get more terrible. But the creeping sense that I was wrong about this became suddenly obvious, and in that moment I felt so strongly that what seemed solid and permanent might be anything but, that things could always change, and that anything that you had—that you owned, that you knew and loved—was just another thing that could be taken away.

"Do you know where he is?" Hans asked.

Edith shook her head and lowered her voice. "We have not heard a word." She looked over at Sophie. "I don't want to spoil such a nice day, but you must understand already that Jews aren't welcome in Austria today." She straightened her shoulders and smiled at Sophie. "Now, let us talk about other things . . . happier things."

Hans and Edith began discussing people they might both know, the way adults automatically do when they meet for the first time. They would clearly be happy to spend the afternoon talking, but there was no need for us to suffer through hours of boring adult conversation.

"Would you like to go into town? I could show you around Prague." I made every effort to sound grown-up and in charge. Sophie smiled and nodded and looked over to her mother, who nodded in agreement. Off we went.

I had imagined this day so many times, waiting for Sophie to visit my city. I led her down various small streets as she seemed to float above the cobblestones with a musical rhythm to her gait—a tilt of the head, a flow of arms, an easy step, crossing one of the big boulevards, gracefully dodging clanging tram cars. I felt more secure and wanted her to be confident that I knew my way, that I belonged here. I was showing off my city. "Don't worry, we're almost there," I said with a grin. "I'm taking you to Vodičkova Street for *karamelový pohár*!"

Sophie's eyes lit up. "Is it a cake?"

"Caramel ice cream."

"I've never had that kind of ice cream!"

She clapped her hands together and ran in front of me, into

the big square. A puppeteer was playing a scene of kids being chased by a wolf. We stopped, and Sophie watched the show intensely, as I watched her. I was transfixed by the blueness of those eyes that seemed always to be sparkling, expressing some inner warmth. The puppeteer was one of the city's best. I'd watched him many times while out with Poppy, who admired his work as much as I did, recognizing a kindred spirit, someone who could create a world with almost nothing, could hold an audience enraptured. The shows were both enthralling and frightening, and the latest feature was a frightful, fanged wolf and terrified child-puppets fleeing its sharp cotton teeth. Sophie looked thrilled and now a little scared and reached for my hand. I wrapped my fingers around hers, feeling protective.

"They almost seem real," she whispered to me. "They remind me of the men who came that night . . ." Sophie's face had gone white and her hand cold. I changed my plan as soon as Sophie finished her ice cream.

"Time for a trolley tour. I'll be your conductor and whisk you away!" I bowed as deeply as I could, thinking about how Hans would do it onstage.

"I knew this day would be a wonderful adventure!"

Score one for Max Mueller! The anxiety I had experienced at Hans's seemed to have magically melted away, and I felt my happiness bubbling up inside me. I wanted to remember the feeling forever. I wished right then that happiness was something you could box up with a string and open whenever you needed it. That's what I would do. I would never forget this moment, capture it like a photograph and recall it whenever I needed to be reminded of how things could be, how full my heart could feel.

The next trolley came along and we took a seat near the front. All the windows were open; a conductor stood on a platform at the rear. "Ladies and gentlemen," I announced, pointing to a castle, "that's where young Max and the Great Viktor Mueller live." It wasn't our home at all, but I pretended it was. "They say a princess lives there too. She's unimaginably beautiful and kind and is loved by everybody."

I felt as if I was like my father, a natural showman. Sophie grinned, along with a few other passengers.

"Do you think I could be the princess, Max?" Sophie asked. "I thought this would only be an afternoon visit." She squeezed my hand.

"Maybe," I said grandly. *You seem like a princess to me.*

The trolley came to an abrupt stop in front of the park. "Let's go for a walk. It's one of my favorite parks in the city."

"I wasn't expecting a girlfriend," I said, feeling more confident. "I've never had one before."

"When did I become your girlfriend?"

She ran her hands along a gate as I paused, thinking that I'd said something wrong.

"If you like," she said, "I'm happy to be just that."

She hesitated awhile, tapping her finger along the top of a wrought iron fence. "There's something special about having a boyfriend . . . or girlfriend," she said. "It's an invisible connection between two people. It's like climbing the castle steps together. Does that make sense? We shouldn't be afraid, because, well, we'll be connected to each other even when we're far away."

I hadn't thought this way before, imagined the existence of such words, or rather such feelings that couldn't quite be expressed, and Sophie had a different way about her, a way of making me understand something new. Already the world seemed a different place, more fragile but also full of possibilities. She was more than just a lovely girl. She was, I decided right there, on that spot in Prague, on that day, the most special person I had ever met, and I was—just as Hans said about music, about what it could do to you—I was taken to another place by the way she spoke. I wanted to write down her every word, to commit them to memory, carry them with me beside that photograph always next to my heart, so maybe her words would become mine. That memory box I had just created was already starting to fill up. I knew that Sophie could help me to understand the world, to feel happy, and maybe I could help her as well.

Because of my brace, I tired easily, and this walk was starting to take its toll. Sophie took my arm.

"I'm with you, Max. I'm right next to you."

My cheeks flushed. My classmates would tease me about having a girlfriend.

"It's our secret. Just ours, and only for us to know."

"When I saw your snapshot, I thought you were handsome. But you're bold too."

"Am I like you imagined?"

"I shouldn't tell you these things, but you are," Sophie replied, swirling around, her dress fluttering. "Yes, Max, I like you very much. There, I said it."

I had never been quite as happy as I was in that moment.

I was floating on air, eyes closed, arms outstretched. I felt like dancing.

"What are you doing?" Sophie asked, as she sat down in the shade on top of a stone wall.

I didn't have an answer. I sat beside her and held her hand. It felt as if it had always belonged there, and I inched closer to her. An elderly couple passing by smiled at us and jolted me back into reality.

Sophie, ignoring them, whispered, "When you least expect it, something happens."

It was a profound message, I thought. *Profound* was a word that David had just taught me, and it perfectly captured what Sophie had just said, like words from my own teletype machine. Sophie *was* the message. She had just arrived, and I didn't want her to leave. Ever.

"I can speak to Poppy," I said. "You can stay with us."

"In the castle on the hill?"

"Well, almost."

"Is Poppy your father?" she asked, leaning toward me as she spoke, smoothing her skirt.

"Yes! The Great Viktor Mueller." I waved an imaginary ivory baton.

"The same man in the castle? You call your father 'the Great Viktor Mueller'?"

"Of course. I call him great, because, well that's what he is. He's great, for sure! There's no one like him. You will meet him, and you'll love him too."

"I'd fancy that," said Sophie, and hopped off the wall. "Onward, Max! We have your city to explore and so little time to do it."

We passed the concert hall, where I had spent so many hours watching Poppy rehearse, and it felt very personal to me.

Sophie admired the building. "Just think how many memories are there, Max. I wish there was a concert right now, and if there were, I'd sit with you and Poppy in your box, and the lights would dim, and we wouldn't have to say much, but just listen, Max. We could listen together, because it's music that we both love—it's music that holds us all together. The ancient Greek philosophers used to believe that, that music held everything together, and I think they were right. We'll have to do that someday, Max, you and I."

"I think we can do that now," I found myself saying with a confidence that I never knew I had.

The National Theater had a stone foundation, beautiful, slender columns, and a stunning, slated roof absorbing the warmth of the sun, and was bordered by towering trees that seemed to accept the building as part of nature, as a natural landmark.

Outside, a poster read, "TONIGHT, JOHANN STRAUSS, CONDUCTED BY VIKTOR MUELLER." There was a photograph of Poppy holding his baton.

"Yes, that's Poppy," I exclaimed proudly.

"Will we find him inside?" Sophie ran her fingers up a balustrade leading to an entrance hall.

"We best go around back," I said, leading her to the stage entrance.

As we entered, a porter greeted us. "Hello, Max. You here to tune?"

"Just to listen," I replied.

"Maestro hasn't arrived, but the orchestra is warming up. You can take your friend to your usual seats."

I felt important and bursting with pride, and soon we climbed the marble staircase to Poppy's box. We took our places in the blue velvet seats and stared down at the players who would take us on a glorious musical journey.

"This must be your palace, Max."

"It's my home."

"And what a lovely home!"

We could see the musicians onstage warming up their instruments, starting and stopping and starting again to find and recapture a secure shared theme and then launch, as if by magic, into *Wiener Blut.*

We sat in the dark, huddled together, Sophie and I, and she whispered, "Isn't it wonderful, Max."

"Yes, I think that's just what it is, Sophie."

"We're musicians, Max, we hear and play every note."

"I have a secret to tell you, Sophie. I can tell the lady is just slightly out of tune."

"The lady?"

"The piano."

"I didn't hear it." Sophie leaned closer to the stage. "You're right, it's just a shade off. How did you know that?"

"I'm a piano tuner."

"You're not!"

"I am, Sophie. I've always had perfect pitch. Poppy is amazed. But it's a gift that has always come naturally. I can hear an out-of-tune note a mile away. I carry these red felt ribbons with me, and they're my tools. When I'm called upon, I slip them between the keys, and they help me register an accurate note and I apply my trusty tuning hammer. I carry that around with me too."

"I'm amazed. You mean you really tune pianos?"

"Of course. I do all the best ones in Prague. And I'll have to attend to the lady onstage before the next performance."

"Your piano is a she?"

"Yes. A gentle, beautiful lady always residing in my father's house."

This was indeed my father's house, and it seemed as if the orchestra was playing for us, and for us alone.

I noticed tears in Sophie's eyes.

"Why are you crying, Sophie?"

"Because it's so beautiful. I heard this waltz in Vienna, this simple, lovely melody. It was played by a street musician in a colorful costume with wild, multicolored ruffles. He had red cheeks and a top hat and an accordion. On the street there were German soldiers, smashing windows, beating people, and I hid in a doorway, just listening to the music, not wanting to see what was happening around me, to my city. A few people stopped for a while and then carried on along their way, doing whatever they were doing, heading off to wherever they were going, and the man just kept on playing. But it was the strangest thing, he simply wouldn't stop, even though some of the German soldiers tried to push him away. But his music prevailed and in time seemed to soften them a little and I saw a tear in his eye. And I wept, too, because I felt the same—a mixture of terrible sadness but also some kind of happiness that this was possible, that this could happen, the music could carry on through all of this. This happiness and sadness, they seemed to be companions, even friends. Max, with words and music, we can make a difference. I believed that then and I believe it now."

Sophie took my breath away. Again, I was stunned into silence. I felt happy, but I could also feel that it was a fragile thing, this happiness, a fleeting moment. I had a strange knowledge of something just then, like a shadow behind me, just out of sight, and I thought of all the parties and the wonderful meals and the walks with Poppy and the talks with him and Hans and the games of football with David and the concerts and everything that seemed beautiful and everlasting, and I knew that the feeling I had right then with Sophie, a feeling of happiness and safety and the sense of belonging and all the good memories, along with the moment that contained it, would pass and I wondered what else would pass along with it. And what would come next?

Outside, the afternoon was edging toward evening. We walked to Old Town and visited a shop called Madam Belinka, where Sophie admired a straw hat with a long, colored ribbon.

"It was made for you," I said, and I bought it, along with a pair of white gloves, with the crowns I earned from my job. They belonged together.

As much as I hated to end the day, we finally headed back to meet Hans and Edith, just as the sun was setting upon my beautiful city. My mother's city and today ours as well.

When we left for the station, Hans gave Edith a crystal paperweight, hoping she would feel better.

"I can't accept anything so dear," Edith protested.

Hans smiled. "Please think of it as a housewarming present for your new home."

He only gave away things that he liked himself.

Shortly later, Hans helped us load the luggage into a taxi and we headed back to the station. As Sophie and Edith took in their last glimpses of Prague, I turned to Sophie and whispered, "If you ever need anything, just let me know."

"I will, Max, I will. And you do the same." Her sky-blue eyes were brimming with tears, like soft rain falling on a sunny day. "We must keep writing. I'm afraid you're stuck with me now."

She leaned over and kissed me on the cheek. It took all the effort I could muster not to blush.

Inside the station, she gave me a handful of hard candies.

"Something special from home," she said. "I've been saving them for you. Something to remember me by."

I hadn't expected anything from her. "Sophie, I . . ."

"Goodbye, Max. And thank you," she said, reaching out and touching my hand as we walked down the platform. Why was she going?

I gave her one of my red-felt tuning ribbons. "Hold it dear. I'll collect it someday."

She took it and put it next to her cheek and boarded the train with her mother.

"Don't leave," I whispered, my words chugging in perfect cadence with the train. *Please don't leave, please don't leave, please don't leave.* And she was gone.

That night, Sophie was the only thing on my mind. I reread all her letters. With her beautiful face and musical voice attached to the words, it was like reading them for the first time. In my dreams, I took her to places that Poppy had told me about. We could waltz in a ballroom with an orchestra playing. We would run over a beach by the seaside, the endless white sand trailing behind us. We would hear Beethoven together at the concert hall. I was lost, lost forever somewhere beyond my thoughts.

I had discovered that loving someone is like falling down a flight of stairs—each step tumbled into another feeling, head-first and upside down, until I was almost dizzy, and when I hit bottom, I knew that each dizzying step was taking me where I wanted to go. I didn't ever need to make my way back upstairs again.

Staring at the ceiling, I planned our perfect trip until I finally drifted toward sleep and, closing my eyes, I had a final glimpse of footprints in the sand before a wave swept over them.

Sophie and I belonged together.

THE GREAT VIKTOR MUELLER

There's a saying in Prague that every other Czech must be a musician, and my father, though German, was no different. As the conductor of the Czech Philharmonic, he loved to perform. Everything he did, from how he spoke to how he carried himself, revealed that he longed to be an actor. He was a natural master of disguise, slipping easily from character to character, a talent that amused everyone around him. He would be a bent-over old man one moment, a flamboyant magician the next. David, Hans, and I would laugh until we cried, watching him play so many roles. He always seemed more alive in those moments; the loss of my mother less sharp, his delight in the moment more vibrant.

From my seat on our sofa, I imagined him as a real wizard, someone who could levitate ten feet off the floor and always land gracefully on his feet. He also could do just about anything. He was my Poppy, but even I occasionally called him the Great Viktor Mueller, even in his presence. He was like seltzer water, bubbling over, refreshing, larger than life. He could speak in rhyme, sing in colors, and see unlimited possibility in the world around him. He was a traveler carrying endless surprises in his bag of tricks.

The Great Viktor Muller always had a distinct sparkle to

him. He took great pride in his heritage, in his adopted city, Prague, as well as in Berlin, the city of his birth. Berlin was a city of poetry and music, he told me over and over. A fine violinist and an inspired conductor, he applied his talents not only to music but to drama. His productions of famous operas were the talk of Berlin and Prague.

He and his best friend, Hans, were sitting in the much-loved Municipal House café one afternoon, when he saw my mother for the first time. He swore to himself then and there, *If I am ever properly introduced to this woman, I promise I'll never look back*. They met that day and he kept his word.

Like all great performers, Poppy was a fantastic teller of tales. One of my favorites was his story of "The Distant and Mysterious Man." It began as a bedtime story, but as the years passed it would be part of our walks and mealtimes, and sometimes when I was younger and taking a bath, Poppy would sit on the side of the tub and tell an amazing tale over the gurgling water and soap bubbles. I eagerly awaited each new installment.

The Distant and Mysterious Man was named Armand Duval, and he lived near the Arctic Circle, just beyond the Hungarian border. Gypsy music played there, under a red-and-blue sky called the Northern Lights. Armand was magical, and had long conversations with his faithful companion, White Dog. Their mission was to collect emeralds and give them to the poor. The emeralds they recovered were stashed in a concealed vault in the Russian sea. The two of them traveled on a steamer ship called *Propensity of the Seas,* and it moved silently, always clouded in fog. And White Dog would always save Armand from the most dangerous situations.

On assignments to find emeralds, Armand was forever trying to outwit his archnemeses, the du Quetman Gang. Time and again, they would kidnap him and leave him to die, but each time, White Dog would rescue him, and the adventure would begin again. Armand always kept an emerald in his pocket for good luck. He loved to read and listen to music, and his favorite food was strudel.

Poppy, I decided, must think emeralds are good luck. He carried one, just a small one, loose in his pocket. But what was luck anyway? Was Armand lucky? He wasn't lucky to get kidnapped so often but was certainly lucky to have White Dog. Was luck something that just happened by chance, or was it a real force, perhaps something that could happen in the shape of a person? I wondered if Sophie was that person, that piece of luck. Listening to the tales of the Distant and Mysterious Man, I realized that the most frightening thing about luck was that you could lose it in an instant.

There were other treasured times, especially when we stepped out of distant fantasy and hiked over hills to admire views of the city and sat on the banks of the Moldau, watching sailboats skim the water and dangling our feet in the cool river until evening, when huge quicksilver patterns mysteriously danced.

Looking at them swirl, Poppy said, "They're telling stories to each other."

"What kind of stories?" I asked.

"Probably about everything they feel. Sometimes calm, then a storm comes along, stirs things up, but most of the time, slow and easy."

"Is that their story?

"Everything has a story."

I looked out to the boats with multicolored sails. "They're pretty, don't you think?" I wondered if they were sailing somewhere or nowhere.

"They're always sailing to the land of somewhere," Poppy said. He could read my mind. "To Camelot or Serendipity."

Serendipity. Where three princes sailed to a land of surprise. So often we fell deeply into pretending.

On Sundays, Poppy and I explored the concert halls and parks near our home. Although we rarely talked about my mother on these days, I knew that we were both thinking about her, and I often imagined that she was there somehow, an invisible but powerful presence between us, keeping us moving and holding us together.

They had met at a French bistro in Municipal House, where formally dressed waiters had ready smiles. Overhead, a spectacular art nouveau ceiling was decorated with Alphonse Mucha's murals. Paintings of slender art deco ladies were everywhere in sight.

I wondered if my mother was among them. The elegant landmark had been a gathering place for artists and writers, the glamorous, since its opening in 1912. It would not have existed without the concert halls upstairs, where my father conducted so often to such acclaim. Over glasses of frothy hot chocolate, my father and I enjoyed every moment together, and that mattered.

We walked everywhere. Poppy would just wave his hand at me when I started to lag. I knew all the walking was to strengthen my legs, and I didn't want to disappoint him. One day we walked twenty-five minutes to Wenceslas Square, along a wide boulevard, to the theater where Mozart first conducted his opera *Don Giovanni.* We stopped for a moment at a statue of Mozart, and Poppy stood next to it and began to sing.

"Attention, everyone, the Great Viktor Mueller!" I announced to the crowd rushing past. With his cane, his straw hat, and his ruffled shirt, Poppy looked like someone special, even if you didn't know who he was.

"*Tra-la-la-la-la!*" Poppy continued, his voice growing louder with every note.

Soon, people gathered to listen. Poppy sang something about love, and I figured I myself could practice in front of a mirror and sing to Sophie one day. As the crowd applauded, I thought about how Poppy was able to master whatever he wanted—music, storytelling, performing. He always told me that I too could do anything. "Max, see the opportunities and grasp them. The world is a place of endless possibilities." And I believed him.

Watching him and listening to him made me feel as though there were no limits to what a person could be and do. That was Poppy's special gift to me. That the world could be mine. It wasn't that different from what David always told me, I realized. Between the two of them, you could believe in anything. Even yourself. Believe in who you can be. One day, after finishing a particularly dramatic installment of "The Distant and Mysterious Man," he turned to me and said, "Dear Max, imagine what the world could be at its best and then help make it that way. Think of the world as a Steinway that needs tuning. Do what you can."

The vintage watch my father gave me tells me that without question, a minute becomes an hour, an hour becomes a day. In that calculus, a day became a year and for all time, I had appointments to keep. When he'd handed me the watch all those years ago, Poppy had said: "Time is the most precious thing we have, Max, perhaps the only thing. Use it wisely." He breathed in, puffing his chest. "Be magnificent!"

Poppy surely believed in himself. And at times like these, all sadness left his eyes, and he was happy. I was beginning to believe more in myself. I had Poppy and David at my side, and the only person missing was Sophie, but she was always near my heart.

HANS KRÁSA SCORES A TUNE

"Call me Hans," he said when I was old enough to say "Professor."

Like my father, Hans's family was originally from Germany. Unlike my father, he was Jewish. Many of the people we knew and loved were Jewish. My father told me that for countless years, European Jews had made extraordinary contributions to all our lives, especially in the arts and in science. "They are part of our lives, Max, and part of you."

I learned from David that for most their history Jews had been expelled from country after country, in the name of religion, from the Book of Exodus through the Crusades right up to now. From time to time, they had found temporary refuge in countries like Spain and France, but eventually they were always forced to leave. David told me that was why a homeland had always been so important for his own family and so many others, to return to their God-given land of Judea. It was somehow a big part of their tradition, as Sophie had written.

"What's it like to be Jewish?" I asked Hans one day. I had no idea what it was like, but I assumed it included being well-educated, reading lots of books, listening to a lot of music.

He paused for a few seconds and then with an ambiguous smile said, "It feels pretty good."

Sometimes Hans isn't very helpful.

Hans was a wonderful teacher, regardless of how vague he could sometimes be. The piano seemed a good way to get kids to like me. If I could play everyone's favorites, then I could win them over. Sophie would like that too.

After a lesson one afternoon, I asked, "Where do songs come from?"

"From an invisible sun," Hans replied, not missing a beat. I liked that answer, even if I wasn't sure that I really understood it then, but it came to make more sense all the time. Because I knew that Hans almost lived for music, that he couldn't live without it, that it was his way of making sense of the world, of telling the world who he was and what the world itself really was. I could never be sure whether Hans would lose himself in composition or find himself there, but creating music was always a playful and very serious time for him.

When Hans composed music, the musical notes looked like children playing together on the page. Sharps, flats, treble, bass—patterns of sound dancing in black and white across the score. Like Hans, I could hear the music as I saw the notes, and every time I witnessed a fresh piece appearing on the page I would imagine him visiting that invisible sun.

"They're a musical troupe, these notes, Max," he said, talking of his latest composition. "They play right into our lives." I nodded in agreement but even Hans could tell my mind was miles away.

"You aren't very focused today. What's her name?"

I hesitated for just a moment. "You know her, Hans. It's Sophie."

Hans had a twinkle in his eye and began running his fingers over the piano keys. Suddenly, they seemed to fall into place, playing a sweet, simple melody.

I couldn't help smiling as I hummed along with the tune. "That's very pretty. What's it called?"

Trilling over the last ivory key, Hans announced with a grin, "'Something for Sophie.'"

Poppy always said that Hans was hopelessly romantic.

Then Hans began to make a few musical notations for a concert he was preparing. *Verlobung im Traum,* his opera based on a novel by Dostoyevsky, was awarded Czechoslovakia's highest honor not long after its premiere at the German Theatre in Prague under the baton of Georg Szell. After the opera and other works, he gained European attention and recognition, and was invited to conduct in the United Kingdom. He told me that he would be gone for a few days.

A LONDON CONCERT

London had not yet taken news from the Continent seriously, and was still dancing in the heady, sparkling bubbles left over from the twenties. Theaters thrived in the Strand, charity balls at the Savoy were in full swing, the economy was encouraging, and on Sunday afternoons, sunbathers with their wooden, pale-blue-and-white-striped folding chairs were out in the city's parks in full force. Anna enjoyed shopping at the boutiques on Beecham Place instead of the larger stores like Harrods and Harvey Nichols, the stipend she inherited from her grandfather complementing her modest salary. She wore smartly designed suits, preferring crisp, freshly laundered white cotton blouses with round collars, showing off her slender frame and ample chest. She was what might be referred to as a Dorset beauty, soft blond hair, clear blue eyes, a peach-like complexion, and not a blemish to be found.

Arriving on the overnight train at Waterloo Station, Hans took a cab across the river and checked in to Claridge's. Having slept well in his carriage, he was refreshed by a shower under an oversized chrome shower head that produced a flow that felt like a heavy summer rain. Nothing worked in Britain better than hot water and baths, and he took full advantage. After laying out his things, he ordered up a full English breakfast.

Sunday afternoon in London was slow and drowsy, languid. Hans had corresponded with Sandy MacPherson, who, as a director of the Royal Academy of Music, had arranged his concert. Feeling alone in an unfamiliar city, Hans found a piano in the hotel ballroom and started to practice. He thought, if only he had had Max to fine-tune it, but it would do for now. He started to play and at once felt at ease, at home.

Across the city, on Fleet Street, it wasn't unusual for Anna to take the desk on weekends, and MacPherson (the staff was always referred to by last names in the editorial trade) noticed she was one of the few people around.

"Working on the weekend? You should be out, Kingsley. All work and all that. The desk will survive a few hours. Come with me, there's someone I want you to meet."

Having studied music, Anna had already noticed the adverts in the paper announcing Hans Krása's performance at Royal Albert Hall. She conjured up an image of an older man with flying gray hair and really had no idea what to expect.

"Keep me company. I'm just going over to say hello."

When they arrived at the deco-appointed hotel, the porter announced that Mr. Krása was "producing uncustomary sounds" in the ballroom one flight up.

With each stair, Anna heard rippling piano music floating down the stairwell. Entering the room, she saw an attractive man in the center, sitting, seemingly unaware that he was illuminated by the dancing rays of dusty sunlight, like some holy figure from a Renaissance painting. He was tall and graceful and she immediately noticed his elegant hands, how gently they touched the keyboard, and wondered if this was the man she had come to meet. In truth she hoped very much that he was.

Hans had been so completely absorbed in his playing that he hadn't noticed that they had slipped into the room, and when he finished, he was surprised by applause coming from two figures sitting in a pair of Chippendale chairs. He was also clearly pleased, this evident in the broad grin that stretched across his face as he approached them.

"I'm Sandy MacPherson, and this is my colleague Anna Kingsley. Hope we are not intruding."

"Not at all, just practicing. Thank you for your invitation, Mr. MacPherson."

"May we sit in and listen?"

"Of course."

"Afterward, we can show you around a bit, if you have time."

"I'd like that very much." Hans took notice of Anna. "Very much indeed." She had eyes that were dipped in ocean blue, a refreshing porcelain complexion that surely commanded a pause in a summer stillness.

Beginning at Nelson's Column, towering above Trafalgar Square, a triumphant symbol of England's past, to the Palace of Westminster on the Thames, and then over to the Admiralty courtyard behind Pall Mall. At Speakers' Corner, where eccentric Londoners proclaimed their views with conviction, Anna casually remarked, "I'm not sure you'd find such free speech in Berlin today." Hans nodded gravely but said nothing. A short while later, they ducked into a workingman's pub called the Swan.

"I thought you might like one of our ales," Sandy said, settling onto a wooden barstool beside Hans. "Not as good as pilsner, I admit."

Hans was cosmopolitan and accomplished, and Anna noticed how elegant and easy he was in everything he did. He walked lightly, with purpose, control, and grace, so different in every way from many of the men she had known, who were as heavy on their feet as in their emotions. His accent was amusing and endearing, very European.

He took easily to a classic pub lunch of cheese, a loaf of fresh crispy bread, and salad when Sandy surprised Anna, announcing that he had work to finish. "My son Andrew has just come down from school. You two carry on. Hans, you will be in good hands. Anna knows London well."

The idea of spending time with Hans certainly did not disagree with her, but she wondered if Sandy was playing matchmaker. Was it all a setup, or was she expected to interview the man from Prague? This must be a social rather than a working engagement, she quickly concluded.

But that thought was quickly contradicted. "Anna, I forgot to mention, Sarah Lloyd won't be back in time for the concert tonight, please cover for her, won't you." He walked out, leaving her bewildered.

A setup, she confirmed to herself.

"I'm not a music critic, but I adore music, and I'll try to do you justice."

"That's very brave of you."

What to do? Anna decided to take her newly appointed charge to a part of London that was a little different and headed to Lambeth. Taking a double-decker bus to the streets of dancing buskers who performed for a sprinkling of tossed shillings, they went to a two o'clock matinee at the Rose and Crown, where Gracie Fields belted out the World War I hits "It Wasn't the Yanks Who Won the War but My Son Billy" and "Wish Me Luck as You Wave Me Goodbye."

Hans confessed that he enjoyed every music-hall minute. "Every country has its own songs and stories, drawn from the people's own experiences," he commented. "America has vaudeville, France has its sultry, smoky songs, Berlin its raucous cabaret. London still struts with good humor."

Anna nodded. "But for how long?"

Hans looked suddenly serious, and in truth *Berlin* was the operative word for Anna, but she decided not to go too far with her reporter's curiosity just yet. "Not too lowbrow for you? I thought a musical introduction to London might be fun. We haven't produced as many great musicians as you have in Europe."

"Oh, I think you have," Hans replied. "I just heard them."

Looking down at her tank watch, something she always wore, a vintage model from the first war, bought at a Christie's auction, she announced, "Just a few hours before your concert. I should be returning you to your hotel."

"If you are coming this evening, and if you are free afterward, would you have dinner with me? I very much enjoy your company."

Anna took a moment to pause before she answered. Would it be unprofessional to review his concert and then have dinner with him? It wasn't a difficult decision. It wasn't as if she nurtured dreams of life as a music critic, so why not? Besides, she had no other plans and, more importantly, no man in her life.

The Royal Albert Hall was a treasured, round, redbrick building with a dome that had, through its sixty years, aged into a green patina. The lights dimmed, the applause subsided. Anna forgot about taking notes, and the reporter's pad sitting on her lap remained empty and untouched. Hans Krása's music spoke to her quietly, and she was overwhelmed by the restrained intensity, feeling at times as if Hans was addressing her directly through his music. She was almost shocked to be reminded that she was not alone when suddenly the house resonated with appreciation, standing as one to acknowledge the simple, expressive beauty of the performance. Hans selected two encores.

For Anna, the experience was magical, transcendent, taking her briefly away from the hall to another, ethereal realm.

Hans had been advised by the hotel's concierge to dine at the Mirabelle in Mayfair. The supper club featured a new French chef. More than a trendy gathering place, it was an elegant setting with a formal garden at its entrance. Unwittingly, he had taken Anna to one of her favorite restaurants. In a quiet corner, Hans ordered a bottle of Roederer Cristal, bottled in clear glass, showing a pale blaze. She thought he looked smart in black tie, and so comfortable in the surroundings, with her, with himself. Anna wore a pale-blue gown, a favorite that had her personality written all over it.

"It was a lovely concert," Anna said softly, trying to downplay the effect that she could tell she was having on him.

For a moment, Hans was silent, looking for a way to enter the conversation.

"Hans, is anything wrong?"

He smiled. "Quite the contrary, it's been a special day for me, thank you. And it's nice to be with you."

"I imagine you play all over Europe. Did you find our English audience any different?"

"Audiences are much the same. Music transcends borders, don't you think?"

"Borders?" Anna knew that she had not expressed herself particularly well and began asking questions with a reporter's verve. "Speaking of borders, any thoughts about Germany?"

"You mean Berlin? I think it will pass. Don't you?" Hans clearly didn't want to discuss politics.

"I think Hitler is mad," she continued, but saw at once that it would be best to drop the subject, if only for good manners. The invitation was for dinner and not an interview.

A menu brushed against a silver spoon that dropped to the floor. Embarrassed, he leaned over and quickly returned the errant utensil to a waiter.

After some consideration, Hans said, "Surely not all Germans are mad, Anna. Just listen to the music of Bach and Brahms."

"Yes, but what about Strauss?" Anna countered.

"Richard or Johann?"

"Yes, music does cross boundaries."

Hans shared a smile. "Shall we dance?"

Anna crossed her long legs and leaned back in her chair for just one last question. "You studied in Germany?"

"Paris suited me better."

Hans talked of how he admired a group of composers in Paris, where he was influenced not only by its music but by Parisian style. He began a carefree, sometimes lazy life there, spending most of his time walking the great boulevards, visiting French brasseries. Anna found herself imagining that he had a grand time courting French ladies, who, engaged by his polite manners, must have fallen for his well-tailored good looks and his music. She reminded herself that it was the music that was important and that it made no sense to be jealous of a man she had known for just a few hours.

"And Prague?"

"Prague is my home." She caught a glint in his eyes. They were deep, dark brown and romantic, even a little mysterious. Returning to the menu, he said he was contemplating a Gruyere cheese soufflé. In an awkward intermission in the conversation, a waiter arrived serving a platter of fresh vegetables, delicately arranged on a silver tray. Petits pois, small honeyed carrots, young green and white asparagus flavored in a lemon sauce, and slim slices of garden zucchini topped with butter.

"They are grown on our farms." Anna admired the assortment.

"I'll have to get a Land Rover and a pair of Wellingtons!"

"A country farmer now?"

"Do you think I could fit in?" His eyes sparkled as he smiled.

"I suspect you might prefer Prague. Has the country changed with so much happening in Germany?"

"Prague is much the same." He paused for a moment. "I think we'll all be safe."

"Forgive me for being rude, but aren't you Jewish?" The pages of her imaginary reporter's notebook kept turning in her inquisitive mind.

"You know more about me than I know about you, Anna. My faith comes from my music. Perhaps my piano is Jewish."

She smiled at the remark, almost a metaphor.

"Don't you think the Munich Pact is a marker? Prime Minister Chamberlain is a pandering fool. We published a photograph of him with Daladier, Mussolini, and Hitler, standing around a table at the signing, and I just can't think of that scene without a sense of shame."

"Perhaps they were just enjoying each other's company."

Anna didn't want to let go, she wanted to know more. It was her reporter's curiosity about the moral equation affecting Jews in Europe, but then finally, politely she conceded: "Forgive me, Hans. I'm sorry."

The exchange of verbal volleys had no clear winner.

"I understand, Anna, and no apologies needed. I usually don't discuss politics."

"Music, then. How can you hear every instrument, and

then bring them together, in perfect combination and tone, the way you do?"

"Music is the way I see the world, so musical notes, instruments, they are my tools. Words are instruments. Don't you feel the same when you write?"

"The same? I don't know, but I do know that I felt something when I heard your music." She had surprised herself. Flirtatious. It was far from her style.

"May I take that as a compliment?"

"You may take it as you wish, but it is the truth."

Leaving the Mirabelle, Hans opened the door of a waiting taxi. "Can I see you home, drop you off?"

Anna shrugged. "Oh, I'm going a different way. But perhaps we will see each other before you leave," she said, pulling on her gloves. "I'm going to the office to file. And don't worry, just music, no politics!"

"Well, good night," he said, with a quick embrace, hoping he would see her again.

The evening had been unsettling, with the push and pull of a new relationship. He watched Anna's cab receding into the darkness until he could only see two red, dimming lights. Returning to his hotel and lying in his bed, he couldn't fall asleep. Anna was on his mind. A song began to play in his head. Then again, he'd always had a sentimental touch. Their day together had gone well, he thought, but the evening had ended on an awkward note. Politics, an uncomfortable topic, was not his game. But he liked her, and their meeting had ventured beyond a casual introduction. However, he lived in Prague and she in London. That was a bit of a distance for feelings to travel.

A SONG FOR ANNA

The following morning, Anna called.

"I wanted to thank you for dinner. I promised Nana that I would take tea with her, would you like to come? I can reciprocate for the lovely dinner you gave me."

At Eaton Square, the brilliantly polished eighteenth-century door knockers gave some hint as to the individuality that lay behind the uniformity of the wide-terraced homes and broad arches.

"My grandmother is a bit eccentric, but I think you'll like her," Anna said as they passed the row of elegant homes. "She's lived here for ages."

Hans asked, "Does she have a piano?"

She looked at him curiously, and then knocked on the door. It opened and a butler in black tails led them into the drawing room.

"Hans Krása, meet Madeline Kingsley." Anna's grandmother welcomed him in a long, pearl-beaded gown, a bit over the top for an afternoon high tea, but anything Madeline chose was commanding, almost regal. Her keen eye sized up Hans as a character for one of her romantic novels.

The flat was filled with English paintings, antiques, and books. A collection of friends posed in sterling silver frames on the piano, which looked perfectly at home in a room that was graced by considerable yardage of crimson taffeta sweeping each side of three windows overlooking the square, and the generous width of the windows allowed patterns of light to reach the pale walls around the room.

Madeline had always retained some British reserve, but the twinkle in her eyes suggested an inner mischievousness, just as it did in Anna. Sensing her daring spirit, Hans knew he had found an ally. He wasted not a moment in recruiting her to support his affection for Anna.

Noticing the piano, he commented, "I haven't seen a Bechstein since Berlin." He knew it would help his confidence. He was nervous before performing.

"May I ask what sign you are, Mr. Krása?" Madeline said lightly.

"Sign?"

"I have an abiding interest in astrology."

"I haven't thought about one," Hans replied. "I was born on the twenty-sixth of November."

Anna tried to interrupt before the planets collided in conversation.

"Ah, good, Sagittarius," Madeline exclaimed. "The stars don't seem to be in retrograde. You have a positive outlook on life. Anna is a Leo. Very compatible. But fair warning, Mr. Krása, the lion is self-reliant. Leo rules the heart with loyalty. She's a very warm girl, once you get to know her."

Anna interrupted in desperation, "Nana, please keep your astrological charting private!"

Madeline paid no attention and commanded a tea service, cucumber sandwiches, crumpets with Seville orange marmalade, and scones with currant jam and clotted cream. The conversation turned to small matters, including the weather.

"Just dreadful," Madeline pronounced.

Hans took this opportunity to brighten the afternoon and, summoning his confidence, was restless to play. He took a seat at the piano and, turning toward Anna as he removed a sheet of music from his inside pocket, Hans beamed. "This is for you."

Then, placing his hands on the keys, came a gentle theme. Madeline couldn't hide her pleasure. "You know the way to the heart, Mr. Hans Krása."

Later, walking through the square, Anna remarked, "I appreciate your sentiments, but you really embarrass me, Hans. I introduced you to my Nana, and the next thing you do is improvise a song."

"Not improvised, but I hope refreshing, the ink barely dry on the paper. That's what I do. I write music."

"For every lady you meet?"

"Oh, no, absolutely not. Only . . . well, for you. It's not my intention to intrude or embarrass."

Anna blushed a little. "I do admit we are a bit unconventional, even direct, but we don't wear our emotions so openly. The next thing I suspect is that you will be reciting a poem, standing on a box in Hyde Park."

"Why not? If the situation demands it."

"You're incorrigible."

"I'm Czech."

"I'm English."

"Perhaps your Nana was right, perhaps our planets are colliding?"

A smartly fitted doorman tipped his hat when they arrived back at Claridge's. A Hungarian quartet played nearby in a grand room off the foyer. Anna realized that the musicians were playing her tune. She couldn't resist a smile. "You did this?"

"Just a way to say thank you," Hans said, handing Anna a page of music inside a white envelope. "It sounds much better arranged; don't you think the quartet adds fullness?"

"There you go again."

"Yes, of course," he said.

Offering his hand, Hans closed the afternoon. As she turned to leave, she saw that on the back of the envelope, he had written:

Anna,

Prague will always be waiting for you.

Hans

When she returned to the newspaper's offices, Anna sat down to read a report filed by an *Observer* correspondent about an upcoming meeting in France that had crossed her desk. It concerned an international conference called by Franklin Roosevelt, intended to provide refuge for thousands of Jews in Nazi-controlled Germany and Austria. It was almost impossible to focus on politics and, with a complex of emotions swirling around inside, she stared at her typewriter for some time, then began to type, surprised by her own words.

`He's a Casanova . . .`

She paused, and then a riff of words fired from her fingers:

`. . . and I'm not some backstage strumpet or stage-door hussy who's` `just going to fall for a tune . . . So forward, in fact a bit rude, a musical manipulation, our song, my song, well, I won't have it. We don't know each other, well hardly, but he is attractive, older, not that that is a bad thing, no, I WILL NOT have it. It's a sweet tune, but he cannot just come waltzing into my life. I'm not Viennese! But . . . he is rather sweet, and it is a very pretty tune . . .`

She called Nana.

"Well, that was a surprise, Anna, bringing that lovely man around to see me. You've not done that before. I like him very much, and I'm assuming he is your new beau."

"Hans said he's waiting for me in Prague, or Prague would be waiting for me . . . Something like that. Nana, I'm unnerved."

"Of course. It's in the stars. Don't be in such an uptizzle. What are you waiting for? Go!"

"Uptizzle? But we just met. I don't know a thing about him."

"I've always had a thing for musicians . . . Strange, isn't it . . . and I'm sure I've passed it on to you."

"Thank you, you're amazingly generous," Anna said with unladylike sarcasm.

"You know more than you think; now stop wasting my time. Goodbye."

With that encouragement, all that was left was her managing editor. Rising from her desk she walked determinedly into MacPherson's office.

"I must go to Prague," she said, closing the door behind her.

"Why Prague?" MacPherson asked.

Standing with conviction in front of the editor's imposing wooden desk, one that was older than most of the reporters on staff, Anna replied, "I think the Germans are moving in that direction. I want to see for myself."

"What makes you so sure?"

"It makes sense, as part of their expansion, but it's also just a journalist's hunch."

"Your review of Hans Krása was impressive. He should be pleased. Thanks for filling in." MacPherson gave a sly smile. "How long do you think you need?"

Anna paused, unsure of whether it would take longer to figure out the Germans or her heart. "A fortnight. And I do have holiday coming up."

"File something for Travel so I can justify the assignment: 'Pleasurable Pleasing Prague.'"

"A bit of alliteration."

Looking up over his glasses, MacPherson shuffled some papers. "We share a bureau with the *Times News Service* near Wenceslas Square. Here's the address. I'll wire them to expect you. Enjoy the concerts."

Before she left the office, she returned to her desk and read the dispatch about the conference in Évian. On her way to Prague, she would attend and file the first of the reports that would justify her trip.

When Anna returned to her flat, it was just after eight o'clock, toward the end of a long summer's day, and the evening light found a bright white envelope posted at her front door.

Anna,

Could you come around? I would very much like to have a short visit before you leave for Prague.

Winston

It had only been hours since she had decided to go to Prague, but as far as she was concerned, her trip was a private matter. Was Nana spreading gossip?

Churchill and Madeline Kingsley had been friends for many years now—just how close Anna dared not think. Anna was miffed. "Why does Nana have to broadcast my every move? I guess I should go and see him, but what on earth could Winston want?"

Churchill had been in the political wilderness in the thirties, taking measures to return the pound sterling to the gold standard, supervising home rule in India, but the one factor that drew him and Anna closer together was their shared and deep opposition to Hitler. He had often and eloquently warned those willing to listen about Germany's pounding war drums. He had delivered an eloquent speech to the House of Commons admonishing Neville Chamberlain, "You were given the choice of war or dishonor. You chose dishonor and you will have war."

Having been passed over as minister of defense, Churchill's warning about Germany had gone largely unheeded.

Arriving at Chartwell, Anna was announced as the great man trundled past bookcases; stern and commanding with implacable determination, he entered the dusty room. The walls were fitted with volumes of leather-bound books on military history, and he walked past an easel on which the oils were still drying, confirming that he had spent the afternoon painting in his garden.

"Hello, Anna," he roared. "Excuse the place for being a bit untidy, Clemmy hasn't finished refurbishing yet." He held up a recent painting of flowers, and briefly, silently assessed his own work.

"I've been out of favor with the government for some time and my paintings seem to be the only portfolio I have these days." He grumbled the remark with a frown, as his large frame settled into an armchair that accommodated him easily. He had the grace to refrain from lighting up a cigar. Anna had sometimes wondered if they were more of an amusing prop than a source of enjoyment. Folding his hands across his waist, he said, "I've known you for a long time, Anna, watched you grow up, and I think we share many of the same sentiments, and most of the same principles."

"Thank you, sir."

"About Germany." He got right to the point.

"I just wrote a piece."

"You're on the mark, and this is one very old journalist to a new one, so to speak," he said in his sibilant voice, rather more restrained, less theatrical than the one he reserved for his oratorical work.

"I'm flattered."

"It's not flattery, Anna, it's the truth. Do you know how fortunate we are to have a great man in England, a truly remarkable man who has just arrived from Austria."

"I know there is an influx of course, so many are seeking refuge. Who in particular?"

"Sigmund Freud."

"The doctor from Vienna. I know something of his work—his remarkable research."

"Indeed. He has revealed and explored so much in his work, and did you know just a few years ago, he published *Civilization and Its Discontents,* writing something that haunts me. *Human beings have the capacity to exterminate people they consider inferior, those who don't serve their cause, down to the last man.*"

There was silence between them for a few seconds before Anna spoke quietly: "That's a very thoughtful statement."

"I fear that it's a warning, a prophesy. History, Anna. History. I think we will all be better off if we check Hitler's death-dealing inclinations."

"There is very much to think about, for every one of us. It is almost as if all of this, everything that is unfolding, is a prelude to a great drama."

"More than a drama, perhaps something very much graver. Yes, if you put it that way, at the very least the prelude to a play, and what we are talking about is a matter of survival."

Churchill reached to Anna's news-gathering instincts. "Since 1933 Freud has examined the great struggle between life and death and how it will be staged. So yes, it is great drama, Anna. Being a Jew, he was targeted by a campaign of persecution and forced to emigrate. When he left Vienna after the gestapo ransacked his home, interrogated his daughter, and seized family property, those bastards even demanded an emigration tax . . . and if that were not enough, he was required to sign a carefully prepared document testifying he had not been mistreated. With a note of sarcasm, he confirmed, 'I can most highly recommend the gestapo to everyone.'"

"I pray you're not recommending the gestapo to me."

"This is an important writer and thinker treated as a common criminal. I know you're going to Prague, Anna."

Nana!

"But what you don't know is that the nation is going to need all the information we can muster. I'm out of fashion just now, trapped between what I suspect and what I know. In short, I've set up an intelligence service, a service in which you could play a role, a vital role."

Anna was curious—more than curious. "I'm a journalist, sir, not some agent working undercover. Who would I be reporting to, MI5, MI15, whatever it's called?"

"I'm running an operation called Pink Tulip." She stared into the keen eyes of the man she'd known since childhood and could see, beneath the veneer of accrued physical weight, the disappointments that were etched into the lines of his face, the air of world-weariness that seemed to weigh heavy on his slumped shoulders, and beneath all that the eager, fearless journalist that he had been in his youth, the master of intelligence. He added with a steady grin, "I hope you'll be with us."

"You seem to have a lot of confidence in me."

"I have a cover for you."

"I hadn't thought of myself as a spy," she whispered to Winston. The notion amused her.

"You'll be working for the Resistance—the Kindertransport program. But essentially, I want you to find an operative. I'll need actionable information."

"What in the world is Kindertransport?"

"Consider this, Anna. If Hitler marches, we're going to at the very least get some of those kids out of Europe. Last night, there was a major House of Commons debate on refugees.

"I've discussed the matter with the home secretary, who has already met with a large delegation representing various Jewish and non-Jewish groups allied under one umbrella organization, the Refugee Children's Movement, or RCM. This group is dedicated to the care of helping children. Anna, I need to know about all Europe. If we enter a war, which I believe we will, it's vital that we have a network spanning the continent. I stand alone, and I had hoped that Germany would be restored to the European circle. That, I am certain, is now a vain hope, and we need to make plans. I need your service over at Electra House. And above all else we need to save the children."

Anna believed that Churchill was angling to become the first lord of the admiralty and a member of the War Cabinet, a position he had held in the First World War. If war came, he would be needed to lead, to be at, or close to, the center of power. She had always been curious, she was leading the European desk, and if a silly fascination with a Czech composer didn't work out, she had an assignment that mattered.

Secretly, she liked the idea. It appealed to her idealism, her desire to be of use, and she knew by her very presence here at this time that her grandmother was connected in ways she could barely imagine. It was a serious assignment, the true nature of which would only emerge if she chose to accept Churchill's invitation. She smiled briefly as she considered this, as if it was possible that she could turn this offer down. She thought about Hans. What would he think of this? Would he ever know?

"On my way to Czechoslovakia, I'll be stopping off at a conference in France, and if I gather any useful information, I'll cable you."

Churchill smiled. "I take it you accept the assignment. I know about the meeting, one of our undersecretaries will be there. But I need more. We'll need someone in Prague, to work with Pierre Burger. And we need a way to report to the nation, without revealing our sources."

"Pierre Burger?"

"Your contact. An essential man, with important connections. Find him, we need inside operatives."

In a little over twenty-four hours Anna's world had been

turned upside down. Before she left, she posted a dispatch to *The Observer.* Her "cover" as Churchill put it. She couldn't know where it would all end for her, for Hans, for Europe. But she knew one thing for sure: she was on her way to Prague.

THE OBSERVER

July 23, 1939

KINDERTRANSPORT

Last night, there was a major House of Commons debate on refugees here in England. The home secretary, Sir Samuel Hoare, met a large delegation, the Refugee Children's Movement (RCM), dedicated to the care of children in Germany and what might be occupied Europe. These agencies promised to fund the operation and to prevent the refugees from becoming a financial burden on British citizens. Each child will have a financial guarantee to ensure their eventual return to Germany.

Representatives have been dispatched to Germany and Austria to organize the operation. *The Observer,* together with the British Broadcasting Corporation (BBC) Home Service, appealed for foster homes, bringing more than a thousand offers. RCM volunteers are visiting prospective homes to make sure that each child will be placed in a clean, respectable, supportive atmosphere and that the expected and understandable stress and anxiety are well addressed. Nicholas Winton, a stockbroker of German-Jewish origin, heads one of the groups financing the operation. As of this writing, he has found homes for 669 children, many of whose parents have disappeared. He has also built a network in Germany through private connections.

The children will travel with a document of identity issued by His Majesty's government and will be admitted to the United Kingdom for educational purposes under the care and authority of the International Aid Committee for Children, an organization with the Queen's patronage. The document requires no visa or personal particulars. Upon arrival in Great Britain, children without prearranged families will be sheltered at Dovercourt and Pakefield summer holiday camps. Britain welcomes these children with open arms and open hearts. One is reminded of the text from the book of Jewish law, *To save one life is to save the world.*

The international conference called by United States President Franklin Roosevelt was intended to offer refuge to European Jews, but instead, with a twist of irony, it appeared the conference would not help after all. There in Évian, delegates from thirty-two countries and representatives from thirty-nine private relief agencies met at the Hotel Royal in the French resort on Lake Geneva, near the Swiss border. Prior to the conference, Roosevelt had made it clear that "no country would be expected to receive a greater number of immigrants than is permitted by their existing regulations." And no mention about the well-being of children. Taking advantage of Roosevelt's qualification, the national delegates, one after another, expressed sympathy for Jewish refugees, while making excuses as to why their borders could not be opened.

Anna learned that what was conceived as a means of

bringing at least some much-needed relief to an emerging and deepening crisis ended in not one viable solution, but instead a serious impasse. After all the promise of international cooperation, the Évian Conference was offering no relief for Jewish refugees, and by legitimatizing the Nazi claim that "nobody wants them," she felt that in time it would be a critical turning point in Nazi-Jewish relations. The conference revealed the centerpiece of Nazi Germany's anti-Jewish policy, and it was clear another solution for the Reich's "Jewish Problem" would eventually surface.

She was offended by such cavalier disregard for humanity, and disappointed, but felt oddly inspired and ever more engaged in her new role, seeing how urgent the work was, whatever it might turn out to be. Next stop, Prague.

RETURN TO PRAGUE

When Hans returned from London, he couldn't stop grinning. He was secretive about his visit, not even mentioning how the concert went. It was so unlike him, a man who was almost as theatrical as Poppy when it came to re-creating moments of triumph or disaster. Instead he would sit at the piano, saying little, but playing a new piece over and over, as if his fingers were glued to the keys.

"What's it called?" I asked.

"Hmmm?"

"The name of your new tune."

"I don't have a name for it yet."

"What's her name?"

"What makes you think she has a name?"

"Just a hunch."

"Anna."

"Who's Anna?"

I knew he had met someone he liked. I was finally getting the hang of this romance thing.

"According to my intuition, she'll be visiting us soon in Prague?"

"How do you know that?"

"A hunch. Inspiration. Maybe?"

Inspiration was on my mind. It was time for a letter.

Dear Sophie,

After you left, I thought you had gone away forever. I hope not. I don't understand feelings the way I understand music, they are all sloshed up inside me. Have you arrived safely at your new home, and how is your mama feeling? I had such a wonderful time with you. I want to come and visit you when you are settled in your new village. When I need to cheer myself up, I play our day together as if it were a movie.

Max

I kept Sophie in my thoughts for the rest of the night and fell asleep looking at her photograph. It was no longer in sepia. I saw the colors deep within it, and the picture, like Sophie herself, had come gloriously to life.

Poppy jumped up from the table and thrust his right index finger into the air after tasting a new concoction of fruit juice made from oranges, lemons, and apples. He was always fizzing with life, with enthusiasm, creating something, bringing his imagination into existence with boundless energy. He had an irrepressible life force whether it was in the kitchen, on a walk, at the piano, or waving his baton in front of an orchestra.

"To life! Now, get your books and we'll walk to school."

I went to my room, trying to remember where I'd put Sophie's letters. I searched my pine desk, tossing books onto the floor. No luck. I searched behind the old spinet that Poppy had bought for my mother, to see if they had fallen behind it.

Nothing. Finally, I looked under my large down comforter, and there they were, right beside my wooden model sailboat. I grabbed them and my books, making sure to snatch my brass army trumpet off the wall, the one with a maroon-and-blue braided rope. But there was a more important thing to do before our musical walk to school.

"Poppy, would you post my letter to Sophie? She's in a place called Terezín."

"Sure, Max." He smiled at me. "I'm curious. Who is she? Are you keeping secrets?"

Hard to keep anything from Poppy.

"We've been writing. We're pen pals, although I haven't heard anything from her for a while. She came to visit one day when you were away working all day. She and her mother had to leave Austria. They couldn't stay there any longer."

Poppy frowned. "Is she Jewish?"

"Yes, but does it make a difference?"

"Of course not," he muttered, and then definitively: "Of course not!" And with that, he gave an expansive wave. "Follow me, Max. We're off to school!"

Poppy didn't say anything more about Sophie, but I was sure Hans must have told him something.

The German School was just a short tram ride away, about thirty blocks, but if the weather was particularly nice, we walked, picking up classmates along the way. Today, the Great Viktor Mueller was improvising a march.

A classmate led our single file proudly, with the colors of Czechoslovakia, a fluttering standard flying red and white with a blue triangle.

"Let's walk smartly, Max. I'd like to hear the sound of your trumpet."

I blew as hard as I could.

"Good morning, Marek, did you bring your drum?"

"Yes, Conductor Mueller," he called, responding with a *boom-de-boom.*

"No skipping, boys, keep in step."

At the tram crossing, he led the ever-growing band with military precision. "Ah, Vaclav, join the ranks, hope you have your clarinet with you."

"All warmed up with a new reed, Maestro."

A block later: "Jan Leopold, your tuba ready today?"

"Ready to play, Herr Conductor Mueller!"

At the corner: "It's Sarah, I believe? We can always use another flute."

David joined us. When we weren't playing football, or hiking through snowstorms together, David played the violin better than anyone I knew. Poppy called him a prodigy. He could hear a score once and perform it perfectly. David was a Topper even when it came to music. The only thing he may have loved more than news and books was a song.

"Welcome, David! Fiddle on, dear man!"

With a *rat-a-tat,* a *boom-boom-boom,* and a couple of *tra-la*s thrown in, the rank and file were led in their joyous procession by Drum Major Viktor Mueller. We arrived at school and followed Poppy as he marched us in and up the stairs and along the first-floor corridor.

Teachers opened their doors to see what all the noise was, and Poppy tipped his hat with a nod to each of them.

"Hello, and top of the morning to you!" He was using an Irish accent today.

I looked over at David. He was busily jotting something down on a small pad, laughing to himself as he scrawled his notes. I anticipated an article in the school newspaper, "Morning Music Procession Causes Commotion and Consternation."

David took his job as editor very seriously. Nothing escaped report.

As we settled down at our desks and got out our books, David turned to me. "I've been thinking about it lately—why don't you join the paper, Max? You express yourself better than anyone I know, and I can always use a good man."

"What about keeping out the riffraff?"

"I'm the editor. I can make an exception for certain riffraff."

"Thanks, David, but I'm behind, studying for exams and practicing piano. And somehow I think your newspaper is going to land you in trouble."

In the last several issues, David had reprinted articles about the political situation in Berlin. One was "Burning Books in Berlin," another "The Reichstag Fire," and one about *Mein Kampf*, "Hitler's Blueprint of Destruction." His editorials were beyond my worldview, and his tutor strongly advised him to tone it down. We went to a German school, and although he was admired for his Czech patriotism, some opinions were bound to get him in hot water eventually.

As for me, I didn't think that Sophie wanted a rabble-rouser as a pen pal. Or a boyfriend.

We were on our way to the station. Most times we walked, but on this occasion Poppy had decided to order a driver. David was waiting for us in front of his house a few minutes later.

The car crept toward the opera house. I strained to hear the muffled yells and shouts along the route, until the source became obvious: People were protesting, waving placards that read SUDETEN GERMAN PARTY while others were attacking them. Two lines of people screamed insults at each other—I felt as if we had suddenly found ourselves in a newsreel. Men and women were pushing against our car, pressed together, and I thought at any minute we would be compressed into a can of sardines. There was shouting and fighting, and I felt uneasy, even a little frightened. The crowd could pounce on us at any minute. There was a sense that news, the things that made the paper, happened somewhere else. But here I could feel that we had drifted right into the middle of a story. We were separated from what was going on by the thickness of the glass in the car's windows.

A man cried out to us, "Please help me," and Poppy managed to open the car's door and with great effort push away a group who were kicking and punching him. He was hurt. It was shocking and ugly. Poppy helped the man up. He was bruised and defeated. The crowd spat on him as blood pooled on the street. A woman screamed. Children cried. My heart was beating fast. I looked over at Poppy who seemed calm and in control.

"Move over, Max," Poppy called as he pulled the man into the cab. On the way to the hospital, Poppy took out his handkerchief and wiped the man's face as he held him in his arms. At that moment, as we continued our slow journey in a shared, shocked silence, I realized how brave my father was. We didn't pick up any sheet music that day, but I learned a bit about courage. The image of the mob burned itself into my mind. I thought I should have helped, too, and felt guilty that I hadn't. There was no excuse. That failure to act stayed with me a long time. In fact, it never left me. From that moment on I understood that you could never just turn away from reality. You had to face it, to report it, help reshape it. And that is something David did too. He reported the truth and at that moment I wondered if I could do the same.

As we left the crowd, David pointed to a man in a black overcoat keeping a ledger. He seemed to stand out from the rest—a faceless man hidden in shadows, but there was something about him that was unmistakably dangerous. It was as if the protest was in color and this man was in black and white.

Looking back in the rear window, the Czech police dispersed the protesters, the streets were cleared, and things were calm again, as if a storm had passed. But we had seen the clouds, they were dark and violent, and suddenly, however brave my father was and I had vowed to become, I felt a little less safe in the world.

A ROOM WITH A VIEW

Poppy clutched a bouquet of flowers as a train marked 1012 from Switzerland steamed into the station.

A lady walked toward Hans, unmistakably the woman that he had been talking about. This was Anna.

While Anna was fluent in German, Hans simply refused to speak the language anymore. Fortunately, our informal reception committee all spoke English reasonably well—it was part of our school curriculum.

"I have always wished to meet a lovely English lady. At your command, your service, your every wish." Viktor bowed. "I am your guide." He presented Anna with the flowers and she beamed.

Then Poppy produced a red-banded porter's hat that I had not seen before and bowed again before placing it on his head. "Madam, I officially welcome you to Prague. I'm here to assist you. These three nincompoops do not know the city . . . an inadequate welcoming committee for a famous journalist. In fact, they lose their way most of the time. Your baggage, madam?" Nodding, her brilliant smile emerged once more. I was keen to know her better. David was so excited he forgot to scribble anything in his notebook. Hans stood to one side, looking handsome and happy.

Poppy the Porter led us out of the station; he waved his

hand, announcing, “Prague has eighty-three churches, and we will visit them all. We make music here too. You will notice a newly varnished violin hanging in the window of a carriage house. Listen to the sounds of a quartet drifting from a room in Old Town. We even write songs to those we love.” He paused looking at Hans. “Prague is alive with music!”

“Before we do so,” Hans politely interrupted, “Anna, I’ve booked a room for you at the Europa, but I have a large guest house on my property with a great deal of privacy, overlooking one of the churches our ‘guide’ mentioned, a beautiful view, and I’d be very pleased if you would stay.”

Viktor countered, “If I may, madam, I am familiar with the best accommodations in the city . . . stay at the Europa.”

“It’s a difficult decision; what do you think?” Anna asked me.

“I would unquestionably stay at Hans’s. The Europa is very nice, but the guest house, I’ve stayed there many times—it’s very private and I see no reason why it would not be proper.”

“Why do you say that?”

“We want you nearby, and besides, Hans is sometimes lonely. And he has the best cook in town.”

I could tell by the look on her face that Anna didn’t believe that Hans Krása could ever be lonely. Sensitive and self-sufficient to be sure, but lonely? I was projecting my own loneliness.

Anna accepted the gracious offer, knowing that Hans was a portrait of a gentleman.

Viktor the Guide exclaimed, “Then it is settled; we’re off to the Grand Hotel Krása!”

The Grand Hotel Krása was a five-star affair, with a living room so spacious it could have been a ballroom. Outside were well-attended gardens, where Hans often collected his thoughts. They were pleasant places to spend an hour or two each day, with colorful flowers matching the seasons. His home had originally been built as the French consulate, until an embassy was needed, and it was expanded into a larger residence with a park, overlooking all Malá Strana, with a sweeping view of the red rooftops leading to the river. It belonged to the Krása family, having been purchased by Hans's grandfather, and had rich wooden floors, wide French windows, and, at its center, a drawing room with two polished grand pianos, where I took my lessons and spent some of the best times I can remember. I knew that Anna would love it as much as Sophie and Edith had. Perhaps even more.

Turning to Viktor the Guide, after surveying her surroundings, Anna announced, "I've made the right choice!"

"Very well, madam," Poppy replied, taking off his hat and resuming the role of my father. Hans and I sighed in relief.

Lucie had set the round dining table in true Czech tradition, on a lace tablecloth, with five different dishes. The eggs à la russe sprinkled with paprika were my favorites, and her chocolate torte was a prize. I remember that the conversation led to the current events on Anna's mind.

"I'm so glad you came, Anna. I didn't think you would, and well, you have made us all very happy."

"You said that Prague would be waiting for me. I didn't want to disappoint."

"Hans plays your song every day, has you on his mind, Anna. I can see why!"

The tables were turned so Hans, for a change, didn't mind when the conversation moved to politics. Anna said, "You must all be worried about your ambitious neighbor, that endless desire to expand in all directions."

Poppy replied in a deliberately lighthearted tone, "I don't

think returning historic lands to the Germans is a terrible thing, they were mostly German to begin with."

"And you're sure it will stop when those lands have been regained? I wonder. Anyway, it's Hitler I worry about."

"We're living in troubled times," David said. "Much is happening, and there's trouble marching in."

"How do you know?" Anna asked.

"I'm a journalist," David said proudly.

"And a pretty good one," I added.

David blushed a little but quickly mentioned Konrad Henlein, an official making fanatic demands, calling for freedom to profess Nazi ideology. Land for the Germans.

"Nazi ideology?" I said without even thinking. I needed to make sense of all of this. As ever, I had to catch up with David.

"It's a way of thinking," David said. "It's the way of dictators and of oppression. One that will destroy free speech, and I suspect will affect us all."

Hans looked uneasy in the face of all of this, but David continued: "The Germans believe they are a super race, and Jews are inferior."

How could anyone believe this? I thought. *How can any of this make sense?* But somehow it had to, and I had to understand it all.

"Should we discuss politics on such a lovely day?"

"You can't just ignore it, Hans," Poppy said. "Being Jewish, I thought you would have a stronger opinion."

"We should read *Mein Kampf*," David said.

"It's a piece of trash, the ranting of a crazy man," Poppy replied.

Crazy or not, it was a book that David had written about in the paper. He had quoted Hitler talking of how Jews were the scourge of mankind, how they must be eliminated, how any kindness toward these people was cowardly stupidity. "*Ein Volk, ein Reich, ein Führer*! One people, one country, one leader!"

"President Beneš is not going to let Germany hurt the Jews, or take over Czechoslovakia as they did in Austria," Hans said.

That's what happened in Sophie's country. I couldn't shake it off. It was already changing the lives of people, people we knew. And it was getting closer, with the flags everywhere, the violence, the stories that I overheard, the kids in my school. Maybe it wasn't just getting closer? Maybe it was here already? All of this was running through my head, and I was lost in my own world for a while until I was shaken from my reverie by my father's attempt to reassure us all: "Those Germans are a bunch of rowdies."

But Poppy is German. Do Poppy and Germany belong together?

Leaving the subject and raising his glass, my father toasted, "Dreams are true while they last, and do we not live in dreams?"

David chimed in: "Alfred, Lord Tennyson. 'I am a part of all that I have met.'"

Anna smiled.

"David has read everything, Anna. He's a Topper!"

"I'm among a community of poets."

Before lunch was over, I knew what was coming. I went to the drawing room to make sure the ladies were in perfect register. I took out my red felt ribbons to make an adjustment, which demanded striking a few notes, over and over.

"What's that?" Anna wondered, evidently hearing notes in the distance.

"It's only Max," David replied with casual understatement. "He's also a piano tuner and, I must say, one of the best."

I suspected that bit of news came as something of a surprise to her.

After dessert, everyone gathered in the drawing room for

coffee. Anna looked at me with what I took to be fondness and admiration. Then taking a seat at one of two grand pianos, Poppy asked, "Do you play, Anna?"

"I took lessons as a girl," she began. "I love to listen more than I like to play."

Standing between the two pianos, with a wide band of light pouring in between them, the Great Viktor Mueller pronounced, "Then you and Max shall play together. Take a piano, and Hans and I will take the other." I had seen all this before, seen my father and Hans fight it out so many times over the keys, their rivalry as intense as it was competitive. But here they would be sitting together.

"That's not fair," I piped up, "you two are professionals. David is a much better musician."

"I play violin, Max. You're the pianist, and you have perfect pitch."

"Yes, there seems to be a lot of perfection in your team," Hans added. "So, I would think you two would make perfect companions!"

I grinned, Anna blushed, and we agreed to do our best.

The battle of two pianos and eight hands started with Beethoven's "Für Elise," and I can tell you now, it began in 3/8 meter, arpeggios in the left hand, which I could play; then Anna took over the modulation to A minor and E major. She really played well. But when the next section advanced to relative major chords C major and G major, Hans and Viktor took over, then back to us for a lighter section in F, to a few bars in C, then back to Hans with a gauntlet of chords that returned to the main theme. We all ended the game pounding the pedals.

I realized I was showing off, but Hans was a great teacher and he often said I was a pretty good student. Sometimes when I played, I stopped and stuttered, but that day, a more confident

Anna pulled me through the afternoon. She was so beautiful that at times I couldn't concentrate on the keys. Who was this other person that had suddenly appeared in my life?

We found the office on a narrow lane that had once been reserved for carriage houses. Anna had invited David and me to visit *The Observer* news offices in Prague. One of David's articles in the school newspaper had caught her attention. It was called "Lebensraum, the Expansion of German Lands," and Germany was indeed on the march. It was part of David's file. He knew and read the papers. He had collected news and facts.

"Don't be alarmed, David, but someone is following us," I said. "Large black overcoat, hat . . ."

David looked around and caught sight of the man, studying his every move and gesture, before he hid in a doorway. After a moment, he looked out again. What did he want? One thing was for sure: the black overcoat was not far behind.

"We saw him at the demonstration."

"You sure that's him?"

"How many men in black overcoats can there be? I'm sure. He's up to no good."

"Let's find out." David ran after him. I trailed behind, leaving Anna in the lurch.

As we reached the corner, the man turned and ducked out of sight. We looked down a few narrow alleys. Gone.

David gripped his satchel, a look of determination etched on his face.

We walked back toward Anna and apologized for leaving so abruptly.

"Whoever that guy is, I don't like it. He's obviously keeping an eye on us, seeing what we're up to. Not to worry. We haven't done anything to deserve his attention. Well, not yet at least," David muttered, almost to himself.

The Anglo-European Agency was my introduction to the news business, and it was just one in a series of surprises and revelations that day. The offices were housed in an enormous newsroom with green machines clattering away in a musical rhythm, starting, pausing, and tapping away again. There were men and women crowded around desks, with hundreds of newspapers scattered in front of them. Each had their own typewriter, each represented a news organization in some corner of the globe. They were writing about the world at work. Collecting information, filing stories, discussing topics, agreeing and disagreeing, making news. Facts were flying around the room, getting ready to land back home on an editor's desk. It was a gathering place, a place of safekeeping for a collective sacred trust, and I felt lucky that we had been invited. David was at home. I loved it all immediately. It felt reassuring. As long as there were places like this, ensuring that the truth was alive, then how bad could things be, how bad could they get?

"Welcome to Prague, we've been expecting you. My name is MacDowell," as he introduced himself to us and to Anna. "You working on the Kindertransport project?"

Kindertransport? More research for me, and judging by his slightly confused look, for David too.

The Observer bureau chief showed Anna the office, and David and I followed behind. "You're just in time for the action."

"Have I missed anything?" Anna asked.

"Some of the boys are on their way back from Berlin. I'll introduce you and fill you in, but in the meantime, have you had lunch?"

"Mind if I invite two friends?" Anna asked, pointing to me and David.

"Are you journalists?"

"I am," David said right away.

Anna smiled. "And Max is on his way to a typewriter if a piano doesn't find him first."

"Are you from London, Mr. MacDowell?" I asked.

"I lived in London for years, but I was born in Scotland. Do you hear the echo of bagpipes, lad?" The bureau chief gave a hearty laugh.

"Are they difficult to play?"

"Not bad, once you get the hang of it," MacDowell replied with a grin. "If you visit, let me know, and I'll personally show you around the Highlands."

Anna kept observing me. I tried to appear beyond my age. I had always wanted to be older, to be smart and clever like David. I was fascinated by the chattering teletypes with stories dispatched from all over the world.

MacDowell booked a table at U Fleků, nearby, down a side street, marked by its noted clock outside the restaurant. It offered a fairly nice lunch, and had been serving beer since 1499, but McDowell mentioned that it was not on a par with English taverns. Waiters with trays of brimming glasses threaded their way between tables. Our lunch was a roast, fortified with dumplings, irrigated by gravy. A green salad meant sliced cucumbers doused in cider vinegar. Afterward, Anna picked up some provisions at a bakery, which included creamy chocolate éclairs for us. We loved her style. She knew just the right thing to do!

Then she stopped in at a bookstore and handed us a *Baedeker's Great Britain*. "You two might enjoy London," she said.

"I'd like to visit London one day," I replied, with a measure of excitement. David joined with enthusiasm. "London!" he exclaimed, "Imagine all the stories to discover, all that history, and everything that's happening right now."

"I'd love to show you *The Observer* offices. That would help you both on your way to becoming journalists, not that you aren't getting there already!"

"Think of all the pianos to tune, Max. We'll be smashing," David replied, affecting a bit of a British accent. "You can bring Poppy along, and Hans, too, and we'll all stroll down Mayfair."

Then on a more sobering note, David asked, "I wonder if they are having the same problems over there as in Germany? Do you think the English are safe?"

Anna nodded earnestly. "I think so, but Europe is riding on the winds of war."

When we arrived back at the offices, a new world opened to me. Anna went to a file that came sputtering over the teletype. Tearing a long sheet of yellow paper from the machine, she took a moment to check copy, then handed it to us. It was from a correspondent in New York, writing about the preparations for the World's Fair, and I was amazed that words could come from so far away.

"Tools of the trade," she said.

Presenting me with her Czech-English dictionary, she took a step closer, bonding our friendship. She was so very generous. "This might help with your English. Part of a reporter's job is finding the truth. Reporting to your readers. Max, you might like to do that one day, like David."

"It's taking time. I guess it's because I'm learning how to begin."

"Just write. If you have something important to say, say it."

"I still really don't know how, Anna."

David interrupted. "If I might add, one word at a time. Keep a diary, write letters, Max. Like writing to Sophie. That was how the first correspondents began, before there were teletypes and typewriters. They wrote letters."

"Whom did they write to?"

"To their editors. Sometimes to themselves."

With that explanation, Anna handed me a small red notebook scored with blue lines. That was my first one. "Write something dangerous," she whispered. "It's fun. And important. Write your memories. Write down what you see and what you hear, what you learn every day. Write your story, Max." She handed me a pen and another pastry to enjoy. David watched carefully. He had an ally.

Then a door opened, and James Addison and Paul Wentworth returned from their assignment in Berlin. Meeting them for the first time, Anna was clearly interested in finding out more from the seasoned journalists.

"I've heard a lot about you from back home," James said. He appeared to be as friendly as his reputation. "I can't believe the old man sent you over. How did you manage that?"

"Charm goes a long way."

"Any left over? I could use some." Paul chuckled.

"I think you do quite nicely. What news of the madman?"

"He's mad, all right, madder than ever. Mad as hell. It's become a dangerous place for Jews and journalists. Want a briefing?"

"Would you?"

Sitting down, Addison reported, "There have been a series of disruptions; here's the latest: Violence and terror are moving fast through Germany. Several internment camps have been set up. Just before midnight last Tuesday, the Gestapo sent a telegram to all units letting them know in advance, and I quote, 'In shortest order, an action against Jews will take place throughout the country.' Then came Kristallnacht. Their synagogues and businesses were destroyed. And get this, the next day, the Germans leveled a one-billion-reichsmark fine on the Jewish population, blaming them for the destruction.

"I guess the Grynszpan affair in Paris preceded that. If you don't know," he continued, turning to Max, "Herschel Grynszpan is a seventeen-year-old Jewish kid who killed Ernst Vom Rath, a fairly important embassy official when he was told that his parents had been sent to a Polish internment camp. The boy was beaten. Taking revenge, Grynszpan shot the guy. And what did the Nazis do?"

"They did what they did. They broke a lot of glass," Anna followed.

"Right. The police were told to arrest anyone they wished. Fire companies were ordered not to interfere, and, imagine this, a thousand synagogues were burned. According to the *Munich Post,* seven thousand shops were looted and trashed. Add ninety-six Jews killed, Jewish cemeteries, hospitals, schools, and homes destroyed, thirty thousand arrested by Hitler's SS, and you have a night out in Germany."

Wentworth chimed in: "Anna, it's time you got used to a new vocabulary: Dachau, Buchenwald, Sachsenhausen. Let me give you Göring's words at his last press meeting: 'I would not want to be a Jew.' There are curfews, restrictions, new laws, and an exorbitant tax for a visa, if you have the connections to get one. And this for sure: life for Jews in Berlin is no longer possible. They are trying desperately to leave, and they need help. It's amazing that, in our time, a piece of paper with a stamp on it is the difference between life and death. Otherwise, Berlin is a terrific city!"

"I've expected something like this for a very long time." Anna was clearly disgusted but not at all shocked.

I understood that these were hard times that were getting worst for everyone—for kids like me and for journalists and Jews—and closer.

Would the music stop? I was beginning to realize that these things were happening, that the world was getting darker and more dangerous, but I couldn't yet know why.

As ever, I looked to David for answers and assurance and could see that, like Anna, he was not at all shocked and we all waited for Addison to report more.

"The *Times* reported yesterday on that one-billion-reichsmark fine for the 'violence' the Jews had caused. Here's the file." He slapped it on the table.

I picked up the file and started reading. David knew much more than I ever could. He was aware that a wave of terror was being unleashed. In his paper at school, he had written about the burning of books. He had also once written about Berlin, pleasing his professors with prose beyond his years. *A city washed in the umber glow of twilight, of children with red wagons and pinafores, of ladies with their parasols on summer evenings, strolling the glittering rims of wide avenues, a city with parties and waltzes, singing beer gardens and Moselle wine, and beech trees, a Germany of almost inconceivable nostalgic fashion.*

I thought of what I had just heard and what I knew already. Sophie and her mother had fled Vienna. I tried to think back to what Edith had said to Hans, that they were no longer welcome in Austria. I reminded myself of my vow to no longer look away. I couldn't deny what was happening. But what could I do? At the end of one particularly wild adventure in which Armand and White Dog had saved a raft-load of African orphans from the raging Zambezi, Poppy had turned to me and said: "Don't be the leaf in the wind, the flotsam on the river, don't be helpless in the storm. Be the helmsman, be the rower, fight against the current, and the wind and the rain, however strong. Stay the course."

I turned to David. "Do journalists have a way of making things okay?"

"I'm not sure that's exactly our job, but we help. We tell the truth as best we can," David confirmed. "Nothing ever happens at the right time. We must be ready. It's the best weapon we have."

"Better than guns?"

"Words are better, the truth is better, more powerful. But actions are most powerful of all."

My world was becoming much larger than I could have ever imagined. It was also becoming more frightening. I was learning more but was also more confused with every passing day. Part of me wanted to know more, to know and understand everything, while another part, the weaker side of me, wanted to go back to a time when I knew nothing, when the world was a small and safe place. But one thing I knew for sure: I could never go back.

On my way home, I knew more than ever that I wanted to watch and listen and learn and report, to fill a red notebook scored with dark blue lines.

Anna realized that the past few days were just a preamble for her assignment. There was no one in the office she could enlist. She knew that right away and needed someone who could anticipate coming events. But who? Apart from a few colleagues, there were still Jews in Prague who denied that there was danger ahead. Anna had Pierre Burger's address in her pocket, and in very short order, she would contact him.

NEW AND OLD FRIENDS

"What can I help you with, young man?"

The man inside the kiosk wore a nameplate on his shirt. SAM RAGGLE, NEWS AGENT.

"I was admiring your selection of newspapers." I took in all the titles: the *Prager Tagblatt*, *Munich Post*, *Lidové noviny*. He had papers in Czech, German, English.

"I can tell you are keen on news. I don't think I've seen you at my stand before."

"Yes, I am. I need to read as much as I can," I said with some authority, "especially *The Observer*."

"That's a good paper. I see you are a worldly reader. The only boy your age who comes around is David Grunewald, and I give him the papers left over."

"David's my best friend."

He smiled. "Well, in that case, I have more confidence in your generation than I have in mine."

"Thank you, sir."

"I've been here for twenty years and I hope to be here for another twenty," Mr. Raggle continued.

"Why wouldn't you be?"

"You know we may be facing a German occupation. I'm not sure what will happen to us all. It causes me a lot of sleepless nights, I can tell you. I could lose my stand. Things are heading in a dangerous direction according to the papers coming out of Berlin. I'm wondering what's going to happen. Here, take a copy of the *Prager Tagblatt*. It's on me. *The Bohemia* is not publishing much these days."

I raced home to read what was inside. As I ran, I saw a heavyset man sitting on a park bench across from the newsstand. His daunting black overcoat caught my eye. Was it the same man who had followed David and me? I wasn't sure. Perhaps there was an army, and they all lived in the same overcoat. I looked again. His black coat matched his black hat, the wide brim shading most of his face. It was a uniform. He was there alone, making notes in a black book. Like David, I had an urge to approach him and try to discover what he was writing. But I had a stronger urge to flee, to get away from this man and return to the safety of home and Poppy. I set off running, not looking back once.

Spreading the paper out on the living room floor, I read the *Tagblatt* page by page, accepting every word. There were articles about everything—features, editorials, advertisements, a calendar of concerts. Would there be news about Sophie, about her new home? Something about Germany? I scoured the paper over and over, reading every piece of hard news I could find and storing it away in my mental file. There was just enough to help me understand things at least a little better. I couldn't find an account of the demonstration that Poppy and I had faced recently, or anything about the violence, about fighting in the streets, about bloodshed, about ideals. I had the feeling that the paper wasn't reporting everything.

Was there a gap between what was real, what was happening, and what was reported? Do the papers tell the truth? The whole truth? Perhaps that was my job. See everything, record everything.

Overcome with unshakable self-confidence, I scribbled away, just as David had told me to, one word at a time. It was important to see everything around me as it was and to write entries about what I saw and felt. I was going to have to determine what really happens and what doesn't, what matters and what doesn't. I was on my way to finding the tools that would be needed one day to become a good journalist.

The Basilica of St. James was tucked away in a fairy-tale huddle of seventeenth-century houses.

I made my next entry.

Against a background where the sky is clear and blue, there was a painted church contrasted by faded yellows.

Inside, statues of angels were flanked by fresh bouquets of flowers. Extra chairs lined every aisle. The pews were filled to overflowing. The Great Viktor Mueller found seats in the packed church.

"Ready for the big attraction?" Poppy asked.

Rising from a balcony was a carved and gilded organ that had been played since 1705, representing a long tradition of keyboard excellence. And on that morning, with the sound of deep Slovak basses, and what Hans called "skirling sopranos," the choir and organist performed one of the seventy-six eighteenth-century masses in their repertoire. Poppy closed his eyes and listened to the echoes swirling around the vaulted ceilings. Behind us were twenty-one altars, and at the foot of each, groups were sitting on the stone floor, motionless, listening to the choir.

Sounds float out through the doors, filling Old Town with music.

Poppy took a moment, explaining to Anna, "It is a product of a troubled history speaking in a very personal way."

There was always a menu of concerts in churches and squares to be enjoyed in Prague.

Hans and Poppy returned home with apple tarts and cider, to finish off the evening playing musical chess, as they called it. They were never happier than when they were trying to outdo each other on the twin pianos.

We introduced Anna to the Steinway boys. They were my "uncle group," those who came over to the "Grand Hotel Krása" once a week. I had already told Sophie about them and was going to include them in my notebook. Uncle Fritz played an accordion; Uncle Bobo, a guitar. Uncle Vaclav played saxophone, and Uncle Karl had mastered the bass. Uncle Anton sang and danced. A few irregular uncles joined them on special occasions, which is odd to say, because they were all special occasions to me.

They weren't really my uncles, but I wanted them to be. Sometimes they played Strauss waltzes, sometimes lively mazurkas, and things really got going when they reached for their playbook of gypsy music. Anton danced, Hans played the piano, and Poppy, wearing a costume consisting of a white ruffled shirt, puffed sleeves, and red turban, took to his violin with such intensity that I thought a string would pop at any moment.

Uncle Vaclav and Uncle Karl were identical twins who often played the same instruments; they looked alike, played alike. They brought a trunk filled with instruments with them, lugging it up the stairs to the flat. Having emigrated from Berlin, they were much in demand in Prague. I'm not the best judge of age, but I suspect they were in their forties, large and balding, wearing white shirts with soup-stained black ties. They completed the musical circle like bookends, and the most fun came when they introduced Anna to a new song from America, with Poppy easily strumming his newly discovered banjo.

Georgia, Georgia, the whole day through
An' just an old sweet song keeps Georgia on my mind.
Georgia, Georgia, a song of you
Comes as sweet and clear
As moonlight through the pines.
Other arms reach out to me;
Other eyes smile tenderly.
Still inpeaceful dreams I see,
The road leads back to you.

The tall French doors were open. Hans called from the balcony, "We have an audience!"

Poppy gave an expansive wave to the crowd that had gathered outside to listen to the improvised American evening. They applauded. The neighbors never complained about the songs or even the pounding and thumping, always enjoying the concert.

"Would you like an encore?" Poppy asked the crowd, urging the Steinway boys to play.

"Yes!" I cheered along with the crowd.

"Here's a song from the great American composer George Gershwin!"

The Steinway Boys performed a song called "Strike Up the Band." And it was a rousing finale. Anna loved it. It was something to write about. Perhaps, after all, music had the power to save us all from whatever was coming. For tonight, at least, I would hold on to that dream.

LETTERS AND DISPATCHES

Anna's visit had been a distraction, and a lovely one at that, but for days now, weeks, I had been checking the post every day, waiting for some note from Sophie, something that would tell me she was all right, that she had arrived, maybe that she was thinking about me a little from time to time. At long last a letter arrived. Bounding to my room, I carefully opened it and looked for how she signed it before I even read the first sentence. *Love, Sophie.* That ending was a good beginning.

November 1938

Dear Max,

We arrived and are settled, and it is much different from where I once lived or what we had imagined. It is an unusual setting with interesting people, many I would like to meet. They have concerts here, which I enjoy, and I still think about you a lot. I loved every minute with you in Prague, and seeing how you spend your time. I'm afraid we have no ice cream here, but that's all right. Looking back to our day together allows me to remember so many good memories and sweet thoughts.

Max, have you decided what you want to do? I bet

you would like to be a composer like Hans, or a conductor like your father, performing on the great stages of Europe to audiences who love music. Am I right? When I first held your hand, it was soft and meant for the piano. I know that touch, as so many in my family are musicians, and I feel the happiness they have when they play, like Hans, I suspect. Music has always been part of our lives, and that is why it is so hard for me to understand why the Germans came to us the way they did—the same Germans who love music—and made us leave. My father was a soldier of sorts who tried to protect us and fight, but he lost. Are you a soldier, or a poet? Then again, with your curious mind, I suspect you might be thinking of becoming a journalist. And you'll make a darn good one too. We need to let the world know what matters most in the day's history. Is it better to win with a song or with words? What do you think? Who are you going to become, Max, when you grow up? For me, I think I would like to find the right phrase for each expression, so maybe a musician or even a poet? But if not, then a nurse like my mother. She likes taking care of me as much as I like taking care of her. I guess I was hoping to find my father here, but we didn't. I think we would like you to be a part of our family. I don't have a father anymore, and you don't have a mother, so in these ways we are alike, and sort of fit, don't you think? Like pieces of a puzzle coming together. I suppose feelings follow us wherever we go. Well, I've always been daring, so I'll try out a poem on you.

I hide myself in a flower.
At first, I thought it best.

You, unsuspecting, are one too.
And I think you know the rest.

I miss you.

Love,
Sophie

I slipped her letter into the pages of my notebook. I wasn't sure how to reply. She was asking me what I wanted to be, and that was a pretty hard question. No one had ever written a poem to me before, and no one had ever missed me. I read it over and over and kept it close by, folded in the pages of my secret journal. It was enough to keep me happy and not so lonely for a while. I thought about her father and her home and music and words; there was so much for me to think about. I wrote back in my best handwriting.

Dear Sophie,

I can't express myself like you. Your letter really moved me. I'm going to have to learn to untie my feelings, they are knotted up like my shoelaces. I need to make sense of everything.

I miss you, Sophie.

Love,
Max

Anna paced the room, thinking that she should send a dispatch for Travel as MacPherson had suggested, just in case she was being observed and monitored by German agents.

FOR TRAVEL: ANNA KINGSLEY

Prague, like London, Paris, and Berlin, is a city that should not be overlooked, but is one still waiting to be discovered. It offers up a confection of poetry and musical delights that centuries have shaped. Throughout, there are serpentine streets, old cobbled alleys, and Baroque churches and palaces in this place of a hundred spires. Red-tiled roofs rise and fall, creating shadows over drowsy courtyards and gently contoured lawns leading to riverbanks. Prague's survival has been a matter of luck. It has not been bombed or sacked, yet, but has a special poignancy inspired by a turbulent past.

The Hapsburgs endowed the city with beauty, painted domes, vistas, and churches teeming with angels surrounded by gilded floral swags.

In the evening, Wenceslas Square is filled with music and in summer, people in evening dress returning from a concert find a curbside stall selling hot sausages on fresh, warm bread with spicy mustard and sauerkraut before closing for the night. Then Prague becomes an almost deserted city, ruffled only by the swish of water carts washing down the streets, and the closing rumble of the last infrequent train.

During the spring's musical calendar, festivals take place, with the opening concert by the Czech Philharmonic played in a courtyard before a splendidly dressed audience. Everyone stands for the national anthem, with its bittersweet opening based on a nineteenth-century song, "Kde domov můj," "Where Is My Home?"

For a music lover, the most thrilling experience is to sit within the green walls of the Estates Theatre and listen to the music of Mozart rising through the gilded tiers of seats to the narrow oval roof, just as it did on that triumphant first night more than one hundred and fifty years ago. And in these uncertain times in Prague, the future has never seemed so precarious. But perhaps in just a few nights or a few days, the Nazis' political agenda will spread across the continent and we will come to know if the city can survive—the magic remains, and music will still play.

THE PIANO TUNER

My new, unwavering interest was news, but my focus was music. Once a week, I received my tuning assignments from Mr. Lorin Mannheim of the Companie Musik, the city's finest music shop. Mr. Mannheim was the most remarkable piano tuner in town. Because he was blind, it was not always easy to make house calls, and from time to time jobs fell to me.

How I acquired this skill I don't altogether know, because I can't remember a time when I couldn't do it. I've always had a good ear, and the mechanics, the technical skill, I learned from this extraordinary man, who knew everything about each instrument ever crafted, from horns and flutes to percussion and strings. He could bang out a Strauss waltz as if his hands were dancing and could restore a neglected instrument like no one else.

At a moment's notice, Mr. Mannheim sat at a piano bench and moved his fingers up and down the keys so fast they were a blur of motion.

"When I was growing up, my parents let me do anything I wanted to do," Mr. Mannheim told me, "and that was a big deal because I couldn't see. When I was your age, my parents felt it was time for a piano. We all have a handicap, and in many ways it makes us who we are." He said this almost if he could see, knowing somehow that I wore a brace.

"Max, you have a special talent. Always remember that an out-of-tune piano makes noise, not music. You're there to make things right."

I studied with Mr. Mannheim, who was as patient as he was kind. My father and David knew that I was learning something special, and with their support, I had soon mastered the craft. To mark the achievement, my father gifted me a small black bag at Christmas, and inside it, my tuning kit, which looked like a set of medical instruments. And I was a doctor of sorts, a musical surgeon. The badges of success for a true piano tuner are the felt ribbons woven meticulously in strands between the piano wires. These red ribbons were always with me, and over time, became my signature.

"Each note has three strings per key," Mr. Mannheim taught me when I first began to learn my craft. "You must first mute the outside strings, so the middle one will sound for each particular note. After you hold it, that's how you count the beats. I actually don't count but I hear them."

I learned to do the same. And with a special tuning hammer and my cherished red felt ribbons, I visited some of the most beautiful houses in Prague.

I soon came to refer to pianos as my ladies, because they were all elegant and graceful and like my mother, a faraway song. It was my love of music and playing the piano that filled so many afternoons with delight. In time, I became known in every pub and concert hall in town.

I particularly liked being alone on a dark stage, just me, my lady, and a work light, and we would speak to each other, note after note, until we reverberated splendidly together.

Tuesdays were my piano-tuning days, and even though I received a few crowns for every piano I tuned, it wasn't so much the money that gratified me, but the glorious compensation of knowing that I was making some contribution to music, not just playing, but making it resonate. I was giving back to each piano her pure and lovely voice. But my job now offered a way to observe people and things. I never paid any attention before. *A tuning journalist,* I thought. A red notebook now found itself snugly secured in my little black bag, keeping company with the hammer and those red felt ribbons.

The large brass plate announced the German embassy, a grand house with a handsome limestone facade across the Charles from Old Town, fashionable and smart. I rang the bell and was escorted in by a housekeeper dressed in a white starched apron. She spoke with a pronounced Berlin accent: "Come with me, Herr Piano Tuner, ja, to the living room."

And soon I was weaving my red felt between the strings, and letting my fingers hit an ivory key. I was at home here, as I always was with my work. A short while later my focus was interrupted when I saw a tall man in a smart tailored German uniform looking down at me.

"Who are you?"

"I'm Max Mueller."

"I'm General Heydrich. How old are you?"

"Twelve, nearly thirteen."

"And you tune pianos?"

"I do. And this is surely a lovely one you have here. It's an August Förster, a very fine grand, sir."

I could tell the general was amazed. People always were. And I took special pains to show anyone who might be interested something of a tuning performance; it always was a way to make friends.

Then to test the notes, I played a German tune, currently popular in the Music Halls called, "Die Liebe macht das Leben schön."

The general enjoyed my playing immensely and called a few members of his service staff into the room.

"An encore, please, Mr. Piano Tuner."

The staff, dressed in their black-and-white uniforms, looking like a chorus, hummed along—the general tapping his foot in time.

They were a very appreciative audience.

"Mueller, that's a German name, not Czech!"

"Yes, my father is Viktor Mueller, from Berlin."

Gratified to hear something of my background, the general said, "Viktor Mueller. Of course." By that I assumed that he believed we had a certain kinship, which I supposed we had.

"I've watched your father conduct in Berlin, Max. He is quite brilliant. You must take after him. Good German genes. My father was Bruno Heydrich, also a composer, so we have much in common. I'm delighted to welcome you to my home in Prague."

"Bruno Heydrich. That's quite interesting. I've studied a few of his compositions with my teacher, Hans Krása. Let me know if he ever needs his piano tuned. I'll gladly do it for free."

"I applaud your generosity."

"Thank you, Herr General. Anytime you need my services, just hit a few notes. I won't be far away."

The tall man smiled, and left the room, calling to his housekeeper to bring some fresh cider and *apfelstrudel*, which made for a lovely afternoon, and after this brief refreshment, I finished my work and left the embassy for my next call. I made an entry in my notebook about this man Heydrich.

Szymon Laks, a composer from Poland who had founded a Polish boys' choir, came to Prague on tour.

Poppy was invited to conduct a Mozart program. To open the

concert, he and Hans would play the Sonata for Two Pianos in D. The Great Viktor Mueller took me aside and paused dramatically.

Another story coming . . .

"There was a young man in Rome called Gregorio Allegri, who composed one of the most beautiful pieces ever written. It was so special that even the pope declared it could only be performed within the Sistine Chapel, that is, until Mozart visited the place and transcribed the entire piece after hearing it once. He was almost fourteen."

We were practically the same age.

"What's it called, Poppy?"

"The *Miserere*. You'll hear it tonight!"

I took Anna. I knew she would enjoy it. Of course, I went onstage for a moment to make sure the pianos were perfectly tuned. They were.

The choir was pitch perfect. Poppy was spot on: it was all so beautiful, and I thrilled to hear it, along with an equally appreciative audience. Anna said, "There it is, Max. There's the power of music. I've always believed that we have a soul, not just individually, but something shared and inexpressible in any other way. I recorded her words in my notebook.

Music gives our imagination wings.

Backstage, I met one of the leading members. His name was Jan, and he had the yellowest hair and clearest blue eyes I'd ever seen on a boy. We didn't speak the same language but managed to communicate in some form of silent understanding.

Finishing the evening, Jan and I walked over cobblestone streets and saw a comet in the sky. I had never seen one before. I suddenly felt connected to something. Was I part of it all?

We looked up and followed its path. It was a moment without words, shared together.

KARLOVY VARY

After Anna had told me about her country, I thought she should know more about ours. I mentioned it to Hans and he agreed. Maybe to a spa town like Terezín?

"We should be invited there first, Max."

"Then, how about Karlovy Vary?" I suggested.

Perfect!

The fairy-tale village was about an hour away by train; it was easy enough, even without Poppy tagging along as a guide. Having been a frequent visitor, I knew the place fairly well. The spa itself was in a narrow valley surrounded by hills, with a river running right through the center of town. The architecture was called Belle Époque, and it looked like a village of wedding cakes. Perfect indeed.

For centuries, the noted and the famous came to take the waters. The bathhouses were magnificent structures and, in the evening, orchestras played in the great square. Poppy told me that people had walked the promenades for hundreds of years. And on this excursion, it became obvious to me that Hans and Anna liked each other a lot. The way they acted was very real. Not so different than me and Sophie.

At the Grand Hotel Pupp, behind acres of gardens and in front of a rim of mountains, the general manager greeted us.

He was formal, friendly, dressed in a double-breasted suit and polished black shoes that shone like mirrors. I could even see my reflection in them.

"Welcome, Mr. Krása," he said graciously. "Would you prefer the Beethoven Suite or the Bach, or the Mozart or the Chopin Suite? Brahms, Grieg?" They had all been guests.

Hans turned to Anna for her choice.

"I seem to be in the mood for Chopin."

"Very well."

My room was part of the suite, and it had yellow-striped chintz curtains and white painted furniture—not exactly my taste, but it had cheerfulness, like Sophie.

The rooms were so large that Anna twirled in and out of them.

"What, no string quartet?" she asked.

"Not even a piano," Hans lamented, until he found one in a salon beside the living room and played a few bars of Chopin's Nocturne E-flat Major, op. 9, no 2.

The music stopped Anna in her tracks.

"You really think I need the cure?" Anna teased.

"I think you're incurable!" Hans replied.

"Well, I'm getting better."

"Sounds promising!"

I sensed they wanted to be alone. Understanding such things, I couldn't blame them.

The waters were said to refresh the spirit. With concerts in the evening and a lot of good food, I looked for something to do. I walked over to the colonnade with my own cup, and every hundred feet or so, I stopped at a drinking station, each with its own name: the Market, the Lower Castle, the Nymph and

Park. It was called "taking the waters." All the while, I thought about Sophie, where she was and what she was doing.

Finally, Anna and Hans caught up, with apologies, as if they had been neglecting me.

I didn't mind. I knew they had spent enough getting-to-know-you time. I would have felt the same way with Sophie.

The next day, I left, feeling sure they needed to be together. The train station was several hundred yards and five minutes away, so I left a note so as not to worry them and sent a postcard to Sophie. Then I returned to Prague.

In my carriage, between being awake and falling asleep, the *rackety-clack* of the steel wheels lulled me into a daydream.

"It's the baths," I said to Sophie; "I've booked a special one."

Sophie was surprised. In the center of a green-paneled room was a huge bathtub, bubbling with hot mineral water. It had been built for Edward VII.

"Built for a king?" Sophie asked.

Without a moment's hesitation, we put on our suits. Daydreams are that way. You can do most anything you want to do.

"There is nothing like a hot bath," I said, stepping into the water.

"Well, after all, we are friends."

"Girlfriend," I reminded Sophie.

Sophie followed, laughing. "You, Max, are the most adventuresome boy I've ever known. In fact, just too bold for words!"

As we were soaking opposite each other, an attendant popped in to check the temperature and left a large pitcher of cold lemonade.

"Lemons from the Orangery."

"Where's that?"

"London, my dear. I shall take you there."

"You are a daring one, Max Mueller. I'm a very proper girl."

We exchanged gazes from opposite ends of the tub.

"This is something I could get used to," I said.

"The baths?"

"No! You, silly!"

Sophie flushed. "It must be the waters."

Under the green iron arches, the sound of a whistle announcing my arrival at the Prague station woke me out of my reverie. On my way out, along the dusty-tiled murals of the station were ladies with silver trays selling inviting-looking sugar-dusted fruit pastries that seemed as though they should be eaten only by gentlemen in white gloves and dinner jackets. They tasted so good that I treated myself to several.

A few days later, Anna and Hans stepped down from the green-and-red carriage at the station. She waved to me, waiting on the platform, and I presented her with an arrangement of flowers.

"Did you have a good time?"

Anna couldn't stop smiling. It was the same smile Hans had when he first returned from London.

THE GENERAL ATTENDS A CONCERT

The most celebrated figure in the city's musical life was Bedřich Smetana, who years ago had opened a school in Old Town Square that attracted pupils from the city's nobility. But Prague's indifference to his compositions, and his disenchantment concerning the future of Czech nationalism, caused the composer to immigrate to Sweden, writing, *Prague does not wish to recognize me, therefore I have left her.* But within five years he returned, having missed his beloved country. Smetana had once proclaimed, "Music is the life of the Czechs," and the evening's performance was inspired by this patriotic composer.

Reinhard Heydrich, a rising star in the Nazi Party who Poppy said would soon be the Reichsprotektor of Prague, had come to pay his respects. David had told me how Hitler was expanding his hold on Europe, and Heydrich was one of his most trusted generals.

Anna invited me to the opening. She was fast becoming my concert-going partner.

"Wait until David hears about this. Sitting in a press box with you, Anna!"

I was so proud that my father was conducting. We got to our seats early. The musicians filed in, with scraping chairs and rustling sheet music.

The orchestra began warming up. A clarinet broke into a quick arpeggio, a flute was running scales. The string section straightened their backs, pulling the bows across their instruments in strange, dissonant tones. I loved this moment. I knew that in a few seconds, all those scattered sounds would gradually find something amazing. Little by little, it quieted down as the moments ticked closer for the evening to begin.

The house lights dimmed. When the musicians were ready, the concertmaster called for an A from the oboe. The Great Viktor Mueller took the podium as if it were his home. Poppy was dressed in his white tie and tails and polished patent leather slippers. The orchestra adored him. He created a direct, electric connection between the musicians and the audience. His conducting was a masterful show, as much an acting performance as a musical one. I was excited. I fought the urge to dance up to the stage to greet him.

For the briefest time, just a single breath, he paused on the edge of silence. He tapped his baton. I always inhaled and then held my breath in that moment, as the first note was played. But then the music, in all its power and instantaneously overwhelming sound, began. His right hand skillfully held the slender wand, as his left hand both responded to and anticipated the music. He caressed the notes and urged still more feeling from the players—turning, gliding, and gracefully speaking to each instrument in turn, urging with his movement every expressive chord and phrase. Sometimes, he even lifted himself up, his heels leaving the platform.

Poppy waved his arms; the music became a direct extension and expression of his swirling ivory baton. A cello chased the violins. Other instruments joined in. The music seemed to fall over itself in perfect cadence. A torrent of notes flowed from bows and wrists, the sound filling every inch of the theater's interior space, right up to the balconies. The orchestra was transported by the sound of Smetana's music, and they played with patriotic fervor. The audience was exhilarated—you could feel it and were a part of it.

During the performance, I noticed that Anna was becoming nervous and uneasy. She kept glancing at the man on my left, who had winked at me. He was clearly enjoying himself immensely. But Anna was uncomfortable, with good reason. It was General Heydrich, just as I remembered him from the embassy, polite and cordial, tall with an angular face and a nose sculpted too long for his other features.

At the intermission, in a large, formal room with pale-blue walls and cream marble columns, we met up.

"Good evening, Herr Piano Tuner." He smiled, and I introduced him to Anna.

"This is my friend Anna Kingsley."

He bowed politely. "You're from London and working on the Kindertransport program."

"*Ich bin*," Anna responded in perfect German.

Kindertransport. It was that word again. What did it really mean? I couldn't find it in my dictionary.

"Hardly needed," the general replied. "We love our children."

I continued speaking with the general in German, asking if he liked the concert. I think Anna was stunned by my easy willingness to engage him in conversation and was unnerved by the general, who was causing a stir in the house.

"Are you enjoying the concert, General?"

"A great evening," he replied. "For Prague, for the Reich."

"It is a great evening and I'm very glad you like music. It's a fine night."

General Heydrich gave a warm smile. "*Ich danke Ihnen.* Thank you."

When we returned to our seats, Anna leaned over and whispered under her program: "Do you know who you're chatting with?"

"Yes, of course. I tuned his piano," I replied.

"He is very dangerous, Max."

"Dangerous, like me?"

"It's not a joke. Be serious. Be courteous and respectful, and careful. Heydrich has come to Prague on Hitler's orders, and if he's in cahoots with Hitler, he's probably not someone we would want to invite to dinner."

After the concert, friends greeted performers backstage with kisses on both cheeks and "wonderful, dear," "moving, dear," "amazing, dear . . ." Heydrich arrived, congratulating the cast, and when he came to Poppy, he was particularly winning.

Anna remained discreetly in the background, a bit unnerved. She was aware of the rumors that had circulated about Heydrich's Jewish ancestry. His grandmother had married a Jew. Because of his background, Anna thought he was more of a contradiction—but a hard-core Nazi.

"I know your son, Maestro Mueller," Heydrich said. "We spoke during the interval, he is an engaging young man. He came around the other day and tuned my piano. Talent clearly runs in the family."

"No one could have done it better."

"It is indeed a pleasure to meet Viktor Mueller, the great conductor, or should I say, the Great Viktor Mueller? Like his father, your son has a fondness for music. I am very much the same. My father was devoted to music as well." Heydrich smiled and adjusted his uniform.

I quickly added, "The general's father is Bruno Heydrich, the composer!"

"Yes," Heydrich said, lifting one eyebrow. "I can't believe that Max should know his work."

"Bruno is a master," I added.

"Do you really think that?"

"I've studied his compositions, as I said. You and I appreciate good music."

Heydrich was pleased and leaned down. "Max, I hope we meet again at the opera. I enjoy your company."

"Thank you, sir."

Then turning to Viktor, he said, "It would be a splendid opportunity to plan a new program for the Reich. Come and see me in Berlin. Yes, come and see me, it will be my honor and pleasure to have tea with the father of the Great Max Mueller. My card, Herr Mueller."

"And may I present the general with mine." With that reciprocal gesture, they exchanged engraved white vellum cards.

The general clicked his heels and with a regimental snap, raised his arm with a "Heil Hitler!" Poppy bowed politely, holding his baton across his heart.

Without a moment's hesitation, I returned the salute, "Heil Hitler!"

The following day, Poppy and I visited Hans for tea, and we were barely through the door before Anna expressed her concerns about Reinhard Heydrich: "What are you doing heiling Hitler, Max?"

"I was being polite and that felt like the right thing to do, the right way to behave, Anna. We do it every morning at school. It's like saying good morning. Some of us compete to see how far we can stretch our arms in the air after taking the pledge in front of the Führer's picture. Everybody except David."

"What pledge?" Hans asked.

Poppy tried to ease everyone's concerns. "Max goes to the

German School. It's the best in Prague, and I assure you it means nothing. Just a German thing. We're musicians, not politicians."

"You shouldn't be heiling anyone, Max," Hans added.

"I didn't mean to offend anyone."

The room was quiet for a few seconds. Poppy changed the subject and put a record of Dvořák's Symphony no. 8 on the Victrola. Then he gave one of his amazing impromptu performances.

"Listen to the music, Anna; it is our life," he said, closing his eyes. "Do you hear every note and every instrument? Music is everywhere. Music is something that we can share and that can help us feel better . . . if times become difficult for us . . . for all of us."

There were instruments left over from a recent evening with the Uncles group.

In a flash, he circled the room and, as he did so, he played the piano, violin, tuba, and trombone.

"Pay no attention to trombones, they like to show off." I knew he was trying to lighten the mood and break the tension between him and Hans and Anna.

Even Hans couldn't help himself in the face of his friend's inspired theatrics. Poppy finished with a dramatic riff on the drum.

Everyone applauded. "Bravo, bravo, the Great Viktor Mueller!"

Viktor never failed to impress. And I saw Anna stare at my father with a look of undisguised admiration.

THE HOUSE ON GOLDEN LANE

Pierre Burger had dual citizenship, Czech and French, but he preferred French style, attitude, and dress. The pension was just off a part of Old Town known as the Golden Lane, a row of sixteenth-century houses near Prague Castle. Each had an appealing charm. One had been the home of an alchemist who had tried to transform base metal into gold, and now was the tasteful twenty-room Pension Burger, where Pierre enjoyed the privilege of accommodating many important Germans, especially Reich generals who brought their mistresses from Berlin for discreet, informal weekends away.

All the window boxes had produced fresh flowers. The foyer was painted with pewter-gray panels, and overhead hung a brass chandelier. It was very smartly decorated with eighteenth-century armoires and gold-leaf mirrors showing off the taste of its owner, a landlord, hotelier, and secret agent. In a hidden room in the pension was the powerful shortwave equipment that Pierre used as a key center for the underground activities and news dispatches to London.

"I've been waiting for you," Pierre Burger announced when Anna arrived at his small hotel.

"I'm sorry, but it's taking some time," she said with a sincerely apologetic tone. "This undercover work should take priority."

"I know," Pierre replied.

"How would you know?"

"We've been watching you."

"Nothing too embarrassing, I hope."

"Nothing at all embarrassing. I'm glad you are here. London is very high on you, and we are so glad to have you as part of our group. It's extremely important work, Anna."

Coming directly to the point, Anna told Pierre she had found someone for Pink Tulip to liaise with.

"Viktor Mueller. Do you know him?"

Viktor had made a deep impression, and she liked his sense of fun. He was unconventional and talented. What Anna liked most was his devotion to Max, and his boundless curiosity. But could she protect him if he joined the Resistance?

"What do you think, Pierre?"

"Everyone knows of Viktor Mueller. He's German, well-regarded, well-traveled."

"I think he has an inside track to useful friendships. Especially Heydrich."

"Friendship and information. But we need operatives, Anna. Can he do what is required?"

"I can't be absolutely sure, but if I had to take a bet, I would trust him."

"You haven't answered my question: Can he manage the hard stuff?"

"Hard stuff?"

"Yes, life and death stuff. Assassination, sabotage, explosives—the ability to risk everything every day, all with the confidence and intelligence of a good actor. I can't overstate how dangerous this all is. You must know this. When you enlist anyone into this work, you must trust that they can do it and that they understand what they are laying on the line for the cause: everything they have and everyone they know."

"I'm new to this game, Pierre. I don't have the answers. I think he's a good man to have on our side; he can move around and socialize with the Nazis. And I want to see him alive. He must stay alive. He has a son."

"Maybe I can arrange something on Kindertransport."

"He's pretty devoted to his father. I'm not at all sure the boy would go. It could compromise things . . ."

"I understand. I've been working hard on the program, and I'm having some success in Germany and Austria. About fifty children. I'm not sure anyone else in Europe really feels the urgency . . . just yet."

"Let me know how I can help."

"Of course. Back to Mueller. We've investigated everyone you have contact with, Anna. I'm sorry to do that but you must realize the stakes in this game. This is not to intrude upon your privacy, but that's the way we work. Intelligence-gathering. I think he could be an essential operative, and in time maybe he can help us. See what you can do to put him in play."

UNEXPECTED JOURNEYS

I was overwhelmed by a term paper I was assigned to write on French history. Why couldn't it have been about England? Anna knew everything.

Poppy surprised everyone: "*Billets de faveur,*" he exclaimed, holding up four train tickets. "Let's all go to Paris!" It was not Anna's first visit to Paris. She had always appreciated everything about the city, and now it seemed to matter more, because it was a city that meant so much to Hans.

After taking an overnight train, we were soon dining at Maxim's, that proud and celebrated Parisian restaurant.

"Named after you, Max!" Poppy proclaimed.

Smart-looking waiters in black tails and white ties introduced a delicious lunch topped with crêpes suzettes. As the French have always known, conversation is the brightest and optimism most accessible when at a table with friends. For a moment, we seemed to have left the headlines behind us. Dinner ended with a toast, "To those we love, to those we cherish, to good times just near."

After lunch, Anna took me swimming in an indoor pool fashioned in teak on the top floor of our hotel, Le Bristol. The deck and even the windows of the pool were reminiscent of a ship, and I splashed through the water like a buccaneer. Then we got dressed and strolled to the Left Bank while Viktor and Hans prepared for their evening performance. Walking across the boulevard Saint-Germain and down to rue de Buci, Anna found an antiques shop with crystal paperweights.

"Are you going to buy one for Hans?"

"I think he will like this one. What do you think?" she said, holding up a particularly intricate piece. The shopkeeper said it was very rare, and made by a glasshouse called Saint-Louis, one of the three great manufacturers of fine crystal. Anna didn't take her eyes off the piece as she spoke, barely above a whisper: "Don't you think it's beautiful, like silent music?"

I said something that day that Anna later told me she never forgot: "I'm learning a lot. About you, about myself, about my world. I hope you never leave us, Anna."

I learned a few things for my notebook as well, one of the most useful being that the best way to know people and a city is through its markets. I saw that Parisians were expressive people, and in the street, everyone was part performer and part spectator; the market was a theater and nowhere was the show better. While we were in Paris, I noticed Poppy and Anna talking a great deal. They were animated, and I wasn't sure what about. But it was an exciting time, free and happy, and my next entry read:

> *These might be called my sunlit salad days. Paris has a thousand amazing places.*

My view of the world was being formed in a series of new experiences. I ran over and played with leaves that were just browning at the beginning of fall. There were old men sitting in the autumn sunlight on green benches, leaning forward on canes, watching. The city was brimming with life and hope, and for those blissful few days at least, so were we.

That evening I wrote a postcard.

Dear Sophie,

I saw the brightest star, trailed by dusty little ones over Paris, and I'm sure that bright star was you.

Love,
Max

Poppy was off to Munich, and before leaving, he described the city as one of his very favorite places to conduct, to be. "Always good audiences in Munich!" I continued shuttling between our house and Hans's. My father and Hans entertained me with music, but Anna was a talking guidebook, telling me about the world, about life, about the changing face of the continent, and about England, with places and historical tales that allowed me to imagine I was there. Sitting on my favorite sofa, I fell into her lap, not missing the opportunity to be close to her and always looking forward to hearing about distant places. She told me about the colorful changing of the guard at Buckingham Palace, and about the other joys available in London, its grand houses, its museums, its parks; then we traveled farther afield over patchwork landscapes in the country to the rugged coastlines of Cornwall, and across to the medieval forests of King Arthur and the Knights of the Round Table. We took long, rambling imaginary walks through centuries-old villages in the Lake District. I took the waters in a town called Bath. She told me about her school, individual colleges along the Cherwell, and about punting on flat-bottomed boats over a rippling waterway with weeping willow trees. She read to me and we stepped through a magical looking glass with Alice.

At Stratford I met Shakespeare, had tea in Anne Hathaway's cottage.

When Anna described London, I fell deeper into pretending, visiting the morning markets in Covent Garden, where farmers brought their fresh fruit and vegetables. But the best of all was a glass house at Kew Gardens, where there was an orangery inside an Edwardian conservatory and beautifully lit over the winter holidays. She described the details with a reporter's accuracy, making the place come vividly alive in my mind's eye. Palladian windows, and hundreds of orange and lemon trees. This was a place where Poppy and I could pick fruit and make fresh lemonade.

"Near the orangery," she said, "is a pond with a squadron of ducks and a flotilla of little boats.

The English poet Percy Shelley floated one when he was as old as you, Max, in a setting that years later was inspiration for his verse."

The war winds were indeed blowing toward Prague, and Anna was asked by her chief to return to London; two journalists had been arrested in Berlin.

> NOT SAFE FOR YOU KINGSLEY STOP
> BEST TO RETURN LONDON STOP
> MACPHERSON

"I hate for you to leave, Anna," Hans said, picking a few late-blooming cabbage roses that had lasted through the summer. "Even our flowers want you to stay."

Walking into the drawing room, Anna deposited the cut

flowers in a slender vase, adding water. "They smell like English cold cream," she said over her shoulder. Suddenly, her eyes widened, and she turned to face Hans. "Come home with me, Hans."

He had a smile, but then his face fell. "England isn't my home, Anna. And even if it were, I can't leave on a moment's notice. Let me just . . . let me have time. We need time."

"Time? You'll soon to be ordered to fly a German flag over your home. Just as in Germany, that flag is going to wave in every occupied country."

She could hardly say more. Anna reached out to Hans, their arms finding an embrace.

"I'd like to take Max with me. I'm worried about him, worried about you all. We have great schools in London. Max can come with me tomorrow," Anna urged.

Hans held Anna close. "Max is a German citizen, Anna, he'll be safe here."

"But you're not safe, Hans."

"I'm safe, Anna."

"Hans, face facts. We can't spend our lives in an idyllic spa. They're shutting down schools for Jewish children, they're passing new laws, property is being confiscated. Even your prime minister is in exile in Britain. Wake up, Hans!"

He walked over to Anna and put his arms around her. "I'll talk to Viktor when he gets back from Munich. I promise."

Then he retreated to his piano and began to play. Anna wondered aloud if this would be the last time she would hear him play. The next day, she was gone.

THE BLACK OVERCOAT

"Hello, Max." Mr. Raggle was piling up newspapers in his kiosk. "I have a good feeling about you, Max. And I have a job for you, if you have time."

"A job? I have one already."

"But you could be very helpful to me, Max. You always read the papers. I like that. It's good for my business, and it's good for your education. I need someone to deliver a few newspapers for me, twice a week, twenty-five or so, all in the neighborhood. I'll give you all the newspapers and magazines that you would like for free."

Endless free newspapers and magazines sounded perfect.

"Aren't you taking a chance on my abilities, Mr. Raggle? I'm just a kid hanging around."

"You're a young man interested in the press. Yes, that is an intelligent interest."

"Thank you," I answered, remembering to be polite. "And I have a bunch of questions from reading the papers."

"Go ahead."

"Do you know anything about this man Heydrich?"

"I do," Mr. Raggle replied. "He's in the news these days. I read recently that he's planning a meeting near Berlin. I suspect he's up to something. There're not many details except dark rumors, something called a final solution."

That solution again? A solution to what?

David would have the answer. I took some papers to him.

"I see you've met Mr. Raggle at the house of information."

"I'm working for him. Now you can have current news."

"Who are you delivering papers to, besides me?"

"I suppose he has his list of subscribers, people like you and me who want to be informed. Do you know anything more about this Heydrich plan? Mr. Raggle was talking about it just now."

"I aim to find out."

I sat down right there and read my first haul cover to cover. All I could find were articles about the Germans, the same story over and over, with names like Himmler, Göring, and Goebbels, and their dedication to "the cause" and their "devotion" to the Führer.

"The German press is just a giant keyboard," David said. "They play what they want us to hear. It's called propaganda."

The second time I visited Mr. Raggle he gave me a few coins for each delivery.

"Be careful," he said, handing me a pile of papers.

"Why do you say that?"

"Just a figure of speech," he replied, but I noticed he was looking across the way. That man in the black overcoat had been there every day, and he was there today too. Even Mr. Raggle noticed him.

I made my way around the city, delivering the papers. As I wove through the streets and alleys I knew so well, I would catch a closer look at the man in the overcoat. He was following me. I tested my theory and took a diversion. Turning left, I walked a little way down the street and turned left again. I looked over my shoulder. The man ducked into a doorway. He was after me, and that frightened me. Would I disappear like Sophie's father? Be taken away and never heard from again?

"Do you know what he's up to, Mr. Raggle?" I asked, pointing toward the black overcoat when I returned, out of breath, to the kiosk. "He's always around."

Mr. Raggle took his time. "I asked you to deliver because some customers don't want to be seen buying papers."

"That's stupid."

"It's really not so stupid, Max. These days it's risky to be well-informed, and riskier to speak out against the occupation. That man and his cronies are particularly interested in anyone who reads the foreign press. I guess he has it in his mind that anyone who does might disengage from the party line, and there's no room to ask questions and seek answers in his world. If he is what I think he is, then he has an agenda and anyone who disagrees with that agenda . . . is going to disappear. I'm convinced of that."

"Then he's a threat. Are you telling me everything I need to know?"

Mr. Raggle sighed. "Just be alert and wary. These are . . . how can I put it . . . precarious times."

I was sure that the overcoat man was interested in me. Or was he more interested in Mr. Raggle, at "the House of Information," as David dubbed his kiosk? Something deep inside me wished he would vanish, but I was beginning to know better, I was learning more each day, the latest contribution to my education coming from an editorial I read, a clipping that David had filed in one of the scrapbooks he kept.

THE OBSERVER

March 16, 1939

PEACE IN OUR TIME!

Edvard Beneš was forced to resign on October 5, 1938, and he left for England, after a trip to Berlin. A new president, Emil Hácha was sworn in a month later. The men of Prague are voicing their anger and their sense of humiliation.

On March 14, Hitler invited the newly appointed President Hácha, a respected jurist and judge, to the Reich Chancellery in Berlin.

In the interest of the country he loved, he traveled by train, in failing health. Arriving at his appointed time of nine o'clock in the evening, without any of the customary respect normally accorded a head of state, he was asked to wait in a cold and uninviting anteroom in the Chancellery. Hitler deliberately kept him waiting for hours, and finally, at 1:30 a.m., he saw Hácha.

"You have two options, my friend and president, for the safety of your country. One is to cooperate with Germany, in which case the entry of German troops will come peacefully, in good will, to ensure Czechoslovakia a generous life. Two, if you should choose not to cooperate, resistance will be broken by force of arms."

By four o'clock, Hácha collapsed with a mild heart attack, and was treated by Hitler's physician. Then he effectively signed over Czechoslovakia to Germany, believing that collaboration was the only way he could help his people and nation.

Germany has taken over Czechoslovakia without

firing a shot. The fate of the most democratic nation in Central Europe would be sealed even before the Munich Conference, when our prime minister abandoned his country's ally to appease Hitler. From the beginning, Hitler called for the union of all Germans. After the annexation of Austria, with three million people living in Czechoslovakia's historically German lands, Germany demanded concessions from the Czechoslovakian government, the goal being to appropriate Czechoslovakia's industrial capacity, its resources of coal and gold, for the expanding Reich military.

The world was changing faster than I could keep track of; my country was becoming different. Every day, squads of black cars with men in black overcoats circled the streets, like crows looking for their prey, something to feed on. David told me that at Municipal House there were long registration lines, with German staff stamping papers. Some had a big *J* on them, for Juden, to identify Jews. This was something that I just couldn't understand. What was the logic? Why were they making enemies of friends, of my friends? In time this would happen to David and his family, to Hans and so many others—hundreds, thousands. It was unimaginable, but it was real. I could feel my eyes opening to the reality facing me, and I was caught between appreciating what my life and the world had been and the horror of what it was becoming. I felt a nausea deep within and thought that I might become sick any second. Life can change, had been changing gradually, but sometimes it turns on a moment, changes in an instant, and my life changed then. I knew that from that day, from that single moment, I was no longer a child, someone who could shut his eyes and wish the horror away. This was how things were, and I reflected that I had to stick with David and be a journalist, to witness it all, unflinchingly. I had no other choice.

One night in our flat I was in the sitting room and witnessed an earnest discussion between Poppy, Hans, and Franz Kohn, Poppy's attorney, who had fought with the Germans in the First World War. He was perceptive and smart, and up to date on what he called the Nazi legacy. "To begin, Hitler is bringing Germany out of a great depression, everyone is working, or in the army, everyone except political dissenters and Jews. Young boys are indoctrinated into Hitler Youth, to fight for the Fatherland. I've seen the kids marching in Munich, banners waving, eyes fixed ahead, keeping time to the beat of their own drums, singing patriotic songs. Their sisterhood is the Bund Deutscher Mädel, the League of German Girls, whose gift to the nation, groomed for domestic life as they are, is that as soon as they are old enough, they will be primed to give birth to pure Aryan children—tall, fit, blond, blue-eyed children for the Reich. As women, the careers they may choose are restricted, and few will be allowed into professional careers, but what matter when they will have the honor of furnishing the next generation in the thousand-year Reich. They are groomed to be 'Hitler's Maidens.'"

"Funny that," Viktor replied. "Blue eyes and blond hair? Hitler has brown hair, brown eyes. Tall? Himmler is short. Lean and fit? Göring is fat. Some pure Aryan race."

"It's a serious matter, Viktor."

"It may be serious but that doesn't mean it's not absurd."

"You have to take this risible man seriously. He's creating a new order, a pure race, and anyone who is mentally disabled or physically handicapped, who somehow or other is not fitting his prescription for a pure race, is to be eliminated. And, Viktor, no Jews."

Poppy looked across at me and sat in silence for a moment or two. "For a short time, every Jew had a choice: either stay and struggle or try and find a way for themselves and their families to leave. Some Jews had access to the very few highly treasured immigration permits to Palestine, held, of course, by the British. Some of us helped in whatever ways we could . . ." The words hung in the air for a while.

David had told me of how, in the long history of the Jewish people, exodus was one of the ways they ensured their survival, and Jews were doing everything they could to get as far from the Nazis as possible. Many were convinced that the Nazis' intention was not to honor their promises to the Jews, a promise of a land of their own, but to destroy them, and that the best solution for those who couldn't get away for whatever reason was to find some way to overcome the imposed hardships until the situation passed.

Kohn visited my father often, handling personal affairs and contracts. They trusted each other. They had been friends since their school days.

"There might be something we can do to outsmart them. We need your help, Viktor. The Nazis are relying on informants and collaborators," Kohn explained. "Birth and census files are being requisitioned, and the Germans are practiced in accounting and record keeping. They're establishing a Jewish museum to provide history and symbols, archives and artifacts of Jewish culture. It doesn't make sense to me, Viktor. Why would the Germans want to recruit Jewish historians and scholars?"

Racial laws and a museum? It made no sense to me at all. But just because it made no sense I couldn't pretend it wasn't happening. I had to listen and try to understand, to try to make some sense of this bizarre, senseless new world.

Poppy pondered for a while and finally said, "I have friends, one friend in particular. Let me see what I can do."

BLOOD AND HONOR

The truth of the new world was approaching in so many ways, closing in on all sides, and the hallways at school were filling with an ever-increasing number of German students in semimilitary uniforms, wearing round swastika pins on their shirts, leather straps across their chests, and red-and-white armbands. Just the sight of the new insignia and these symbols was enough to trigger that deep, sickly fear inside me. The pressure to join their Hitler Youth meetings was growing. They wore brown short pants and shirts with the same *HJ* armband that was worn on the German League jerseys.

"What does the *HJ* stand for?"

"Stand for?" one of the boys replied. "Don't you know, Max? *Hitlerjugend. Blut und Ehre.*"

Hitler Youth. Blood and Honor.

My new classmates walked taller than ever, exuding a confidence, a sure belief that they were superior to me, to everyone. I feared them now and wanted nothing to do with them.

We were set for the final game with the German League. I went to my locker to pick up my jersey, only to find five of them pinning David to the floor. David howled with pain when they stamped viciously on his arm. This time I didn't stand by. Forgetting my tricky leg, I launched myself at the pack and I was held down by three of them while the other two repeatedly hit out hard, punching me in the stomach. Finally, our teacher Mr. Rudolf ran into the room and screamed at the boys to stop. I spat out blood and David helped me to my feet. We were sent to the infirmary.

"What happened to you boys?"

David turned to the nurse. "Nothing. Just a little disagreement about football." He refused to speak out, as he was figuring how to carry on this fight another day.

She bandaged David's arm, but that didn't stop the game.

"Come on, Max." David winced. "We're going to take them on. We'll show them."

I was swept up by my friend, enthused by his spirit. On our way to the field, David skipped over the cracks in the sidewalk.

"Why do you do that?" I asked.

"Superstition."

David, bruised arm and all, played his heart out, almost winning the match, but the final whistle sounded too soon. We lost the game, but I gained something that day, a new respect for David, for who he was and what he stood for.

They played a victorious Nazi anthem on the field. We both refused to heil Hitler. And for the first time I really understood something about his courage. It felt like a small act of defiance.

Weeks later, there were fewer students than usual in class; David's seat was noticeably empty. Where was he? Mr. Rudolf walked nervously around the room.

"There have been some changes," he said, concern and something far deeper etched onto his face. "Some of our students have been transferred."

Transferred?

Mr. Rudolf shrugged. "It's a new law. New rules."

"What rules? Where's David?"

"It's better this way," Mr. Rudolf said, taking me into the hall. "He's at a home called Mrs. Blomberg's."

"Where are his parents?"

"That we don't know . . . yet. They were taken away."

"What?"

"I feel badly for our school, even for the Czech All Stars," Mr. Rudolf stammered.

"What do you mean?"

"They've been disbanded, only the German League will be allowed to play. They're champions, you know."

Some champions. Some rules. The ground beneath my feet felt ever less stable with every passing day. Anything could change. Anyone could simply disappear.

THE INCREDIBLE EVELYN BLOMBERG

I couldn't come to terms with what had happened. I could make no sense of it at all, and I just couldn't shake this feeling of a cloud looming over me, over us all, becoming darker and more ominous with every passing day. How could I get on in my life without David? We were always together. We would talk and share a meal, it was our time. Occasionally he used me as a sounding board about his next editorial, how to fight the good fight.

I missed Anna. I worried about David, and that night I asked Hans about Mrs. Blomberg.

"Evelyn? I know her, Max," Hans said. "She runs a place for orphans and Jewish children."

"David's not an orphan. What does this mean, Hans?"

For the first time I saw a note of anguish in his face.

"She has David!" I said, desperately grabbing his hand and pulling him out the door. "He's my best friend. We've got to go and see him!"

"Easy, Max. I'm with you."

Mrs. Blomberg's was in the Jewish Quarter, and as soon as she opened the door to us she wrapped Hans in her warm embrace.

She was a plump woman with the largest bosom I had ever seen browsing beneath a generous apron.

"Come in, come in, my dear Hans! And who is this?" she asked, sweeping back her silver hair.

"I'm Max Mueller," I said. Without waiting a second, I almost shouted, "Where's David?"

Mrs. Blomberg took my hand and pointed upstairs. "He's fine. I think you know some of my other new kids, too, Hans." Her red cheeks and cheery face were somehow reassuring.

She leaned toward him, and I could still hear her whisper. "We need accommodation for the new children arriving every day."

Hans nodded and handed her a bulging envelope.

What was that about? I wondered.

"The Germans take their parents away and drop the children off here," she continued in a hushed tone. "Jews are being interned all over the country. They are being rounded up, Hans. No one is safe, and every day I wonder if I'll be here tomorrow."

"This is crazy," Hans replied, shaking his head in disbelief.

Crazy, indeed. I couldn't believe that my best friend had been forced from school, his parents taken away just like Sophie's father.

We walked through the old house which, like many in Prague, had been modestly restored. Hans and Mrs. Blomberg kept whispering as we made our way from room to room, and Hans greeted many of the children.

I found my moment when Hans and Mrs. Blomberg were deep in conversation and raced upstairs.

Poking my head through doorway after doorway, at last I found David's room and my friend was sitting alone on his bed, waiting for someone. The room was stark, with just the essentials. Nothing warm or cozy, but cold and functional. Before I could ask how he was feeling, David said, "My parents are gone."

His face was drawn, and it looked like he hadn't slept for days.

"I know, David, but do you know where they are?"

David shook his head. "I was going to ask you and Hans. All I know is that they're missing, Max." His eyes welled with tears. I couldn't bear to see him like that.

"Is this all because you're Jewish?"

"Just that, Max. Hard to believe."

"Parents can't just be taken away. Not in Prague. It doesn't make sense."

"They were a bit too political. They saw Hitler and the Germans for what they are, brutal, and they wrote and distributed pamphlets against the occupation, defending human rights. That's what we Jews do. We've always tried to right a wrong. And I guess that's a part of me too. We get in their way."

"I must be in their way too."

"Not necessarily, Max. You're German."

"Does that make us any different?"

"These days it makes all the difference."

I thought quickly, trying to conjure up something, anything, to make it better. "You can come and live with me until we find them. We spend most of our time together anyway. I've got to get you out of here."

David smiled weakly. "Max, thanks, you're a pal."

"I brought a newspaper, maybe there's something about your parents."

Turning the pages, we didn't find anything, but what we couldn't fail to notice was that the *Tagblatt,* a German liberal newspaper, had taken a dramatic editorial turn. There were articles about German purity and an unflattering caricature of a Jewish man. At last David let the paper drop from his hands as if he might be tarnished by its toxic content.

"For a moment, I thought that you may have left for London. I heard that there was a transport arranged."

"Max, it's great they are saving some kids in Germany. But it couldn't take everybody and, besides, we have to be here to fight the good fight."

I put my arm around my friend's shoulders. "We'll find your parents, David. Leave it to me." I spoke with much more assurance than I felt.

"What's going to happen to the school paper?"

"We'll start another one and call it *Mrs. Blomberg's Gazette*."

"How is your father?" David asked.

"He's back in Berlin playing a concert."

"I wouldn't want to be in Germany right now. There are whispers, stories about people, people like my parents, disappearing without a word. All kinds of people. Jews, Communists, people who just don't like Hitler. My parents, Max. Where are they? They would never leave on their own. They were arrested, I know it."

"Don't worry, David. I can already see the headline: ACE REPORTER FINDS PARENTS." I tried to lighten the conversation.

"Now that's a story!" He tried to smile.

Hans shouted up the stairwell, "Max, we better get going!"

I went downstairs, yelling behind me, "Don't worry, I'll be back tomorrow, and I'll bring some supplies."

David waved from the top of the landing. "Great to see you, Max. And my parents . . .?"

I sounded as confident as I could: "I'll find them."

"You promise?"

"I promise."

I pretended that David didn't have tears in his eyes.

Before we crossed the street, I appealed to Hans: "We have to do something."

"Something? Something about what?"

"About David's parents. They've disappeared."

Hans stopped in his tracks.

I stared at him for a while and he looked so lost. I gently nudged him in the ribs. "Don't you go and disappear on me, Hans."

It was a stupid lighthearted remark, but it carried a bit of truth, not only for me, but for him. There was a brief, awkward pause, and then Hans smiled and looked me in the eye. "I'll stop in the police station later. I know the chief."

As we walked, Hans started to hum quietly.

"Why are you humming, Hans?"

"To cover my anxiety, I suppose. Humming a tune might make things better. When I stop composing in my head, I think things are taking a bad turn, so I hum."

"And you think that works?"

"I'm not thinking, Max, I'm humming!"

WHERE ARE THE GRUNEWALDS?

The police headquarters was filled with German soldiers and a few men dressed in black. At the desk was a Czech policeman, wearing a blue uniform appointed with brass buttons. He was so large that he seemed in danger of bursting out of his jacket.

"Hans Krása!" The policeman's greeting was as big as his waist.

"Still playing the tuba?" Hans turned and shook hands, and said to me, "The chief is the star of the police band. They're lucky to have him in the band and we're lucky to have him looking over us. For now. Gregory, can you give me a minute please?" Hans moved closer to the officer and whispered, "Can you find out anything about Hanna and Jacob Grunewald? They're professors at Charles University, friends of mine. They're missing."

"Missing?" He spoke in hushed tones. "Friends of yours? They could be Communists," Gregory continued quietly. "A lot of protesters from a group called the White Rose Movement at that university. Not popular with the Germans these days. I'll see if any of my men know anything."

Gregory signaled to one of his aides. The man left the room and, after a few minutes, returned. "We don't have any information," he said. "If it is the SS, we have no jurisdiction. They may be part of the last roundup."

He took Hans aside, out of earshot of everyone in the station.

"The White Rose? Is it possible? Do you think your friends were a part of it? Do you know anything?"

I looked blank and Hans whispered, "The White Rose is a Resistance group working against Nazi Germany, made up of students and professors. They could have been part of it, and if they were then they could have been taken away. Anyone belonging could pay the price for standing up for what they believe. I have one of their leaflets."

He began to read.

"The policy of the National Socialists is to control all communication, the news media, police, the armed forces, the judiciary system, travel, all levels of education from kindergarten to universities, all cultural and religious institutions."

I thought for a moment and said, "That means . . .?"

Hans winced a little. "That means that no one is safe."

We looked up and saw another of Gregory's colleagues handing him a report. He scanned the document and then leaned over to Hans. "Well, it seems they also had a visa for the family to leave the country, but the papers were forged. Not good, Hans. Not good at all."

Then Gregory turned and said confidentially. "They were taken for questioning to a place called Sachsenhausen."

"Come again?" Hans whispered back.

"A camp for political dissidents. I'm sorry if they were friends of yours, Hans. But this is a dead end as far as I can see. I've no authority in this matter. This falls squarely under Heydrich's command. Good luck, my friend."

Hans was clearly upset, and he started to hum again.

I caught a glimpse of a man in a black overcoat, slipping inside an alcove in the background. Was it the same man? Who was he? Did he have anything to do with David's parents' disappearance? The thought was another dark cloud.

Gregory took him aside. "Be careful, Hans. This is a bad time for Jews."

Hans nodded and said goodbye. As we left the station he interrupted his humming briefly to lean toward me, as he straightened his collar in the face of the growing wind. "This is a bad time for everyone."

With all urgency, I appealed to Poppy as soon as he came home: "David's parents are at a place called Sachsenhausen. General Heydrich is in control. Maybe we can help. Maybe you can. There must be something . . ."

"Whoa there. Slow down, Max. Heydrich *is* our friend."

How could that be? David was afraid of him, hinted that he was involved with terrible things. But he was kind, even friendly toward me, and he did love music. Was that enough? David was wrong this time. Poppy seemed to think the general was a fine person, and he was never wrong about anything.

Poppy smiled at me, encouraging me to smile back. "And if he knows anything, he'll help. I'll speak to the general and make sure they are okay."

"But they're Jewish. They are all being taken away. What's happening to them? I see it every day. Lines, desperation, fear. It's all around me, Poppy. You don't see it."

"Of course I see it. They'll be okay. I'll make a plan. Trust me, Max."

The Great Viktor Mueller always had a plan. I had to have faith.

PUT IT ON THE PROGRAM, VIKTOR

Staring at the fleshy jowls of Mirco Bonifac, the artistic director of the National Theatre, Viktor Mueller spoke quietly in an office on the top floor of the theater building. Bonifac had a secret panel in the office that opened toward the stage. Yards of red velvet fell over a wide window, a rich fabric that had once been a curtain in the great hall.

"I have some information," Viktor began. "Reinhard Heydrich, who I've heard will be appointed Reichsprotektor of Prague, is the son of composer Bruno Heydrich. His father-in-law, Hofrat Kranz, founded the Dresden Conservatory. I just met with him in Berlin." Viktor smiled encouragingly.

"You don't say," the director responded.

"I do say. And he loves music!"

"Excellent. That's a good indicator of character, in my opinion," the director commented. "We should get ahead of the power-game and be ready for any eventuality."

"The best people love music."

"Max tunes his piano over at the embassy."

"He does a fine job, that lad of yours, Viktor."

"It took Max to tell me that Heydrich's father is Bruno Heydrich."

"You don't say!"

"I do say."

The director tried to squeeze into his much-too-small Louis XV chair but was only able to perch uneasily on the edge. Viktor was fascinated by this awkward balancing act. Bonifac took out his handkerchief and mopped his brow, a habit he had, whether he was sweating or not.

Viktor continued, "We should welcome him to Prague. An Evening with Bruno Heydrich!"

Bonifac slapped his hand on the table in front of him: "A marvelous idea. Put it on the schedule, Viktor."

"We'll include his D-Major symphony, op. 57, a favorite," Viktor added.

Viktor's face lit up. A part of a plan. A concert with a few short weeks to organize everything.

"Hans, aren't you coming with us?"

I knew he had no intention of going to the concert. It was a stunt, he had said, something appealing to the German High Command, something to show how thoughtful the Czechs were. The event had been announced all over the city by the German propaganda machine; all the patrons were set to attend.

The day of the concert, a motorcade of eight Mercedes sedans pulled up in front of the two-hundred-year-old German Theatre. The late afternoon sun shone with cold brilliance on the cobblestone streets. Leaves from the sycamore trees fluttered to the ground as the cars came to a halt.

From just inside the lobby, I saw General Heydrich and his wife step out of an official black car to be greeted by Director Bonifac. "Welcome, welcome, welcome," Bonifac said, clapping his hands before escorting them inside.

Finding my seat, I looked up as the general and his wife settled into the director's box. A Nazi flag hung from a balcony. My body tensed, but I had to have faith that all of this made sense. The hall was conveniently filled with people with Czech-German backgrounds, to make sure of a warm reception for *An Evening with Bruno Heydrich.* General Heydrich, standing in a neat gray uniform, spotted me and waved for me to come his way.

Knowing what I had learned from David, and given the constant presence of the black overcoat, it was probably not smart to defy a Nazi general. The atmosphere in the hall was warm and receptive. I felt sure that the main reason the audience had come was to hear my father conduct rather than to hear the music of Bruno Heydrich.

On the way to the first tier, I wiped my moist palms on the front of my trousers. I'd never sat in a royal box before and was impressed by the sight of a butler wearing white gloves serving finger sandwiches and chocolates.

"Max," the general said, tapping my shoulder. "May I present my wife, Lina, and my mother, Elisabeth, who has come from Dresden for the concert."

Lina extended her hand and nodded a smile. She was wearing a suit and platform shoes that made her appear much taller than she was. "Max. It is a pleasure to meet such a fine young man who loves concerts."

Heydrich's mother was severely blond, fair, and German. Supported by a cane with a silver handle, she was elegantly dressed in black lace.

Leaning toward the general, I said, "It must be nice having your family here."

"You can't imagine."

Reinhard Heydrich was not only in charge of Prague; it was

also his responsibility to defeat any resistance to the Nazi Party. I was seeing him in a new light. He was tall and effortlessly warm and engaging, yet something in his face seemed sculpted in stone. I had learned a lot about him from David in recent days: his methods were arrest, deportation, and murder. From the beginning, he had carried out attacks on the Jews during what was known as "the Night of the Long Knives" in Germany. He was friendly and engaging while at the same time proud to be known as a man with an iron heart. I felt something dangerous lurking behind the genial smile that seemed almost fixed on his face.

I was playing a role and reached for every bit of Mueller charm I could muster up. In my way, like Poppy, I had a plan.

"My father told me this is going to be a great evening," I said. "It's going to be thrilling to hear the music your father composed, General. Now we'll all be able to enjoy it."

I was sitting there and imagined myself as a character in a film being improvised on the spot. I felt that I was a performer and knew that I had to get my lines right. I was, after all, the son of the Great Viktor Mueller. I told myself over and over, *Max, be calm and friendly and convincing. Nothing to worry about.*

Before the house lights dimmed, I took my chance. "I wonder if you can help with a small matter, General?"

"Of course, Max, how can I help?"

"My best friend, David Grunewald—well, we play football together, and he's great . . ."

"The Czech All Stars."

"How did you know?"

"I'm fond of sports, always interested." The general spoke blandly.

"His parents are missing, and I think they are at a place called Sachsenhausen. He's a good son. A good person. My best friend."

The general replied coolly, "Just a formality, Max, I'm sure. Are they Jewish?"

"Yes. They teach at Charles University."

"That's a fine school. I'll consider it and see what can be arranged. But these are complicated times. I'm sure you love your country, yes?"

"Of course I do."

"It is essential for all of us to look forward to a new order."

What kind of order is he talking about?

"A new day for Germany, the start of an era that will last for a thousand years."

A thousand years? A thousand years of what? I thought as the house lights dimmed and the audience stood as the orchestra played "Deutschland, Deutschland über alles." "Germany, Germany above everything."

There was a hush and the audience applauded Poppy's appearance in the darkened hall, with only small lights glowing from the sconces on the walls. He tapped his baton emphatically and the orchestra launched into a rich melody. Heydrich never shifted his gaze from the stage, his eyes increasingly misty. *My father is a music maker, a great music maker,* I thought. *No matter what happens in the world, music is beauty and my father is part of that.*

When the final stanza was played, the musicians stamped their feet on the wooden floor in a loud rumble, a customary sign of appreciation, and before the house lights came on, the Great Viktor Mueller invited Reinhard Heydrich to the stage. The general urged me to follow.

Poppy presented the general with his slender white baton as Heydrich smiled and placed his hand over his heart. "I will never forget this concert, Viktor," he whispered. "Never. You've given my father a great honor."

"A pleasure," Poppy said, leading us off the stage.

"You're not only a great conductor but a thoughtful man," Heydrich said.

"*Haben Sie vielen Dank,* Reinhard. With deepest appreciation."

"I want to speak with you privately about something from which we all will benefit," Heydrich commented, taking Poppy aside when we went backstage. "I know how valuable you are, Viktor."

After a pause, Heydrich added, "Viktor, the Fatherland is on the march to greatness. You're a Berliner."

"Of course." Poppy straightened his shoulders.

The general presented his card. "When you are back in Berlin, bring your violin and we'll play together."

Poppy and I made our way outside. It had turned cooler. Ladies dressed in long silk gowns and men in black ties with white scarves around their shoulders huddled along the sidewalk under the marquee, waiting for cabs.

"Will Heydrich help?"

"I think he will."

"This evening was an opportunity to lay the foundation for a useful relationship. Strategy, Max. Strategy. The long game. The general wants me to come around for a meeting. This could be useful in so many ways for us, for the future."

Poppy couldn't fail to see the doubt written across my face. He ruffled my hair. "Max, have faith in your father. This was a great evening, a great and important evening made better still by being with you."

"Why didn't Hans come?"

Poppy spoke in a quiet tone. "Because he is Jewish, Max. This is not a safe time for Jews."

"But surely this doesn't mean people like Hans . . . and Sophie."

I pulled up my coat collar as a gust of wind blew through the winding street. "I guess that's the reason that David is no longer at my school."

Poppy bent down and lowered his voice. "A lot of Germans don't like Jewish people. It doesn't matter how good Hans and Sophie and so many others are—"

"And David . . ." I said.

"Yes, David too. They are all good people. Look, many people don't like Heydrich."

"What kind of a man is he? Do you like him? Is he a good man?"

Putting a finger to his lips, Poppy glanced behind him as if expecting to find Heydrich hiding behind a lamppost. He shrugged his shoulders. "Is he a good man? Max, what's most important right now is that he can be useful."

"Do you want to be his friend? You even gave him your baton."

Poppy looked deadly serious. "Adaptability, Max. Sometimes we adapt to situations, however strange or difficult they may be. We must figure things out and find ways to survive, and we should do this without giving up all the things that make us who we are. I'm dealing with Heydrich in a cordial way, and I hope that he'll conduct himself as a fair and honest man, Max." He looked away for a while and then turned back to face me, nodding: "Tonight was important."

Poppy buttoned his coat and put his hands into his pockets. We stood in silence on the sidewalk, our breath forming a vapor between us.

Finally, he broke the oppressive silence. "It meant a lot to his family. Yes, I thought it was a nice thing to do, the right thing to do," he said. "I have to do things in a certain way."

I narrowed my eyes as I looked up at my father. "Which way is that, Poppy?"

I always looked to Poppy to do the right thing. Always.

"Do you think he can help David?" I asked.

"Please know, Max. I am going to make sure we are okay, all of us, and I will help David, but you must understand, it's complicated. You must believe that I'll never let you down."

I nodded uncertainly. I wanted to believe him, but I wasn't sure I could altogether. That was a scary thought, but one that I couldn't push away. Everything was changing. My world was shifting on a delicate axis. I could never doubt Poppy, the very thought was terrifying. If I lost faith in him, then who was left? What was left?

Poppy looked up at the star-filled sky, and cleared his throat: "You know, Max, most of the Czech musicians didn't want to play this evening, but they did it for the love of music. Your mother was Czech. I may have been born in Germany, but we're all Czechs in spirit and we can always offer a gracious welcome. We have to keep the houselights on."

Poppy dropped me off at Hans's before again leaving for Berlin; my room there was beginning to feel like my real home.

I couldn't get Poppy's words out of my mind. I realized that three of the most important people in my life were Jewish. Hans. David. Sophie. Was Sophie safe? With all that was happening, I hadn't been thinking about her as much as I usually did. When was the last time I received a letter from her? It had been too long. I thought back to the day we had spent together, retracing our steps in my mind. Were my thoughts and feelings for her still there? They were, all of them, stronger than ever. I needed to contact her.

Dear Sophie,

I don't understand everything that is happening but what I do understand I don't much like. I am writing about what I see and feel in my notebook and I aim to do something about it. I hope that you are safe and I know that somehow or other we will be together again. I think of you all the time.

Yours,
Max

I kept up with the papers—politics still confused me, but I couldn't get away from the cruel truth that my country was alone and in danger. And if my country was in danger, then I was too.

I felt alone both inside and outside myself. Sometimes I thought that I would die before I understood everything around me.

PLAYING FOR HITLER

The piano playing woke me, and, putting on my robe and slippers, I headed to the kitchen.

Hans was playing in the drawing room. "I'm working on an opera. Oh, and another thing . . . you'll be the star."

I was bewildered. "You're joking. Me a star?"

Hans smiled broadly as he looked up from the piano. "Oh no, I'm perfectly serious. It's called *Brundibár*."

He rippled the keys.

"I'm writing something for the kids at Mrs. Blomberg's. It'll occupy their time and be a distraction from . . . everything." Hans's eyes darkened. "It'll be fun for them to perform, give them something they might enjoy."

"An opera! You really want me to be in it?"

"I most certainly do. It's about a person named Brundibár, a character who owns the marketplace. He, by the way, is just like Hitler and doesn't want the people in the village around. With the help of a fearless sparrow, a keen cat, a wise dog, and a chorus of children, they chase him away, singing a finale in the square. They send him packing. I'm going to need a clarinet, accordion, piano, percussion, violins, a cello, and a hurdy-gurdy."

"A hurdy-gurdy?"

"Yes, a hurdy-gurdy," he said, his eyes bright. "Some people call it a hurley-gurley, more melodic, sounds nicer. You've heard them on street corners. A box you wind with a handle that plays tunes. Not many around, but it is essential to the story. I'm getting Frantisek to do the sets; he'll locate one."

Frantisek Zelenka was an old friend of Hans's. He had designed the production for his first opera at the National.

"Who's going to play Brundibár?"

"You are."

I was lost for words. "Mmm . . . me? I, well, I don't know, Hans."

"You'll be perfect, Max, and yes, it's the starring role. Listen!"

He produced a theme that sounded like a carousel in a park. It was the prettiest song he'd played for weeks.

"That's nice. But Hitler?"

"That's just the point! Brundibár is appealing, even though he has a lot of terrible ideas. But the play has a double meaning. It depends how you see him. Some of the most interesting things are like that, aren't they, Max? Two people can look at the very same painting and see something quite different. It's the same with Brundibár. I look at him as a pretty good guy. I promise you, he's a fabulous character."

"But I'm not like him."

"You're a born actor, Max, just like your father. You've got that spark in your eye, that amazing appreciation for everything around you. You'll wear a top hat and a fake moustache. He's a buffoon, you'll be fine. It's only make-believe."

Hans just continued playing.

"I don't like pretending, I don't like moustaches, and I'm not a buffoon. How long have you been writing this?"

"Playing a buffoon doesn't make you a buffoon. It makes you a performer. And I've been thinking about it for a time. Then I began writing it all down on paper at five o'clock this morning, and in a few weeks, I'll finish up; then we'll cast and start rehearsals."

"Does Mrs. Blomberg know about it?"

I wasn't sure about Hans's opera, but I wanted to tell David. I missed him. The Topper was my partner in everything.

A PLAN FOR VIKTOR MUELLER

Berlin 1939

Viktor Mueller always had a plan. He was intent on forming a stronger friendship with the general. His offices were close to the State Opera House in Berlin, and with cheeky confidence, he called on Reichsprotektor Heydrich. As he presented the general's card at the entrance, he was detained.

"Do you have an appointment with the SS-Obergruppenführer?"

Unabashedly he replied, "Kindly announce Viktor Mueller, violinist." Opening his case, he showed the guard that it carried no machine gun the way gangsters' violin cases did in movies.

A few minutes later, Viktor Mueller was greeting the general.

"Viktor," Heydrich said, giving Viktor a warm handshake and returning to his place behind an ornate oak desk. "Nice of you to come. Please, sit."

The general gestured toward a large, ebony and leather chair to the left of the door. Heydrich was immaculately dressed in a well-pressed gray uniform with a silver-and-black Iron Cross pinned to his chest. One could not imagine him in civilian clothes; he would be out of sorts, out of fashion, out of step. He was born in his uniform. His manner was considerate with ingratiating overfamiliarity. "You are not only a great conductor but a thoughtful humanitarian," Heydrich said. Viktor had not thought of himself in this way. "You created a plan to help those poor Jews in Prague with a program to support the Reich. We need talented workers. I hadn't thought of it. Your idea was efficient. We're very grateful." After a pause, Heydrich added, "I see you understand, Viktor, that the German Fatherland is on the march to greatness. You're a proud Berliner."

"I'm German. Indeed." Viktor sat even straighter in his chair.

"And you remember how things were. All the Jewish financiers ruining the country."

"I remember hardships. I remember difficult times. I remember the music, great musicians, many of them Jewish. But I am not sure what this has to do with the racial laws?"

Heydrich laughed and shook his head. "Viktor, our Nordic soul defends our noble character against racial and cultural degeneration. We are a pure race, and I have nothing personal against Jewish people, or their artistic friends, but they don't serve Germany's interests. They are not German, and they should leave. The Führer wishes them to do so."

"But with the extraordinary contributions of Jews, the zeitgeist in Berlin was a great cultural renaissance. Take Brecht, his *Threepenny Opera*."

Reinhard thought for a few seconds. "Lotte Lenya was terrific."

"She was magnificent, the play and the music were magnificent. And Piscator changed theatrical techniques and production, brilliant!" Viktor continued, "I studied under Erwin. You are a man of culture, you know that he was the first one to project newsreels behind actors onstage. We revolutionized drama at the Nollendorfplatz. Revolving stages, treadmills. And Max Reinhardt, a magician creating atmosphere and illusion, in a way we had never seen before. We had forty theaters in Berlin alone. Of course, you know all of this already."

"Those were indeed heady times," Heydrich began, "but as in Rome, there's a sinister counter-renaissance undermining our essential German character. With much decadence the city was sullied, became sexually unbuttoned. I visited some of the cabarets—so many homosexuals and transvestites. And those art galleries. Dadaism. I never quite understood it; a lot of nonsense, if you ask me."

Viktor nodded his head.

"Then stand proud with me, Viktor. We have a chance to restore democratic nationalism; it is our right given by destiny. We lost our rightful lands!"

Heydrich stood up and began pacing the room.

"The Treaty of Versailles was an obscenity, a stain on the history books, with unreasonable demands for Germany to repatriate, to accept sole responsibility, as if we had caused the war!" Heydrich shook his head. "We had to make substantial territorial concessions and pay reparations and in return, there was unemployment, impossible inflation. You had to roll millions of reichsmarks to the bank in a wheelbarrow because they were worthless. We lost our identity, our pride. Our movement is to restore the Fatherland to greatness! But, Viktor, if I may return the compliment, you're a man of history." Viktor said nothing but gave a mirthless smile. Heydrich stopped to spin a globe on his desk. "Now is the time for us. I wish you had been with me at the rallies in Nuremberg and seen the Führer's speech, the parades, the cathedrals of light."

"I was there."

"You were?"

"Yes, before I became a conductor, I was a violinist with the Berlin Philharmonic, and principal soloist when we played at the Luitpoldhain-Dutzendteich. A nicely received evening."

"I would have liked to hear you play. I adore concerts. Of

course, you already know that," Heydrich said, *ta-tumm*ing and waving his hands in musical punctuation.

"We share a passion for music."

Heydrich held Viktor's gaze. "We share more than that. We share a passion for Germany."

Changing the subject, Viktor said, "The season is beginning in Prague. I'll arrange tickets for you."

"I understand they are difficult to get, oversubscribed."

Viktor was aware that Heydrich could have any ticket he wanted, but he and the general continued to play the give-and-take.

"Do you prefer orchestra or a box?" Viktor asked.

"Orchestra, of course. The closer the better."

"The acoustics are better in the middle of the house."

"I prefer to be close to the orchestra. I like to watch the musicians perform as well as listen."

"I'll take care of it."

"I have something to show you. I've treasured the violin all my life." Heydrich opened a simple black case. "A Stradivarius!"

"No!"

"Yes!" Heydrich clapped his hands together like an excited boy.

Viktor walked over to the case and admired the instrument. He knew that Stradivarius violins were among the most exquisite, expensive musical instruments ever made, boasting an extraordinary sound due to the craftsmanship of Antonio Stradivari, who crafted these magnificent, rare instruments in his shop in Cremona, Italy. They were musical gems. Other violin makers had attempted to duplicate them without success, never achieving the same precision, the same sound. Made from maple with special glues and varnishes, they were impossible to replicate. With only seven hundred made, each violin was a musical treasure. After tuning the strings, Heydrich began to play Tchaikovsky's *Violin Concerto*. Viktor had no intention of being upstaged. Retrieving his more modest instrument, he played along with the general.

"I am surprised," Viktor said, "I didn't know you played, and so well! Bravo."

"Call me Reinhard, please."

"Then, Reinhard, you may call me Viktor; we are fellow musicians!"

Heydrich offered a restrained chuckle while walking around his desk to a cabinet, which he opened to reveal a small bar.

Accepting a brandy, Viktor asked, "How did you ever come to acquire such a magnificent instrument? I could never afford such a thing."

"It's on loan from a violinist in the Philharmonic."

Viktor knew at once it was a lie; Heydrich had stolen it. His theft was an insult to all musicians, but Viktor had to be careful not to show any offense. The instrument belonged to Artur Levin, an accomplished and much-admired musician. Mueller knew this because Levin's name was fastened to a small engraved plate on the case. Violins were deeply personal instruments; each one belonged in some profound way to its player, residing in their soul.

"I'm very glad you came, Viktor. I've been thinking about you, and, now that we have had our warm-up, we must get down to business. I want to offer you a position on my staff."

"And I wish to offer you a position in my orchestra, Reinhard, Concertmaster of the Philharmonic. Czech or Berlin. Always good to have something to fall back upon, Mother used to say. You never know, hard times . . ."

Heydrich grinned broadly and then seemed absolutely serious. "Ah, Viktor, I have no fear of hard times. I think we can look forward to good times, great times. Together, making music and making history."

Viktor finished his brandy and placed the crystal glass on the desk. He then packed up his violin. "I'm performing tonight; I'll leave two tickets at the opera house."

"Thank you. I'll ask Lina to join me."

Viktor presented his card. "When you are back in Prague, bring your violin and we'll play again." Heydrich gave a little laugh.

The general saluted. "Heil Hitler." Viktor, hesitant at first, smartly returned the salutation, adding a little dash by clicking his heels a bit more sharply than Heydrich. He would have preferred to return Heydrich's casual Nazi salute with a handshake or bow. But it was not to be. And one small gesture at the end of an important meeting was a price worth paying in this long game.

GREETINGS!

An official document marked with a German seal arrived for Herr Viktor Mueller.

When Poppy unsealed the envelope and read the contents, he dissolved into laughter.

"Max, well, there you have it. I've been conscripted."

I jotted the word *conscripted* in my notebook. My vocabulary was expanding by the day.

"I'll save you the trouble of a dictionary. They want me. I'm in the German army now."

"How can that be? We live in Czechoslovakia."

"We're German citizens, Max, and they're calling people up."

I never thought of Poppy joining the German army. I couldn't imagine it. We were a family of musicians, citizens of music. Like so much these days it just didn't make sense. I couldn't imagine the Great Viktor Mueller in the military. *But why . . .?*

Finishing my thought, Poppy said, "I have no intention of being part of Hitler's Reich. This is not exactly what I had in mind. I'm going to speak to Heydrich about it. But it may be useful . . ."

"What about David's parents?"

"Ah, yes, I have something for him."

"Good news?"

"Very good news!"

He handed me a piece of paper.

The Lucerna was a classic turn-of-the-century cinema in Prague, with velvet cushions, richly painted walls, and silver lighting fixtures from 1920.

David and I got together for the first time since I had visited him at Mrs. Blomberg's. I tried to visit him more often, but a curfew had been set, and surely I was being followed. Despite no longer being in school together, this was an opportunity when Poppy arranged for tickets. We met up in front of the theater.

"I have news!" I was out of breath. "Your mother and father were released and given the last two permits to Palestine, they're on their way there."

David was lost for words. "Can this really be true? They're safe?" David could barely get the words out.

"Yes, yes, Poppy told me about it just last night."

"Max, how did it happen?"

"He arranged it."

I didn't have all the details but gave him the official paper. His parents had not wanted to leave him behind. I also handed him the letter that they had sent with Poppy.

Dearest Son,

You cannot imagine. We had to go quickly, our only choice. If we hadn't we would have been shot. Please know that your mama begged and pleaded to stay. I had to consider what you would have wanted us to do. We could leave only after a promise that you'll be protected and safe.

I believe that with all my heart. We love you so much and we live for a better time. One day, one day soon, the conflict will be over, and we'll be together in Palestine. Be strong, my son. Please forgive us. Bless you, David.

Your devoted father

David put down the letter and said nothing. At last I spoke: "Poppy has promised to look after you. He made a sacred oath."

"I miss them terribly," he finally said in a pained whisper. "It had to be as difficult for them as it is for me. But at least they're safe now. I'm grateful to Poppy."

"They're going to be all right, David. You will see them again, and I guess that in the meantime, you'll have to just put up with me."

"That may be more than I can take."

"Well, it won't be for long."

"Is Poppy working for the Reich?"

"I don't know what he's doing, except he has some kind of plan. We have to trust him."

"Well, he was able to help my parents, and I won't forget his kindness. Your father did something extraordinary!"

There was some small sense of security in knowing what Poppy had done, and he did something that proved he was still the Great Viktor Mueller. Perhaps things really would be okay after all.

A LITTLE PANACHE

"I think it's time to remove that brace of yours," Poppy said. "You're doing really well, walking better, leg stronger, looking good to me, Max."

"You've helped me arrive at this moment, Poppy."

"You've arrived by yourself, son, and I'm proud of you." Poppy bent down, and removed the straps.

"You're not going to be a target for any Nazi."

"I'll feel funny without it."

"Then only the special shoe. It will help you adjust."

The Great Viktor Mueller always made me feel better than I was.

"That was something great you did for the Topper," I said, again thanking my father for helping David's parents.

Poppy smiled broadly. "And you must tell David not to worry because he always has us to help him."

The Great Viktor Mueller always dressed carefully for important occasions. Today, he decided on a charcoal-gray coat with darkly striped trousers for his meeting with Heydrich at his Prague office. I sat down with my books and my notebook.

My journal was fast filling up and I had invested in three more identical ones. I was committed to my new interest in writing. The more I read and the more I wrote, the more sense I was making of my world.

When Poppy returned later that evening, I breathed a sigh of relief. We went into the living room, with its many photographs of actors and musicians staring down at us, each housed in a sterling frame. I loved studying the photos, memorizing the assorted loops and swirls of each autograph and inscription to my father. I flopped onto my familiar beige couch.

Poppy gazed out over a balcony, the railings heavy with trailing ivy, to the courtyard beyond. He sighed and strolled over to the antique wooden table. He kept a red box on top, filled with his slender ivory batons. He caressed one before facing me.

"What happened?" I asked. "What did he say? Must you join? What if you were to—"

"Easy, slow down, Max."

Poppy walked over to the sofa, deep in thought. He moved a towering stack of sheet music to the floor and sat down next to me. "I don't want you to be afraid. I am the Great Viktor Mueller, remember?" He waved his baton in the air.

I leaned my head on my father's broad shoulder. "You're joining the army? Surely Heydrich can get you out of it."

"The general wants me to take the rank of captain. From now on I will be the Great *Captain* Viktor Mueller. I'll spend time in the cultural ministry in Berlin as his personal deputy."

"But that's crazy! You're a conductor; a music man not an army man."

"I'll be supervising productions," Poppy said, "beginning by organizing a suitable entertainment for the Führer's birthday."

"Hitler has birthdays?" I asked with some bitterness.

Poppy chuckled. "Everyone has a birthday and everyone

loves a celebration, Max. And besides, you haven't heard the best part. I get to wear a full uniform, befitting my rank!"

There was a hat rack in the far corner of the living room, holding Poppy's prized collection: the elegant black top hat, the bright red fez, the debonair gray homburg, the dark brown fedora, the yellow straw hat, the felt trilby, the English tweed country cap, and the one I most admired, the *Three Musketeers* hat with an extravagant plume. There were many more, with new ones appearing whenever Poppy returned from another grand adventure. Some of my favorite stories revolved around them.

"Take my fedora. It was made by the famous hatmaker Giuseppe Borsalino himself. They called him Pepe, and with style he strolled the *via* every evening after dinner in Alessandria.

"And the fez! King Farouk—king of Egypt—told me to always wear the tassel on the left. I don't know why, but I would never question the king of Egypt and the Sudan. I was in Cairo. We drove through the desert in the king's red Rolls-Royce convertible and sailed down the Nile and into Cairo in a felucca. Glorious days.

"Now, the Panama hat . . . I loved Panama, but I acquired one of their hats in a small town in faraway Ecuador."

I knew all these details by heart. Each story had been recounted so many times, but I welcomed every telling, as if being reintroduced to an old friend.

"A superfine Montecristi, the signature on the finest Panama hats in the world. They have over twenty-five hundred weaves per inch. Twenty-five hundred. Each one took a year to make! And whenever I got thirsty I filled it with water; imagine a hat so fine that it can hold water. Very hot in Ecuador.

"The trilby is from James Lock of St. James in London. It's just the sporting brim for a gentleman. Kind of jaunty. A little panache."

Poppy always selected a proper cane from a group in the umbrella stand. Some with silver handles. One even had a built-in sword.

He loved to pretend. He couldn't help it. He was a born actor, a master performer. I wasn't surprised that Poppy might want to dress up in a German uniform. I just hoped that he wouldn't take that role too far. Poppy reassured me and said that it was "immeasurably worthwhile."

I collected new words wherever I found them, and now I knew that some things were just *immeasurably worthwhile.*

"Captain Mueller at your service. How do you like it?" Poppy strolled into the living room. He had been fitted by A. S. Schneider, Heydrich's personal tailor in Berlin.

Poppy looked taller than usual. His light-gray jacket, square-shouldered, with gold braid and engraved buttons, had a red insignia with the rank of captain. There was a black stripe falling like a ribbon down the side of each trouser leg.

Hans said, "Viktor, you look like you just stepped out of *The Nutcracker.*"

"Very observant, Hans. It's my new uniform!"

"Are you serious, Viktor?"

"I joined up," he announced.

"Are you crazy? In the German army?"

Hans blinked.

"I didn't have much choice, Hans. I was drafted. Surely Max mentioned it."

Hans became deadly serious: "You always have a choice. It may not be easy, but it's still a choice. You've chosen to take on this role, and it's ugly and dangerous. Viktor, this is an insult.

What are you thinking? This is a betrayal not only to me, but to yourself. You're a collaborator, Viktor. And I'm ashamed."

Collaborator? I didn't know the word, and I quickly took out my dictionary.

Was Poppy a friend and associate, or a defector and traitor?

"The Reichsprotektor needs my help for the cause."

"What cause?"

"Thingplatzes."

Hans frowned. "What are Thingplatzes?"

"They're platforms for staging performances from German history and mythology."

"And this is your cause?"

"I have to be practical, Hans. I'm a German, not a Nazi."

"You report to one . . . your new friend."

Hans stood up from his chair.

"We will get through these hard times, Hans. I'll get us all whatever we need. My rank carries a lot of benefits. I mean a *lot*!"

"A *lot*? And what will you do to earn us these benefits? Round up Jews? Take away citizenship? Enforce curfews? Who are you, Viktor? Who have you become?"

"Hans, we're best friends. I conducted your first opera. We're not politicians. We're not soldiers. We live for music."

My father sounded as though he was pleading with Hans.

"Not the music you're playing, Viktor. No. No."

While Poppy and Hans argued, my feelings were trapped somewhere between them. What did all this mean? Where should my loyalty lie? Where should I place my trust? I had never seen Poppy and Hans exchange a harsh word. Now they seemed to be on different sides. What had my father become? And whose side would I choose?

"Let's put this grotesque show aside for a moment, Viktor. How about Max? You know what I think is a good idea? There's a program, Kindertransport, to rescue children of Prague. If we don't take advantage of this, you and your new Nazi friend are going to fill Europe with orphans, and then who knows what will happen to these kids?"

Poppy growled. "I know all about that, Hans, and it's for Jewish children. Max doesn't need to leave. Max is with his friends. I want him nearby."

"And what about David?"

"He feels his place is in Prague, After all, he's a newspaper man, and he's a curious boy."

"And where will you be, Viktor? In Berlin?"

"Don't I have any say in this?" I asked.

Before an answer came, Poppy took my arm and led me toward the front door. I looked over at Hans. He was tapping his foot in anger, his face dark with tense emotion. I didn't know what to do or say.

"I'll see you in a few days, Hans," I called. "Have you found a hurdy-gurdy?"

"Not yet," he muttered.

Poppy stopped and gave a sigh. He went over to Hans, placing a hand on his shoulder.

"We've been friends too long," Viktor said. "For too many years. We can't do this."

"I'm sorry." Hans stood up and walked out of the room.

I had tears rolling down my face.

"I'm doing this for Max! For all of us . . ." Poppy called after him.

He watched Hans retreat toward the drawing room, shaking his head. Under his breath all I heard him say was, "I'm sorry."

PLAYING THE HURDY-GURDY

A lot of the kids were gone. I was feeling even more alone. Poppy knew how concerned I was, especially that he and Hans should fight and disagree. I was caught between the two, somewhere between loyalty and friendship. I didn't know how to handle the situation, and tried to push it aside, but it disturbed me deeply. It was an uninvited, unwelcomed gloom that wouldn't leave.

To make things better for me, Poppy took me to a performance featuring the Comedian Harmonists, a clever singing group who were all the rage in Berlin and were now appearing in Prague. We ran into Heydrich unexpectedly and he invited us to come around and see the new offices he had recently set up in Prague.

I was reluctant to go along with Poppy. I didn't want to feel disloyal to Hans, but Poppy was, well, Poppy. I persuaded myself that Heydrich had been nice to my father, and that David's parents were safe. Maybe deep down he was okay. After all, if Poppy had faith in him . . .

Wearing his uniform, with a long gray overcoat falling just short of his ankles, the Great Viktor Mueller and I arrived at Heydrich's headquarters in Prague Castle. Poppy flashed an official pass that allowed him to go anywhere in the city.

The grand hallways had paintings in carved gold frames.

There were painted cabinets and, overhead, a long line of chandeliers from generations of Austrians and Hapsburgs. Each was suspended from a bright-yellow ceiling with crystals that sparkled like diamonds.

We walked into a room that had finely stitched rugs with medallions at each corner. The walls were mahogany, and the ceiling was painted with constellations of stars—silver stars glinting out of a deep–royal blue sky. It was the first time either of us had ever seen the magnificent rooms inside the castle.

The general nodded at my father and turned to me. "Welcome, Max. Any new concerts lately?" Heydrich spoke in a pleasant tone.

"As a matter of fact, I'm playing a character based on Hitler in a new opera. It's called *Brundibár*."

Poppy's eyes bulged, and he glared at me.

"My friend Hans has written it and I'm the star." I could hear the note of defiance in my voice.

General Heydrich's eyebrows rose. "You aaaaare?"

"It's a children's musical, and I need a hurdy-gurdy, like they have in Old Town; it's a square music box that plays tunes."

Heydrich smiled. "Max, you're stirring memories. Yes, I know hurdy-gurdies. It's so ironic. My father wrote an opera and I recall a refrain, 'We all dance to the tune of a barrel-organ.' Yes, I like that very much."

"I have to find one for the show."

Poppy questioned me in a low whisper, then turned to Heydrich, and then again back to me. Hans hadn't told him anything about his opera. So, for once, Poppy didn't know everything going on in my life, but he played along.

"Ah, the Führer is in an opera? Amazing. This Max of yours is something, I wish I had a boy like him. Viktor, take my car at once. Max shall have his hurdy-gurdy."

On the way down to the courtyard, Poppy asked, "Max, what is this nonsense about playing Hitler?"

"I have the lead in Hans's opera."

Poppy shook his head.

"If you're in the German army, Poppy, I can play Hitler." I was being deliberately provocative, just wanting to test his reaction.

"We'll speak more about this later. For now, we can't disappoint the general. To the hurdy-gurdy store!" He hailed a taxi and the driver set off toward town.

The Companie Musik had more than the standard assortment of brass and strings; it carried entire families of instruments. Three crowded rooms led to a warren of dimly lit spaces. It was a fantasy land for me. I had been there so many times and was forever grateful for all the hours that Mr. Mannheim had taught me how to tune pianos. We liked each other very much. Poppy admired the trombones lined up against the walls, and the gleaming brass trumpets that hung from ceilings. Violins faced violas, all stretching along an old and tired corridor. There were saxophones, clarinets, flutes, and horns, and I imagined that they were all once played in parades. They were all there just waiting to come back to life, to march again. I had always felt at home here, among the instruments and knew that my father did too. I wished he hadn't been wearing that uniform. It struck a sour note among all the gleaming brass and gold and wood, and I wondered if Mr. Mannheim would somehow sense it, would hear the distinctive brush of the stiff uniform, pick out the hard click of the military shoes against the aged oak floor of the shop.

Conducting the squads of instruments was the music master of the establishment, my blind business partner, Lorin Mannheim, greeting us with a wave of the cane that he carried at all times.

"Mr. Mannheim," I asked with the greatest respect. "Do you have a hurdy-gurdy? I need one for an opera and Brundibár."

"Not many around these days, but you are in luck, Max. I got one in recently. Poor fellow became ill, and it was just too hard for him to stand all day." He went into a back room and returned with a pristine hurdy-gurdy. It was expensive, but when Poppy explained the project to him, he made a special price. Perhaps Mr. Mannheim had been intimidated by my father's new position if he had indeed detected it. I hoped not. Perhaps, being my friend, he made a special concession.

Demonstrating how the instrument worked, Mr. Mannheim said, "You'll appreciate this, Max. Tunes are encoded onto the barrel using metal pins and staples." He spoke with calm authority, as he always did, with the bearing and confidence of an engineer, his every move precise.

"We'll only need it for a short time," I promised.

Mr. Mannheim fine-tuned the cylinder and polished the cabinet and the bright brass handle on its side. I watched his hands feeling and searching carefully, observing every detail.

"Is there a particular tune you need?"

"Max can tell you," Poppy said, caressing the instrument with his hand.

"I have it here, Mr. Mannheim."

I took Hans's sheet music out of my knapsack.

"Shouldn't be any problem at all. I'll have my son play it for me, and I'll pin a roll."

When we picked up the hurdy-gurdy a few days later, I turned the crank, and it played a theme from *Brundibár.* The instrument felt alive in my hands, and I played the theme over and over. There was instantaneously an unusual feeling about this piece, both melancholy and exhilarating. I was thrilled by the moment and a grin spread across my face.

It had been too long since my father had seen me smile.

"The Mueller boys are back again," Heydrich exclaimed with a chipper grin. He studied the hurdy-gurdy with misty eyes, admiring its condition.

"Play for me, Mr. Brundibár."

"I'm a little rusty. That is, I haven't gotten the score down yet."

"Give it a go," the general said. "I would like to hear you play."

The general and Poppy took their places in comfortable chairs.

From the center of the room, I turned the handle, the tune began, and I sang the refrain:

"Now, you kids, don't make a riot,
When I am here, please be quiet.
Here I am, I'm your star,
Mr. Charming Brundibár.
When I'm here and wish to play,
Sing with me and shout, Hooray!"

"Fantastic, Max!" Heydrich slapped his hands enthusiastically. "From piano tuner to star. You're a natural!" He chuckled lightly and my father, too, smiled. But the moment was short-lived, as Heydrich got right down to business. "Viktor, the Comedian Harmonists are the talk of Europe. I'd like them to sing at the concert for the Führer. You know them?"

"They really are talented!" I jumped in.

"Of course," Poppy confirmed. He looked a little unsure of himself, something that I was not used to seeing: "Yes, but . . . you do know that three of them are Jewish?" Poppy sounded uncomfortable and apologetic. Why should he have to apologize?

Heydrich gave a peculiar smile. "I'm sure you can work it out. We Germans appreciate talent. The group, so unusual. So interesting."

"Very good then."

"Viktor, why don't you take Max with you to Berlin? I'd like for him to see our city and sing for the Führer."

Sing for the Führer? How did I get myself into these things?

As we left Heydrich's office, I turned to my father. "Are you serious about this plan, Poppy?"

"You could use the experience, an out-of-town tryout. After all, you're playing his double."

"Does this feel like a game to you, some kind of joke? I don't even know what to say to you, Poppy. But I'm sure that I'm not going to do it."

"Please, Max. Do it for me."

He was emphatic and that frightened me a bit. Why was he so insistent? There had to be a reason.

"Okay," I finally said. "Poppy, I'll do it for you."

"I understand it's an opportunity," Hans said quietly when he learned the details of the show's unexpected premiere. I knew singing *Brundibár* for the German High Command was not how Hans had imagined things would go.

Hans sighed. "We'll see how it plays. As I said, the opera

carries a double meaning and that meaning can be taken in different ways. This will be a test."

"I'm not sure I can carry it off, Hans. It's not just the performance. It's in front of Hitler himself. How am I going to feel singing for the most feared man in Europe?" I was not just unsure, I was in a panic about it. Poppy had waved off my concerns, but I knew Hans would listen.

"Let's look at it as experience. You need to get your legs in front of an audience. I know it's one we don't like. Just pretend he's not there, and sing for yourself, Max, and for me. Ignore who he is. You know my feelings, and I know yours. It's our music that counts, and the song carries a message. When you're turning the handle on the box take your time, take the stage, win your audience. You can do it. That's why I chose you. My music will be right there along with you. So, through my music I'll be standing beside you all the way. And besides, you'll be singing about hope and victory. Not for them, but for us. You will be singing a song of resistance and rebellion, resisting from within, and you will be doing it without the Germans even realizing. You know, Max, it just may be the perfect debut for you and *Brundibár.*"

Suddenly it all made sense. I had been afraid but I was starting to think that I had courage to move into unfamiliar territory.

Brundibár *and I belong together.*

THE SWEET AIR OF BERLIN

We flew over checkerboard patches in a thousand shades of green. The treetops towered above Tiergarten Park. Far below us was the golden figure of Winged Victory, whose two-hundred-foot column was ringed at the base with the barrels of French cannons captured during the Great War. Poppy had told me about the city of his birth my whole life. And now at last I was here.

Poppy turned his gaze from the plane's window to smile at my wide-eyed amazement. "Welcome to Berlin, Max!"

A taxi met us at Berlin's Flughafen airport.

"Where can I take you, Captain Mueller?"

The driver was thinly mustached, wearing a wool cap, brimming over his face.

"You know my name?"

"I used to drive you to the theater every so often in the old days; you weren't wearing a uniform then, of course. Does the name Frankie ring a bell?"

"Yes, I remember Frankie."

"I used to substitute for him. Have you been away long?"

"I've been living in Prague."

"Ah, you people in Prague. You have no idea how good we have it here."

"Really?" Poppy said, settling into his seat next to the driver.

I sat in the back, listening closely, taking in every word, every nuance. I was intent on getting the hang of reporting. David had told me that a journalist always pays attention to details. He also told me that a good reporter knows how to listen in.

"Sometimes a reporter needs to be invisible as they listen to the conversations around them. You learn things when you listen in. Especially if the people speaking don't notice that you are paying attention." David loved to give me tips.

"Eavesdropping, you mean? That doesn't sound ethical, David."

"Sometimes a good reporter needs to follow his own ethics—the ethics of getting the truth. Remember, Max, you must report the truth. It's the highest obligation of a reporter. But to report it, you have to find it."

David's words echoed in my head as I sat in the taxi listening to Poppy talk with the driver.

"We Germans are on such good terms with the Nazis that after I park my cab at the garage, they insist on driving me home in their army trucks."

"That's nothing," Poppy replied. "In Prague, we not only drive you home, we invite you in and give you champagne, and there you can drink and smoke all you like. Afterward you can take a long, leisurely, warm bubble bath in our tub."

"Propaganda," the driver said with a snort. "Do you mean to tell me all this has happened to you?"

"Not to me," Poppy confessed, "but it happened to my sister!"

The driver laughed uncontrollably. I also laughed at the joke, even though I hadn't the foggiest notion what it was about. A mere courtesy, as Poppy would say.

Poppy loved *mutterwitz*—humor directed against authority.

"Captain, what brings you home?"

"I want to show my son Berlin."

"You've come just in time. I'm not sure how long Berlin will be Berlin."

The taxi dropped us off in the heart of town, and we set out on a leisurely walk to our pension. With a sense of nostalgia, my father showed off his city.

"One of my favorite things is something all Berliners pride themselves on, Max. It's a German sausage with a special sauce. There's a stand at 171 Ku'damm. The longer name is Kurfürstendamm and it's the most famous boulevard in all of Berlin."

It was a very wide avenue with couples promenading past fashionable shops, gated homes, and outdoor restaurants. And in contrast, on this famous street was Poppy's favorite stand. Poppy knew what I liked, and every bite was a treat for me. It was the best grilled sausage and potato salad I had ever had, and I was quick to add a mention in my notebook.

We walked down Unter den Linden, another fashionable boulevard, that had been widened earlier in the thirties to accommodate military parades and that was now crowded with poets and students, musicians and pretty girls. Poppy ran history for me: "In the twenties, the whole world camped on our doorstep, to watch theater, argue about art, and listen to our music. I was a part of it all. We called it *Berliner Luft,* the air of Berlin."

He reminisced, gazing at the people wandering past: "I remember going to plays and operas. You can learn a lot by just watching. The beautiful actress Marlene Dietrich used her incredible legs and smoky voice to enrapture crowds with the song, 'Ich bin von Kopf bis Fuss auf Liebe eingestellt,' a sultry 'I'm Ready for Love.'"

Just off the Ku'damm was the Romanisches Café, with a glassed-in terrace and revolving doors. The bistro was a favorite haunt of Poppy's, and he was well remembered there. He introduced me to the oversized proprietor, Wilhelm Furst.

Furst was happy to see the Great Viktor Mueller. "Your father came for lunch dressed like an American cowboy with leather chaps, silver spurs, and a ten-gallon hat, and other times like a London stockbroker with a bowler and furled umbrella. The patrons loved him. His performances were always better than the cabaret downstairs," Furst said wistfully.

Poppy told me that the playwright Luigi Pirandello came to this café when he arrived in Berlin. He had gone in search of a production for his famous play, *Six Characters in Search of an Author*. Had he come just a few years later, he would have found the Great Viktor Mueller, performing and holding court.

The time passed quickly and after dinner we went to the Pension Schmidt, Poppy's preferred place to stay in Berlin. He introduced me to its landlady, Frau Schmidt, who, I thought, was built like a world heavyweight champion.

Hearing Poppy explain that she was held in high regard by the performers of Berlin, as she attended theater four or five nights a week always dressed to the nines, Frau Schmidt blushed and gave Poppy a small pat on the arm. Her laughter matched her full frame.

"No opera or play can succeed in Berlin without her approval, Max. So, mind yourself!"

"Oh, Viktor, you are so kind to humor me. Surely, I don't have that much influence."

She gave a little wave of her hand and walked off to see to other guests.

"She's a diva," Poppy said.

"A diva?"

He leaned over and whispered, "Max, Frau Schmidt is a star herself. She is a celebrated talent and can make *Brundibár* a hit!"

"Poppy, do you think so?"

He nodded as I watched the sizable retreating form of Frau Schmidt going upstairs. She looked an unlikely star to me, but Poppy seemed very sure.

The fourth floor boasted enormous rooms where patrons stayed. Our room was round, with curved bay windows and massive oak doors fitted with silver-plated door handles. The bathrooms provided an ideal environment for vocal exercises. I could hear sopranos and tenors singing scales bouncing through the halls and walls. Of course, the Great Viktor Mueller joined the musical community right away. In a tenor voice, he sang snatches of Verdi and Puccini recalled from old opera recordings and tried to duplicate the style in improvised and inaccurate Italian. Above the showers and flushing toilets, he invented fruity vocables, *la-la-la-laaaaaa-amore!*

"*Guten Morgen,*" Frau Schmidt called out the next morning, her arms opened in an expansive greeting. Breakfast was delicious, and she expected her guests to eat as much as she did herself, insisting that Poppy and I work our way through freshly baked rolls, cold cuts, cheese, butter, and homemade plum jam. Following the meal, Frau Schmidt had a custom of reading tea leaves for her guests, an art she said she had learned from a band of gypsies.

She examined my cup and, after a moment's contemplation, announced, "Ah, yes, I see a fine young lady in your future."

Sophie!

"How does she know that, Poppy?"

"Some people have a gift."

Poppy nodded at Frau Schmidt. She gave a laugh. "Don't jest, Viktor, I've read your future many times. And you know the surest way to see the future is to see the past and present with clear eyes. I've seen your past, Viktor, and as to your present, well, I never would've foreseen this outfit you're wearing."

She raised an eyebrow in disdain and wrinkled her forehead. "But I suppose there are reasons."

Poppy had told me the night before that Frau Schmidt referred to the Nazis in a tone she usually reserved for tenors who sang flat. I could tell now that she wasn't happy that her old friend was working with the Germans. When Poppy carefully explained to Frau Schmidt that he was just working for the Ministry of Culture, she shot a dubious look his way. My father clearly loved Frau Schmidt and respected her opinion, and it was equally clear that she had serious doubts about her old friend. Somehow, I had to make sense of this tension, and had to remind myself of that tough lesson I had learned over and again in recent times, that some things just didn't make sense. What if things were no longer right or wrong? Maybe that was the truth about the new world in which we were living? Maybe understanding this was part of growing up? I didn't know. But I did see how the very word *Nazi* made Frau Schmidt frown with distaste.

Frau Schmidt invited us to the opera that evening. When we arrived, the ushers treated her like royalty. Whenever Frau Schmidt applauded, the sound resonated through the theater, but if a note failed to reach her standard, her silence was fierce. I noticed some patrons gauged her reactions before giving their own. If she laughed, the house boomed with laughter.

Afterward, we all went to a café on the Ku'damm for a final assessment of the evening. I focused mainly on demolishing a vast portion of a chocolate torte with an accompanying mountain of whipped cream.

"Are you performing in Berlin, Viktor?" Frau Schmidt asked. "You do so many things we love: conducting a concert, directing a play."

Poppy beamed. "Not at the moment. But I plan to do all I can to make sure we have pleasant evenings."

For Frau Schmidt, concerts were the reason for her existence. "An audience can only make a performance better, especially when they applaud in the right places.

"Passions these days still run high inside and outside the theater. We think about the world, we talk of art and politics. Still, we have the Schiller Theater, the Philharmonic Orchestra, and the State Opera. I have the feeling that the whole show is being put on for my benefit, except when they sing those awful army songs."

She wrinkled her nose. "Well, it's still a lovely town. I won't leave Berlin unless they throw me out, and even then, I'll only go on the last train."

"My affection for Germany is conflicted," Poppy said while walking along a tree-shaded path in Grunewald Forest, where he had spent much of his childhood.

"I was born here, yet I feel that I'm an outsider," he confided. "Still, we return to Berlin to see how the old town is getting on. When I was young like you, Max, my Berlin was a beautiful city. I had a secret ambition to be part of the Prussian cavalry. I used to watch an old field marshal trotting by on his morning ride in this forest. He must have been about sixty, old school, silver-haired, straight as a tree, a big flowing moustache, and a bit of an actor. From that moment, I wanted to be like him, to be dressed like him, on his majestic horse, medals gleaming on my chest."

I tried to reassure myself that for Poppy it was about the show—the performance—and not about the ideas that were bubbling beneath them. Then I found myself thinking that this was not so reassuring after all.

When we reached the woods, Poppy said, "This could be a setting for *A Midsummer Night's Dream*."

"Mendelssohn?"

"Good for you, Max."

The woods exuded a peaceful sense of solitude, and I felt as though I was in one of the most beautiful places in the world. Suddenly Poppy was quiet, lost in his own memories. And beside him, I was lost in my own worries.

INTO THE LIMELIGHT

The following evening, I saw *Max Mueller as Brundibár* listed in the program and knew there was no turning back from the State Opera House.

"Are you sure I can do this?"

"Max, all great artists get butterflies," Poppy assured me. "Let them fly away and you'll enjoy the moment."

I was part of the bill that included the State Orchestra and Das Meistersextett, elegantly dressed in white tie and tails, and formerly known as the Comedian Harmonists: the group had been renamed after Heydrich requested, after all, that only their non-Jewish members perform. So much for "working it out."

Standing in the shadows, I peeked into the hall from behind the curtain. During intermission, the orchestra played music by Richard Wagner, Hitler's favorite composer.

There were hundreds of tiered golden boxes, and in the dress circle, Hitler was with his lady, a woman named Eva Braun, surrounded by a group of well-dressed officers, all appearing as though they were posing for a photograph.

I remembered what Hans had said: "Pretend they're not there. And remember why you are there, what it means, what it really means."

The curtain rose on the second act and I was introduced. I

didn't know if the applause was for my father or partly for me. The audience had been ecstatic to welcome the Great Viktor Mueller back to Berlin.

Before the footlights, wearing a moustache and a top hat, rouge on my cheeks, I felt alone at first. Alone and frozen. But then, something happened, something magical. I felt the distance between myself and the audience vanish, as if we became one somehow. It was something that my father could do effortlessly. It felt as though I could do it too. I was a true performer after all.

A yellow spotlight hit me, and as I placed my hand on the brass handle of the hurdy-gurdy, there was a hush. I turned the instrument slowly at first and then a little faster. I was no longer at all afraid. I felt that I belonged there. I had a job to do and the words began to flow from me, clearly and powerfully, over the stage and directly out to the audience.

Music played, and I sang the second stanza from *Brundibár,* my voice loud and assured.

"Music's for the poor and wealthy,
If you wish to remain healthy,
Listen to my songs and dances,
They will satisfy your fancies,
Waltz and polka, fox-trot, gallop
All my nice tunes give a wallop!
Dance to them, go slower, faster,
Welcome, please, your music master,
Good and kind, strongest by far
Here I am, your Brundibár!"

The performance over, I held my breath, exhaling with relief when I saw the audience rise from their seats, clapping, demanding an encore. But I didn't have one. So instead I just sang the song again, and after another round of applause, the orchestra played an *oom-pah-pah*-ing beer-barrel polka, as I pretended to play along. The audience, including Hitler and his generals, clapped along with the music.

Frau Schmidt was in the crowd on that April night. I heard her call, "Bravo!"

Her voice soared over the crowd. I had won her approval.

The Great Viktor Mueller had given the Führer a birthday celebration, and he'd apparently enjoyed the show. I had been part of it, and I felt that I had been divided in two. Part of me felt shame and confusion and another was proud of my performance. But I kept hearing Hans's argument with my father and felt that I had been a part of something that didn't include me at all.

"Last night really was a triumph. We've been invited to the Berghof," Poppy announced the next morning, opening a packet delivered by courier and sealed with red wax.

"Berghof?"

"Eagle's Nest. It's Hitler's home in the Bavarian Alps."

"Wow, are there eagles there?"

Poppy sat in an alcove below a window in our room.

"When do we go?" I asked, hoping I wouldn't have to sing again for the Führer.

"*We* don't," said Poppy. "This is a trip I must make alone."

I frowned. "But, Poppy, I—"

"Max, enough!" he said, whipping around to face me. "This is a unique and unusual time. I want you back in Prague."

He took a deep breath.

I scowled and pushed my potatoes around my plate.

"I'm playing Hitler, shouldn't I meet him? Study him up close?"

"You're playing Brundibár, and you're just fine. Take it from me, Max, that is as close as you need to get."

Not an hour later, there was another knock at the door. Frau Schmidt had come to say her goodbyes. She also handed Poppy an envelope and a briefcase with a camera inside. I caught a glimpse of the camera, and a letter before Poppy slipped it inside his jacket pocket. It read, *For your eyes only.*

"Goodbye, dear Max," said Frau Schmidt, walking over to me. "It was a delight to meet you and attend your debut."

"I hope you visit Prague someday. We have a wonderful opera house."

Frau Schmidt smiled. "I would love that, Max."

She turned. "Viktor, I wish you Godspeed."

Poppy embraced her, and excused himself from the room, returning a few minutes later.

"Poppy, what's that letter?"

"Nothing, Max, just a message. A note of good wishes."

"And the camera?"

"I have some pictures to take."

He sighed and looked away, effectively ending my questions.

Poppy was getting close to powerful, dangerous people. Too close.

On the way to the station, we passed by a theater on the Ku'damm. The last production Poppy had directed in the same theater was a musical by Bertolt Brecht and Kurt Weill called *The Rise and Fall of the City of Mahagonny.* He had told me that in the last act, Mahagonny goes up in flames, destroyed by actors carrying signs reading, LET'S DESTROY THE OTHER FELLOW. The final refrain was a chilling reminder because it had been banned a few years before, when Stormtroopers, Germany's special assault troops, marched past.

Now a concert by Wagner was being performed by Berlin's famed Philharmonic conducted by Wilhelm Furtwängler. His name was prominently displayed on the marquee, and Poppy knew him well.

"He's regarded as one of the greatest in Germany. But recently, we've had our differences."

"You're both great conductors, how do you differ?"

"Furtwängler was critical of Hitler's appointment as chancellor, and I very much supported him. But as the Third Reich took hold, he compromised, to save his orchestra."

"Was he a collaborator, Poppy?"

"He did what he had to do, Max."

"What's the difference? Aren't you doing the same, doing what you have to do?"

A long silence fell between us.

I posted a letter to Sophie, because I was thinking about her at every turn. After waving goodbye to Poppy standing on the platform, I was still wondering what could be so important to send me home alone. The endless rhythm of the wheels over the tracks offered welcome distraction from these concerns.

Opening my notebook, I was hoping that I was learning to write better, even copying articles I'd read, imitating style, of course not original, but it was a practical lesson. It felt like the drills in football training, practicing moves and set pieces. I was learning and honing my craft.

Passing ice-cold lakes outside of Berlin's great green forests and birch trees. Putting my face to the window, I see two children are ice-skating along an endless ribbon. They skate as fast as they can, trying to keep up with our train. We speed beyond them; they reach their arms toward me, waving goodbye. We pass a picture book of houses. I'm leaving a country and I have the feeling it will be a long time before I return.

The birthday festivities were moving south and so was Viktor Mueller. The private train taking him to Bavaria was known as the Blue Train. It was green with gold lettering on the side of each wagon, spelling out BERLIN-MÜNCHEN-SALZBURG. The carriages had blue upholstered velvet chairs, table lights with rose lampshades, blue curtains, and crystal fixtures. Leading the carriages was a locomotive pouring out streams of white smoke, and a gleaming gold watch pulled from the conductor's pocket was a sign that the journey was about to begin. There was a whiff of delicious sauces from the mahogany-paneled dining car, and the endless rhythm of the wheels over the tracks. In a few hours, there were mountains, and on the other side, another landscape, another life. Every car had attendants dressed in starched white jackets with a gold eagle signifying their rank.

Viktor pushed a porcelain button on a brass panel above a polished table. A porter appeared. Any request could be serviced and satisfied. A bottle of brandy was served.

The hideaway chalet, designed by Hitler, was high in the Bavarian Alps. On the second floor, from a pine-paneled living room, a terrace with large red umbrellas opened to the outdoors. Inside, past a telephone switchboard, was a study with books, and in the center of the room, a globe of the world. Beyond it, a floor-to-ceiling window opened to views that stretched forever. Wearing lederhosen and embroidered braces, with Eva Braun at his side, Hitler gave a clipped bow to Viktor Mueller. He was face-to-face with the man who wanted to impose his will, to conquer the world. Viktor asked himself how he could be there. What could justify this visit? He wondered, what if there was an explosive planted inside his camera? One click would be all it took. He dismissed it as a fanciful notion.

The Führer was comfortable around children, especially the blond, blue-eyed kids playing on the terrace who were the children of his personal photographer, Heinrich Hoffman. Eva Braun had been Hoffman's assistant when Hitler first met her. Viktor spoke with Hoffman about the latest Leica he was sporting. "Best lenses in the world," he said. It was true, Leica lenses gave the sharpest contrast between black and white and were made with precision.

He stayed in the background taking lots of pictures, with the camera Frau Schmidt had given him, a Rolleiflex with a double-lens system. General Heydrich had secured an invitation, and Hitler was pleased to have a great patriotic conductor attend this gathering. For Viktor, there was the unmissable chance to observe Hitler, to study him, see up close this peculiar, nervous charisma, this clash of imposing, overwhelming self-belief and something close to neurotic anxiety. This man, of whom Viktor was taking candid images, was another Germany, not the personification of his beloved country.

When he let his camera drape from its strap around his neck, the guests approached him with every courtesy and professed the pleasure they took from his conducting and his son's assured performance. They were fascinated with the barrel-organ. He smiled as he accepted the praise and fielded the questions about the future of German music.

At lunch, he was seated at a table hosted by the Führer, a vegetarian who ate mostly salads and vegetables. Viktor had little appetite for the food, for the surroundings, for the company.

Afterward, some guests retired to a private viewing theater to watch newsreels.

"Come, children," Eva called. "We shall go for a stroll, for the air."

Eva Braun was a natural beauty with bright-blond hair. She was full of energy, wearing a sundress patterned with blue cornflowers and a matching sweater. The whole afternoon unfolded like a strange fantasy, the walk through the stunning Bavarian countryside, the rarified mountain air, an extraordinary setting, the seeming friendliness of everyone there, Viktor capturing much of it through the lens of his camera, making him feel like the observer of something, a peculiarly ordinary drama unfolding in front of him. And just for him. With every click of the shutter, the mechanical routine of changing reels of film, he couldn't shake the sense that this could be a very different process, each click echoing within his imagination as the squeezing of a trigger, the detonation of a device that would mean instantaneous oblivion for him and everyone there, the Führer and his cohorts, but also the children, a single event that would freeze this image forever.

Late in the afternoon, still in his dream, still the observer of this emerging movie whose ending he could have dramatically changed, Viktor shook Hitler by the hand and thanked him for "a most joyful, inspiring day," and as he turned to leave, Heydrich took him aside confiding, "I'll see you back in Berlin."

Entering the Chancellery, the general and the captain were glad to be indoors on a late summer day.

"I hope you enjoyed our afternoon, Viktor?"

"It was a remarkable occasion. Thank you, Reinhard. Something to remember always."

"I didn't know you were a photographer. A man of many talents! It's a picturesque setting, I must agree."

In the center foyer, there was an architectural model of Germania, the planned capital that Hitler had designed and given to Albert Speer, his architect, to realize. The model had been replicated in marble and was white, as if under an early Berlin snowfall.

"You're a great success, Viktor. You were at home there, among devout patriots and we are indeed a special few. We have much to look forward to. You'll have an office just next to mine, even if you won't be spending much time in Berlin, but when you are here, it's important that you be at the center of operations."

The offices of the Third Reich all had alcoves with doors to rooms that were home to the generals, and at the end of the long corridor was an impressive office, one with a large white-marble swastika displayed above a wide oak double door. When the captain was invited to attend a meeting in an adjacent conference room, it was so large that the great round table at its center seemed empty, even when it was surrounded by generals and aides. He placed the generals in two categories, the short and the tall. The shorter ones, like Himmler and Goebbels, aimed for power and were more aggressive and dangerous, while Göring and Rommel were much taller, and appeared relaxed.

Wondering how much time he would be needed in Berlin, Viktor spent most of his stay there carrying out Heydrich's promotional plan. But it was in these headquarters that he would collect information. Gossip, conversation, plans—all of this would be valuable to his role. He had secured an arrangement to dispatch information in an invoice packet to Pierre Burger in Prague by way of a trusted Berlin news agent, who delivered the *Berlin Post* to Prague each morning by train, a five-hour journey each way. Other reports, not demanding urgent transmission to London, he would personally give to Burger.

Viktor was standing in Heydrich's office, mentally running through the logistics of his secret work, when his thoughts were interrupted by Heydrich's declaration: "We'll be marching into Poland soon.

Viktor was unsure that he had heard correctly: "Poland?"

Heydrich stood up from his desk and strolled across to the window, staring out at the platoon of soldiers on a routine drill outside, the hint of a smile playing around his lips as he announced solemnly, "The show is about to begin."

A THREE-DAY VISA

London was suffering from an unusual spell of hot weather. Running to St. James's in spitting morning rain, Anna dashed into her office looking for a place to deposit her umbrella. On her desk was a letter from Max Mueller inviting her to an opera. It was not only Hans she missed, but Max, and in the back of her mind, a visit with Captain Mueller would be helpful, a chance for current updates on an impending, inescapable war. Chamberlain, in all his naivete, had returned from Berlin, negotiating concessions with Hitler, waving a white piece of paper to the reception committee at the airport, proclaiming, "Peace for our time."

Borders were closed to anyone wishing to leave German-occupied territories. Journalists and diplomats could still visit, but Anna's editors thought it a foolish risk and that she was either the most poorly informed person at the paper, or the most courageous. Churchill thought otherwise. There was still the Kindertransport program he had authorized. In any event, there was always a reason, a cover, an excuse, and whatever it was, nothing was going to stop her from returning to Prague.

David had a million questions when I arrived back at the Grand Hotel Krása.

"Did you write everything down? How was Berlin? Tell me, I want to know."

"It was amazing. I felt more like a world traveler than a journalist."

I didn't mention the concert, or that I had sung for Hitler, or that Poppy had gone to Eagle's Nest to do whatever he had to do there.

"There's a forest in Berlin named after you David. You must go someday."

"A whole forest? A park maybe, but a forest?" David loved the notion.

Then to my immense surprise, I spotted someone easy on my eyes. It was Anna!

"If you won't come to me, then I guess I should come to you," she announced flushed with exhaustion.

Hans's house quickly returned to its former brightness with Anna in residence. Bunches of fresh flowers appeared in every room, and Lucie celebrated her arrival by baking a chocolate torte.

Anna seemed particularly happy to see Poppy, who looked after her with great courtesy. Hans was occupied with so many last-minute details for the show. But his happiness more than matched mine. That she had come, and indeed how she had done it, was a mystery.

Opening night came too soon. I spotted David in the orchestra, and he gave me a wink for good luck. Anna and David were always nearby when I needed them most.

František Zelenka had transformed Mrs. Blomberg's living room into an engaging stage. He managed to hang lights with gels overhead, creating a dramatic atmosphere in an unusual space. It was a house that had become a home and a home that had become a theater. Zelenka had built a set and provided props. I could smell gauze and grease paint. At the center of our makeshift stage my hurdy-gurdy stood alone under an oval yellow light, waiting to be played. It was a magnificent setting. Most of the small Jewish community remaining in Prague came. David played violin in the orchestra and supported every scene with a thumbs-up. Mrs. Blomberg wiped away a tear, not a sad one but one of unescapable joy. The show was such a success that we should have played in the biggest theater in town. I was sure it would have won another prize for Hans, but there was no other place we could perform.

My only disappointment was that Poppy was called away. Had he appeared, however, he would have done so in uniform, and I think the cast and audience would have been uncomfortable. I would have been uneasy and still unable to reconcile the father I knew with the one who was serving in the German army.

But he sent a telegram with love and good wishes and made sure a shipment of refreshments arrived for the occasion.

The evening was a glorious success but a bittersweet one for three reasons: the show was over, Sophie was not there, and Anna, who had arrived a few days earlier, was returning to London almost as soon as she arrived.

"You were quite wonderful, Max. You belong on the stage."

I still couldn't get over the fact that Anna had thought enough to come, to travel so far. Could it have been just to see *Brundibár*?

The next morning, I went around to the shop Sophie had loved and selected one of the few hats remaining on the shelf, a round straw one with a brim showing off a spectacular ribbon. Perfect for Anna, I thought.

Hats were becoming my trademark to the people I cared about most. When I presented my gift to Anna, she was quietly pleased, put it on at once, adjusted it to a rakish angle, and then rewarded me with a huge grin.

"Max, you're a charmer. I am so sorry it is such a flying visit, but I've only been allowed a three-day visa. But I intend to make every minute count."

Before she left, she asked me how I felt about Poppy being in the German army, working with Heydrich. I could tell that she was concerned. I told her that I knew it was for our future.

Hans averted his eyes from me, staring out of the window instead. "You are our future, Max."

I tried to assure them that Poppy was a good man, doing his best in very difficult times, but I don't think they understood, Hans at least.

She turned to him. "I've heard Hitler is going to march. If Germany invades Poland, no more concessions will be given and the sequel to the Great War will be on. David and Max belong in London with me."

She took his silence as an agreement. "I'll contact Whitehall."

She made the call at once and five minutes later came back into the room, trying to look calmer and happier than she was. She rationalized to herself that it was too late, and Viktor would never have agreed to it anyway. She wanted to believe that David and I would somehow be safe in Prague.

"I understand how much you love your friends, Max. It's always comfortable to be with those you love most."

She may have been telling a white lie, to herself as well as to me, but it didn't matter. I believed without a doubt that Prague was the place for me.

But was it? My confidence was shaken when I saw men in SS uniforms speeding through the streets in black cars decked out with red-and-black swastika flags. They would stop and arrest people for no reason. I saw the man in the black overcoat sitting casually on a bench in a park, making notes. Then another, and another, all over the city. They were everywhere now. They were as much of a presence as the clock chiming the hour in Old Town. I was becoming increasingly scared, scared for myself and everyone around me. What made it so unsettling for me was that I realized I had every reason to be frightened—and it would be crazy not to fear what was happening, not to fear the men in overcoats and everything they represented. And then I had a recurring nightmare. What if someone my age, just like me, were picked up in one of those cars? Anna had to leave and had to leave fast.

A SUNDAY AFTERNOON

On a perfect Sunday morning a few months later, the sun shone down from clear sparkling blue autumn skies over the British Isles, but it was unlike any other Sunday I had ever seen. Before the day was over, Germany and England were at war for the second time in the twentieth century.

As September began Germany invaded Poland with these words from their leader: "I have secured for the German people the land they are entitled to in Europe." With Austria and Czechoslovakia's western Sudetenland taken, the conquest of Poland was just another notice from *Mein Kampf.* Powered by a vision of distortion and falsehoods, propaganda minister Joseph Goebbels issued an unequivocal warning: "Germany is forced to find a solution to problems that can never be solved in peacetime." The Polish army was destroyed in two days. To honor their treaty obligations, Great Britain and France had declared war.

Outside my window in Prague, streaming rain. Rain bouncing like silver coins, rain making puddles, rain spitting over red-and-black flags, rain sliding down garden leaves, rain splashing sidewalks, rain running with couples, rain peeping over red-tiled roofs, rain sloshing old ladies, rain dripping from broken black umbrellas, rain under footfalls, rain no longer laughing, no longer dancing. Rain everywhere.

The following Tuesday afternoon, the very flowers—once rivers of pink tulips bordered by cold green grass, planted by the Dutch ambassador in Petínské sady—bowed their heads. The heavier presence of the Nazis changed the spirit of the city, spreading an uneasy truce, and causing further intrusion into my world. It changed my will.

After school, on my way to an assignment, I found my bicycle smashed, the wheels buckled, the frame bent beyond fixing. I confronted a gang of classmates standing nearby, wearing Hitler Youth uniforms with red-and-black bands around their arms.

"You did this to my bike?" I asked, pointing to the damaged wreck.

"Why would we do that?"

"I don't know. Only you know that, but I'm on my way to work and I need my bike."

One of the younger boys, from the year below, mocked me, "*Dad de dah de boom*, the piano tuner is on his way to work."

One of the bigger boys tried to snatch my black tool kit, but I was determined to save my red ribbons with my life.

"You don't need that, it's only my lunch." I diverted their attention with my subterfuge.

"You won't be eating lunch anymore if you continue to hang out with Jews."

"Do you guys like doing this, hurting people? Does it make you feel good?"

The ringleader stepped forward. "Yes, it does. We're a new world order."

"*A new world order?* Can you even hear your own words? Do you understand them? It's your world, not mine."

"Max, you're German, and you'd be better off if you didn't associate with our enemies."

"Enemies? You call my friends enemies? I can be friends with anyone I like."

"That's where you're wrong, Max. Not here, not now," their leader spat, and they ran away, leaving a yellow star on my broken bicycle.

If I hadn't known it before then, I knew in that instant that I didn't belong there any longer. Nothing and no one was safe anymore. There was some tiny consolation in the fact that I had saved my tools. But a much bigger question remained: Where *did* I belong? Where could I be safe? I didn't want to hide; every part of me wanted to do something, to stand up to them, to fight. I couldn't take them on, they would kill me. Who could I reach out to? Who could I speak to? My father was away. I rushed over to find Hans just as he was setting out for a walk. We strolled together, but soon I wondered if skipping over the cracks in the sidewalk could bring better luck.

"I'm worried, worried about everything, Hans—about my father, my friends, about you."

"I'll be okay, Max. Where's your bike?"

"I'd rather walk with you, Hans."

"Why do you do so much skipping?"

"Because I'm good at it. I learned it from David. It's just a superstition, avoiding cracks in the pavement. Keeps you safe. Lucky."

"Is that true?"

"They say it is."

"Well, does it work?"

"I don't think so."

We went to Mrs. Blomberg's to look for David. He would understand, he would help. He always did. Because of all the commotion, many of the streets were blocked off and I hadn't been able to get there in days. Posted on the door was a notice marked with a black German eagle. The place was empty except for Mrs. Blomberg herself. She looked distraught, deeply depressed.

"The Germans were here. They've all been taken. David's gone. The word is that the children have been shipped to Terezín."

It was the first time I heard Hans raise his voice. "Bastards!"

I was confused. Why was Hans so upset if they had they gone to Terezín? I reasoned that if any place was safe, it would be there. But *was* any place safe? I wasn't sure of anything anymore.

Mrs. Blomberg did her best not to convey her anxiety, but I could sense her unease in every word, every gesture.

Hans was stunned, his face pale and drawn. Finally he said, "At least we managed to secure passage for many of the younger kids on the Kindertransport program."

I was deflated. "David has got to be okay."

"It's difficult, Max, but we must have faith," Hans said. "Try not to worry. We're here for each other and who knows—if they are in Terezín, that might actually be a lot better off than living in Prague right now."

Back at his place, Hans packed a bag. "I'll be back in a few days, Max. I'm going to make sure everyone is okay."

He collected a few things: mementos, photographs, and clothes. I knew that Hans was trying to protect me as best he could, but I wasn't stupid, and I could see that something else was going on. This was not going to be a weekend in the country. I was consumed with worry for David. And Sophie.

As he prepared to leave, he turned to Lucie, taking her plump hand in his: "Stay with Max, at least until I return."

I was struggling to hold back the tears: "Hans, take me with you."

"For now, this is the best place for you. Trust me." He kissed me on the forehead, shut the gate, and was gone.

Hours passed and Lucie had fallen asleep on the couch. The only sound in the house was from the blades of a fan overhead whispering panic. The Great Viktor Mueller appeared in the doorway. Finally, he had come home.

"They're gone, Poppy!"

"I know, Max. Lucie sent me a wire."

Poppy extended his arms and I ran to him. He held me tight until I stopped crying.

COME TO TEREZÍN!

> Come to Terezín! Apartments, attractive facilities with excellent cuisine, concerts, and a spa. Would you like your accommodation riverside or on the square? Bring casual dress to be sure, and walking shoes, tennis racquets. Bring the children along for the parks, schools, and playgrounds.

Travel bureaus were offered commissions to promote the plan with color brochures. Living conditions, especially in the Reich, were becoming intolerable; for some time there had been rumors of deportations to "work camps" in the east. Many Jews had emigrated; most wanted to go to Palestine. The only agency left in Prague allowing a limited number of permits had closed. Quotas to other countries, like the ten thousand allowed by the United States, had long been filled. In occupied countries, borders closed, and for the hopeful who remained behind, a temporary home in Terezín sounded promising. Apartments would not be as spacious, but the facilities were attractive, offering good food, staff physicians, nurses, and spa specialists. Making deposits, future occupants filled out questionnaires. It all sounded so persuasive, so appealing. They arrived with their parasols, in their summer dresses, winter capes, top hats, and frock coats to their new home. Plans and provisions were underway, so why not bring the children along for the parks, schools, and playgrounds?

Meeting the requirements were partners from mixed marriages. Because of the "racial laws," a few were considered non-Aryan if one grandparent was Jewish. At the top of the list were Jews who had distinguished themselves in their professions, including the army; they were called *Prominenten.* Many were diplomats who were given favored treatment, including the prime minister of the State of Saxony, the mayor of Le Havre, the president of the Dutch Red Cross, the surgeon general of the Austrian Imperial Army, and a French minister of justice. Added to the impressive list were scholars and academics, artists, actors and singers who had performed for the Kaiser in better days, and even Viktor's great friend, the concertmaster of the Czech Philharmonic.

The brochures advertised that the Germans were offering Terezín as a unique place for special Jews; the rich, the powerful, the brightest, and most talented. In exchange, they had to turn over every asset for "safekeeping." Until the conflict was over. Many families felt a sense of relief. The cream of European Jewish aristocracy were signing up.

I thought it might be a good time to speak to my father.

"This place, Terezín, what is it really like?"

"It's called 'Hitler's Gift to the Jews.'"

"Why a *gift*?"

"There are Jewish people—musicians, artists, soldiers, people from all professions—who fought in World War, and they need a place to live."

"A place to live? But don't they have homes? Sophie did."

"It's a political thing—some people are considered enemies."

"Surely David and Sophie are not enemies," I said, "and if they were, why would Hitler give them a gift?"

"Max, it's complicated."

"Too complicated for me to understand?"

"Maybe too complicated for anyone to understand."

"Why hasn't Hans come back?"

Poppy shrugged. He had no answers.

"Is it a nice place, this village?"

Still no answers. One thing I knew for certain: I was going to find out the answers to all my questions.

October 19, 1939

Dear Max,

I would have written sooner, but Mama has been ill and we don't have enough medicine for the sick. I spend a lot of time at the hospital and try to keep busy. Please think of her, Max.

Love,
Sophie

So much had been on my mind since my father began wearing a German uniform, so many questions inside my head like balls in a bagatelle. I had received so few replies to my letters, leaving me lost, unmoored, looking for direction, sailing to nowhere. On one of our now infrequent Sunday walks, we stopped in the middle of a dirt path and I turned to Poppy, taking a deep breath.

Okay, here goes nothing, I thought.

"I don't know what you're doing in the army, Poppy." I spoke with as much courage as I could muster up. "You told me you had to do things your way, but I'm not sure I feel right about your way. Things are different, Poppy. The Germans have taken over Czechoslovakia. You've told me that and I understand that. Prague is occupied. I've heard all the stories about protesters and dissenters just disappearing. Hans and David are gone now. People are getting killed in the streets. My papers and my notebooks and the occasional letter from Sophie are the only companions I have left. Where is Hans? What is happening to all the Jews? How can I make sense of it all? And how are you making it better?"

Poppy sighed and sat down on a nearby bench. He patted the seat next to him, putting his arm around me. "There are all kinds of people. But we come from a long tradition; our country has produced some of the best artists and musicians in the world. I took you to Berlin because I wanted you to see where you came from, and I think you know it's a beautiful city. "

"Prague used to be beautiful too." I was as angry as I had ever been in my life as I uttered those words. What good was a city to me or for any of the people that we loved?

"Max, it will be magical again. Sure, we have different points of view, and friends can disagree. That doesn't make them bad. You've met Heydrich. He's an okay fellow. I know how much he likes you. We should remember that he helped David's parents. I've been thinking about the best thing to do until this thing blows over. What worries me is that I'll be traveling a lot more. Hans is not around, and I need someone to care for you. I think I can work with the general to bring about better things, to change things, to reshape things, to change the course at least a little bit. Perhaps a lot. I really believe that, Max. You might think about being with your friends, David and Sophie. I want someone to keep you company when I'm away, Max."

"Can't I be with you? I'm not much trouble."

"Of course, you can. You and I belong together like Armand and White Dog. I'm just thinking of the short term."

I was torn. The telegraph keys in Old Town were sending me a message. I shifted a decision back and forth. One word said it all. *Sophie!* And I could bring medicine. Terezín was just an hour's drive away. I wanted to be with my friends. Anna had said, "Best to be comfortable." And if Hans was planning a production of *Brundibár,* I didn't want anyone else playing my role. But there was one essential thing that was more important. I didn't want to be just a bystander in this world. If I was going to be a journalist, I needed to know more. I needed to know what was going on, and to find out if I could make a difference. What was happening to my friends, and the Jews? Poppy had his plan which I didn't understand, and maybe never would. But I had mine too. We were two different people. We were also very much alike. I had to determine facts for myself. Besides, I wouldn't be gone for long. The decision had been made.

"I won't be making any deliveries for a while, Mr. Raggle."

"You're leaving for Terezín, but why? You're not a Jew."

"It's not so far away and Poppy feels I'll be better off, because he won't be around a lot of the time. I have lots of friends there."

"I'll miss you, Max, you're a young man I can trust."

"Mr. Raggle, you already knew I was leaving?"

"I hear things. I *am* in the news business. Will you write, let me know how you are doing? It's important."

"Sure. Will you send me the papers from time to time?"

"That might be difficult, too dangerous, but I have a favor to ask." Mr. Raggle invited me inside the stand, speaking quietly. "You can be helpful."

"What do you have in mind?"

"When you get the chance, when you have something to say, whatever it is, write a short note letting me know how you are and about life in Terezín."

"Why should that be so secret?"

"We don't know too much about the place. We certainly don't know enough, and I don't think things in Prague are going to get better for a while. Life should be better up there, so that might be good news for you and your friends, for everyone there, the good Lord willing. But in the meantime, as much information as I can gather will be useful."

"Is it dangerous?"

"Well, always be careful. You'll be sending me information. Address anything you can report, send to *Sunshine*. And don't tell anyone."

"Sunshine?"

"There's a green box with a white crest where the milkman collects and leaves milk three times a week. Be sure you mark the envelopes *Sunshine* and place them inside the box, they'll get to me. Sign them *PT*."

"What does *PT* stand for?"

"It's just a secret code, Pink Tulip."

I hesitated for a moment but then the opportunity of becoming part of a news team came to mind, an investigative reporter, a journalist. The stakes were high. With my accounting, a plus outweighed a minus. Another turning point.

"I'll do it for you, Mr. Raggle, but I also have a favor to ask."

"How can I help?"

"I need to take some medicine, boxes and boxes, they don't have enough up there."

"I'll see to it. But be careful, the Germans wouldn't be too keen on all this."

I wondered what I was now: a journalist, a smuggler, or a secret agent?

I had to acknowledge I was moving into dangerous territory. Could I do it? I had no reason not to trust Sam Raggle. And, besides, if I didn't, what kind of person had I become?

PART II
TEREZÍN

AN UNCERTAIN JOURNEY

November 14, 1939

I settled into the tan leather seats of the general's open-top Mercedes, acting as if nothing at all was bothering me. I carried my most treasured possessions as if they were secrets locked up in a hidden, secure vault. My watch, my hurdy-gurdy, notebooks, red felt ribbons, and my black tool kit. Surely there would be some pianos at Terezín I could tune and earn a few crowns.

I thought that I just might see things that I'd never seen, and experience life that I'd never dared imagine. I can't say I wasn't scared. But I had become good at pretending.

Poppy told me there were funds, should they be needed. He gave me rolled-up banknotes inserted into an empty fountain pen and a can of baby powder, which I hid in a pocket. I sat in the backseat. He spoke to the driver before turning his attention to me. Our eyes met through the glass. I willed myself not to feel so alone.

"Poppy, I . . . I'll miss you."

"I love you, Max. I'll always be beside you wherever you are. Always. I'll see you soon, or my name isn't the Great Viktor Mueller!" He used the over-the-top voice of a circus ringmaster, the way he'd always done to entertain me. He smiled, but his smile had sadness etched into the edges. "And tell Hans . . . well, tell Hans to take care of you."

My father leaned forward. I had the sense that he wanted to tell me something else, something more, but before he could speak the driver started up the car. I couldn't tear my eyes away from Poppy, waving at me through tears, blowing kisses, and forcing a smile until the car was out of sight.

Next to me was my hurdy-gurdy. There were four large boxes marked BOOKS FOR THE LIBRARY, a consignment that Mr. Raggle had arranged for me. Inside the boxes was a supply of medicines. I didn't know how he had procured all these, but despite my curiosity, I knew I was better off not knowing.

I wiped my eyes and began to think about where I was going. General Max Mueller felt the wind brush his face as the open car reached a rolling green landscape. I couldn't help waving to the farmers we passed. I thought of something I had recently read: *On the other side of chance is discovery and if you don't go there, you'll never find what you're looking for.*

Eventually, the whistling air and the hum of the Mercedes lulled me to sleep and I didn't wake up until the car came to a stop.

The Mercedes arrived at a small village of neat gingerbread houses with slate roofs, lining narrow cobblestone streets. Many had flower boxes, which added a homelike touch that one might see in any small town in Europe. An inn, a church, a café, and a converted bakery, which served as the administrative office of the man I had come to see.

I had traveled thirty miles south of Prague to Terezín. The town was originally a resort reserved for Czech nobility. Next to the village were the forbidding walls of the famed fortress. It was called Theresienstadt then, created by Emperor Joseph II of Austria in the late eighteenth century and named in honor of his mother.

"Max Mueller, yes? I'm Commandant Siegfried Freidle." He spoke Czech easily, and clicked his heels together before asking me into his office. He was so tall that it hurt my neck to look up at him, but the man's smile was warm and reassuring. "And you brought books for the library. Much appreciated, Max. I'll have them delivered right away."

"But . . ."

An SS guard appeared, and slashed the top open for inspection. Inside were layers of *Mein Kampf,* Hitler's infamous manifesto, his blueprint for a new Germany.

I had never read it, and perhaps I should have, instead of having David fill in the blank spaces.

At first I was amazed and then I realized that the books had done the trick. I was relieved. The simple deception worked.

"You're a thoughtful compatriot, Max."

Freidle had been given the responsibility of organizing Terezín from the beginning. His shoes were polished to a shine, but his office was in total chaos. Teetering towers of papers threatened to consume the small clearing on his desk. Sitting down in a dusty, standard-issue chair, he pointed me to an armchair in the corner that had seen better days. Moving a pile of letters and a box of stamps before taking a seat, the major said, "So, Max, your father says you like music. Do you know this one?"

In this bizarre setting, the commandant closed his eyes and sang in broken English,

"You're the top!
You're a Waldorf salad.
You're the top!
You're a Berlin ballad."

I was surprised by his love for popular songs and nodded my head. And amazed that American lyrics had found their way to Terezín. Were they out of Poppy's repertoire?

"There's another I'm particularly fond of. One of my favorites." He cleared his throat and sang,

"We'll take Manhattan,
The Bronx, and Staten Island too,
It's lovely strolling through . . ."

He was on key, and rather sweet. But I wondered if he was singing a lyric or predicting the future.

"I have a degree in engineering but my great passions are American music and movies. Yes, like *Alexander's Ragtime Band,* and of course the tap dancing of *42nd Street.*"

I loved that music too. I had made my first new friend at Terezín. Things would really work out here after all.

"You'd never believe it by the many files around my office, but I manage to get things done. Within months of the first construction detail arriving, I made sure facilities were in place for carpentry, farming, a bakery, and a kitchen."

"That's impressive, Commandant."

"Yes, well, I understand you'll only be here for a little while, Max, but please come to me for any needs. Any needs. You'll be confined to areas inside camp: the post office and special barracks. Each area is named after a city back home. Hamburg is where you will find Hans Krása in his studio. Hanover is where your friend David Grunewald lives."

Commandant Freidle explained the details for my stay from an itemized list. "I've arranged for you to help out at the post office; you will have school in the mornings. You'll be staying with our postmaster, Fritz Branka, and his wife, Ava. They live next door in a duplex. They're Czech and have been here for a long time. Lucky for me Ava's a superb cook. A superb cook. We take most of our meals together."

"Do we have fresh milk here?"

"We get milk from the farm a few times a week. It's left in the green box just outside the Brankas' door. I'll ask Ava to leave a note for the milkman to order an extra bottle."

The secret dispatch box!

"Mrs. Branka taught school before the residents relocated, so you'll have classes with her each morning." Humming another tune, he glanced up at me. "You'll enjoy your time here. The Brankas will be pleased—Ava is a lovely lady. I welcome you, Mr. Max Mueller."

"Not to be disrespectful," I asked with a bit of hesitancy, "but I was hoping I could live with Hans Krása. I often stay with him in Prague when my father travels."

"My apologies, Max, it is not allowed, not allowed," Commandant Freidle replied. "You should live with the Brankas. I know you'll find it a comfortable arrangement and I'm following General Heydrich's special instructions. Do you know the general well?"

"We attend opera together and he's a friend of Poppy's, my father." I hoped I was speaking with the appropriate modesty. I could tell how impressed Freidle was by the way he said Heydrich's name.

"Yes, Viktor Mueller is famous. I've watched your father conduct many times."

"I'm sure you would like to meet him when he visits."

"I met him once before but yes, I'd like very much to meet him again. I know you are here under, well, unusual circumstances, unusual circumstances, considering you're not a Jew."

The Jewish issue again. I didn't comment and I was curious

to know whether the commandant repeated words on purpose, for emphasis, or if it was a kind of verbal pause so he could catch up with another thought. Urgent questions burned in my mind. Questions I needed to answer, to record in my notebooks and report back to Sam Raggle.

"I want to see my friends as soon as I can. They're important to me." I hoped I was sounding reasonable and patient.

"When you've settled in, you can see your friends. It's a good plan, yes? It is my duty to follow regulations and to assure General Heydrich of your well-being. You'll be able to spend some time inside the gates."

Some time wasn't going to be good enough for me; I intended to spend most of my time with David and Sophie. Beyond that, I was going find out just about everything I could for Sam Raggle.

"Are there regulations?"

"Security," Freidle said, collecting papers from his desk.

"But aren't we secure?"

"We are secure because of the regulations."

"My friends are the reason I came here."

"There's flu going around in camp right now and we best wait a few days. I want you healthy."

The major pushed his chair out, and I realized I didn't have much of a choice but to agree to Freidle's wishes by settling in first.

"Now, we shall meet the Brankas!"

Outside the gates, the Branka couple lived in a courtyard of small houses, beyond was a view of the river. Down the street, across a flowered field, were farms with fertile land growing vegetables. On the other side, there was an off-limits area called the Little Fortress. A jail for political prisoners. I wondered if I would find out more about it.

Ava Branka flung open the front door before the commandant could even knock. "Hello, Max! We've been waiting for you." I'd barely stepped into the house before she handed me a cup of hot chocolate. Despite myself, I felt right at home.

She was a pretty woman with gray-blue eyes, curly brown hair, a bright complexion, and rosy cheeks. Her cotton dress seemed a little too long, falling just above her ankles.

"Please enjoy, our young guest," Freidle said. "We'll discuss music and movies again soon."

He headed out the door.

"Yes, I'll show you your bedroom now," Ava said cheerfully, leading me upstairs.

My room looked comfortable at first glance. "This will be just fine, Mrs. Branka."

"Please, Max, I'm Ava."

There was a small couch that pulled out to a bed, nestled in an alcove near a large window, as big as a door. I surveyed the decor of lace curtains fluttering against flowered wallpaper with little vines of roses on a cream background. It was probably not something that I would have chosen for myself, but it was refreshing in an old-fashioned sort of way.

"I'm learning to speak better English from a friend, Ava, and I would like to keep practicing so I can become fluent."

"English will we speak. As much as we can. You and me," she said, nodding up and down. "What do you read to like? We should make plan for class."

Her expressions fascinated me, as if she had found a language all her own. She seemed like a nice lady. We would learn the finer points together.

"Do you like poetry?"

"Poetry! Yes," I exclaimed.

"Happy for me, as well. Much to think about. In ninth century China, a person of cultivation knew many poems and could quickly with recall, present an 'occasion of ideas,' and occasionally, they made up their own." Ava spoke in English as though she was translating words in her head, but I immediately cherished the idea of an "occasion of ideas."

I smiled at her. "Made up a poem on the spot?"

"When they did, they were given honor and respect."

I nodded. Sophie would certainly be impressed if I could do that. I could hardly believe I would see her soon. She was nearby, we both were in the same place, and that, if nothing else, made this a place I wanted to be. Nothing had changed, only a location. I wanted my first words to her to be reassuring, to come straight from my heart. I felt as nervous as I had on the day we met. Sophie and David were just around the corner. My time had come, and I was both excited and scared. Excited to see my friends. Scared of . . .

Ava Branka broke into my thoughts. "The tradition spread to Italy and Europe to poets called troubadours."

Troubadours. Now there was a concept I could get behind.

"Fritz sends a poem every day," she said, smiling. "Just a few lines, which like me very much."

Catching the notion about "the occasion of ideas," I thought how great it would be to learn to express myself in the same way they did in China. Maybe I would become a troubadour, making my way from place to place, traveling the world one poem at a time!

Making our way into the dining room, housing a large bookcase, I asked, "Could Sophie and David take classes with me?"

"Who are they?"

"My friends."

"This could be something to do, Max. Books. You read books?"

"Not as much as David, but I do like to read. Do you have a newsstand nearby?'

"I'm afraid they're not allowed."

Why not? Here was my first piece of information for Sam Raggle.

"My husband, the postmaster general, is a man of letters who likes to read. He speaks nice. Here are books; would like German or Czech?"

"Do you have any in English?"

"I have American book, very good. I'm sorry for my English. Sometimes I order my words in different way."

"Ava. You make perfect sense to me."

"Good. Yes, I have book about Mississippi, America, *The Adventures of Huckleberry Finn.*"

She handed it to me as I plopped into a chair and began reading at once.

The very first line jumped out at me:

> You don't know about me without you have read a book by the name of *The Adventures of Tom Sawyer*; but that ain't no matter. That book was made by a Mr. Mark Twain, and he told the truth, mainly.

What was *The Adventures of Tom Sawyer*?

I didn't know, but it was one more book for me to read.

It continued with a notice from someone called G. G., who was identified as the chief of ordnance. The notice demanded that no one try to find a motive, moral, or plot in the novel, or else they will be prosecuted, banished, or shot.

At first the book seemed to be set on creating more fear than I needed right then. But there was something about it, about the tone. It was like being spoken to by an old friend, and as I flipped through the pages past the introduction, I began to feel in safe hands with the writer. Mark Twain. I liked the sound of the author's name—it was all very different and somehow very comforting. Twain's novel fitted neatly along with my notebook. I would be able to carry it with me wherever I went. I was certain I was going to meet some important characters. I knew at once that I had to keep Mark Twain with me always.

I was sure we belonged together.

I began to read more, but the words started floating on the page. I must have drifted off because the next thing I knew, Ava was shaking me awake. She wanted to introduce me to her husband.

"Come with me, Max. I want to introduce you to husband special."

Fritz Branka was in his office. He was older than Ava, with a face weathered by the seasons.

"Are you the postman?"

"Postman, gardener, carpenter, and sometimes poet. I work indoors and out."

I immediately warmed to Fritz. He had a certain energy, and there was kindness in his eyes. The jacket he wore had polished buttons and a badge announcing his position. His hands were in constant motion, searching for something to do, something to read, something to deliver.

"I understand you're a general!"

He smiled easily. "Not a real general, just a postmaster general."

"May I call you 'poet general'?"

Laughing, Fritz leaned over and said, "Could you help me after your morning classes? There's not much mail, but I'm sure you would be good company."

"Don't you get a lot of mail here?"

"Not much. Packages come in, and, except for a few cards which the new arrivals send, few letters go out."

"Why?"

"Regulations."

"I've heard about regulations already. What kind are these?"

"Don't worry. You won't have to find them, they will all find you. You'll see."

I suspected there were going to be a lot of rules, and when they arrived, I'd better make note of each one.

I noticed a red sealed packet stamped CONFIDENTIAL.

There could be a lot of information.

"I'll help you, General, in any way I can."

"What languages do you speak?"

"Czech and German, and I speak and read English."

He raised his eyebrows. "English? I know well. Twenty-three Skidoo!" he said.

I didn't have the slightest notion what Fritz was talking about, except I noticed a *Handbook of American Phrases and Slang* in his pocket.

After dark, I asked if I might take a walk. "Fresh air."

"Stay close by. There's a curfew."

Ava opened the door for me.

Curfew. My first regulation.

At the first turn, I carefully surveyed the area, to make sure no one was around. I started toward the box, then a German officer appeared down the street, clearly in a hurry, making his way toward and into a nearby building of some sort, his quarters, I imagined. I waited, catching my breath. When he was out of sight, I discovered an important destination. The box. It was waiting for me. It would be my most important link to Prague.

I sent my first dispatch to Sunshine.

> I'm here. No newsstands anywhere. I haven't been able to get into the camp yet. A lot of regulations. I'm living just outside with a couple called the Brankas. I think they are good people, and I've met Commandant Freidle. We seem to get along, but I'm careful and cautious. The books are safely delivered, but only after an inspection. My eyes and ears are open. Until next time.
>
> *PT*

Looking around again, to make sure I hadn't been seen, I left it in a milk bottle to be collected when the milkman made his next drop.

Ava was available if I had a question, and the icebox was always full. Poppy had seen to that. She prepared all the meals, and Commandant Freidle joined us. Her cooking was almost as good as Lucie's.

I was desperate to find my friends. But I was learning patience. My instinct told me to just take in my new surroundings and try to relax, if possible. I had never been away from home for a long time before, let alone away from Poppy. I wanted to think he was beside me, but he wasn't. Anyway, thoughts of Poppy weren't as comforting to me as they had once been. I needed to grow up, to be brave—I needed to find a way to be calm.

In my first days there, I focused on what I could learn. I had to create a mental map of the place, to discover the nature of my new home, if this was going to be home. There was a lot to absorb and a lot to try to make sense of. For starters, I was pretty much the only person here really out of choice, however limited my choices might have been. I'd read the brochure, but what kind of place was this? Had we all been duped? Just outside of Terezín I took a closer look at the warren of cottages—yellow buildings with red roofs, and columns of windows with green shutters. Acres of rolling hills and a rushing river bordered the village. It had once had thirty-five hundred residents. It seemed that they had left their homes to make room for the new arrivals. The Germans had kept to its original German name, Theresienstadt, but everyone there called it Terezín. A hotel called the Kameradschaftsheim accommodated a group of officers in residence. They wore the menacing black uniforms of the SS, the secret police.

What was clear to me was that I was on the outside, and I needed to know what it was like to be within the walls, within the camp. I had caught brief glimpses of the camp when I walked up to the gate. Watching a few people milling around, I saw a girl wearing a hat. *Sophie?* The girl looked tired, her face smeared with grime, her dress dirty and worn. It couldn't be her, could it? I needed to be sure, and strained to see her, but she turned a corner and I lost her.

Whatever doubts I was starting to have, I told myself that Poppy wouldn't send me somewhere that wasn't all right, that wasn't safe. But I wasn't altogether reassured by my inner voice. Still, I had my own teacher, a nice room, and it was only a matter of time before I would see my friends. I kept repeating this to myself over and over, as though by thinking that I would be fine, it would all be fine.

Working at the post office was an advantage. I would be the first to know if a letter arrived from Poppy; but before one came, he surprised me with a visit. It was as though Captain Mueller had stepped off a stage. He was wearing a new dark-gray tunic and looked rather impressive.

I hadn't quite adjusted to my new surroundings yet. I knew where I was coming from but I was unsure about where I was. I still had so many questions and was in search of answers.

"When you left, Max . . . when you drove away, you looked so grown up, bigger than any field commander. I miss you a lot."

"I'm not so big, Poppy."

"In my eyes you're big, nearly a man already." Poppy picked me up and hugged me. "See, I can barely do that anymore."

Setting me down, he looked around at my new home.

"Tell me, how are you?" he asked.

"I'm pretty good, Poppy. How are things in Berlin?"

"I'd rather be in Prague."

"Why? Things are not so good there. Has anything changed?"

"A lot of changes, Max, and all very complicated."

"How? You keep talking about complicated. Too complicated to understand? Too complicated to explain to me?"

"Max, I just can't . . ."

"I think you could, Poppy, if you really wanted to. I know so little. What little I know makes me think that I'm still finding my way. But one thing that I do know is that you're carrying a lot of secrets."

That brought a broad smile. "Then, Max, you know me pretty well."

So, I wouldn't be getting many answers. Instead, Poppy offered up the cakes and fresh fruit he'd brought with some cold cuts and a loaf of black bread from Berlin. Ava prepared dinner, adding her special potato salad.

Sitting at a large table, Poppy asked Ava, "Is Max a good student?"

"Of course."

"Ava knows a lot about poetry and writing. She even speaks wonderful English. She gave me the American novel *Huckleberry Finn*. I like it a lot."

Ava beamed at me.

But as kind as the Brankas were and Freidle seemed to be, I wasn't going to just pretend that everything was somehow normal. "I can't wait to see Sophie. You know she's living here." I observed my father, but he wouldn't meet my eyes.

"Now, don't be rushing, Max. Give it time. You never know who else you might meet. You never know what might happen."

"You told me that when you met Mama you never looked back."

"One look was all I needed. But she was one of a kind."

"So is Sophie," I said frankly.

"Have you seen Hans?"

"At the end of the week. Major Freidle says I need a few days to adjust, and he doesn't want me to catch the flu that's going around the camp."

I watched my father closely.

"And *Brundibár*?" Poppy inquired. "I bet Hans is working on a new production."

"What is this *Brundibár*?" Ava asked.

"You'll see, Mrs. Branka," I replied. "Look forward to a great evening at the opera! We first performed it in Prague, on a small stage, but it deserves to be in the biggest theater around. It was written by Hans Krása."

"Yes," she said quickly. "I know his work. It's very wonderful. He's here in Terezín?"

My father didn't comment. I spoke on his behalf: "Hans was my father's best friend. They composed and worked together. A grand collaboration."

I faced down a stare. "Hans *is* my best friend. We'll work together again someday soon."

I was glad to hear that. But I was still trying to overcome any doubt.

Poppy rose and began to gather his things. "I'll come again before you know it, Max. And we will go away for a weekend together."

"Why do you have to leave so soon, Poppy?"

"Max, sorry but I have commitments and concerts!" He tousled my hair, the way he always did, ever since I was a child. But I didn't feel like a child any longer. "But don't worry. I'll be back before you have time to miss me."

"Poppy, can you bring some newspapers the next time you come?"

"Foreign papers are banned, and I don't subscribe to the papers in Berlin."

"But why?"

"Just doesn't make great reading."

I somehow knew not to push it further. "Then can you get me some photographs of movie stars?"

I thought of Poppy's personal collection and knew that he had contacts at the Ministry of Culture. *This could be very useful indeed,* I thought.

"Any particular ones?"

"Well, American musicals mostly, Busby Berkeley ones would be ideal."

He nodded, and I embraced him one last time.

After Poppy left, Freidle showed me a clipping that he had somehow managed to obtain.

THE OBSERVER

December 17, 1939

HITLER'S BAND

The relationship between the National Socialists and the Berlin Philharmonic Orchestra began in 1933, when the world-renowned orchestra came under the control of Hitler's Propaganda Minister, Joseph Goebbels. They serve as Germany's flagship cultural ambassadors, performing at the Nuremberg Rallies, the opening of the 1936 Olympic Games, and on Hitler's birthday. At the heart of the orchestra is the iconic conductor, Wilhelm Furtwängler, who is enjoying exceptional privileges. Distinguished Jewish musicians no longer play under his baton. Notably missing in the orchestra's bill is Jewish composer Felix Mendelssohn. Last week, Viktor Mueller arrived on an unseasonably cold day in Berlin to lead the orchestra. He was accompanied by some of Germany's noted generals. They came to celebrate Remembrance Day, to honor the nation's fallen in The Great War. A German national living in Prague, he is by all accounts Hitler's favorite conductor and aide-de-camp to Reinhard Heydrich.

Where had Freidle gotten this clipping? Poppy had told me about Wilhelm Furtwängler when we were in Berlin. My father didn't discriminate. That much I knew, and yet what he said and what he did were different. Who he was and what he was, all of this, was still a puzzle and the task was to put the pieces together. That was how I had to see this whole experience, everything was part of a puzzle and everything must fit there somewhere. I had to discover where I belonged, where Poppy fit in and if we were still together. I just couldn't think about Poppy excluding anyone from his orchestra or not playing compositions by Jewish composers. But how much did I understand about what my father was up to now? How much did any of it make sense? There was one thing I couldn't ignore and that was the fact that Poppy hadn't shown me the article. Was he embarrassed? Had he changed? He wanted Freidle to see this, but not me. In time, I needed to complete this jigsaw puzzle.

Lessons with Ava were in the kitchen at a round table, with blue-lined pads and Eberhard Faber no. 2 pencils, the same as I had at school.

"I have ideas for class," Ava said. "You are liking Mr. Huckleberry Finn?"

"I am, a lot." I had been carrying the book around with me everywhere, reading and rereading various passages. I had only gotten through the first few chapters, but I was hooked.

"I hoped you would," Ava said, arranging her notes neatly on her desk.

"We'll have a fine class. This Sophie is the girl your father mentioned?"

"Yes, Ava, and I'm going to see her soon. Well, I think I

might have seen her already actually, through the gates, and if that was her, I suspect she might need a few things."

"A new dress, you are looking, and clean clothes, some colognes."

"How did you know?"

"Max. I'm not falling off truck, and I am happy to do such a thing. My niece left grown-up. Yes, we will fix something nice for visit. Tomorrow, I will wash and make clean dress for Sophie."

The following morning a large packet marked for me came by special courier at the post office.

It was marked in bold lettering that read: CONFIDENTIAL.

Inside, I was relieved to find black-and-white glossy production stills; photographs of movie stars dancing through fountains, dressed in sweeping silk evening gowns and smart black ties and tails. They were from some of the great Hollywood musicals. *Top Hat* and *42nd Street.* Poppy had come up with a few hits. I told myself that I mustn't lose confidence in the Great Viktor Mueller. I showed them to Fritz and we came up with an idea. It was a way to make sure we stayed on Freidle's good side. I asked him to help me autograph them, but Ava had better handwriting. We dictated what she should write, and she inscribed each one in her very best script.

Fritz and I waited for the right moment to slip into Freidle's office. A photograph mysteriously appeared on his desk.

For Siegfried Freidle,
Dancing with you,
Busby

HAMBURG BARRACKS

Finally, in February, an all-clear to explore Terezín—the flu epidemic was over.

Past the gates, a building with tiled roofs housed the officers' quarters. Each group of the other buildings had a park, a quadrangle, and green lawns, and in the center a large square for parades.

From a bird's-eye view, the camp was an eight-pointed star. Double-brick walls surrounded the place. At one end, there was an abandoned church, and at the other a coffeehouse and a few stores. Some buildings had been converted into a hospital, library, and a Jewish administration building. Czech guards, wearing green uniforms and tan boots, were posted at every corner. Along the way was a private sidewalk used only by German officers and officials.

I could hardly keep up with my footsteps.

"You can go that way," the guard pointed.

The private sidewalk?

"Can you direct me to Hamburg Barracks?"

A guard with steel-gray eyes shifting abruptly from side to side pointed the way across the square.

A note on the door said, *In the library.*

Towers of books stood precariously on tables and in pine

bookcases. Spotting Hans at one of the tables, I held the moment for a while before I raced over and embraced him.

"Max, Max, what are you doing here?" Hans leapt to his feet.

His smile failed to hide the sadness in his eyes. He looked older, tired.

"These books," he said, "every one of them, has had readers who have resided between their pages. I've become a guardian of literature, and that's not a bad thing. But there are no books by Jews. Heinrich Heine, Zweig, Proust . . . all banned. Strange that a great writer can no longer be a great writer because he's Jewish. This is the world now, it seems. But, I'm pleased to see you. Shocked, but pleased. Tell me, Max, why are you here?"

"Because I couldn't wait to be with you. I thought you might need a piano tuner?"

We stepped into an outer reception room. A few threads trailed from his tweed jacket. He moved quietly as if not to disturb any objects around the room.

I punctured our silence: "Are you feeling okay?"

"I keep busy," Hans replied, his hand over his jacket, shaking off the dust, "stacking books in the library. Someone has to organize them."

"And you got a fresh delivery last week?"

Hans stared at me and smiled. "Ah, so it was you? Well done! As soon as I unpacked the top layer, I sent the medicines over to the infirmary."

"Are you teaching? Maybe we can get a production of *Brundibár* going."

Hans looked away from me. "Things aren't so easy here. Most of the cast left Prague on a Kindertransport and we have no piano."

"How can you be without a piano?"

"I compose in my head, when I'm alone. I suppose I'm

lucky. I could have been assigned to a detail in the carpentry shop or the laundry."

"Detail?"

"Work details. It's a way of life here, Max. Things are as they are."

"Where's the spa?"

"Some spa. Come, Max. I'll show you my studio. You can tell me how you came to be here."

"Poppy wanted me some place safe while he was traveling."

Hans frowned and shook his head. "Somewhere safe? And of all the ones available he chose this place?"

"No, I did. I convinced Poppy, and he agreed. I'm not sure if Poppy understands what is happening to the Jews. Surely, he knows the situation in Prague, and for you, David, and Sophie. The way he is, working with them, working with the orchestra, working with the restrictions . . . that's not Poppy, Hans. At least not the Poppy we know. I don't know what's happened to him. But what I do know is that while I am here I have work to do. I need to find out all I can, and I hope you'll help me. And I need to be with you and David and Sophie. I want to see you every day. And I want to play Brundibár. I want to do a lot of things."

I finally saw a smile come to Hans's face. "It's good to see you, Max. A part of me wishes you were somewhere, almost anywhere else. But another part of me is glad that you've arrived, that we're together again. I can look after you, we can look after each other. We'll go about this together."

With that, I felt better again, better than I had for a while. We really could make it work? Hans had a modest flat: two rooms where he'd arranged a few photographs of his friends; there was a picture of Hans, Poppy, and me—the three of us crowded around a piano. There were the same things he had packed when he'd first left for Terezín. It made sense to me now; he knew he would be away for a while. Pages of sheet music—Chopin, Mozart, Strauss—these had been keeping him company. These were his treasures. A paperweight from Paris was on a corner table.

Taking a moment to freshen up, a familiar Hans appeared with his silk robe draped around his shoulders, with a touch of citrus following him. I guessed it was a way of reminding himself of who he was. I saw the Hans I'd always known.

I couldn't wait any longer to ask. "Have you seen Sophie Mahler?"

"Oh, yes, your girlfriend. She'll be delighted you're here."

Wow, news travels fast.

"I'm working at the post office."

"Post office?" Hans asked. "There now, you've taken a detail." He placed his hands across his chest. "I'm sure you'll make a fine postman."

"How's David? Is he writing? Playing his violin?"

"David has found his place. It's not the same, but it's something."

"We're together, all of us. Poppy asked about you."

Hans looked away and said nothing.

VEDEM

Wasting not another minute, I made my way up to the third floor. Entering a large room, I found him working at a wooden desk, wearing his green eyeshade, sporting his long maroon scarf. He jumped up from his chair when I entered. His grin matched my own.

"Max! I don't believe it!"

"Well, I made it."

"How did you get here? Where are you staying? How is Poppy?"

"A car brought me here. I'm living right outside camp, and Poppy, well, I don't exactly know. But I'm here. That's the most important thing for now. We're together again, me and the Topper."

"Well, this is great news, Max. It's simply great. But I'm . . . I just don't know what to say."

"Hey, you're my best friend, and I want to know how you're doing."

"Max, for now I just couldn't be happier. My best friend in the world . . ."

"Now, I'm at a loss for words. But we'll find the words together."

David seemed taller, thinner, older. Much older. He was

still sharp in gray flannel shorts, a white-collared shirt, navy sweater, and vest. But he was wearing something new: a yellow star on his chest.

David caught me staring. "I hate it."

"I don't know, David. This may sound stupid, but I'd be proud to wear one."

"Well, it does sound kind of stupid, and you really should know that wearing a star is not some badge of courage."

"But I'd be more like you."

"Are you sure of that, Max?"

I noted something across the room. "Is that your violin in the corner?"

He forced a smile. "My other constant companion." Taking it out of its case, David played a plaintive tune to welcome me. Even at Terezín, David was the Topper.

"Poppy says you play better than anyone he knows. Now I know why."

"Well, Max? How are you finding this place?"

"I haven't seen the spa yet."

David let out a whoop: "Spa? Forget all the promotion, Max. It's pure propaganda. None of it is true."

"None of it? What do you mean? What do you do here?"

David shrugged. "What do we do? What we do here is we manage. We do what we must do. No options. We get through one day at a time. There are rations, not much to eat. Things here are not getting any better. But we get up. We get dressed." His voice broke off. "A lot of the kids paint. That helps . . . a little."

He pointed to an art gallery of crayon drawings, houses and families in oranges and blues, yellows, and purples, jumbled together around the walls.

"There is a school, then. That's something, isn't it?"

"You're looking for the silver lining in the clouds, Max.

Maybe that's not a bad thing. But you're going to have to look hard. There's no real school here, just a few improvised classes for the youngest. Max, there are a lot of regulations for everyone here. What we can do, who we can see, even attempts to control how we think and feel. And that's hard to regulate. Terezín was supposed to be Hitler's gift to the Jews. Well, there are some gifts you really don't want to receive. This is a place where it's hard to live. That's the truth. But, Max, as I said, we get up, we go on, we manage, we hope, we pray, and even find a smile occasionally. But there's contrast. There's a counterpoint."

"Tell me."

"You'll meet some of the most extraordinary people here."

This place was so different from everything that it was supposed to be, all the promises. Sam Raggle had to be told. My detail was expanding.

"Have you written to Sophie?" David asked.

"I have."

"She'll be around tomorrow. And she'll be surprised to see you. Sophie helps with the paper when she can. I've organized one called *Vedem*. It means 'In the Lead.' We provide news, well some news, for Terezín. More than five thousand people are reading it. And we can only produce one copy of each edition. Think of it, Max, that's some circulation, some readership. Funds from Jewish relief agencies help with food and clothes, and paper."

Flipping his eyeshade, David resumed his routine as if we were still at home, as if we were still at work on the school paper. "I need a good reporter. Since you're here, you can be my eyes and ears. You ready?"

"Of course. But tell me, have you read anything good I should know about?"

"In Czech or German?"

"How about in American?" I asked.

"American?"

"Yeah, American. 'How's ya get here? Maybe I better not tell, because dey's reasons.'"

"You're reading *Huckleberry Finn*? It's an education, Max, that's a great book." David smiled.

"Ava gave me a copy."

"Who's Ava?"

"My teacher."

"Your teacher? Where?" He frowned.

"She's a good woman, and plenty smart. I think we can learn a lot from her. It's an opportunity to read and know more, at least for me. I would have never known about Mark Twain if it weren't for Ava."

"Well, you're reading about freedom."

"I haven't gotten that far."

"You will, and when you do, you'll find prejudice, like we have here."

"How so?"

"You may not like the sound of this, Max, but right now we're niggers. We're like Jim."

The word jolted me.

"What's happening here, what's happening to us reminds me of the slaves who were bought and sold, separated from family, who lived lives of pain and suffering, but at the same time, wherever they were, they found a way to survive; they could sing and pray and somehow endure, even overcome unimaginable hardship. Yes, it's an ugly word but that's what we are here and now—niggers. I hate the word, I hate the thought. You know it was the last word black men heard before they were lynched. Imagine that, Max." David spoke with an intensity and a fury that I had rarely heard in his voice. There was more to this place than I had imagined, and it seemed that there was much more to Huck than I knew so far.

"It's a good book," David said. "An important book. We should always look for what matters most, Max. Sometimes you can find the answers. You have to have the right books of course."

He took me down a flight of stairs to a large hall occupying the entire second floor, a row of narrow beds in a room with high windows every ten feet.

"Here's where the Jewish kids live. Young kids from all over Europe. They're out on a field trip with Sarah now. You'll meet her. We're trying to make things normal, at least to make them seem as normal as we can. We do it for the children but for ourselves as well. We've got some great people around. Have you ever seen *The Blue Angel* with Marlene Dietrich?"

My heart skipped a beat. "Is she here?"

"No, but her costar, Kurt Gerron, is, and he's made a lot of movies."

"What kind of movies?"

"As Twain would say, that's for your learnin', boy, and for *Vedem* to publish." David spoke with an exaggerated American twang.

I was running late. I still hadn't seen Sophie, but I had to get back to the Brankas' and couldn't be late for dinner.

A BLUE STAR

Camp Commandant Freidle joined us for supper, and I had to stop myself from bombarding him with questions as soon as he walked through the door. Pouring myself a cup of pea soup from a silver ladle, I couldn't keep silent any longer.

"Can I wear a yellow star?"

"No, no, it is not for you, Max," his hand stopped in midair as he tried to sip from a bowl of *erbsensuppe.*

"How about a blue one?"

"Blue?"

"I'm color blind." It sounded reasonable to me. "The guards can identify me on sight. Security, Commandant."

Blue was Sophie's favorite color, I remembered.

Freidle was quiet for a moment. "Yes, Max, it does make sense. You can wear a blue one."

I pushed my luck.

"Can you help get a piano for Hans? He is a great composer, as you know, and—"

"A piano?"

"There's no piano anywhere in the camp . . . in the village."

"How is that possible? We're German! Are you sure we have no piano?"

I shook my head.

"No piano," he mourned.

Lifting my head and stroking my chin slightly, I played my next card. "I'm sure my father would want us to have one. I know how much you appreciate music."

Freidle nodded. "We will see what can be arranged. How are you finding your lessons with Ava?"

"I like her a lot! She's smart and pretty."

"A boy of kindness." Ava blushed.

"I'm sure she is as good as any teacher you had in Prague."

"You seem to know a lot about me." I tried to sound jovial.

"I know about your interest in music, your pals."

"I have just one more request." I was testing my powers of persuasion. Clearly, I was privileged here. I needed to know how privileged.

A slow *hmmmmmmm* emerged from the commandant.

"Can my best friend, David, join my class, if it's all right with Mrs. Branka?"

"What do you think, Ava?"

"It would be good company for Max. Maybe he would like to invite Sophie too."

"Who's Sophie?"

"She's my girlfriend."

"Why not? It's nice to have classmates," Freidle said in an agreeable sort of way.

A few days later, another photograph found its way to Freidle's desk. Ava's handwriting was becoming even more artistic.

To Siegfried,
We are your biggest fans.

Regards from 42nd Street,
Ruby Keeler and Dick Powell

I was beginning to make progress, but with matters of the heart I was quite hopeless. More than anything I looked forward to seeing Sophie again. I felt confident one minute and not ready for the next. I seemed to be falling somewhere between anxiety and happiness. Was that falling in love? It felt to me like the kind of stuff that songs and poems were made of.

Making my way up the stairs to the *Vedem* office with a box under my arm, I was caught off-guard by a wonderfully familiar voice: "That wouldn't be Max Mueller, would it?"

I held my breath. I wasn't ready to respond as quickly as I should have. I couldn't find any words at all. Cornflower blue eyes looked up at me. "Sophie!" I exclaimed. Then I stuttered, "Th-they wouldn't let me come any sooner."

"No need to explain." She grinned. "We're just today out of quarantine. The last in the whole camp."

Above us was a skylight between the upper landing and the afternoon sky. She took my hand and again I couldn't think of a thing to say. All the words that I had planned vanished. It had happened too soon and yet not nearly soon enough. I glanced at my watch. The magic hour, twelve o'clock, noon. I would never forget the exact moment, the exact minute, the exact time.

"Come with me, Max."

Reaching the top of the dusty landing, I noticed Sophie's favorite dress was torn and dirty and sporting a yellow star. Even so, she was just the same as when we first met, her features softened by the light of a late afternoon sun filtered through the glass. She was perfect, and I realized that I didn't need to say anything, that there were no words to express how I felt at that moment.

"Well now, Mr. Mueller, I've been waiting for you."

"I came as soon as I could."

"I knew you were here."

"You didn't. Who told you?"

"Word gets around when somebody like you arrives."

"Any other secrets?"

"Just between you and me. It's up to us to keep them or break them."

"I'll be keeping mine."

"And you brought medicine for the infirmary."

"You know about that too?"

"Sulfur, drugs for pain, bandages—a welcome gift, Max. We live in constant fear of a typhoid epidemic breaking out."

"It wasn't so hard."

"Except you could have been arrested on the spot. I can't tell you how amazed we were to find it hidden under copies of that . . . horrible book."

"I imagine Hans can use the covers to disguise some other books in his library."

"Is that the reason you came?"

"Sophie, I'm here because of you. There are some other reasons, but you're the main one, the real one."

"Are you sure, Max?"

"I'm very sure."

"We have a lot to catch up on. So much is happening here."

"Are you listening to music? Are there concerts we can attend?"

"Some of the finest musicians in Europe are here."

"And they are all Jewish?"

"They are, and we can all cling on to the hope that we're here only for a short time. Until we can make it to our homeland."

"I'd like to make that trip with you. We'll add some background music. Just like the movies."

"You are a romantic."

"I think you have turned me into one."

She beamed. "I want to introduce you to Sarah, my best friend. And Rabbi Leo Baeck, you'll have to meet him too. Don't ask me about him now—it's too much to talk about right this second. But when you meet him, you'll know why he's so important."

"Where are you living, Sophie?"

"Over in our barracks. We're some of the luckier ones."

"Lucky?"

"It could be so much worse, but still, Max, we were expecting so much more."

"I've been learning about the gap between what you were promised, what everyone was promised, and what you have all been given. But tell me, how's your mother?"

"She's . . . well she'll be happy to see you. I hope soon."

"I'm not sure I understand this place."

"Have you seen David? He'll fill you in."

"I plan to join his staff."

"That's great. Particularly if you have special privileges here."

"Special privileges?"

"Of course, Max. You're special, you know that, I mean you're different. You must understand that."

"I hope not. If you mean not being Jewish, then I'll find a way not to be so different."

Sophie touched my cheek.

"Max, the way to learn things is to keep your eyes open, really open. Now, just look around you and you'll soon see how things are. And in the meantime, I want to know more about what you've been doing. How is your father, the Great Viktor Mueller?"

I paused before answering. "That is a simple question, but I'm not sure the answer is so easy. Poppy is doing a lot of things. I have a lot to tell you."

"Do you think he can send more medicine? It's desperately needed."

"I'm sure he can."

She placed her head on my shoulder, and I liked that a lot.

"If I'd known I was going to see you today, I would have worn my hat."

"I'm glad you didn't forget me. I wrote you all the time."

"I never received any letters."

"What?"

"I really didn't. Things are different here, difficult in so many ways."

"Surprise! I have a job; every letter will be delivered from now on."

"How can that be?"

"I'm working at the post office."

"Really?" She laughed.

"I'll be making some changes. Just consider me special delivery."

"I don't see a stamp."

I kissed her. "There's your stamp. Letters are important, not just who they're from, but who receives them, especially from someone you're waiting for. I happen to have a package to deliver that just arrived."

I gave her the box that Fritz had wrapped, making it official. It contained some nice new clothes from Ava, two pretty dresses, pencils, paper, needles, and thread.

"Who's it from?"

"Hmmmm. No return address."

"You're something special, Max Mueller."

"If that's true, then you make me so."

A GRAND ARRIVAL

There was a message from Freidle posted on my door.

Max, meet me tomorrow morning before class. Bring Hans Krása along. I've made arrangements.

Arrangements?

I got up early and went to collect Hans. We met Freidle and crossed a road to a long stretch of wet lawn rolling down to the river and a rickety old pier. The air was chilly.

"Nice morning," I said, rubbing my hands and adjusting the new blue star that hung on my gray cotton blazer. Hans stared at the patch of rich periwinkle, and turned away, saying nothing.

The mist shifted, bringing a cooler wind and a touch of clear sky. Just as the sun broke, rays of light bounced across the water. Right on cue, we heard the strains of Haydn's *Surprise Symphony*. A narrow barge pulled by a tugboat came into view over a floor of fog. On the deck, a man played a piano. It was Hans's own grand that Camp Commandant Freidle had brought up the river from Prague. The film-loving commandant had staged a showboat! I had seen musketeers with swords jumping from rooftops, heroic aviators dodging each other in epic battles, casts of thousands dancing down staircases, but a floating piano being played on a barge slipping over water through a curtain of weeping willows?

Freidle turned to me with an oversized smile. "You see, my boy? Hollywood."

Hans didn't speak, but I saw a tear on his cheek.

"I think you're pretty good, Commandant Freidle, pretty good."

His "production" deserved a reward.

The following day on the commandant's desk was a gorgeous photograph of Hedy Lamarr, with a note written in an elegant flourish:

Dearest Siegfried,

My darling. You are the most special man I've ever known.

Hedy

I didn't think he would have known that she might be Jewish.

Freidle's staff began asking him about the actresses featured in his office, and each inquiry was answered with an understatement. He had probably figured where they were coming from by this time, but he played along.

"Oh, that's just Hedy."

Eventually they were all framed and formed a special Hollywood gallery on his wall.

But most important, over the following months, pianos began arriving in a more conventional way. In fact, a spinet even showed up in our quarters, and I couldn't wait to get back to my craft.

There was a milk dispatch the following morning, and I had more to report. Incidental news about the Brankas, my job at the post office, impressions of the village, and a dozen regulations.

Sunshine,

We've gotten Hans a piano. David is okay, and he's editing a paper here called Vedem.

PT

Although, I hadn't had a chance to gather specific incidents, I added a footnote.

Terezín is strange; not what I expected. Many people look lost, hungry, tired, confused. They are doing what they can to get by. I can't really tell you quite what this place is yet, but I do know what it isn't. It is not a spa. I'll let you know more as soon as I know more.

I waited until evening, scanning everything around me to make sure no one would see me. When I was sure it was all clear, I dispatched my note and slipped away. I was doing something, and I had to believe that in some small way it was making a difference. I was a reporter, but I didn't quite know all the facts.

At our first class, Sophie looked pale and exhausted. She had stepped back into my life, and it was more than a movie. It was real. I could hardly find words to express how the colors she brought with her were painting my world. But written in her face were the everyday worries of her life. So many hours at the infirmary, looking after her mama, the need for medicine, a clean place to sleep. Sophie deserved so much more, the freedom to breathe, to be happy, to be alive, to believe in something. I needed to help her, to allow her the promise of something different, something better.

David shook me from my reverie by asking Ava about Germany and the Jews.

"Why are we being driven away from our homes?"

Mrs. Branka probably thought that we should not be discussing politics. She tried to answer: "It's a political situation."

"But we've been taken from our homes," David persisted. "Isn't it a matter of fanaticism? Of toxic, virulent anti-Semitism?"

I turned to *virulent* in my dictionary. No question about it. The Germans were spreading hate.

"David, much you say is true, and I assure you the matters bothers me greatly. I'm Czech and not German," Mrs. Branka replied, trying to regain control of our small class.

David wouldn't let up.

"The Czechs are just saying, 'Come on in. You want to kill a few folks, fine, hang those red-and-black flags, looks great, after all we need a few swastikas to decorate the landscape. You want to destroy an entire culture, come on in. Oh, we're just Jews, it doesn't matter.'"

Mrs. Branka did her best to respond. "There are a lot of people in Germany who don't support what you're saying, David."

"I'd like to meet some of these good people, Mrs. Branka."

I could understand David's concerns but I felt uncomfortable that he was confronting the wrong person.

Sophie jumped in quickly. "I agree with David, Mrs. Branka. My father was a professor, just like you, standing for decency, and he was courageous, part of the Resistance, but he was silenced."

Ava did something I wasn't expecting. She came over and put her arm around Sophie. I wanted to do the same.

"As long as I'm here, I'm going to help. We're all doing the best we can, Sophie. I do believe good people like you will carry the day. Let's think of the poet William Blake. 'We become what we behold.'"

David looked at her. "So if that's true, what are we becoming?"

Ava met his gaze, unblinking. "I think we can decide about what we want to be."

Classes continued with David firing questions, determined not to give up on finding the truth. Ava could only do so much. She couldn't explain a lot to us. If word got out about her personal sentiments, and our questions, she would not have lasted very long. Our lessons became cherished times for us all, oases of calm and reason, places where we had the freedom to try to understand more about the world and about ourselves. With Sophie's help we came to discover, and began accepting the art and literature Mrs. Branka introduced us to, subjects that would enrich our lives. In their own way, all of this would help us learn how to survive, and how to look at things in a different way, to decide who we were, who and what we could become.

That night, I turned to my bedside table, where Mark Twain had become my reliable companion. There was a passage all about how people think differently, a discussion between Huck and the black man he befriended, Jim.

> "Well, it's a blame ridicklous way, en I doan' want to hear no mo' 'bout it. Dey ain' no sense in it."
>
> "Looky here, Jim; does a cat talk like we do?"

MEETING LENI RIEFENSTAHL

Near the cabinet room, ever-delusional Joseph Goebbels, the notorious propaganda minister, sat dwarfed by a desk as exaggerated as his imposing Berlin office.

"There's someone waiting to meet you: Leni Riefenstahl."

Viktor was surprised. He had seen her perform as a dancer and actress prior to her liaison with Hitler, before she became one of the premier film directors in the world. Her films, *Triumph of the Will,* for the 1934 Nuremberg Rally, and *Olympia,* the documentary on the 1936 Olympic Games, had become legendary, seen around the world, winning gold medals in both Paris and Venice.

"She admires your work, Captain."

"What does she have in mind?"

"A collaboration. Two great artists. She is waiting for you in your office."

When Viktor introduced himself, he was amazed how small and slight she was, and how her face was reminiscent of the kind seen in so many classic films. Confident and comfortable, she sat in his small but well-appointed office, surrounded by signed photographs of all the musicians he admired.

"Captain Mueller, at last. I've admired your productions."

"Thank you, Fräulein Riefenstahl."

"Leni, please."

"Leni, yes, of course. Let me say how impressed I am by the way you have revolutionized film, how you see through the lens so differently."

Riefenstahl had practically invented tracking shots, and inventive pans from cranes, and even built trenches to shoot upward with elongated shots. She had a cinematic eye and had single-handedly given film a different perspective. She had five hundred searchlights form a circle at fifty-foot intervals, shooting into the sky at night forming a cathedral of light creating an image that was not only impressive and unforgettable, but burned forever into the minds of everyone who was there.

He continued. "You'll have to come to Munich next week. There will be a premier of a new production."

"I know your work, Viktor. I believe the Führer would like for us to work together."

"But I am not practiced in film. I know a little about stagecraft, but film is a different medium, one I've not explored."

"I appreciate your use of multimoving stages, film projection, and music integrated into your productions. I want to do the same. What I envision is seventy-millimeter film to project on very large screens, and I will need one of your amphitheaters to create this kind of cinema. Special speakers and projectors. I have a plan to have both moving screens and moving projectors and integrated live performance. I know film; you know theater. I need your knowledge and technology, and I need to understand the way you direct your cast, to create emotion. I want to do on film what you do onstage, to engage and capture my audience."

"Have you the authority for this?"

"Our Führer has allowed me to work in complete freedom, just as he has done for you. He would like for us to work together."

Viktor knew Riefenstahl was a great artist, but he was curious. Was she just a gifted filmmaker in love with her art? Or an instrument of the Reich? Or simply a supreme pragmatist, an opportunist? And what was he himself?

She seemed to be eavesdropping on his thoughts: "We are very much alike and have much to share."

Viktor navigated the conversation into a different direction. "I've heard that you believe that Hitler is the greatest man who has ever lived."

Riefenstahl spoke with extraordinary calm: "I'm not a member of the Nazi Party, Viktor. Hitler gives me the chance to create a message for and about Germany. Are you not doing the same thing? Are you not brilliantly expressing yourself, with opportunities and almost limitless tools such as you have never had before? What artist, what true artist, could resist this chance—the chance to fully realize yourself, your vision. You're a great talent. When you're not directing, you conduct great orchestras. I've watched you. When you are on a podium, you express yourself like a dancer. Your hands dance."

"I am flattered, but I suspect you're here for a greater, clearer, very different purpose. What do you really want from me, Fräulein Riefenstahl?"

"I want you to coproduce my film *Victorious,* which will play to the entire world when the war is over. We should begin planning now."

"Yes, we should start planning."

The meeting left Viktor thinking about how involved he was in propaganda, how much longer he could carry on doing what he was doing. How much of this could be justified? How many more concerts would he direct? One thing he did know: he had made a deal with the devil.

A PERFORMANCE

I received a special invitation. It was from General Heydrich and on elegant stationery tied with a ribbon. Poppy had engineered a musical production, and I was to go. I opened the envelope in the *Vedem* newsroom with David at my elbow.

"Ah, an invitation from the Reichsprotektor himself. You'll have to report on this event, Max," David said. "Pay attention to everything, everyone. Remember, you can't expect an easy explanation. But if you really are a journalist now, you are part of a tradition of truth-seekers." Leaning closer, David spoke softly, "Time to put your long pants on. Be a man. Be a reporter, Max. Be my undercover man. There's no one else. I trust you. Find out whatever you can. It's so important." And then softer still, "Lives may depend on it."

In the distance, hundreds of searchlights beamed into the sky. It was an open-air theater. The sound of a hundred drums—first a roll of snare drums, then timpani—reverberated and built and joined together in an overwhelming rhythm. An orchestra played, accompanied by a chorus of three hundred. One group sang and the other responded, as though it were a mass, a holy celebration—an overture to the event itself, conveying Germany's heroic glory.

The general had also invited Commandant Freidle to the premiere. It was the first time I'd been out of Terezín since I'd arrived nearly three months ago, and the chance to see Poppy was more than I could have hoped for. Dresden was near the border, just an hour's drive away.

Arriving at the amphitheater, I was more interested in finding my father than in anything else. I endlessly scanned the audience over hundreds of rows of seats, looking for his face. They were all waiting for the performance to begin, sitting quietly, obediently, their expressions glazed. Freidle was overwhelmed.

"This is incredible, Max," he kept repeating under his breath. "Incredible!"

The audience members were intoxicated by the spectacle. They thrilled by the production, especially the final scene when a godlike figure representing Hitler was lowered into view. The event concluded with a celebration of the greatness of the Fatherland.

The orchestra played the national anthem, "Deutschland, Deutschland über alles," and they all jumped to their feet. They wept and fervently sang along. It was a staggering thing to see. But throughout the performance I felt a peculiar sense of isolation, as if I was the only one not moved by the grandeur of it all. I didn't feel in any way connected, not to anyone. I was fighting the urge to stand up and scream that this was nonsense. How could they believe this spectacle? After a thunderous ovation, the drums started again, and the Führer's adoring fans brought the evening to a close.

Nearby, I saw the mysterious presence of the black overcoat scribbling in his black book. I felt completely ill at ease in this vast crowd and wondered if I was also the only one who saw his sinister, spectral presence. Was he writing about the event and Poppy? It bothered me to see him keep appearing wherever I went, always lurking in the background, an ominous shadow. Looking away, I tried to erase the dark silhouette from my thoughts. Why was the black overcoat there? Why was he everywhere? Was he real? Was I conjuring him up, projecting my fear, my deepest anxieties?

At last, it was all over. Poppy found me. He pulled me close in a hug and didn't let go for nearly a minute before stepping back and beaming. "Well, Max, what did you think of the show?"

Before I could answer, Commandant Freidle pushed past me to shake Poppy's hand, pumping his arm up and down, as if he'd just met the Führer himself. As they spoke, I saw General Heydrich moving in the crowd with his wife. He waved to Poppy and came over. I stood a little taller.

"Did you enjoy the performance, Max?" he asked. "Better than opera, yes? We always meet up at great events. I'm glad to see you."

"And you as well, General. I appreciate Poppy's work."

I hoped that sounded genuine enough. I did appreciate it. But did I *like* it?

"Viktor, the Führer is invigorating the Nazi message, to resonate for a thousand years. Your Thingplatzes are the churches of National Socialism."

Heydrich turned to Freidle and they chatted lightly. Poppy stepped away and spoke to a man I had never seen before. Poppy beckoned me to come over. "I want you to meet Fritz Gerlich, the managing editor of the *Munich Post.* He's come to interview me."

The Munich Post*! A big-time journalist.* I could almost feel David at my shoulder, urging me to take notes, not to miss a detail.

"A pleasure, Max," Gerlich said, his face unreadable. He turned back to Poppy. "And congratulations, Viktor Mueller. I've been a fan of yours for a long time. I attend your concerts every chance I get."

Poppy smiled but Gerlich did not return it, instead speaking in deadly earnestness: "So I must ask how you got involved with this nonsense?"

Poppy frowned. "*Nonsense?* We're both German; it's our culture, our history."

"Are you serious? German culture or the Nazi message?"

"I'm a musician. Music is my country. I am not part of the Third Reich," Poppy protested, stepping closer to Gerlich.

"You may not be but your production suggests God is. Whatever you say you are, it appears you are a votary, supporting everything Hitler stands for."

Votary. *Good word. I'll look it up.*

Glaring at the man from the *Post,* Poppy replied, "I was asked to take on the project to construct amphitheaters for productions worthy of the German tradition." He cleared his throat and dropped his voice. "My work does not make me a Nazi."

"Well, what does it make you then?" Gerlich said with contempt.

I was upset. Even at his most furious, Hans had never spoken to my father like this.

"Viktor Mueller," Gerlich said, "you are a great artist but you are disgracing yourself as an acolyte of the Reich." He spoke as though he were passing sentence on a criminal.

Acolyte. Another good one for my collection. My father's face was white as Gerlich spat out his words.

He glanced over at Heydrich, still chatting with Freidle nearby. "I should remind you, Mr. Gerlich, to be careful what you say in these times."

"I know that very well." Gerlich spoke quietly. "I go a long way back with Adolf, and I can promise you, Hitler is betraying the German spirit. My offices have been ransacked, I've been threatened. The *Post* is the last paper standing up for free speech, and as a journalist who respects a great artist, I can say, Herr Mueller, that I'm deeply disappointed that you are part of an anti-Jewish, anti-Christian propaganda crusade, all to glorify a criminal. You will learn, as I did. I'm truly happy to meet you, but I am deeply sorry for what you do. And I bitterly regret what you have become."

He turned and disappeared into the crowd. I watched him in stunned silence.

"Poppy? Why did that man say all those things about you? Is it true what he said about Hitler?"

Poppy held me close. "It's not so important, Max. These are testing times and tempers can run high. What is important is that I can see you again. I'm so glad you came and I'll be coming to visit more often."

"But, Poppy, if Hitler is a criminal and you're building him up, and the Germans hate Jews, it seems as if . . . I mean, what about Hans, and David and Sophie? Do you think they're—"

"Max, you have the makings of a fine journalist, but for now, I must ask you to believe in me."

I wasn't sure what he was asking, but I pushed that thought aside. I was still hoping that Poppy would help my friends. "Do you think you can get more medical supplies to us? We need them. People are suffering there, Poppy, and that can't be right, can it?"

Poppy nodded and turned around as someone patted him heartily on the shoulder. There was nothing that the Great Viktor Mueller appreciated more than admiration for his work.

"I must go, dear Max. Travel safely, keep believing, and I

will see you soon." He gave me a last hug as he was swept away into the crowd.

"Bye, Poppy," I called to his retreating back. I looked around me. People were wearing swastika armbands and badges. Their mood was exultant. But I had a terrifying feeling of nausea deep in the pit of my stomach, an anxiety that was growing bigger all the time. Poppy was a man in a Nazi uniform, wearing a swastika badge, the symbol of National Socialism. What had he become? Who had he become? How could I believe in him?

A PAIR OF STEEL-RIMMED SPECTACLES

I was relieved to get back to Terezín. It was the only home I had. Reporting to David the next day in the *Vedem* office, I gave my account. "It was unlike anything I've ever seen before." David scribbled notes as I spoke. I told him about the crowd, the mood, the near-hysterical singing of the German national anthem.

"Hitler descended like a god, to save Germany." I shuddered a little as I spoke.

"You saw your father, though?"

"Yes, I saw him." I spoke flatly. I knew David understood that I didn't want to talk about Poppy.

Thinking of him and his Nazi production reminded me of my own. *Brundibár* had a brighter message. Poppy had his production—I would have mine. We needed to do something, just to show each other that we could, to remind ourselves of who we were and who we could be. It became clear to me then that this was important, for all of us, even for Poppy too.

"I can only imagine what an overblown production it was. Did you get the message?" David asked. "These enormous productions are there to send a message. It's Hitler's propaganda machine. It's all show. Searchlights and drums are just a prelude to rolling tanks and marching troops."

"Do people always swallow propaganda?"

"When it's done well, yes, I think they do." David spoke somberly.

"Have you ever read the *Munich Post*?" I asked.

"Fritz Gerlich is the best editor in Germany."

I was lost in thought.

"It's all a lie, Max," David said, reviewing his notes. "Everybody lies for a purpose, some good, some bad."

"Tell me about the mail, Fritz. People send letters, a few others receive them. I don't see much activity."

"It's difficult, Max."

"What do you mean? I keep hearing that things are difficult. This is the mail, isn't it? We send the letters out, don't we?"

"They go to headquarters," Fritz replied.

"Why?"

"It's considered sensitive material."

"You can't be serious, Fritz. Why is there a post office? Sophie never received my letters. I can't believe that happened. When you write a letter, you assume it will arrive at the other end."

"I'm bothered, too, but it's just the way things are. I do my job. I suspect the censors do theirs."

"The censors? They're reading all the letters? It's not right, Fritz. Letters are personal."

"No, it's not right. But it's the way it is."

I had to report to Sam Raggle. I had to write something that would be read only by the person it was sent to.

I spied a red packet with a Berlin postmark.

"What's in the large envelope?"

"It's marked confidential, Max. For the SS, and in my custody until I deliver it."

"But what's inside?"

"Not for us to know. We are here to do our jobs, not ask questions. Questions can cause trouble."

Asking questions was my mission, and trouble was already swirling all around me. Censors, the SS, my father. When Fritz left the office for a moment, I did what I had to do. It wasn't lying, it wasn't stealing, it was asking a question and finding the truth. *Isn't that what journalists do?* I could hear David's voice in my head, urging me on. Carefully lifting the seal off the packet, I saw documents and newspaper clippings. This was information that Fritz had and never told me about. Clippings about my father, Berlin, the war. There was one in English, and the name Gerlich leapt out at me. The SS were even tracking foreign newspaper reports.

THE MAN WHO SAW TOO MUCH

Fritz Gerlich saw events before they happened. He was editor of the Munich Post. No longer. He grew up in Munich, studied history, and earned a doctorate. With poor eyesight, he depended on distinctive steel-rimmed glasses, a characteristic that came to identify him.

Staunchly defending his country's response to the aftermath of Germany's defeat in the World War, he offered unwavering support throughout Hitler's rise to power. When the Nazi agenda expanded into radical racial laws, Gerlich would have no part of it. Hitler had promised to peacefully restore and rebuild Germany, with rights for all its citizens. In time Hitler betrayed and blatantly lied to Gerlich.

Coupling his radical views with anti-Semitic policies—seizing property, internment camps, and

> violating the rights of Germans without trial—Hitler's deceptive actions were clearly illegal. The *Post* was warned, but still the paper reported on political murders, on Hitler's willful falsifications of history, and on the propaganda stunt using the newly constructed Thingplatzes to promote the German message. Gerlich realized that at the core of Hitler's credo was the ideal of racial purity. He wanted his fellow Germans to understand that Hitler's way—freedom of the press suspended, free assembly forbidden, civil rights violated, and any protest a crime punishable by death—was not the German way. Gerlich fought until Stormtroopers burst into his newspaper office last week, beat him senseless, and dragged him off to a concentration camp. Then, a few days ago, his wife received a message and a package. The Nazis had killed the journalist who had seen through them all. Inside the package were no words, just his blood-spattered, steel-rimmed spectacles.

I could hardly catch my breath. The man who had so recently been talking to Poppy had been murdered. Murdered for reporting the truth. Gagging a journalist. Who would be next? I couldn't control my trembling hands as I resealed the envelope. I was horrified. It was a cover-up. It wasn't betraying Fritz's trust that I was ashamed of, but the news about the death of a good man. This was the man with whom my father had argued so bitterly. My first instinct was to send a message to Raggle. It was murder. It was wrong. Gerlich represented the best of us, the last defender in Germany of the free press. And if they killed Gerlich, they would kill Sam Raggle, or me—anyone. I knew I must hold on to who I was. Yet I was sure that Raggle must have known and what could he do? After weighing the consequences and risks, I decided not to dispatch the report.

The stakes were rising and the scales were tipping up and down. How could they be rebalanced? The next few days I found myself just sitting across from the gates of the camp, waiting for Poppy. But he never came.

THE EMPERORS WITHOUT CLOTHES

Berlin 1940

For weeks Viktor had the event under surveillance. He knew that the occasion was a big one.

The generals were having special uniforms made. All of them.

They were going to be in a reviewing stand for Berlin's Victory Parade. And Hitler was to have a ceremony afterward, celebrating his leadership. Every photographer in Berlin had been enlisted for the event. Newsreel cameras would be on hand. The generals would be at their very best, elevated and contemptuous. As a warm-up, a show of force, goose-stepping troops, platoons of tanks, the navy, the air force, military bands, the works.

But before the parade, the ceremony. Every member of the high command would receive a new medal, the Silver Cross, adorning their uniforms. Photographs would be circulated to every newsroom.

The idea came to Viktor when he was being fitted for the occasion by A. S. Schneider.

Over lunch, he suggested to Pierre Burger, "I have an idea. It appeals to my sense of drama. While I'm not practiced in bombs, what if we attack character by humiliation?"

"I have no idea what you're talking about, Viktor."

"I've been thinking about the generals. A small gesture for tomorrow's parade could bring a surprise, not so dangerous, but dramatic."

Pierre was curious.

"For the last month, each of the generals has been fitted by my tailor, A. S. Schneider, for new custom-made uniforms and each have added personal adornments and accessories. There must have been many fittings for each general. Every detail must be flawless. Ribbons, medals, leather straps. Schneider has been charged to cast new medals for the occasion. As you might know, Schneider is the best tailor in Germany; Heydrich introduced me to him."

Viktor had been to the establishment many times and knew the entire uniform drill. Hitler preferred brown khaki, while Göring opted for a loose-fitting gray tunic; Heydrich wore a more slimming line with black stripes to highlight his tall good looks. No matter the fabric, each uniform featured a red armband with a circle of white, a black swastika at its center. Himmler demanded black, ever since he commissioned Hugo Boss SA in Bavaria to design and manufacture the uniforms for the SS. They matched his large black SE Mercedes and fleet of German-made Ford Eifels, with their blue spotlights mounted on the driver's side, that scurried around Berlin arresting people.

"I'm not sure how this intelligence is going to help our effort, Viktor."

"Attack by humiliation. You know bombs; I know costumes," Viktor replied. "They are impressive," he continued. "Glamorous new uniforms to satisfy every ego. A new distinguished medal to confirm self-esteem. The uniforms have been made from the finest wool in Austria. They include brass buttons from the Krupp works and are tailored by Germans, not Jews, even though Jewish tailors have been the best in Germany for a hundred years. Hitler doesn't want them sewing his uniforms because they would only soil German honor. There are uniforms and medals on order."

"Yes . . ." Burger was confused but intrigued.

"I've observed that the generals, the most powerful men in Germany, have long adopted the posture of military flaneurs, playing a game of make-believe in their long gray overcoats and black-booted costumes. I know a bit about impression management. I'm not only a musician, but I've studied and directed theater."

Then Pierre became amused. "You amaze me, Viktor. Well, we deprive them of their roles!"

"Exactly! It might not be such a stunning achievement. But a lot of fun."

"A personal statement from us to them," Pierre responded.

"A bit of black comedy."

The next day, as each general awaited his moment of glory, Viktor Mueller and Pierre Burger carried out their mission: "Attack Humiliation."

Viktor would carry out his plan by intercepting a German army truck assigned to make deliveries at the various hotels accommodating the high command. Calling ahead, he spoke to A. S. Schneider's assistant. "This is Reichsmarschall Himmler's office," Viktor announced with authority. "Please have the goods ready. My couriers will be picking them up at exactly five o'clock this afternoon."

"I didn't know Himmler was a Reichsmarschall," Pierre said.

"Neither did I." Viktor laughed. "It's easy to embellish a plan when you know how."

Backing the truck to the delivery dock, the uniforms were placed under a canopy in the rear.

"May I sign for them, please?" Pierre reached for the

clipboard with the documents. He added his signature with a flourish, delighted by the honor. Viktor stayed in the truck, approving Pierre's improvisational skills.

It was a daring adventure with imagination, Viktor was well schooled in theater, and Pierre became a willing cast member.

The uniforms disappeared just as thousands of Jews and political dissidents had vanished. Himmler conducted an investigation. No smart new uniforms, no Silver Cross medals, no planned ceremony. Goebbels was furious. Germany's generals were, in a sense, undressed. The emperors without clothes had something to remember.

Finally Viktor felt he had accomplished something. Nothing big, but something.

SNOWFALLS

Falling back into my structured routine, the months passed as I continued my lessons with Hans, working on Schirmer's *Book Three,* advancing into chord progressions. This had become my new life. Terezín was home now.

"Isn't it time for us to stage *Brundibár*?" I finally asked Hans.

I thought it might help to do something constructive, creative, and defiant; it might soften the miserable, oppressive thoughts about my crumbling country.

Hans thought for a while and then spoke slowly, "It's going to be difficult to assemble a cast, but with some luck, I know where I'm going."

Where were we going?

Poppy was now truly absent from my life, but Hans was still there, steady, never lost, driven by optimism. I couldn't shake the thought that Poppy was wearing the same uniform as the men who had murdered Fritz Gerlich.

The lowering clouds were almost touching the roofs of Terezín's buildings, announcing the beginnings of winter. The days were getting shorter and darker. I remembered how a few years earlier, after one of Prague's many snowfalls, Poppy had invited David and me on a walk in a forest near the city. We were fitted with snowshoes, making a clumsy trek through the silent, white woods. The three of us puffed along in single file across the mountainous snowdrifts. It was too cold to talk, and each of us was lost in our own private world. Suddenly, it occurred to me that I was far from home, far from the road, and miles away from the path back. Worst of all, it was almost dark. I had a moment of panic thinking that we had strayed off the snowy track.

Father, son, and best friend, with no food, walking through miles of snow. But Poppy walked confidently, easily defeating the forest.

Catching up with David, I whispered, "If we don't make it back, there's no one on Earth I'd rather freeze to death with than you and Poppy."

David grinned. "Thanks, Max. You always know just the right thing to say."

Poppy interrupted my thoughts. "Well, boys, there's the road!"

When I thought of Poppy now, it was as though he was somehow lost in winter. I needed my father. But until Poppy came back to me, I knew I could lean on Hans. Hans had always been there throughout my life, and he was with me now. Whenever my thoughts got too dark for me, I resorted to playing some piano as a distraction. Today, Sophie came to listen to me playing the piano.

"It's very pretty."

It was a song from *Brundibár.*

"Aren't we lucky to have music? A song creates a story—it can take you to new places. It can take you back to somewhere familiar and warm and safe. It's always there for you."

"See how you can express yourself in music and words, Max. I think you'll become like my father. He could write a poem one minute, then tell a story in the next. He really loved people. I miss him every day."

"He'd be proud of you, Sophie. Every day. The way you help people at the infirmary."

"It's my job, Max. They help me get through the mornings. We help each other, I guess. I know I'm asking again: Do you think Poppy can help us get more medicine? It's really important."

"Of course; I'll try." I was hearing less and less from Poppy and yet, I didn't want to let Sophie down. I was going to figure out a way.

David had begun testing me, giving me written assignments. This morning was no different.

"I have a job for you, Max. Take Sophie, she knows the ropes."

Sophie took my hand and led me across the square to a café. There we found an empty stage surrounded by tables with red-and-white checkered tablecloths.

"Why the blue star?" a voice bellowed. Looking up, we saw a large man in the darkness above, dressed in a black, heavy wool sweater. He was on top of a ladder, hanging lights in the makeshift theater, to stage small performances. That rickety ladder just managed to hold his colossal frame.

"To identify me," I said. "The name's Max Mueller."

I heard a laugh and the man's face came into view as he peeked out from the shadows, chomping on the end of a cigar

I leaned over and whispered to Sophie, "Is that who I think it is?"

She smiled and nodded.

"No need for secrets, son, we're all friends here. Kurt Gerron at your service," he said with a huge grin and a wrinkled brow. "So why the blue?"

"I could say I wear a blue star in tribute to a great actor who starred with Marlene Dietrich in *The Blue Angel*." I couldn't believe I was talking with one of the most famous actors in all of Europe.

Gerron laughed. His was no ordinary laugh; it exploded out of him.

"Oh, you're good, son." He sighed and put his beefy hand over his heart. "Ah, Marlene," he gushed.

Looking down, "Is that you down there, Sophie?"

"It's me."

As he balanced precariously above, I had a better view of him. He was an immense man, about forty, with a ruddy face and a shock of flaming red hair; his balloon-like body rippled, overflowing his shirt and pants.

I pulled out my journal, making notes.

"Do you prefer film or stage?"

"Stage. Next you're going to ask about my best role."

"How did you know that?"

"Because I'm a director, and I anticipate what's coming next. And I'm used to talking to reporters." He leaned over the ladder and winked at Sophie.

"What was your favorite role?"

"The police chief in *The Threepenny Opera*. I played Tiger Brown. Did you ever see it?"

He immediately burst into song with such enthusiasm that he nearly fell off the ladder. Sophie and I ran over to steady it.

"Und der Haifisch, der hat Zähne
und die trägt er im Gesicht
und MacHeath, der hat ein Messer,
doch das Messer sieht man nicht."

"That was great, Herr Gerron!" Sophie called.

"I'd take a bow, but it's hard to do from up here."

Once more his laugh echoed throughout the room.

"Have you ever been to Hollywood?" I shouted up to him.

"Marlene asked me to come, but I didn't want to."

"Why? You'd be great in Hollywood," Sophie chipped in.

"Think so? Didn't figure I'd fit in. Why are we shouting?"

That brought yet another laugh from him.

"Do you fit in here?" I asked.

"There are better places for fitting in. Does anyone? Would anyone want to?" I wanted to ask him more about this but decided that would be better discussed face-to-face, rather than shouting up a ladder.

"What are you doing up there?"

"Hanging lights for a show. Our trio is performing tonight. They imitate the Andrews Sisters—they're famous singers in America. Ours dress up like them. They have blond wigs, paint their lips red, snap their fingers, and jive. I call them the Aryan Sisters." He gave a short, harsh laugh.

"I wouldn't want to miss that. Can we come?"

"You'll be my guests. Front row seats. But I've got to set up these lights."

"Is lighting difficult?"

"Yes, it can be difficult. But it's important, kid; it creates mood. If I had my way, I'd carry them with me all the time."

"I guess you paint scenes with them and different lighting adds contrast?"

"You've got that right, Sophie. They help make a dramatic scene. What is life without shadows, and without so many delicate shades?"

"Maybe you could help with *Brundibár*. Bring your lights," I said.

"What's *Brundibár*?"

"It's a pretty good show. I can tell you all about it sometime."

"You must, you must!" he shouted. "Now, I must get back to work before this ladder collapses. I might be an actor, but I still can't play skinny."

"Goodbye, Herr Gerron," I said. "A pleasure."

"Hope to see you again soon, Max. You, too, Sophie. Perhaps on solid ground."

I took Sophie's hand, and together we ran back across the square.

David was sitting cross-legged on his lower bunk, grinning. "Well?"

"You should have seen Max fire questions. He's a real reporter."

"You got in a few, Sophie. You're helping me . . . well, you're helping me more than I can say."

"I thought I'd give you some help, to get you going."

Giving me a kiss on the cheek, Sophie announced, "I'm late for the infirmary. Can we meet later?" She scooted out of the large room, which was our office on the top floor. I touched my face where her lips had pressed. For a moment, I forgot where I was. That was what we were up to, playing this balancing game, surviving by forgetting where we were, if only for a while, and then the rest of the time really trying to work out what was true, about us and our surroundings, the reality of where we were and where we were heading. Learning, remembering, forgetting, remembering . . .

"Max! Hey, Max!" David was standing in front of me, waving his hand.

"What?"

"You're a team."

"And why not?"

David flopped back onto his bunk, and I settled into a nearby chair. I reviewed my notes and wrote about Gerron. I had the newsroom to myself. I finished up my piece and read it through. I was insecure about my first interview, and just having Sophie there gave me confidence. She had to know. What was I without her? I thought about that for a while and then before I could find an answer I reminded myself that I didn't need to, because I was near her right now and wanted to be with her always. Feeling surer of my ability, I was ready to take on another job.

"David, I'd like to visit Rabbi Leo Baeck."

"Do you know anything about him?" David looked at me inquisitively.

"No, but Sophie said I should meet him, so I'll find out, right? That's what an interview is for," I replied.

"Well, get on with it then, we'll hold space."

"I'll have to prep myself."

"That's what good reporters do."

"Right. I'm on my way." I tossed a wave. "Award-winning journalist at your service." That was one of the secrets that I learned about how to make it here. Being busy was better than worrying all the time. I had a purpose. I wanted to fill my time by being useful—to David, and Sophie, and Hans. The more I learned, the more I understood, the more help I could be.

I met up with Sophie outside the infirmary. I finally asked her all the things I'd been wondering about since our conversation about being *different.*

"Sophie, what's it like being Jewish?" I hoped for a better answer than Hans had given me.

She looked at me seriously. "It seems an odd question. But maybe it's not so odd . . . the way things are. I don't know, I suppose that I just am," she said. "Why do you ask?"

"I don't want to feel like an outsider. You said I was not the same as you . . . how?"

"I didn't mean it that way. I meant you have never experienced what it is like to be Jewish."

"Is it such a contrast? My pals are Jewish and we seem much the same."

"We try to have a good heart."

"I try to do that, too, Sophie. See, no different."

Sophie was quiet for a moment. "The difference is that I wear a yellow star, Max. That's a big difference right now and nothing can change that."

I felt foolish, trying to fit in with my blue star. I knew that I had to stop playacting and take a new approach.

"When things go badly, there's always a need for somebody to blame. Hitler says we're the reason. It makes it easier for him to think we're not important, we're not good people, we don't count. But we do. We all count. We *are* different. Countries have persecuted us for years. It happened in my country; it happened in yours. Palestine is our home, where we came from centuries ago. Mama always felt we would be better off there, we could begin a new life, and that's what Rabbi Baeck believes too."

"That brings me to another question: What's a rabbi?"

"You're getting good at interviewing, Max. He's a teacher. They are at the center of our lives. All through our history, they traveled from village to village, bringing news, offering healing words, restoring faith. It may be the most important thing that we have, the last thing that we're left with, that we have hope, that we have faith, that we have courage. And God has promised us one thing."

I looked across at her: "What's that?"

She smiled, stroking my cheek sweetly, and then said with a wink: "Next year in Jerusalem."

AN APPOINTMENT TO KEEP

The rabbi's apartment was just across from the library. When I arrived and knocked, the rabbi threw open the door and pulled me in with open arms.

"Welcome, Max. Sophie has told me much about you!"

His watery eyes twinkled with pleasure. He had soft gray hair and a matching beard, making him appear older and wiser than I had imagined. He had a calm and easy way of speaking.

"It's very nice to meet you, Rabbi. I've heard many good things about you too."

"I'm pleased to know that. Makes my job easier. I like being liked."

He led me into the apartment. The place smelled musty, and I wasn't sure if it was from all the books stacked around the room or from the windows being closed. The rabbi opened one and a breeze swept in.

"Max, you're just in time, like fresh air. Have some grapes. Can you believe they grow grapes in Terezín? A miracle. Maybe the Germans will make wine and offer it up for church Communion."

He seemed amused by his own thought. We settled into comfortable chairs.

"Max, you're not Jewish. What are you doing here?"

He spoke quietly and looked me straight in the eyes. His eyes were kind and insistent.

"I'd like to be Jewish."

"And why is that?"

"Honestly, it's because of the Jewish people I've known. They have welcomed me. It's a spirit that goes beyond my friendships. I want to belong with them."

He stroked his beard with thoughtful composure. "Well, then, I bless you Jewish."

"Just like that?"

"Just like that. We have something in common, yes, a family of sorts."

"I've heard about your lectures. I'd love to come and hear you speak."

"You're welcome anytime. I'd like to know more about you."

"There's not much to know really. I'm a reporter. I'm a sort of musician too. But I'm supposed to ask the questions."

"And I'm a rabbi, I'm supposed to give answers."

"Is that what rabbis do?"

"We can only try. Yes, we can only try." He looked away for a moment.

In the next few minutes, I learned a short version of his story: Rabbi Baeck came from a tradition of rabbis. His father had been one. Brought up in Poland, he became a prolific writer, scholar, and philosopher. In the thirties, Europe's Jewish community turned to him as a defender of Judaism.

"Can you tell me about where it all started? Judaism, I mean."

"That is a big question, Max, and a direct one. Well now, where to begin? I guess we can begin with our biblical origins—with the Old Testament. With Abraham who walked in a much different direction, bringing the world out of darkness. And then comes Moses, giving a moral compass, showing us all how to perfect one's self and the world."

"To perfect the world? I don't understand. If the Jews work to perfect the world, why do the Nazis hate Jewish people so much?"

"It's funny they should do that, don't you think? Maybe that's close to the heart of it all. But back to your question: Hate is a product of fear and there is a lot of fear in the world right now. People who are afraid want power in order to calm their own fears. They have uncertainty and doubt, and they need someone to blame. Our culture is different from theirs, our religious beliefs are different. Difference can create scapegoating. And here we are. Just when we settle down, we're driven out of our homes. It's been going on for over three thousand years."

"It doesn't make sense. Aren't you chosen?"

"That's an interesting concept. Since the very beginning we've written the story of stories; we Jews considered ourselves chosen, because we were blessed as agents of God. Sometimes I wonder just how chosen we are, rejected by so many in history. But we have always managed to survive. Maybe that's being chosen. It's a mystery, don't you think? And mysteries are good, too, Max. We don't always have the answers, but we always need to ask the right questions."

"Yes, that's what my friend David always says. May I ask what brought you to Terezín?"

"That's a question I can answer. To serve. Yes. I frequently court the Nazis' displeasure, which brings me a measure of satisfaction," he said, raising an eyebrow. "Before coming here, I was summoned to Gestapo headquarters one Saturday and I declined. On the Sabbath, I go to services. This did not please them. Now to another subject, you like music?"

I wasn't sure I fully understood, but I nodded. "Yes, I do. Don't you, Rabbi?"

"A blessing. If you listen, you will find some answers. You don't just listen to music, you respond to it, and sometimes even ask it questions. And in our quietest moments, it can whisper answers."

"Answers?"

"But you have to be ready to hear them."

"Do you play an instrument?" I asked.

"I like to listen to music. We always have a cantor in synagogue. The cantor is the singer who leads the chanting of prayers."

"And you read lots of books."

"That's what rabbis do. We are learners as well as teachers. We must continuously learn if we are to teach, to lead. We spend Saturday mornings in the synagogue; we read, we study, we think, and we ask a lot of questions and study the Talmud."

"The Talmud?"

"It's a book, our book."

"Is it a secret book?"

The rabbi contemplated for a moment. "Not so secret; it's our history and our commentary, often with three points of view. It's a book of law, on how to live, how to make decisions, how to solve problems."

"Aren't two points of view enough?"

The rabbi's smile turned into a hearty laugh. "I don't think so. For example, does a candle burn brighter in the morning, afternoon, or at night?"

"At night."

"Are you sure?"

I thought for a moment. "No, not so sure."

"Then you must think about it. I read one page a day until I finish. Then I start again."

"How long does that take?"

"About seven years."

"It takes seven years to read that book?" I couldn't think of anything that took seven years.

"Indeed, Max. It's a manual to help live a better life, and very often we have more questions than answers. The Talmud shapes our culture, and it's been around for a long time. Perhaps someday you would like to know more?"

"Why not?"

"Max, you're becoming Jewish by the minute! You ask *why not,* not *why.*"

I was starting to think that being Jewish was like being a reporter. It depended on how you asked questions, and which questions you asked.

"We Jews are somewhere between hope and history and there's more to it than just being Jewish. You should be closer to your friends, and you need to have that covenant. To become Jewish, you're given a letter."

"What kind of letter?"

"It's not just a letter, it is an assignment. That's the way we do things. It's an appointment to keep."

"I'm here to interview you. Isn't that an assignment?"

"It is written in the Torah, our portable operating manual that we have been carrying around for thousands of years, that we all have a responsibility. We reflect, we react. It's an unshakable truth. We dream, we feel, we look at the world inside out, and not outside in. And it is up to you to decide what your assignment is. Along the way there are messengers, and you will be smart to recognize that they are pointing you in the right direction."

"What is your assignment, Rabbi?"

"It starts in the heart, that's where the appointment begins. What you do defines who you are."

Everything fell into place for me at that moment, another reason confirming why I was there. There was fear, always fear, and it was real. But now I had something solid to lean on, to think of, to aim for.

"Tell me, Rabbi. What does 'Next year in Jerusalem' mean?"

"It's said at the end of our Passover every year. It's a wish we all carry."

In the meantime, Terezín was an appointment. *Brundibár* was my assignment.

PROGRAMS AND COMING ATTRACTIONS

Many entertainers came to Terezín from Berlin that year, where revue and cabaret were immensely popular. Even the Steinway Boys arrived—I had mixed feelings. I was glad to see them but sorry they were forced to come. As ever in my life sadness and happiness seemed to coexist, to be partners. Perhaps sadness and happiness were closely related, and perhaps it was our duty to ensure that the shade of sadness didn't altogether blot out happiness.

But the Steinway Boys were there and became part of our strange new world. It was a place where, somehow or other, the arts managed to thrive. Small theatrical productions became road companies performing in attics and courtyards. And there were so many performances. All of this was so important, allowing us the luxury of forgetting for a moment—overlooking so many needs: food was scarce, medicine scarcer, everyone in the camp was becoming thinner with every passing day, cheeks becoming hollower, skin paler, bodies wearier. Unlike most of the people there, I had it better, and I knew that. I felt guilty. But as the days passed, and I thought more about Rabbi Baeck, I made my decision. I would throw in my lot with my friends, with the Jews. Other than Poppy, these were the people I loved. I only needed to reflect for a moment on why I was here. I thought about "Next year in Jerusalem" and really understood it as a statement of faith, a declaration of hope for the future, for what could be and how we could make it be. To leave would be to admit defeat, to give in to despair. My decision was made. I was now fully committed, and that commitment might not be without consequences. How could it be? It wouldn't be easy, but my commitment to Terezín was solid. I was no bystander, but part of what I could call my community. In the moment that I made that resolution I was happy in a way that I couldn't quite define, in a way I had never been before. I knew one thing for sure: I belonged.

I thought of all these activities that were there to create the illusion of normal life. They were designed to keep people busy, to keep minds active, and to help stave off the darker thoughts of our everyday reality.

I wanted to produce *Brundibár*. I *had* to. I explored every venue. I had to find a cast. I had to start looking. Thirty kids who could sing. This would be my answer, to shine some light into the darkness. This was my mission, my assignment.

Weekly gatherings filled attics, and there was never an empty chair. Many Czech guards came and enjoyed the talks. Speakers were free to lecture on most subjects, if they weren't too provocative. Each week, Sophie and I picked one to attend; afterward we interviewed the speakers for *Vedem*.

One we liked more than any other was Pierre Levy, a mysterious Frenchman claiming to be a former professor of Egyptology at the Sorbonne. As it turned out, he had only worked as a proofreader for a travel publisher, and, in that fact-checking capacity, had learned about Egyptian history. No matter, he was fascinating. Wearing a red fez, he took his audiences sailing on feluccas down the Nile, to explore the pyramids and the riddle of the Sphinx.

"She is guardian of the Great Temple, and to enter, any passerby must know the answer to the riddle."

Being a showman, he added, "If you want to know the riddle, come next week."

He described the pharaohs in detail, and, in the spring of 1941, for a grand finale to his lecture series, Pierre attempted a belly dance after enlisting a friend who played a Turkish *bağlama* to accompany him. Everyone knew he was a phony, but everyone loved him.

David added the listing as "Comic Relief" to the weekly diary of events.

Karel Švenk was one of Prague's most treasured entertainers. A well-known personality, he was a star in a company called the Club of Unused Talents. After producing musical revues in the attics of Terezín, he now headlined the coffeehouse. It had become Terezín's premier cabaret venue.

Sophie, David, and I went to see his latest performance. It featured his most popular work, *The Last Cyclist*. It was a biting satire, and we settled in for some fun. A ruthless dictator took to the stage and proclaimed that cyclists were the cause of all his country's problems.

"If any cyclist cannot prove their families were pedestrians for at least six generations," the dictator proclaimed, "they will be deported to an island."

Cyclists made the best victims, not those who rode wagons or cars, but those who rode bicycles.

Sophie leaned over and whispered to me, "I guess I'm a cyclist."

David nudged me. "Hey, I am too. Who knew that cyclists could be so dangerous?" The meaning wasn't lost on any of us.

Long after everyone had gone home, Sophie and I sat under the stage rafters with a candle lighting the room, doing what any candlelight-watchers might do: we snuggled up to keep each other warm.

"Sophie, if you loved someone who was terribly sad what would you do?" I asked, smoothing an errant hair behind her ear.

She wrinkled up her nose. "I'd try to do something that would make them happy, something that would mean something to them."

I sliced an apple that Ava had given me and offered half to Sophie. She took a taste and turned. "I suppose I'd help that person as much as I could."

"Exactly."

"Are you up to something, Max?"

"I'm thinking about what I might do for Hans. He keeps to himself most the time. I need to do something for him, for me, for everyone."

Poppy had his production. I was going to have mine.

I spoke to David to figure out how we might finally get a production of *Brundibár* going. To find thirty kids.

"You've been a part of it from the beginning. But things aren't easy around here. Take *The Last Cyclist.* The Germans are closing the show."

"Why are they doing that?'

"It's always censorship. They cut out anything that doesn't promote the Nazi message. *The Last Cyclist* pokes fun at how the Jews are blamed for everything that has ever gone wrong in Germany. I'd like to write an editorial for the next edition defending creative expression. But I can't."

"Why not?"

"It would be censored."

David said with a wry smile. "But, remember, even if we can't write, we can still observe, and we can tell one another what we witness and what we think. They can stop us publishing, but they can't stop us thinking. At least they haven't figured that one out yet."

THE SHOW MUST GO ON

As the year passed, I still had *Brundibár* on my mind. Of course, the Nazis wouldn't want a production if they thought the Führer was defeated at the end. But they might love it if they found another meaning to it. The Germans could see Brundibár as a scheming Jew who is run out of town by a cast of villagers—villagers who cling to the virtues of the German nation. I remembered what the rabbi said about different points of view. Hans was brilliant at crafting messages. And our production would go ahead with its double meaning. This is what it was meant to do all along. For the villagers, victory over traits that pollute the German nation. But for the Germans, a triumph over a crafty Jew.

"I know someone who can play Annika. Sophie!"

"Do you know her range?" Hans asked.

"She can sing and I know she can play the part. She's an amazing musician."

"Then bring her for an audition."

I spoke to Sophie. This was an opportunity for us to be together more than ever. I knew that her performing would cheer her mother as well.

"It's good of you to come to sing for me," Hans told Sophie when she arrived the next day.

"I'd be delighted to do just that, Maestro."

Sophie handed over a piece of sheet music. "Key of C, please."

Hans nodded and Sophie turned to sing to me. I felt as if I was the only other person in the world.

"Ihr Blumen, was seid ihr vom Tau so schwer?
Mir scheint,
das sind gar Träne."

By the time she repeated the chorus about flowers and tears, Hans was applauding. Her voice was perfect, commanding every note and phrase.

"Sophie, how did you come by 'Das klagende Lied'?"

"I'm a Mahler," Sophie said, smiling. "It's a sad song, but I've always felt it's quite beautiful."

"Yes." Turning to me, Hans said, "You're a talent scout, just like your father. Sophie, you have the part."

Sophie beamed.

One by one, we were beginning to assemble a cast, and when we were ready, we would need a larger stage. Hans said that if you believed in something, it might come true. It sounded a little corny but, well, at least it helped.

THE TRACKS OF PROGRESS

Over the loudspeakers came an announcement from Commandant Freidle.

"A new arrival platform has been built for Terezín. Two miles of tracks made with AG Hoesch-Krupp steel were constructed by our workers. We admire their accomplishment. The extension will make it easier for our guests, who will no longer have to walk two miles from Bohušovice Station to Terezín."

Guests?

"Medical personnel selected the strongest in the camp," David told me. "I'd love to print this, but I'll have to make do with telling you. It was backbreaking work to build the tracks. They were at it in shifts around the clock. Freidle made sure to keep the workers healthy with better conditions and better food, so they would be fit and in the best condition to accomplish this plan. Look at what it says there above the gates. *Arbeit Macht Frei.* Work might not set you free, but it will keep you fed for a while."

He paused a moment or two to let the words sink in. "It took a former Olympic star to build that station. The special project detail was headed by Fredy Hirsh. He won a gold medal in Berlin before the war. He was a national hero. Now look at him: he's just a Jewish laborer."

David looked into the distance as he spoke: "You know, even the SS respects him. Fredy immigrated to Prague after life became intolerable for him in Germany. Like so many Jews, his deepest wish was to someday live in Palestine. Maybe next year for him and all of us, Max? He has always been a leader, a Jewish pioneer. He's attractive, charismatic, a super athlete. Kids look up to him, because he's devoted to them. They're part of his life, they love him."

I thought for a while and smiled. "I think I love him too."

Freidle was deeply pleased with the completion of the new track and platform. German soldiers in dress gray, and Czech guards in freshly pressed green uniforms, stood to attention. A regimental band was first to arrive in a carriage, playing the German national anthem and making it sound crisper and clearer than the tinny version usually heard from the loudspeakers.

The soldiers cheered, and the band followed up with more military tunes.

A few of the stronger children were cleaned up for the occasion. They stood at the platform presenting bouquets of flowers to the committee. It was a warm and clear day. Refreshments were served and for the first time that they could remember, there were sandwiches, cake, and apple juice. They were devoured by those who could get their hands on them.

"Do you think things will be better now? People are slowly starving, but maybe there will be enough to eat and enough medicine in the infirmary. Will this place ever become what it was supposed to be, what we were all promised it was going to be?" I asked David a slew of questions, but I felt stupid even as I asked them. It was like I was a five-year-old asking for a bedtime story from Poppy, the latest adventure of Armand and White Dog, wanting to lose myself in a fantasy for a while.

David didn't hesitate before answering, "No, it's all a show."

I snapped, "I want to speak to one of the guards then, tell him that we know this is phony. Ask him what he had for dinner last night, was it the same watered-down soup and stale bread that the camp gets? I'd tell him . . ."

David interrupted my rant in full-flow: "Max, exactly how stupid are you? That might make you feel good for a second or two, but they would send you to the Little Fortress in a minute flat. And you won't be reading it in *Vedem* anytime soon, but the Little Fortress is not somewhere you want to go, trust me. From what I see, the people who come back from there look a whole lot worse than they did before. And from what I hear, some people don't come back at all. At the very least you'll lose your privileges, and then what? What help can you be? We can work in other ways. We must be clever. We have to use our anger as energy to fuel us."

I spoke to Mrs. Branka when I got back to my room. "These kids at the ceremony are really undernourished! And I have to get food to David and Sophie. Yes, they get something better when they come to school, and we're lucky to be here with you, Ava, but for Hans, and the kids, I have to do more for them, I must."

"I'll see to it we get some fruit to the children, Max. I have a connection. I will help in some way."

"That would be great, Ava. Anything at all. And maybe some oranges for the infirmary."

A few days later, Sophie wondered where the boxes of food had come from. I think she knew. It was another small victory. It made things just a little bit better for a short time.

THE FINAL SOLUTION

Exactly three years earlier, in January 1939, speaking to the Reichstag about the fate of European Jewry, Hitler had delivered a menacing forecast of what would become the final solution:

"Today I will once more be a prophet! If Jewish financiers within and outside of Europe again succeed in plunging the nations into a world war, the result will be the annihilation of all the Jews in Europe." No one really listened, but he was deadly serious.

The Führer did not detail what he had in mind at the time, and the idea soon became the Reich's policy. Hitler gave his generals broad authorization to carry out his wishes.

Then the final solution was implemented. Reinhard Heydrich had been planning for years and issued an invitation to German government lawyers, generals, and officials for a special weekend gathering at Grossen Wannsee 56–58, a comfortable lakeside villa not far from Berlin. Fifteen men, many with doctorates from German universities, came to Wannsee to launch Aktion Reinhard. These bureaucrats, wrestling with a question of logistics, resolved the matter and oversaw the implementation of "a final settlement" of the Jewish Problem in places called Belzec, Treblinka, Auschwitz.

Churchill was living in the Cabinet War Rooms under London's Whitehall, the underground complex that housed the British government's command center throughout the war. The facility's Map Room was in constant use and was manned around the clock by officers of the Royal Navy receiving information that produced a daily intelligence summary for the prime minister. Churchill's office-bedroom included BBC broadcasting equipment which he often used to address the nation.

"Well, here I am, Anna, directing the war," Churchill said as she entered his quarters a few months after Aktion Reinhard's announcement. She noticed an encrypted red telephone in an adjacent area near Churchill's office-bedroom enabling him to speak securely with President Roosevelt in Washington.

"Very nice to see you again, Mr. Prime Minster."

"I read your accounts religiously, Anna! You're a fine journalist. But you don't need an old man telling you that. Madeline, by the way, has been a great addition to the war effort."

"Nana?"

"Yes, your grandmother. You're quite aware she believes in astrology, excessively so perhaps. And she will help defeat Hitler. She's my astrology advisor, if you can imagine such a thing."

"Madeline Kingsley? Really?" Anna was not actually that amazed. She knew the full intention of her grandmother's personality.

Churchill smiled warmly. "It's not so foolish. Astrology guides Hitler more than his generals do. He doesn't plan a battle without a reading. He's been obsessed ever since an astrologer in Vienna advised him that a great leader who has his same birth date will emerge. Hitler charts; I plot. I would hazard that he pays rather careful attention to the stars, but what harm can it do? So long as I keep my focus on, shall we say, rather more concrete matters of war."

She was cheered remembering that Nana was first to suggest that celestial positioning might influence her relationship with Hans, who had been relocated to Terezín. What must it be like for him there?

"I'm glad she is helpful to you, Mr. Prime Minister, but like you, I am thinking of more earthly things, and I'm deeply concerned about the Nuremberg laws and the concentration camps. What we know is unspeakable. And I fear that what we don't yet know is very much worse still."

"I know full well. The architect is Heydrich, Anna, and we have a 'solution' to remove him. We are counting on Anthropoid."

"What?"

"Anthropoid, Anna, is a mission."

"What can you tell me about it?"

"Anna, it's absolutely off the bloody record. It's part of the Political Warfare Executive, up at Electra House."

Anna had a direct line to PWE, where Viktor Mueller's dispatches were received and evaluated.

"Five Czech Resistance fighters have been training to parachute into Czechoslovakia to kill Heydrich. The operation has taken months of planning. Pink Tulip is not aware of the details, Anna, and we must keep it that way. Your man, Mueller, must NOT know specifics. It's essential for the mission, for his own survival, for his continuing usefulness to the cause. He's been tested already. It would have been a fortuitous opportunity to blow up the bastards during his visit to Eagle's Nest, but that wasn't to be. But he took some damn good pictures. It helped us frame a place that up to then I could only imagine. And we all loved the uniform caper.

You can't overstate the value of making the top brass look ridiculous."

Anna had to admit she had been amused. "But why shouldn't Viktor know?"

"Because he's the only man to lead us to Heydrich, and he can open the door without even knowing that's what he's doing. That's invaluable and there's no need to take any chances for any leaks. It's a top-secret assignment, Anna. There is a trove of paintings requisitioned by the SS for Göring in an estate outside of Prague, near Lidice, and the field marshal wants the collection to be shipped to Berlin. Mueller is planning for their transfer. We have provided him with the details, and with Heydrich arranging the acquisitions, indeed a perfect deception."

"Prime Minister, I can't afford to lose him." She cleared her throat. "We can't."

"Well, there may be ways. Only Heydrich himself will be targeted of course."

She understood that these decisions had to be made, but she felt sick at the thought that she had just watched Churchill roll the dice in a game with so much at stake, not least Viktor Mueller's life.

OPERATION ANTHROPOID

When Viktor arrived, he was impressed by Heydrich's home in its storied setting. The general had always wanted to live on the lake, and he had found his perfect summer retreat.

"The air, Viktor, ah, the air so clean and pure! It does one good."

The small white villa had a skylight over an indoor garden. It belonged to Max Liebermann, who had collected French works and himself become a noted artist. It meant nothing to Heydrich that Liebermann's family had been sent packing to Terezín.

The studio had been stripped of the former occupant's belongings, and all that remained were rays from the sun warming the solarium. In many ways, however odd, this thought struck him: There was something within Heydrich that Viktor liked. He had found a side of him that was kind and empathic, but he could never reconcile his view of the general which made him notoriously ruthless, cold, brutal.

"It's a lovely place, don't you think, Viktor?"

Viktor Mueller admired the artist. "Imagine, a German Impressionist as good as the French." He knew that the irony of what he was about to say would be lost on Heydrich, or overlooked—or did his friend accept Viktor's idiosyncrasies? "And if he weren't a Jew, he would be a genius!"

"How true, Viktor! How true!" The general slung an arm around Viktor. They enjoyed a laugh together. "So now, Viktor, you have discovered a treasure trove of art stored in a town near Prague, from the Louvre? How did you come by this information?"

"I have sources."

"You are clever, Viktor!"

Viktor Mueller danced around the story, making it plausible. His information had in fact come from London, that there were paintings stored in the cellar of a home he knew just fifty kilometers from Prague.

"Hermann will be delighted. He loves art," Heydrich remarked. "Come, would you like to ride with me, Viktor? It's a nice day, plenty of fresh air."

"I thought I might take a small truck, and then take the paintings directly to Berlin. I think we should keep the operation under wraps."

"Very well, Viktor."

"We'll have two motorcycles escort us. Just to be safe." Viktor handed over directions and a small map.

The motorcycles, Viktor's assigned truck with a closed canopy, and Heydrich's open-air Mercedes sped through Germany into the small roads along the winding Bohemian countryside. Viktor Mueller found the day agreeable and refreshing. He was relaxed, a soldier but also a consummate performer who was managing to keep two opposing sides happy at once. It was a good day's work. It would just take a few hours to reach their destination. He wondered again why intelligence was turning over these paintings to Göring. It was a bit peculiar, he thought, but then again it surely made sense for Berlin to take advantage of the vanquished, the spoils of war—self-serving greed. And it made sense for him to be furnishing them with this treasure, to become ever more valued, more trusted.

Then he heard an explosion and, looking in his rearview mirror, saw that Heydrich's car was a smoking wreck of metal.

The driver of the truck slammed on his brakes, and Viktor ran to Heydrich, found him wounded, and held him, trying to stop the blood gushing from his mouth. There was smoke pouring from the automobile. He yelled for one of the enlisted men to help him get Heydrich into the truck and get to a hospital. The escort screamed through the countryside. Then Heydrich whispered, with red blood spilling from his lips, "What happened, Viktor?"

"You're going to be all right, my friend. Just hold on."

Why hadn't he been told? *Why . . .? Anna!* And then he recalled the final message that had arrived, unsigned, saying that the works were of paramount importance, were priceless objects, and that he must ensure that no harm came to them in transit, that he must travel in the truck, and as he sat and watched the life slip away from Heydrich, a man he had once admired, who had been his friend—someone in disguise, someone who had deceived him, someone who had brought unimaginable heartbreak and cruelty beyond measure in the name of Germany. How could a patron of art and a lover of music march to a different tune?

Then he thought of someone much different—*Anna!*

A broken man, exhausted and practically unconscious, was in my bed at the Brankas'. What was going on? Who was this man and how had he come to be here? Studying him closely, I saw that he was a Czech soldier who could easily have passed for a boy not much older than me. He looked at me with a wild gaze.

At last he spoke, his voice hoarse, "I've taken your bed."

"I don't mind," I could barely get the words out.

"Kind of you," he said in his throaty whisper. "I'm Andrej."

I crouched next to him. "What happened to you?"

Before Andrej could answer, he trembled and began dripping with sweat. "Where's Ava?" he asked.

"She went into the village. Don't worry, she'll be back soon. Had to get some things."

"How long will she be?"

I took a cold towel and wiped the soldier's face. My hand shook slightly, and my mind was racing.

He looked briefly uncertain and then let out one barely audible word: "Resistance."

"What you're doing is serious, I'm sure of that . . . and secret."

Just by being there I was complicit in whatever it was. Some instinct told me that I had to stay, I had to tend to this man, and he was Ava's brother, so what alternative was there than to remain with him and help in whatever way I could? There was no going back. And I had to know what happened to him.

His leg was in a makeshift splint. And it was badly broken causing him excruciating pain. I mopped his brow and he responded to the gesture with a pained smile.

"We got him," he said. "We killed the son of a bitch."

His words stopped me cold. What was he saying?

Over the next few days, he slipped in and out of consciousness, but by the fourth morning, a healthier color had returned to Andrej's face. Ava began to breathe a bit easier.

"I can't thank you enough for everything you've done for me. Surely, you want your bed back?"

Andrej was propped up reading a book.

I smiled. "You need it more than me; I'm fine on the sofa. But now, can you tell me what happened to you?"

"I was part of the Resistance, Max. We assassinated a Nazi general."

"*What?*"

"I can only tell you what took place during the mission."

I knew that I was now moving ever more decisively in the direction I had chosen for myself, no longer just an observer—a journalist, but something different, something more active. "Tell me as much as you can."

"I know I can trust you. Ava tells me you're a good man. Someone should know what happened—someone must tell the story. Outside Wannsee, a small town near Berlin, there's a villa where the Germans planned the final solution, a plan to eliminate the entire Jewish population in Europe. It was one man, General Heydrich, who directed the meeting."

The world briefly stopped and my mind was immediately racing in so many directions at once.

"I'll tell you all I know. I committed the file to memory; it's part of my training. The general was the chief executor of a plan that he had nurtured for years, one that had come to be accepted by the Nazi leadership to solve the Jewish question."

The Jewish question? Now someone had told me straight out.

"A way to get rid of all Jews. Even ones who are only part Jewish. Eliminate every one of them from all of Europe. The final solution."

My head was spinning and I fought my body's urge to run, to throw up. I had to focus, I had to think clearly and understand everything. "How do you know this?"

"I was part of a group that planned the assassination and I trained in London for an undercover operation known as Anthropoid—just a part of the Pink Tulip plan."

Pink Tulip? That was what the *PT* abbreviation stood for in my messages to Raggle. This was overwhelming. At that moment I knew that I was already involved in all of this.

"So, you assassinated General Heydrich? You see . . . I know him. I know who he is."

"I've told you too much."

"No, please. Tell me more. You have nothing to worry about from me. I promise."

"We had an inside operative, a friend of Heydrich who arranged to collect paintings. They were hidden away in the countryside. The paintings had been requisitioned for the German leadership, especially for General Hermann Göring, Hitler's vice-chancellor. He is a serious collector of art. All of this was planned by intelligence in London. On the way, we blew up the bastard's car. That was *our* final solution."

I could hardly say anything. I wasn't sure how I felt about Heydrich's death. We had spoken in a friendly way about our shared love of music. I couldn't quite make sense of it all. He had been murdered in cold blood. But he had been part of something so terrible.

Andrej continued, as if relieved to share the whole story: "He had a specific route, and an open car, so we tossed a grenade as he passed. Except for me getting wounded, it went off exactly as planned. But there was a German captain, Viktor something, who ran over and tried to help him. I suppose he thought that he was worth saving."

I felt my heart skip a beat, but I gathered myself and tried to sound calm: "Viktor? Are you sure that was his name?"

"The general called out to him, 'Viktor, help me.' The captain held Heydrich in his arms as he died."

Viktor, help me!

I was shocked at how directly and calmly I spoke. But it was absolutely clear to me. I didn't hesitate because I knew that what I was saying was honest, was true: "I appreciate everything you've told me. Andrej, you're a hero."

Then Andrej just vanished. That evening after dinner, the Brankas listened to a radio that was forbidden inside the camp and was tuned to Radio Prague, which confirmed that some days earlier, Czech Resistance fighters had carried out a top priority mission to kill Reinhard Heydrich during his commute in his open-top Mercedes. I was struck by the macabre thought that it was the same Mercedes that had brought me to Terezín. The announcer reported that the men, who had tossed hand grenades, mortally wounding Heydrich and his chauffeur, hid in a nearby church. Three were killed in the priory after a gun battle with the SS. One escaped.

Ava and Fritz exchanged worried glances. I knew now and forever which side I was on, but found myself left with a burning question, *Whose side is Poppy on?*

I sat in the Brankas' kitchen with Ava, Fritz, and Freidle, listening to the report of Heydrich's funeral on a beige German Bakelite radio with a standing slim antenna. Freidle surprised us with an outburst. "Heydrich's death will be avenged! The SS will take retribution in the name of the Reichsprotektor."

I was sure to keep my gaze fixed on the table, to avoid making eye contact with Ava or Fritz. I was suddenly and urgently aware how just one tiny slip could change everything forever.

The announcer's voice was suitably grave, and I leaned closer to the radio so that I didn't miss a word.

> "Today, June 4, 1942, Heydrich's body has come home to Berlin for the last time. It is a silent and somber occasion, honoring our great general. A hero has fallen. Flowers and wreaths cover the Chancellery. Drums roll in a military ceremony parading through the streets of the city. Thousands weep. The Führer and Reichsmarschall Göring pay their respects to his wife, Lina, with their young sons and daughters standing by her side."

The general I met at the opera, the man who was friends with my father, was dead. But I had come to understand a simple fact: It was clear to me that the man who loved music and the Reichsprotektor were two very different people. Once again, I was struggling to comprehend Poppy's position and his loyalty to Heydrich.

TRANSPORTS!

I shared my worries with David after sneaking over to visit him at the barracks. It was close to midnight, and I had taken great care not to be seen. David was looking thinner now, as was Sophie. Thanks to the Brankas' generosity, at any opportunity, I smuggled some extra food to them. I could only hurt thinking how it must feel to be hungry. They never complained—their rations were never nearly enough, nor the snacks when we were together at the Brankas'. Every day, I felt the darkness and the hunger closing in on them. It was as if they were slowly disappearing, slowly receding from me like an outgoing tide.

"Where have you been, Max, under a rock?" David asked. "We're all in danger. The Nazis will make us pay for Heydrich's death."

"David, why didn't you spell it out for me when I first got here? Is it because I'm German and not Jewish?"

"I tried to, Max," David said desperately. "It's difficult being Jewish, because we don't have all the answers. That's part of the design. If we had the answers, we wouldn't be philosophers or poets. We think we understand God. We understand nothing. What I do understand, Max, is that your father is a captain in the German army. He was a close friend of Heydrich's. He's working for Hitler, for God's sake! Will your beloved Poppy have me killed?"

Stunned, I leaned over to David and whispered, "Don't you *ever* say that about Poppy. He saved your parents from certain death. He promised to take care of you. He would gladly die before he saw anything happen to you."

"Are you really so sure, Max? Are you? I'm a Jew. Do you know what that means now? It means we're enemies of the German state—every one of us. How can you be sure of your father anymore?"

"Because I am a part of him with everything I am."

Was I shouting? David just looked at me in sadness and anger.

Even as I was arguing with David, I struggled with my own conflicted feelings. I had to be right about Poppy—I couldn't bear the alternative. But there was so much I didn't know, didn't understand. As I gathered my thoughts, we were interrupted by yelling outside. We peeked through the window and saw people lined up in the shadows with backpacks, tool kits, and canteens. Rows of people were moving out of the gate, their pathway lined with torches stuck in the ground. SS men loomed between the torches. Desperate voices echoed throughout the streets long after they were out of sight.

There was a man standing in the background, wearing a black overcoat, taking notes, watching, I whispered, "There he is!"

"Who?"

"The man in the black overcoat."

"He's the gestapo, Max," David hissed.

"What does he do?"

"He keeps an account."

Was he the same man I had seen back in Prague? At last I realized it made no difference.

"Is he a reporter? One of us?"

"No. No, Max, he's one of *them*."

"What's his name?"

"His name isn't important. They may as well have no names."

"Does he kill people?"

"He causes misery and suffering. The SS does his dirty work."

"How?"

"Transports. Labor camps, mass killings. That's it, Max. Sophie, Hans, me . . . there's no telling who's next."

Transports.

"Poppy will keep us safe, don't worry."

I struggled to believe this myself. A part of me no longer did.

"Forget it. The clock is ticking, Max."

David's voice was bitter.

"I have to tell Freidle."

"Don't you think Freidle knows? What do you think this place is, Max? I don't want to end up next in that line. We can't report a damn thing. Does anyone know what's happening here? Is the same happening all over?" The truth of his words practically stopped my breath. The Nazi machine was a vast spider's web, entangling all of us. There was nothing we could do to stop what was happening in front of our eyes.

Maybe there was at least one thing I could do. I had to get word to Sam Raggle.

For Sunshine:

People are being taken away, disappearing in transports to God knows where. Conditions here are now even worse, even more overcrowded. There is not enough food and not enough medicine. People are dying, starving. We won't all make it. I wonder if any of us will now. The man in the black overcoat is everywhere. It's dark and frightening and you must help us. Please tell the world.

PT

For months after Heydrich's assassination, the SS swarmed the camp by night like fireflies. Winter came again, a new year bloomed, and they continued to take people in alarming numbers. I was determined to find out exactly what was going on and, seeing a light burning late one evening, I went across to Freidle's office.

"Where are they going?"

He shuffled some papers on his desk, then impatiently looked up at me as if my questions were an inconvenience. "Who, Max?"

"All of the people who leave by train . . . the transports."

"Work camps to the east, Max. There's a monthly allotment that has to be met, ordered by the SS. Over four million of our troops have invaded the Soviet Union. There's a war being waged right across Europe. Workers are needed in the east. It's a simple matter of logistics, Max, and nothing for you to worry about. Nothing but bureaucracy, really, shifting the workforce to where it's urgently needed to support the cause in which we all believe."

Not all of us.

The general scraped his chair forward, landing with a thud, then delicately tapped his fingers. Freidle spoke with assurance. And what was it all about? Was it really something relatively innocent? Or was it just that I was desperate for every single verified fact? I had seen frightened newcomers marching to the administration building to be deloused. Maybe Terezín had been hell all along, and I just hadn't realized it. I had been selective. I felt like kicking myself. Was I seeing only what I wanted to see? I heard David's words about mass killings ringing in my head.

Freidle continued, "It's not easy, Max. I'm losing control since General Heydrich was assassinated. I'm not getting the supplies I need, and we're too crowded. I promise you, Max, I'm doing the best I can. We must keep morale high. Only the strong survive. Survival is a choice."

"Do we really get to choose? And does Poppy know about all this?"

The commandant stared at me. "You're a good German, Max. Your father is a good man. Jews are enemies of the Third Reich. It doesn't matter where they are being sent. It doesn't matter if they ever come back. In fact, better if they don't. They are our enemies."

There it was, as clear as daylight. I'd been willing Freidle to be different. But that was the boy I had been, the child I could no longer be. Here was the truth, clear and unmistakable. I couldn't leave it alone. I couldn't remain silent: "Really? Can that be true? How could they be enemies?"

"Max, be sensible. See things as they are. Reassure yourself with the fact that you aren't included. You're not a Jew. Forget about them, they have nothing to do with you."

Heydrich and now Freidle? The goodness that I had seen in them, the kindness, the sophistication, it was all a big lie that I had told myself over and over again. Now I had to be really clear about the questions that were in front of me. What if the deep whispers really were true? What if the transports really were a one-way trip for Jews? What could I do? What could I accomplish? I had to think of Sophie and David and

Hans. I had to find a way to protect my friends, to protect the people I deeply loved. That was my resolution, one I would never change.

I gave a nod and left the office.

At night, the whole atmosphere of the camp was quiet. No voices, no clatter, no wailing siren, no tinny announcements from loudspeakers, no footfalls on the cobblestone streets. I was on my way to Ava's, when someone jerked my collar, pulling me off my feet.

I was slammed downward, my knees crushed against the cold ground. The air was pushed from my lungs. A man glared down at me, the man in the long black overcoat. Pulling me up, he dragged me behind a tree and thrust his finger into my chest. "I've got my eye on you, Mueller. I'm watching."

I tried to catch my breath, fighting the spreading panic. "What do you want?"

"Your Jewish friends."

"Do you know who my father is?"

"You little bastard, you think you have special privileges because you're German and because of your father? People like you are undermining our efforts—you and the Jews. We know what you're doing. We know about the green box."

"Green box?"

"The milkman has been arrested. We have a home for spies."

The Little Fortress!

"You don't have any proof. Who I am and what I do is none of your business."

"It is my business. And here's proof."

He slapped me across the face, hard.

"Don't hit me again."

Then with a strength I never knew I had, I pushed him away, and ran as hard and as far away as I could but I couldn't run fast enough. He caught up with me and threw me to the ground, kicking me again and again. Then without saying a word he turned and walked away.

I made my way to Ava's. Falling in the front door, I limped up the stairs. She was on the top landing. She frowned and touched my bruised cheek. "Max, what's wrong? Who hit you?"

"Some Gestapo monster."

Ava's lips tightened.

"He told me to stay away from my Jewish friends, he said that I was a collaborator. I wanted to fight back and kick him as hard as I could."

Ava's face turned white.

"A collaborator? What does he know?"

"Nothing. Don't worry. It's just my friends that he's worried about, the company I keep."

"Be careful, Max," she said, applying ice to my face. "I'm glad you ran away. It showed much more courage. You could be shot if you had not."

"I have to do something. I don't know what, but something . . . for my friends. Surely you understand this better than anyone, Ava. I was trying to get information out, but that's not possible anymore. There must be a way to make a difference."

Poppy, Sam Raggle.

"I have understanding of our secrets, Max, but be careful. They can do anything they want. Just watch with awareness. It's all you can do."

A shadow followed me, and it wasn't my own. Before, I had felt a threat hanging over my world—a sense that danger was lurking just out of my line of vision. It was present but I couldn't quite make out what it was—a menace that I couldn't quite describe, something nameless and shapeless. Now it was coming ever more sharply into focus and I was beginning to know precisely what I was afraid of.

REMEMBRANCE DAY 1943

On that very same unseasonably cold, overcast night, Captain Viktor Mueller arrived at the theater. He brushed off the beads of wet mist that had gathered on his gray overcoat. At the stage door of the Berlin Philharmonic, now known as Hitler's Berlin Band, the porter guarding the backstage entrance saluted, "Heil Hitler." He was always glad to see the great conductor. "Good afternoon, Captain. The orchestra is waiting for you."

The captain carried a medium-sized brown leather suitcase, with two secure straps with brass buckles at each side. Inside the polished luggage were three bombs.

"Can I check your bags?" the porter called to him.

"No, thank you. Personal belongings."

His instructions were to place a bomb before the performance in each of the grand boxes in the great hall where the German generals would be sitting at the Remembrance Day concert. Pierre Burger was a demolitions expert, and had shown Viktor how to activate the timers, just by lifting a switch. It was not something that he wanted to do, it was not his style; he didn't want to blow up any part of the State Opera House where members of the audience would be killed. The hall was a sacred place; it housed all that symbolized everything for Viktor Mueller, and that was music. He moved into the shadows of the first tier, where he found boxes 412, 413, and 414. Each contained six chairs with gold-leaf and red-velvet seats.

In front of each balustrade, he would reach around to find a circular rim of pipes holding theater lights with gels that would softly illuminate the stage during his performance. He was uneasy and even offended. Why had Churchill ordered this action? He wanted no part of killing, at least not yet, even if it meant eliminating the German command in one sweeping fatal disruption and he felt the electric charge of his heart skipping a beat when he heard the approach of security guards, and their German shepherds.

"Captain," said a voice through the darkness, followed by a barking dog. "Need any help?"

Viktor froze briefly but was composed, practiced enough in the management of preperformance nerves to think quickly: "No, I'm just making sure the lights are in place." He pointed to the spotlights projecting from the pipes in front of the boxes.

"And please, if you don't mind, German shepherds scare the life out of me. Can you keep them at a distance?"

The guard laughed. "Of course, Captain, they are not here to attack, just sniffing out explosives. You never know these days."

Moving silently to the outside perimeter, he had to get his suitcase out of range. Otherwise, he would be shot then and there. What in the hell was he doing carrying bombs anyway?

Viktor knew he had to abandon this mission immediately. It was over and he would make sure to return the suitcase to Pierre.

In his dressing room, a valet had carefully laid out his white tie and tails. As he dressed, Viktor was relieved, and slipped into his polished patent leather slippers. He loved wearing formal clothes; they helped him prepare for a performance because they represented a custom and tradition that was part of him. He had lived almost entirely for his music, but all that was changing.

Wilhelm Furtwängler knocked on his door. Viktor had always respected this man who was a great conductor. But he knew his sentiments. Furtwängler had decided to remain in Germany, ignoring politics. Unlike Viktor, he was not in the German army, but their relationship with Adolf Hitler and the Nazi Party was a matter of concern to both, and part of the bond between them. Furtwängler had never joined the Nazi Party, nor did he approve of it; much like the composer Richard Strauss, he made no secret of his dislike of the Nazis. And like Viktor Mueller, the Nazis treated him with respect because he was an important cultural figure. Their concerts were held within occupied territories and were broadcast to German troops to raise morale, and tomorrow's concert was useful propaganda that would be broadcast all over Germany. It was Remembrance Day for Germany's heroes. Furtwängler looked curiously at Viktor's brown leather suitcase, but any thoughts about it remained unspoken.

"I deeply regret you are not conducting Mendelssohn, but it wasn't approved by Goebbels. It upsets me greatly that we can't play his music. It's a terrible struggle, Viktor, but we are still responsible for German composers; we hold the legacy of Bach and Beethoven, of Mozart and Schubert."

"But Mendelssohn? Of course not. We understand this, we two."

"Yes, we can only do the best we can, in our own way." Furtwängler's voice was hollow, there was a tone of defeat there. He had compromised with the Nazis to save the best orchestra in the world. He had gotten financing and the support he needed, but Viktor saw he had lost something along the way. "I'm pleased, Viktor, pleased that you've come; it's an important event."

The orchestra loved Mueller. His style of conducting was a

masterful show, and they had not only played for many of his productions, but also toured Europe together. The orchestra never thought of it as propaganda, only as performance. Each member of the orchestra treasured music for what it meant to them, how it connected them to one another, to the composer, to the audience. It was more than a profession to them; it was a calling and each performance was an experience during which just for a moment, they could take solace through a series of notes, through ineffable ideas that could find expression only in this way, these urgently needed reminders that there was beauty in their unsettled, unstable world.

"We do what we must do," Viktor replied. "Music is not a voice of the state; it is for the people."

But the Berlin Philharmonic was Hitler's favorite orchestra, Viktor Mueller his favorite conductor.

On Remembrance Day, Viktor Mueller had a lot to remember. They would all be in attendance: Hitler's generals, the whole lot—Göring, Goebbels, Himmler, Hess, Keitel, Rommel. And they would never know how close they had come to a violent end on that night of music and celebration.

All the members of the orchestra were onstage warming up. The house lights dimmed as the concert master, one of the first violins, indicated to the principal oboist for a tune note for the orchestra. An A was repeated three times, for the strings, the woodwinds, and again for the brass.

Then Viktor Mueller entered the stage with two soloists, a soprano and baritone. He lifted his baton, and like magic, the evening began, the orchestra began to play.

He knew the Führer would have preferred the religious ritual of Wagner. In counterpoint, he had decided on Brahms's *Ein Deutsches Requiem*. He loved the beauty of the piece, and the choir, and in many ways it reminded him of Max, who loved the melodies as much as he did. *Max,* he thought, *what have I done to you? What bargain have I made?*

The music overcame time. It was a higher calling. Tears came to Viktor's eyes, from the music and from the deep well of his memory. When the concert finished, the great hall was quiet. Then came the traditional rumbling of the musicians stamping their feet in appreciation and respect for their conductor. The long accolade finally trailed off, leaving just the sound of a German officer's footsteps approaching the stage to present the Great Viktor Mueller with an envelope containing a handwritten note: *The Führer thanks Viktor Mueller for Remembrance Day and the tribute to the fallen.*

After the performance, at a café, over coffee, Viktor confided to Pierre, "I can't do this sort of thing."

He handed over the suitcase that had never been activated. "I don't want any part of blowing people up. I can't do this. I simply can't."

It was a missed opportunity, Pierre thought, but some part of humanity within him understood. It was more than destroying uniforms, more than humiliation. It was life and death. He knew he would have to condition Viktor for tougher action and it would take time.

Pierre placed his coffee cup carefully on the saucer in front of him: "Viktor, I know that you are a good man, a great conductor, a sensitive artist. But this is the world as it is and you can't turn away from the facts. Every day, Jews, political dissenters, Catholics, and others are being rounded up and sent to camps, and for slave labor. We must find ways to stop it. Doing nothing is no longer an option. There's someone I think you should meet. Another good man, a courageous fighter."

"Who is he?"

"Raoul Wallenberg."

SANCTUS

On a miserable morning at Hanover Barracks, David was hunched over a desk, editing the next edition of the paper.

Sitting down beside him on his bunk, I said, "Well, I've got some news, but we can't print it. I'd be dead by morning."

"What are you talking about?"

I told him about the man in the black overcoat.

"I can't believe those bastards think they can just—"

A siren blasted through the camp, a noise always followed by an announcement, an ominous one: "*Everyone remain in your barracks and away from windows.*"

Immediately, we raced across the room, disobeying the rules, risking punishment, especially for David, fewer rations, or none at all, our foggy breath from the freezing barracks almost blurring the view. We saw the line—a group of children who were holding hands in the pouring rain. Torn and dirty clothes hung from their bodies as they walked alongside a column of SS men. Closely guarded, they were led to the infirmary building for the usual disinfection and delousing, a rule for everyone. Huddled together, they had refused to undress or wash or to have their wet rags exchanged for dry clothing. Where had they come from? Some of the kids were strangely familiar to me. Where had I seen them before?

A letter arrived at the post office from Colonel Eichmann in Berlin addressed to the SS. I was hesitant to ask Fritz about it and finally my curiosity prevailed. I opened it in secret. It was about the children. After my encounter with the black overcoat, and covering for Ava's brother, all bets were off.

It couldn't be.

Resealing the letter, I rushed over to the barracks as fast as I could make it back to David. He was fiddling with an old typewriter, trying to get it to work. Hopping from one foot to the other and rubbing my hands together, I protested, "Must it be so cold in here, David? I think my brain is frozen."

It was a dumb, rhetorical question. I understood that fuel, like everything else was in pitifully short supply now. David tightened his ever-present maroon scarf. "Okay, what do you have for me, Max?"

"The children are from Poland."

"How do you know?"

"Don't ask me. I just know. They were taken from their parents. I know these kids! Hans conducted them at a concert in Prague. Except for you, we were all there."

"Are you sure?"

"I'm positive, they are part of the Szymon Laks group." My teeth were chattering.

"Did you ask Freidle if he knows anything?"

"I doubt if he does."

David shook his head. "He is not a very helpful Nazi, is he?"

"Nope, but he's the only one I've got."

I discussed the children with Sophie. "They're tired and dirty, hungry; they're beaten down. We must help them, Sophie, we've got to do *something.* I've found them! We must give them a sense of purpose, of belonging, if only for a while. We have to do it for them and for Hans, too, because, finally we've found the voices for *Brundibár*!"

I ran over to Hans's quarters and told him.

"Are you serious?"

"Hans, they need this. We all do."

I started my campaign.

"These kids are special," I told Freidle, arriving at his office. "They have a gift that I know you'll appreciate. They need to sing and people need to hear them."

There must have been something in my words or how I spoke them, because at once the commandant gave permission for me to help in any way I could.

Then I was on to Dr. Citron, the doctor who had come with the group. He had been assigned to their care. I learned about the Warsaw Ghetto.

"It was called the Jewish District, *Jüdisc Wohnbezirk,* over four hundred thousand Jews confined within an area of not much more than three square kilometers. Most residents starved or were sent to the camps."

I looked at him, bewildered. "Why didn't they fight back?"

"They did, but it's hard, if not impossible for a ragtag band of starving, barely armed men to stand up to let alone defeat a powerful army with tanks. They were overwhelmed and hoped for safety inside the Great Synagogue. The Germans set fire to the ghetto. Countless thousands of people burned on the spot. It's unimaginable but it's true."

I couldn't take in what I was hearing. I was physically sick.

"We managed to save some of the children."

"How?"

"Through tunnels and with the kindness of strangers on the Aryan side. They were sent here. This is their sanctuary."

Good God! Terezín was their sanctuary! A place where people were starving and dying and getting transported to labor camps. I was horrified by the thought that this place was better than where these children had been. What had they experienced? What had they lived through? What had they seen?

I went to visit the children. There was someone in particular I needed to see. I walked through the barracks until I found him.

"Jan, it's me, Max. We met after your concert in Prague, and we saw a comet in the sky."

The blond boy said nothing. But I knew it was the same boy I had met what seemed a lifetime ago. I remembered those clear blue eyes, even though they now seemed lost and vacant.

"They're traumatized," Dr. Citron said. "God knows what these young people have been through. They won't talk. They're mute. All of them. I've tried, but not a word. The only thing we can do is feed them, clean them, take care of them until they find their voices."

In the end, Sophie came up with a plan. She couldn't speak their language, but music could. Hans found a spinet in the village that had been acquired for the guards' quarters. It was old and rickety, but had not altogether lost its polish or its tone. I helped him move it over to the barracks, and within five minutes of concentrated tinkering, I had helped this beautiful battered instrument regain its tone.

With the kids cleaned up, they gathered around Sophie. Then she spoke to the children in a way they all understood. She struck a resonant D. Nothing. She followed with a D major chord and bass line. It echoed throughout the barracks. There was a long silence.

She struck the key again.

A single voice came from the boy with the yellow hair. A pure and lovely sound broke through, then another chord, another voice, with each chord other voices, until a full glorious choir came alive.

"Well done, Sophie. Well done."

Hans returned to the piano. Freidle stood in the back with a few guards in the shadows. Sophie took a seat along with Ava and Fritz nearby.

The children sang Mozart's *Sanctus*. We wept. I had not heard the canon before. Their voices were exquisite, and at this moment Terezín was filled with light. It was that invisible sun that Hans had described to me long ago. Music had not gone away. It was still there for us. We had now surely found the voices Hans needed for *Brundibár*.

Could this be an opportunity to get a production going? Freidle could get things done, and I had an assignment for him. Returning to the commandant's office, I made another appeal, hoping my powers of persuasion would convince him. I wasn't sure what tack to take with him, but decided to sound as confident as I could.

"You've built a station," I offered boldly. "Do you think we could build a stage?"

"Stage? What for?"

"It's an assignment."

"Assignment?"

"Yes, we all need an assignment, and this is one for an opera."

"Why *opera*?"

"Because we can do it, and perhaps we need to do just that. We have a camp orchestra, and music is part of our tradition. Don't you think it could take the performance to a whole new level? We have great composers here. We have a cast. And you heard those voices! Something to lift our spirits."

"And what is this opera about?"

Rabbi Baeck's words about the importance of different perspectives rang through me.

"It's about the qualities of the German character. I think it would be a great achievement, and with your showmanship, it will be 'A Siegfried Freidle Production.'" As the Great Viktor Mueller himself once told me, a little flattery never hurts. I tried not to think of Poppy; it was too painful. I pushed him to the back of my mind, only recalling what could be useful.

Freidle started making doodles, taking pencil to paper. Within minutes he had sketched the rough outline of a stage.

Before we could even start rehearsals, the children left unexpectedly, just as they had arrived, on a wet, gray afternoon. The wooden barracks were silent again.

"They were told to remove the yellow stars from their garments, and those who were old enough were required to sign a pledge of silence about what they had seen and experienced," David said. "They were sent away. No one has been told where." David could hardly get the words out.

I determined that the only thing to do was to send a letter to Poppy. I couldn't write fast enough—my fingers were cramping up.

> *They sang for us. It was beautiful. Remember the concert in Prague? We had a cast. Surely you can help. They were taken away.*
>
> *Max*

Fritz read the letter, slowly shaking his head. "I think it is best we don't mail this to the captain. Speak to your father when you see him."

"I'm not sure what kind of war he's fighting. Surely there's something *we* can do to help these kids?"

"Max, the orders came from the High Command."

"Berlin?"

I looked and saw the secret red packet that had arrived.

Fritz was unusually silent, almost prayerful.

"You seem pretty sad."

"I'm going to tell you something that you don't want to hear. They were sent to a camp called Auschwitz. SS Colonel Adolf Eichmann had conducted negotiations to send the children to Palestine, for a great sum of money put up by the Jewish Relief Committee. However, the entire operation was canceled on orders from Himmler, who pocketed the money paid for their safety. On one of the holiest days in the Jewish New Year, Rosh Hashanah, the kids were sent to a place . . . to a place I can't imagine. None of us can."

"How do you know?"

"I opened the red packet from Berlin."
He quietly recited part of an English poem to me.

"Come, my friends,
'Tis not too late to seek a newer world."

He sighed, turned his head, looked out the window.

"To sail beyond the sunset."

He stopped there. When later that afternoon I told David, he whispered the final line of the poem:

"To strive, to seek, to find, and not to yield."

BLOCKS OF ICE

A great snow had fallen in Terezín, and it was cold, unimaginably so. David and I slipped through the ice-covered streets, making our way from the library to the infirmary to deliver to the patients a few books, protected under our coats. It was difficult negotiating the frozen streets, our hands numb, our breath heavy, from a heavy snowfall with rain and sleet.

In the distance outside the kitchen was an irregular winding line, silent and unsheltered, dark against a backdrop of snow. The people were queuing patiently, silently, waiting for a bowl of thin, watery, unseasoned potato soup and a piece of black bread. Separate from the crowd, slumped against a snowbank was an old man staring at the two of us as we approached. Four members of his family—an elderly woman, a middle-aged man, and two children—had left their places in the line, looking for him, calling for him, finding him, wailing to help him—"Please, Eli, come back," they pleaded.

The man was unmoving. We each let go of our books, which dropped to the ground, and in a moment beneath the freezing rain they became blocks of ice with a thousand words frozen inside.

David ran toward him.

He was unable to get up, could not shift his feeble limbs.

He looked up, but his gaze could no longer find its focus. His body was aged and impossibly thin, his teeth broken and brown, his gums bloody.

He managed to whisper, "Please help . . ."

David and I struggled to lift him up, but we saw that his eyes were now fixed, his body limp.

He was dead. A dead man standing. He didn't need our support. We let him down slowly onto the snow as his family gathered around him, keening in a shared, raw grief.

Within moments the Kapos, the hated Jewish prisoners known for their brutality, came, wearing white armbands with inverted green triangles. They had been assigned by SS guards to carry out administrative tasks, collecting garbage for incineration and taking away the dead for cremation.

David had told me the day before that these corpses were burned like fuel to provide heat for the village. It was too much to bear. Garbage and dead corpses used to provide heat for the living.

"Get back," one of them shouted to me and David. The cart arrived, the body was thrown into it with a thud, and it departed again. It was a scene of inexplicable grief, and a sound that none of us would ever forget.

It was not the beginning nor the end. I never turned on the heat in my room again.

Another transport arrived at the platform, a group of Danish Jews delivered on this grim conveyor belt. The tracks brought, and the tracks took away. Every day was becoming harder, the place dirtier, the conditions worse, food and water scarcer, disease more prevalent, faces more resigned, the nights darker, and fear reached into the everyday reality of painful, undignified death. We were busy staying alive; the quality of life was distant and far away, part of a forgotten dawn, fading into lost sunsets. Secretly I wondered if I would ever see another.

I learned from Fritz that the Germans had organized plans at the Chancellery to send nearly all of Denmark's eight thousand Jews to Terezín.

"New supplies will be arriving. This is good news, Max," said Freidle.

"What supplies?" I asked. "Eight thousand people? Where are they going to live? What will they eat?"

"New barracks are being constructed."

David and I had become experts at finding the best hiding spots from which to observe the goings-on around camp.

"Can I come along?" Sophie asked.

I was reluctant. I didn't want her in harm's way in case we were spotted.

"Oh, Max, you're being so protective. Just because I'm a girl?"

"Because you're you, Sophie, and you don't have to take risks. I want to protect you. That's part of my assignment."

She grinned. "I want to see what you and David are up to. We're a team, remember."

Sophie insisted on coming along, and since she stayed close by, I thought it was okay. I was extra careful to watch out for the man in the black coat, and on the day the train arrived, we took cover behind a low wall near the tracks, watching the Danes ushered into a nearby courtyard, where freshly set tables had been arranged, piled high with food and drink.

"David, who do they think they're fooling?" I whispered. We moved to a nearby building.

"Is that herring and aquavit?" David asked, shaking his head.

Then the loudspeakers began playing a familiar Danish song,

"That's the 'The Champagne Galop,'" Sophie remarked.

Was this real? It felt more like a scene from a film.

Sophie spotted a man that she had once heard perform, Peter Deutsch, the conductor of the Royal Orchestra in Copenhagen. He was a short distance away, and she pointed him out.

"Many of them look tired; some are probably ill from their journey. I should get back to the infirmary. I suspect Mama will be needing a lot more help with a short supply of nurses. It always happens with new arrivals. We have to check for typhoid."

"Be careful, Sophie. I'll see you later."

David and I continued to listen as the music played. Then we retreated to a darkened arch and watched this strange scene. I was so caught up that I pretended I was conducting.

"You're being ridiculous, Max."

But I felt the music, I heard every instrument—soft strings, brilliant brass, all of them speaking to each other, leaving and returning in perfect harmony. I couldn't help myself, waving a slender stick as my baton to an imaginary orchestra, playing under my direction. I was madly keeping time when I felt a tap on my shoulder, turning only to find Commandant Freidle staring down at me. The secret hiding spot wasn't so secret.

Then my heart leapt. Just past Freidle was Poppy!

I ran into my father's waiting arms, and Poppy held me tightly. It was hard for me to do, but I had to accept that he was my father. Our embrace was so familiar, so warm, yet at the same time unsettling and painful. With just one hug, I realized the terrible longing that I had tried to suppress, to deny, remembering all those long hours that I had spent hoping he would come, praying for him to come and reassure me that everything would be all right.

Poppy gave me a big smile, one I had long forgotten. "Oh, Max, how I've missed you."

"Poppy, I—"

Commandant Freidle clapped his hands together. "Shall we go to the luncheon?"

"I've some work to do at the office," David said, walking off, but not before catching my eye. He hadn't acknowledged my father.

Poppy and I walked over to the courtyard as Freidle strode from table to table, asking the Danes if they were enjoying the afternoon.

Once the welcome was over, the Danes were hustled into the administration building for room assignments. Then they were fumigated for disease. Like animals. From that moment, the life they had once known would end. They'd be required to leave their baggage in the hall. Their belongings would be promptly searched for valuables. In exchange, they would be awarded yellow stars.

We made our way back to Fritz and Ava's house. Freidle excused himself, and Poppy and I settled down at the kitchen table. He sighed and took off his hat. He'd changed a lot. His hair was grayer and his shoulders sagged.

I noticed a slight tremor in his right arm.

Poppy caught me staring. "I'm fine, Max, just so much work. As soon as I finish one project, another begins."

"When will it end?"

"I don't know, Max."

He rubbed his head.

I couldn't take it anymore. I stood up and walked over to him, the Great Viktor Mueller. I leaned over and stared into his eyes. "It's all a trick, Poppy, and I think you know it. This place was never a spa. It's getting worse, you can see how crowded it is. And now the transports. You know about transports, don't you? You know about the children from Bialystok, near Warsaw?

They were taken to some place called Auschwitz. Where is that? *What* is that?"

Poppy said nothing. I tried to read what the silence meant: Was it shock? Guilt? Shame?

"I thought you would save them, Poppy, but you didn't. Now the Danes. It's all fake. I remember all the stories you used to tell me about the Distant and Mysterious Man. About courage and good deeds. I thought you were a better man, and that he, the hero, might be you, Poppy. It was our story, our secret. And you want to know something . . ." I pointed a finger at his chest. He stared at me, his face betraying nothing. "Every Dane will be given postcards to send to their friends back home, about their great reception was and how good it is here, and you know what I'm going to do, Poppy? I'm going to tear them up, because it's not true! We've got to find a way to get everyone out of here."

Poppy broke his gaze, placing his hands in his lap. "Max, I—"

"No! I don't want to hear any more lies. This place started with a couple of hundred people, and how many now, thousands? They come and go. To where? Do you know their destination? Tell me, Poppy, show me. To the theater, to a concert? Were you taken to administration and deloused when you came? And you supported this place so much you were okay with me coming here!"

I threw a chair to the ground.

"'A gift to the Jews,' they said. The Nazis kill children. Some people are starving and freezing. There's not enough food for everyone, or clothes, or medicine, or fuel. Why, Poppy? Some of the barracks are so crowded that they have hard wooden beds stacked together four-high. Not like the ones you and I sleep in; and this is their home? This is how my friends are treated? What kind of father are you? What kind of man? Is this what my mother would want? Is this how you honor her?"

"Max. There are things at work that you don't understa—"

I interrupted. I couldn't allow any explanation, any excuse.

"No, *you* don't understand! I came here, Poppy, because you promised me it would be a great place to be with my friends. Just for a little while. Well, where have you been for 'just a little while'? It's been a long time, Poppy! You deserted me to produce shows full of lies. You're a selfish man, Poppy. More selfish than anyone I've ever known."

Poppy's eyes streamed with tears. I didn't care. I needed those tears. I needed to know that I was being heard.

"You've hurt us, Poppy, that's what you've done. You forgot me, and you forgot your best friend. You betrayed Hans. I'm not proud of what you've done. I'm ashamed of being German, and I'm ashamed of you."

Poppy's right hand shook uncontrollably and he covered it with his left. He stood up from his chair. "Get your things. I'm taking you with me, Max. We're leaving."

"No, it's too late," I said, stepping away from him. "I don't know who you are. And *I* don't desert my friends. I am on their side. Not yours, Poppy." My voice was suddenly heavy with grief. "Not yours."

Always in the past, one of Poppy's preeminent gifts, one that carried a real sense of meaning and presence, was his ability to express himself with an eloquence that was supportive, engaging, illuminating, truthful. However much I needed reassurance, I was older now—no longer the boy who he could enchant.

I turned my back on my father and walked away.

Standing in the hall, I held my breath until I heard the front door close, then running down the hall, I threw open the front door. Poppy's sedan was already fading into the distance.

"I don't know what's real anymore," I said. "My mind is all jumbled."

Sophie held my hand. "Max . . . we're real. This . . . this is real. Here and now is real. Maybe that's all we have, maybe that's enough. We escaped, Mama and I, from a terrible place. I lost my father, Max. I've accepted that he's gone. The suffering you can't imagine, the humiliation that we were subjected to. My mother being spat at in the street while I held her hand. Things are difficult here, terribly difficult for all of us. But I am with you and that is everything for me now."

"Think of what we've had and what we've lost; and in all of this confusion . . . Poppy . . ."

I couldn't believe what I was about to say. Taking a breath, "I don't love him anymore, Sophie."

"Max, he's your father. Don't reject him. Don't give up. If we hold on, who knows what will happen? There is still space here for music and for dreams. I've always wanted a house, and I can make it exactly how I want it to be. A place to cook, my own room, a piano." She reached out. "Will you come live with me, Max? All we can do for now is be closer to each other."

I thought about Poppy and my eyes burned. But he was gone now, and I had to try to forget. "Yes, we'll find a place to call home."

TALKING TO A TREE

David knew how I was feeling. He had understood the truth long before I had been able to, and he knew I needed a distraction, so he gave me a new assignment.

"I'm not up to it. About the last thing I want to do right now is interview anyone."

"Are you giving up, just like that? You're a journalist, looking for answers until you can find no more. And part of the job is writing about other people, about what you observe and feel. If we speak to someone else, we can always learn something. Everybody has a story."

"About death?"

"And life. That's what reporters do. They dive back in, no matter what."

He wasn't going to let up. I grabbed my notebook, said, "Fine," and stormed out of the office and down the stairs.

Viktor Frankl was talking to a tree outside a building called Block B IV. Before approaching him, I studied the young doctor. I'd developed a reporter's knack for sizing people up. He wore glasses that tried in vain to conceal his tired gray eyes. He was tall and much too thin, his white coat hanging from his slight frame.

When the doctor saw me, he extended his hand. "You're Max Mueller."

"You know me?" I stepped forward and greeted him.

"You're Sophie's friend, of course. She's told me all about you. She and her mother help me a lot. Edith's a good nurse."

"How are things in the infirmary?"

"I believe we could save a lot more lives if we had supplies. Sulfur would help. But most medicine goes to the German army. I'm doing all I can with what I have."

"I take it you weren't able to treat patients at your clinic in Vienna, so you came to Terezín."

Frankl laughed. "Yes, I figured a spa vacation was just what I needed. You're probably wondering what I was doing when you arrived."

I smiled. "Clearly, you were in a discussion with that tree."

"I come here to clear my head when I have a moment. I take care of a ward inside that building there—patients who have been traumatized, patients that you never see. I've recently heard about killing squads called the Einsatzgruppen. I'm not sure if anyone can ever recover after what they've seen. I hear their stories, stories from a few who have managed to escape. Hundreds are taken from their homes, shot, and left in a ditch. There's a young boy from the Ukraine, a sweet boy, but he hardly talks, and when he does, I hear about what he has seen, things that nobody his age should see, nobody of any age anywhere should see, crimes against humanity. I can't imagine it. He won't tell me his name, and there's so much I want to know. I'm lost for words and answers, and that's why I talk to trees these days."

"What do you talk about?"

"My wife," the doctor said sadly. "I talk about Katharina, that was her name. I see Katie's smile in my mind, her encouragement. To me she represented all that is good. I think we saw truth together. Truth, Max, just when you think you have found it, it skips out on you. It's elusive."

"Why? What happened?" I asked as gently as possible.

He seemed not to hear me, lost in his own thoughts. "I try to understand how anyone, including myself, who has nothing left in this world can hold on."

The doctor shook his head. "But we do hold on and . . ." He sighed. "I remember when we first came. We walked, stumbling in the darkness, over stones and large puddles in the daylight, along a road leading to the camp. Hardly a word was spoken. As we staggered along, she whispered to me: 'We must find a way. We must always love each other.' I guess we live in expectation; but when the last page is written, it doesn't matter how we live; it's not what we expect from life, but rather what life expects from us. I think that is some sort of truth. Here at Terezín, we have a responsibility to help each other. We consider truth one step at a time."

"Have you found it?"

"Oh yes, that's why I look to that tree. It will shed its leaves and be reborn next spring, and it will be green and alive, living through another winter. My wife was not so fortunate. She died and I couldn't save her. But she lives on in a way. It's a matter of the soul. The soul inside you never dies."

"Trees, do they understand? Do they have souls?"

"I think so. They are simply beautiful and ask for nothing but to be nourished and appreciated. They understand more than we know. While we're around, we need to love each other, Max, and understand more about where we are coming from so we can find where we're going. Hold on until we get home."

Home. Barbed wire and guards. Outbreaks of typhoid? The suffering all around increasing every day. I had the desperate feeling that I was on a train traveling toward hell. At other times, I thought that we had already arrived. No matter how difficult things were already or would soon become, how could I help? Could I change things somehow, change the course of events at all? When life around me became too confusing, I rationalized that sooner or later the war would be over. It had to end sometime, and I had to hold on to that thought. There was so much to do, so much to build, so much to rebuild. I had somehow or other to cling on to hope. If those around me were carrying on as best they could, living lives of bravery and hope, then what right did I have to give up? The courage to carry on hoping felt like the only thing left. Not to give up on my assignment.

Then Sophie introduced a plan that slowly unfolded.

"I want you to meet some people."

On the second floor of the children's block, just under David's office, Sophie led me to Sarah Markova, her dearest friend about whom she had written to me before I'd first arrived. Sarah was small and fragile and had studied in Russia. When she was too old to dance at the Kirov, she earned her degree in psychology at Moscow university. With more optimism than her slender body could pack in, Sarah managed to teach one child at a time in the tiny livable space below the *Vedem* office. I didn't know how she managed, except she loved the children, and that was her driving force. The kids were like trees, I thought, asking nothing in return but to be nourished, to be given the chance to express themselves and to be appreciated.

I knew what it was like being separated. But these kids had no idea where their parents were, nor who they were. Maybe it was better like that, I reasoned. It had to hurt. Yet they appeared to have found some happiness. It had to be like a seesaw. Hurt and happiness. Up and down, back and forth, hoping to land on the happiness side.

While I had a special situation, teaching had been formally banned at Terezín, and materials like books, pencils, and crayons were in short supply. But Sarah was determined to give the children some bit of hope in their daily lives. She created activities—playing games, performing skits, and singing songs. In these multinational surroundings, language wasn't a problem. She was tireless in her love for these kids.

"I'd like for Max to meet the children and see their home." She figured *home* meant a lot of different things to a lot of different people, a place to feel better, and free. Home for me? I would have to make do with my imagination.

They were a mismatched bunch from all over Europe. But they clung together.

"We're all a family," Sarah said. "We may look different and speak different languages, but our feelings are the same. We really are very much alike. All of us."

To welcome me, they stood in a line holding hands and sang a Georgian folk song called "Suliko." It was a song that Sarah had taught them. Their voices were so pure; they could have been a professional choir. I knew that they could be the cast for *Brundibár.* They took their places, sitting cross-legged in a semicircle on the floor of the barracks, not saying a word. I hoped that they would respond to the idea of a performance.

"We're going to be putting on a show and you, all of you, would make a perfect cast."

One piped up, "We've never put on a real show before, we only pretend every so often."

"That's just it, you can play and learn different parts . . . that's all that acting is: proper pretending."

"Is it hard to learn lines?"

"It's really easy, and a lot of fun."

Putting on a theatrical voice that would've made the Great Viktor Mueller proud, I introduced myself as "Mr. Make-Believe."

"Sometimes," I said to them, "pretending makes the world a special place. You can be anything you want to be, in the land of make-believe."

"Is it an actual place?" one of the kids asked.

This was something I knew about. "If you believe, you can be a dancing elephant in the jungle."

Placing a jacket over my head, I waved a sleeve as if it were a trunk and pranced around the room. I found a multicolored jester's hat, put it on my head, and attempted a handstand, surprising myself when I tumbled over. The room rang with the children's laughter.

"Or even be a clown."

The kids *ooooooo*ed at this feat.

I asked, "Can you draw a picture so I have something to remind me of our visit together?"

The children huddled in conference with Sarah and Sophie, and after a few minutes, giggled. A few came forward with paint. They colored my cheeks pink, exaggerated my mouth white, smeared a bright red blotch on my nose, and pulled the floppy hat down on my head. They cheered. I became a walking painting, a performer in the land of make-believe. And I knew that finally I had a cast.

Sophie came over to me. "Max, the kids adored you. Sarah says you have *dusha.*"

"*Dusha?*"

"Something in the heart of every Russian. A kind of mystical identity, a sense of your soul having a place in the world. It's hard to translate."

Feeling a bit Russian, I supposed it was a good thing. And if it was, Sophie surely had more than me.

"*Dosvedanya.* Until we meet again, and thank you," Sarah Markova vigorously shook my hand. *Dosvedanya.* It sounded like a word I wanted to dance to, and so I grabbed Sophie and tried to twirl her around, and the children clapped. I took flight on a blessing. After washing up, I didn't waste a minute and led the kids over to meet Hans.

It was a good day.

Fredy Hirsh, who was inseparably connected to the children at Terezín, had made believers of them all. He was head of the physical education program and convinced everyone there how important it was to condition themselves physically and mentally for building a Jewish state. Living in a Jewish homeland was the dream of every Jew at Terezín.

"Palestine is a land of olive groves and lemon and fruit trees as far as the eye can see," he said. "It's always warm; you can do as you please. It's a place to take long walks through history, a place to be proud, a place to be free."

A place to be free? If that was true, I understood why David and Sophie were so keen to go. David longed to join his parents. Although I wasn't a Jew, I thought I might like to go with them. That Russian word, *dusha,* seemed to describe the Jews too.

"Max, I have a statement for *Vedem,*" Fredy said. "Take it to David for me, please: Tomorrow, Palestine. Believe me." As I turned to go back to the newspaper office, Fredy called, "Be sure to put on the *Vedem* calendar that the football season is still on, practice continues, we welcome players at all levels. Come on out and join the team!"

I entertained the thought for a minute. Could David and I revive the Czech All Stars? Probably not. At least I had the memory.

WHEN YOU LEAST EXPECT IT, SOMETHING HAPPENS

Taking the mail to Commandant Freidle's office, a voice called to me.

"*Guten Morgen. Wie Gehts.* How are you, Max?"

Frau Schmidt!

I couldn't believe it! She had come all the way from her celebrated hotel in Berlin! Had she come to commandeer the office?

"Is that Max Mueller coming to see me?" she asked, keeping her stern composure.

I was speechless. How had she gotten here? My spirit brightened in an instant.

"How? Why?" I asked.

Her face almost broke into a smile. "Thanks to my excellent housekeeping skills, I've been sent to assist Freidle. Things are terrible in Berlin, and I made sure I was on the last train out." She leaned closer to me and whispered, "The Nazis thought I was hiding Jews. They were paying guests, like anyone else! But imagine! They charged me as a conspirator. I put an end to that notion, with friends in the right places. I convinced them that I could be of service to the Fatherland. They agreed that with my talent to run a hotel, I could help out at Terezín."

She gave a huff toward the tumbling stacks of paper and cluttered shelves. "No one could have predicted how much of a mess this office is! It will take the fine hand of the Motherland to get it organized! Absolutely no excuse."

"Frau Schmidt, things have gotten pretty bad here."

Her thoughts were somewhere else.

"How is Captain Mueller? Where is he now?"

Unable to say anything positive, I mentioned that he had visited a few times.

"He'll be along any day. I don't have my reservation book with me, but I'll let you know. And keep mum, chum." It was an expression that I had never heard before. Frau Schmidt probably picked it up from one of her guests.

"I don't think we agree on much anymore," I told her. "Poppy's not the man I remember, not the father I had."

"Now just hold on, ducky."

Another phrase to add to my notebook!

"Ducky?"

"One of my visitors in Berlin was from Nottingham. He played the bassoon and was rather fond of the word; but enough about that, I have a letter from Viktor for you."

At first, I couldn't bring myself to read it. That night I did.

December 12, 1943

Dear Max,

I'm sad how we left each other. Regardless of what you may feel, you are still my son. I know we may disagree, but that should not stop our love for each other. I'm assured that you are safe. I wish I could tell you everything, but I can't. During wars, families are separated, we all make sacrifices, but we must stand up for what we believe. I saw Frau Schmidt, and she will be coming to Terezín and will give you this letter. I know that since the death of Heydrich, things at Terezín are bad and I expect to have a meeting about the matter in Berlin. This is not the German way. Many good people, even kids, have been recruited for the war effort; for many there's terrible hardship. Be brave and strong, Max. We stand together. Someday I hope you'll understand.

With my love,
Poppy

The German way? We stand together? How? Everything about us was different, except for one big thing: Poppy was still my father. That didn't mean so much anymore. *Stand together?* I couldn't. Poppy was standing on different ground. I had chosen where to stand, on good days and bad.

When I next saw Frau Schmidt again, she called to me: "An artist friend of mine is here, a famous painter, and you might like to meet him. He stayed with me at the pension in Berlin and he's a talented man, though he leaves paint all over the place. He needs a friend; his name is Norbert Troller."

BRUSHSTROKES

I saw the opportunity for an interview and advised David: "I think a piece about Troller would be great. You could publish a few of his drawings. He's well-known."

I recruited Sophie, and we found the famous master on a park bench, sketching a few buildings. Troller was wearing a velvet jacket covered with pastel dots and spots, each dash of color marking him as an artist. He was painting with his focus fixed on his canvas.

"Do you have a few minutes for an interview? I'm Max Mueller and this is my friend and colleague Sophie Mahler," I said, hoping I was exuding authority.

"I'm not sure I have much to say," Troller answered, never taking his eyes from his painting.

"Maybe you tell stories with paintings."

"That I do."

Sophie and I were fascinated by his jacket. He flashed a quick sideways glance at us.

"Why are you looking at me and not my work?"

We both shrugged.

"I always wear this gown. A bit of a habit I suppose; if I am not wearing it, I don't paint."

"You've always been an artist?"

"An artist, yes. I like to see things my way, not the way they are. That can be helpful sometimes."

"I studied art in school, and someday I'm going to learn more." Sophie had no doubts. "I'm sure it takes more talent than practice, or is it more practice than talent?"

Troller looked around and smiled, then returned his gaze to the painting, tapping a touch of color to the canvas.

"I was trained to be an architect, but I'd rather paint; it's a much better way to participate in life."

"Yes, I'm going to learn," Sophie said. "I can play music, then I'll paint, and then I'll listen, and then paint again. I'm always amazed how you can capture feeling. It's the greatest gift. How you see everything from different angles, so many shades of color, seeing life realistically or upside down."

Sophie never failed to surprise me with her enthusiasm.

"From my perspective, it's the light," Troller said. "And that carries a bit of music. Early morning and late afternoon, the colors are softer. Do you have a favorite color, Max?"

"I've never thought about it."

"And what about you, Sophie?" He nodded his head toward her.

"Light blue," she said quickly.

"Good. You're a lady of the sky, an optimist. Everyone should own a color; you can find blue in a thousand shades, and if you add a little tint, well, that adds something more. Take red, and add a hint of white, and pink surprises you. Take blue, add red, and welcome purple."

He put down his brush.

"Let's try again, color?"

"Beige," I decided.

"Interesting. You can do many things with beige. It's almost neutral but still it has its own personality. From light tan, it can take many directions. It offers more opportunity than blue or gray. Come visit me in my studio in Berlin Barracks. There you can see my drawings and you might like to select one for *Vedem.*"

He packed up his paints and Sophie and I followed him to his studio. He had painted his walls with a Palladian arch and a balcony reaching out onto a landscape in Tuscany. Sophie gasped when she saw it.

"It's called *trompe l'oeil.* The Italians are masters. The painting is so true to life that it looks real. But that's all art, isn't it, a technique to trick the eye, yet tricking it into seeing things as they really are and not merely as they appear to be. That's a really worthwhile trick."

I could almost breathe fresh air and feel the light sweeping in. Sophie beamed. And twirled around. "I can feel the colors."

When we left, Sophie almost sang as she declared, "Norbert Troller added color to our black-and-white world."

Brimming with excitement, and with Frau Schmidt following right on my heels, I approached Freidle's office.

"Commandant, we have a celebrated artist here, and I think he can be of great value to you. Has Frau Schmidt told you about Norbert Troller?"

Freidle nodded at Frau Schmidt. "Yes, but how can he help, Max?"

"Well, for starters, the whole camp is awful." I just came out and said it. "I mean awful. Even your office is tired."

Frau Schmidt put her hands on her hips. "It is a mess."

"Norbert Troller can design anything and make it terrific," I said. "I mean, not that it's not nice already, of course . . . I . . ."

Freidle got the message: "I don't disagree."

He looked around as if he was discovering for the first time how untidy his office was and had always been.

I relaxed and continued, "He's not only a painter, but an architect and designer, someone who can design anything!"

Frau Schmidt wagged her finger at Freidle: "Siegfried, it's impossible to keep you neat and organized, but if I have to inspire you with a kick in the tookie, I promise you, I will."

Freidle finally turned to me. "Arrange it. It's a start."

"I'm on the case, Commandant!"

I was feeling a sense of energy. Everyone needed an assignment, and while still working on a production, here was another one. Troller took on the challenge and began producing drawings for a desk, bookcases, and a wall for files and documents. He painted samples on little cards, easy pastels for the walls and contrasting color for the moldings. With a decorator's eye for detail, he refurbished Freidle's office, living quarters, and conference room. In a few weeks, we didn't recognize the place. The commandant was over the moon, and soon Troller was given other work.

Troller was a man of many talents. I called him "an artist for all seasons." He could design, draw, build, construct, and paint, with so much talent that even Frau Schmidt was in awe. His passion, however, remained painting portraits and landscapes. Freidle commissioned one of himself in full military regalia.

For the unveiling, Freidle gave a small party in his office, and the guests enjoyed baked cakes and drank fresh cider that Ava had made. Only the most privileged members of the camp had been invited. Fritz, Frau Schmidt, and I admired the portrait in its ornate gold-leaf frame.

"I wouldn't want Hermann Göring to see this," Freidle confided to the assembled group. "He might take it for his own personal gallery."

"He has one of the biggest art collections in all of Europe," said Frau Schmidt narrowing her eyes. "Most of it stolen."

"We must hang the portrait in the post office—on loan of course," Fritz suggested. "If not, it should be part of the permanent acquisition in the Alte Nationalgalerie in Berlin."

"No, no," Freidle replied, "I think it is more fitting in my office, more fitting. You and Frau Schmidt have introduced greatness! We have our very own Rembrandt."

Frau Schmidt nodded. "A tidy office makes for a tidy mind," she proclaimed.

When visitors arrived from Prague and Berlin, they admired Norbert Troller's paintings in the anteroom to Freidle's office. Frau Schmidt thought Freidle purposely placed them there because Germans were fond of pastoral landscapes. A few drawings turned into a cottage industry, and Troller was busy providing Freidle with a steady supply of paintings. They were all duly sold to visiting party officials from Berlin. Troller had his assignment. The "art fund," Freidle called it, and it was a profitable arrangement. Frau Schmidt wasn't sure where the proceeds went, but she was sure Norbert Troller's landscapes would soon be hanging in every home in Berlin.

Soon, Troller received a letter ordering him to appear at Himmler House. Himmler House was where the SS were, along with visiting officers and officials. Troller was ordered to design a taproom and a lobby conforming to a Bauhaus design. The existing rooms were shabby, and Troller, much to his annoyance, was compelled to adapt a plan to a military theme.

With my faithful tool kit and my beloved ribbons, I was commanded to keep its glorious Steinway in tune. Playing and tuning once a week allowed me a time of respite, a time of escape, away from the anxiety and the hunger and the illness, a time to get lost in my craft.

To keep Freidle's landscape gallery well stocked, Norbert could paint outside the gates of Terezín anytime he wanted. I was appointed to supervise him, which amounted to being his keeper. I was to watch him and warn of any attempted escape. They'd picked the wrong man for the job; if he'd tried to escape, I would've given him a map and a pat on the back.

A favorite place to set up his open-air studio was a park-like setting outside the village. It had well-tended lawns and grass-covered slopes, and Norbert sketched every house and every tree. When the afternoon folded into a quiet time of day, I figured that life was created in those meadows. It seemed a place that God must have walked through from time to time, while taking a detour from Terezín. Between my work tuning the Steinway and these idylls with Norbert, I felt fully alive for the first time in months, even years. I was reminded that there was a place and a need for color and space and beauty in every life.

During our expeditions to satisfy the inventory of Freidle's gallery, Troller saw a house with a gabled yellow roof. He pointed his brush as if to paint a stroke in midair, not unlike waving a baton. The house had a shaded lawn with leafy oaks and maple trees. It was a scene so perfect that Troller immediately set up his easel. While he was at it, the owner appeared, walking from the wide doors across a path to a cart used for farming. He saw us and came closer, peering over Norbert's shoulder at the sketch of his home and hay wagon.

"Are you from Prague?" the man asked.

"Um . . . no," Troller said, with a practiced economy of words. "Just nearby."

"My name is Pavel." He offered his hand and I shook it.

"I'm Max, and this is Norbert Troller."

The man nodded and left, returning a few minutes later with a package containing two loaves of bread, tomatoes, and slices of smoked meat, a well-received gift considering our food rations. A man appearing and then reappearing with a gift—it all seemed mysterious. And yet I felt safe.

"I don't like those Germans much," Pavel said. "I hate what they do. I hope that something good to eat will help."

I grinned. "Wow, we should come here every day!"

"Pavel, you are much too kind," said Norbert. "May I present you with a sketch of your home?"

"Do you think you could paint my family, especially my wife? She's beautiful."

"Of course, my new friend," said Norbert. "But please understand the commission will take several weeks to capture the light and mood."

I took the hint. I wanted to enjoy treats for as long as possible. "I can assure you, Mr. Pavel, you will treasure it always."

Within the hour, we were tucking into freshly baked pastries filled with wild strawberry preserves. It was the best deal we ever made.

Two days later Sophie sneaked away long enough to be with me and walk over fields of cornflowers that stretched into the distance as far as the eye could see.

While Troller painted, we lay on the grass, shoulder to shoulder, holding hands, enjoying the beauty all around us.

Sophie rubbed her nose along my neck.

"Cut it out, Sophie. You're tickling me."

"I can't. I have no control."

"Norbert will think we're kids."

"Well, aren't we?"

I sat up and looked at Sophie. She wasn't a kid anymore, and neither was I.

"It's really a pretty setting, isn't it?"

"It reminds me of a poem I once read, Max—it's like floating on daffodils. If I could collect all the poems in the world on a long sheet of paper, I would roll them up and give them to you."

With just a hint of a smile, she combed my hair away from my forehead. I wished Norbert could have painted us there together, capturing our feelings, so they would have lasted for all time. Then I thought, that's what memories are for. I saw a detail that I had seen in one of his paintings, a beam of light shining onto a field through a gray and platinum sky. The heavens paused for a moment. That moment was that glimmer of light. A landscape of unspoken words made visible.

ON THE WORD OF THREE WITNESSES

On a cold, crisp morning—it felt like the coldest Terezín had ever experienced—Rabbi Baeck called David and I to his study. When we arrived, he introduced us to a man named Milos Brunner, a Czech engineer who had recently returned to the camp.

"Sit down," said the rabbi. "You must listen."

Milos nodded at us. We sat down on the rabbi's worn couch and waited expectantly.

"Fredy Hirsh is dead," he said.

I gasped. "But I don't understand."

I hadn't seen Fredy in weeks but hadn't thought much of it. David sat quietly, always a thoughtful listener.

Sighing, the rabbi said, "Max, a few weeks ago, Fredy and some older children were transported to a place known as the Reich Area, a settlement called Birkenau. It's a family camp, part of Auschwitz."

I had heard of this place from Fritz.

Milos frowned. "It's a dreadful situation. I've just returned." He moved closer to the rabbi. "They're using Zyklon B on the prisoners—women and children alike."

The rabbi dropped his head into his hands.

"What's Zyklon B?" David asked.

"It's a commercial name for cyanide pellets. It's being used to gas thousands of Jews deported to Auschwitz."

"Wait, slow down, what do you mean, *gassing Jews*?" I asked.

David sank deeper into the couch.

I was unable to comprehend the news of this.

"I was there, Max," said Milos. "It's for the final solution. Zyklon is poured through small rooftop openings into rooms packed with Jews. After a few minutes, the screaming stops."

It was beyond my imagination. It was too much to take in. How could this be true?

"Why? What happens then?"

Trying to soften the news, the rabbi came closer. "They're dead, Max. They're all dead."

Milos told us that Fredy had impressed the SS, speaking perfect German, and with his manners and dress, had managed to set up a home for the smaller children. While the family camp was separated from the complex, Lieutenant Colonel Adolf Eichmann appeared with a man called Dr. Mengele. He'd already shown a special interest in the children, especially twins. He began making selections for scientific experiments.

"Eichmann and Mengele?" David asked, his face white.

"Karl Adolf Eichmann," the rabbi said, "is the man who keeps the trains rolling all over Europe. He's a model bureaucrat and a lover of systems. A classic subordinate following orders. But he's no fool. He's studied all aspects of Jewish culture, attended synagogues, visited our homes. He even made Jewish friends, who trusted him."

The rabbi took a few moments to gather himself before he continued. "Many . . . many thousands, tens of thousands, unimaginable numbers of people, of human beings have died at the hands of this monster. It is what he does that makes him what he is. I met him on one of his visits. He studied Hebrew and speaks a bit of Yiddish; it was Heydrich and Eichmann who ordered the Jews to be rounded up and forced into ghettos and labor camps, following orders from Hitler. They followed the orders with alacrity."

"Now to Josef Mengele. He's called 'the Angel of Death,'" said Milos. "A doctor who was wounded on the Russian front and volunteered to go to Auschwitz. A slightly built man, deceptive in every respect, and not what you think of when you imagine evil. There's scarcely a wrinkle in his uniform, he's perfectly groomed, not a hair out of place, his dark green tunic neatly pressed, his face well-scrubbed, boots polished, his death's-head SS cap tilted to one side, you can't miss him at the Auschwitz station, surveying his prey. He greets everyone at the train and with a simple gesture, a flick of his cane clasped in gloved hand, he seals their fate, with a casual wave; death to the left, life to the right."

Milos extended his arm, imitating Mengele. "One woman, faced with being separated from her child, screamed and scratched the face of an SS man forcing her back into line."

Milos drew an imaginary gun.

"Mengele shoots the woman and the child without any hesitation and sends the rest from the transport to the gas chambers."

David gasped.

"Mengele is Satan incarnate," Milos said. "He appears to be a gentle, affable man, a sort of father figure. 'Have a chocolate,' he says. It's hard to believe he's the same man performing grotesquely cruel scientific experiments that I can hardly talk about. Fredy learned all about him and staged a revolt. The kids were doomed; they were taken . . . taken away and never returned. Fredy was with them."

We were silent. David was shaking, unable to take this in. I laid my hand on his arm to steady him.

"Max," said the rabbi, struggling to regain his composure, "there was a debate in the Talmud: Would the world be better off if God had never created mankind? Much to my surprise, the commentary concluded that maybe God should not have created man."

"No disrespect, Rabbi," I said, "but thousands of Jews are being murdered. God couldn't be a factor here."

"But God—think of the hand of God, Max, one that can be open or clenched into a fist."

"What are we expected to do?" I asked, jumping up and pacing the room, thinking of Viktor Frankl's words. "Why do we exist?"

"That's a big question. We exist to live life as best we can, to be virtuous through all adversity, to give and to contribute to each other. Part of our culture is steady hope. We are being tested, every moment, every day, in the face of everything that we endure and see others endure, and somehow, some way, the hand of God points us in a better direction."

David stared into the distance, rocking back and forth, still not speaking.

Milos hung his head in despair.

The rabbi offered a prayer in Hebrew. I didn't understand it, but I knew what it meant by the resonance in his voice.

I looked across at him, looking for some utterance, some message. "I just can't see God in all of this. It's too much for me. I feel desperate, and all around I see the same blackness."

The rabbi paused a while, reflected, and finally spoke, quietly, so we had to lean in to catch every word: "God is here. God is in everything, in every moment. Things look dark now. They are as unimaginably terrible for those who hear them as for those who witness them. But the brightest light casts the darkest shadows, and there is always, always, a light of hope, and people must know the stories of those who didn't survive, who couldn't make it, from those who somehow did. David, Max, you must remember this story."

"How can I forget?" David said, coming out of his wave of shock.

"A great writer once said that those who can make us believe lies can make us commit atrocities," the rabbi said.

David scrunched up his face, trying to place the author.

"Voltaire," the rabbi said.

Turning to David, I said, "If we can't publish these things, how will anyone know?"

David shook his head, his eyes closed. "Maybe they never will."

"Where was God?"

"Where is man?" David asked.

"You may not be able to document all that you see and know about in *Vedem* now," said the rabbi. "But someday you will. You have a calling now, another appointment. Max, it's written in the Bible that a battle must be told 'on the word of three witnesses.' It's in Deuteronomy. You have heard this story, not to weaken you, but to strengthen you. You have become a witness. That is who and what you are. If you are the only one who lives . . . you are our witness."

I decided that I had to tell Sophie, we kept nothing from each other, but when we met, I lost my resolve, I couldn't.

"What is it, Max?"

"I . . . I just wanted to see you. It's not a good day."

"What happened?

"It's just a lousy day."

Sophie put her arm around me, offering an unswerving steadiness through her embrace. "Come on, Max. We'll get through it together."

I couldn't manage to say anything more. I trusted that if God could really open the heavens somehow, somewhere, I had to go along with that. Where was the rest of the world? Gone. Disappeared. Swept away, leaving not a shadow behind. There was just enough to keep us all going. I couldn't take it all in, and I had to keep believing we would still be together, waking each morning to find ourselves a little older and one day closer to the end of all this.

Fritz denied knowing anything about gassing.

"Surely there has been some information in the red packet."

He stared at me blankly.

"Tell me, Fritz."

"It's beyond comprehension, for all decent people. I don't want to talk about it."

"You once mentioned Auschwitz to me."

"Yes, but I didn't have details."

"You knew something, and you didn't tell me?"

"How can I speak of such an outrage?"

"I want to know more about it, Fritz."

"It's true."

"For God's sake, Fritz, someone has got to stop it. We can't stand by and do nothing."

"What do you propose we do, Max? Head toward Auschwitz and put out the fire? Sure, I'll do that with you, but how far will we get? Max, we need an army. An army of soldiers with guns, journalists with words, people with prayers."

I wanted to fight back. But not in prayer. The darkness returned. Little food and clothing. People, already thin, were becoming thinner by the day. Most of the residents believed their friends had only gone east to work. Rabbi Baeck said it was best to keep the news quiet. I wasn't sure I agreed, but then again, what good would it have done to tell every living person at Terezín? For the time being I said nothing.

I was wracked with doubt. I couldn't sleep, I couldn't eat. Had I done something wrong? Had I offended God? The pages of Twain spoke to me:

> And I about made up my mind to pray, and see if I couldn't try to quit being the kind of a boy I was and be better. So I kneeled down. But the words wouldn't come. Why wouldn't they? It warn't no use to try and hide it from Him. Nor from me, neither. I knowed very well why they wouldn't come. It was because my heart warn't right . . .

One night I just couldn't shake off the conviction that the people I loved had been taken away. I had to reassure myself, to make my heart right, so I left the comfort of my bed and, heading out into the chilled air, I silently patrolled the streets and squares of Terezín, ducking under every sweeping searchlight, avoiding the ominous, watchful guards. I took every precaution not to be caught after curfew—that would be the end of me.

I felt haunted, somehow convinced that I had lost my friends to the work camps, to the chambers. *No, it couldn't be,* I tried to reassure myself as I trudged on, my frozen hands buried in my pockets. But was I sure? I had to dismiss this awful thought, one that refused to leave my anguished mind.

Slipping quietly around corners, I considered the barracks, first Hanover, quietly checking on David. I was relieved to see him sitting at his desk, buried in his work, lost in thought. I moved on to look for Hans, and there he was, as ever lightly playing a composition at his piano. Is this what they did at night? Did they ever sleep? Or were they a quiet, watchful presence, staying up protecting all good people from the dangers that came in the darkness?

When I arrived at Sophie's barracks, running past wooden slats to window after window, I saw bunks of sleeping bodies, but hers was empty. I panicked. I invoked every prayer in my being, *Please God, let her be here. Let her be well. Let her be okay. Let her be alive.*

I guess I believed in God after all. I reassured myself that she must be at the infirmary, but the wards were empty, with only the sounds of an occasional, rasping breath clinging on to life.

I fell into a wave of grief, despair capturing every thought, leaving me certain that Sophie had been taken from me forever, that she had been snatched silently away. I walked on, occasionally slipping and stumbling on the frozen ground, not caring whether I was seen or heard; what did it matter now?

I stumbled to the railway line and I stared down the length of the tracks, looking through a slowly rising, ghostly fog for some clue, some meaning, something to say where she was. I found only the darkness of the cold, unforgiving night. I couldn't allow myself to think that she, the person I loved more than anyone, anything in the world, was gone. I waited. Silent. Still.

There had been no transports that night.

I returned to the infirmary, hoping that maybe I would find Edith. I peered through another window. The sun was rising now, its rays melting the frost on the panes. The water gathered into rivulets and ran down the glass like tears. Then I made out the profile of someone moving in the ward, like a vision, a prayer answered. It was Sophie. I felt overcome, overwhelmed by a deluge of relief and happiness. She was there. She was alive. My friends had lived another day. I had made it through the darkest and coldest of nights and we were all still there. I wasn't altogether sure whether I was reassuring myself or lying to myself. But at that moment, in that brightest of mornings, I stood there alone, facing the new winter sun, my eyes blinking against the fierce light and whispered, "I am not alone in this world. They will survive. They must."

Just before I returned to my bed, I paused and sat down at the piano downstairs. For the longest time, I looked at eighty-eight ivory keys and each one was calling me. It was still early, but I couldn't resist striking just one key, a middle C, and I heard its sound that resonated and carried its sweet note across the cold, dark night air. And before I knew it, as mysterious as anything that ever happened to me, came back a chord, an answer. I hit my key again, and after an unanswered moment, it returned, a magnificent chord, full and alive and vibrant. It had traveled back. At that moment, it had been heard. I knew it had to be Hans responding in a way that both of us understood. We were both alone. Not so far away from each other that we couldn't share this glorious response, speaking to each other in the middle of the night, striking notes of prayerful encouragement, each giving the other the reassurance that everything would be all right.

UNEXPECTED CIRCUMSTANCES

The intolerable conditions could no longer be kept secret. Frau Schmidt saw the dispatches that had been sent to Freidle's office from the Chancellery. The international press was publishing stories about German crimes against humanity.

I would soon learn that a "news dealer" in Prague, who knew every international editor, had sent a letter to the International Red Cross describing the conditions in Terezín, the impossible overcrowding and the lack of food and medicine and all other necessary things. It was received by Peter de Pilar at the headquarters in Geneva.

Apparently, Hitler was troubled about Germany's reputation in the world in a war he was losing. Particularly troubling to him were reports about his model concentration camp. A stain upon German character was unacceptable. The Führer was annoyed.

"Your father is an amazing man, Max," Freidle said when I arrived in his office. Frau Schmidt nodded her head, heartily agreeing.

"He convinced the German leadership to allow the International Red Cross to visit, after stories were leaked to the world press."

Poppy's plan! Could this be what he was trying to do?

"How did he do that?"

"The major is persuasive."

"Major?"

"He's been promoted. And the High Command have insisted that German honor be restored and preserved."

What honor? I said nothing and kept listening.

"The directive is 'Fix Terezín.' With your father's urging, Terezín has been made a top priority. It was intended to be Germany's gift to the Jews. There will be dramatic changes."

Winter had passed, and surely spring was not far behind.

CURTAIN GOING UP

On a brilliant dappled sunshine day, Poppy arrived outside Freidle's office. The last time we were together, I had turned my back on him. Now I was facing him. He was still my father. "Is it true, Poppy? Is it? Did you convince Hitler?"

"We'll get it done, Max. Hitler will make good on his promise."

"Why should he?"

I wanted to believe Poppy.

"World opinion, Max. His legacy."

"What about Zyklon B?" I demanded.

"How do you know about that?" Poppy turned away. "It's a terrible thing. Unthinkable."

"Poppy, promise me . . ."

Without waiting to hear me out, Poppy said emphatically, "I will do what I can. Whatever I can."

"But you're not around to protect us, Poppy."

"I may not be here, but I am always with you. And I am always thinking about you. And I am here now to protect you. Wherever I am, whatever I am doing, I am doing it for you, for Hans, for all of you."

With every fiber of my being, I wanted to believe him. But my faith wasn't yet restored. I couldn't forget what I had learned in these recent days, months, years. I was growing up and the world had changed in a few short years. Poppy was different. Could things be the same again? Could my vision of the world and of Poppy ever go back to the way it was before? It seemed impossible.

Poppy braced himself. "Now, walk with me. It's time to see my friend."

When we entered Hans's room, Poppy said, "There won't be any more transports from Terezín."

Hans wrapped both arms around him.

"Viktor, I always had faith in you. Even when I didn't."

Poppy smiled. "What about *Brundibár*? It should have been the longest-running musical in Terezín by now."

"It's been a long road, months, Viktor. Delays, disappearing people and facilities, changing circumstances. We've had a few postponements, but we have talented kids, we have Max, we have a cast, all pulling together. We still need a big stage."

Poppy grinned, and for a fleeting moment it was as if the three of us were back in Prague. "I'm going to fix things, and you're going to see what I can do. Leave it to me."

Poppy collected his satchel.

"But you'll be around, right, Poppy? To check on the progress we've made?"

"Of course, Max. Everyone has orders, and I have mine. Even if from a distance, I will be watching you. And I'll be back before you know it."

I studied his face. "Poppy, I'll be your right-hand man. I'll make sure everything is going smoothly."

I had to be sure Poppy was the man I thought he was, the man I hoped he had always been.

He gave me one last hug and got into his sedan.

"We both have a lot of work to do. I'll see you in a few days."

I waved until the car disappeared. There it was again: steady hope. I had to try to hold on to it.

Frau Schmidt and Norbert Troller were responsible for overseeing the reconstruction, applying their skills with enthusiasm. Substantial funds were given for the project. *Vedem* could print that the World Jewish Congress had donated over a hundred thousand dollars for the restoration, and the Jewish Rescue Committee in Budapest and the King of Sweden gave an equal amount. Berlin sent a letter of thanks and encouragement, noting how much "the conditions will be improved for those we care about."

"The Führer's disgusted!" Frau Schmidt said. "The whole Terezín concept was bungled thanks to a dunce called Eichmann who is now relegated to lesser duties." She commented that he had had an unremarkable education. When he joined the Nazi Party, he was appointed head of the department responsible for Jewish affairs. He was practiced in killing people.

The SS had no supervisory standing in the work and Frau Schmidt was given a broad range of authority for the project. Transport offices were closed. Boxes of files were removed.

New offices called "Die offizielle Verwaltung für öffentliche Arbeiten" took their place. The Germans always had long sounding official names, and the DOVFOA was not an exception. Eventually the office was simply called the "VolkFarben," *the people's colors.* Things were changing, moment by moment. I felt a sense of hope, however tentative, returning within me and all around me.

"I need two thousand paintbrushes," Norbert said.

Two thousand paintbrushes arrived from Poland.

All the residents volunteered. Everyone carried one in their back pocket. Frau Schmidt and Freidle gave assignments by color.

Park benches were given a new coat of green, living quarters beige, hospital wards white. The *Vedem* offices were fitted with desks.

"Isn't this amazing, Max?" Sophie said, making rounds at the infirmary. "It's as if the camp has been reborn!"

"Your mother appears to be better," I said, watching Edith moving around the ward, organizing much-needed supplies.

"I caught her humming today. I still can't believe that your father did all this, Max. But after all, he is your father, the Great Viktor Mueller. And he's a compassionate man. How could we ever have doubted him?"

I allowed myself the smallest of smiles.

Frau Schmidt kept the mission simple and, as the ultimate hands-on housekeeper, she knew how to handle details.

Even the Czech guards began to take pride in the effort. With a chorus of "Can we help too?" they joined the labor force. The sidewalks were spotless, freshly painted green disposal cans placed on every corner, and a red telephone booth set up next to the post office. Only no phone was ever connected.

"Fritz, let's fit the entry with brass mailboxes!" Max said, walking into the post office.

He added some of Ava's stationery and stands with stacks of white paper. "Some fancy pens?" Fritz asked.

"Great idea. Montblanc?"

He laughed. "In your dreams."

Doors were sanded and varnished, tables polished. A crew made sure that lamps with green shades were installed in the library. The dusty room was transformed into banks of color, with brochures announcing *Terezín on View.*

"You know, Max, I think I have a calling," Freidle confided.

"My office is a workshop. Project managers come in and out, construction workers pore over plans. That's what engineers do."

The wall where his portrait had hung had been sacrificed for blueprints pinned to every available space.

Norbert popped in. "Hi, Max; been over to the new concert hall?"

Brundibár! I jumped up and raced after Norbert, leaving Freidle in my wake.

Hans had announced a full rehearsal schedule. He had already orchestrated the music and was now making individual parts for the players. Sets were built, lights hung, and the cast given "sides" for their roles.

All the kids wanted to be in the show and everyone took part. There was crew and chorus, props and scenery, even a makeup team. *Brundibár* was the most anticipated event in Terezín. And there was to be a special performance for the International Red Cross. Hans was in high spirits, surrounded by his cast . . . make-believe was in full force. For a moment, fear and horror stopped, and I made myself believe that the hell-bound train had changed direction, that things had indeed been fixed, been transformed. We all wanted to believe that all of this—the assignment in which the whole camp was busily engaged—was good and real.

"Max! There you go again, forgetting your lines," Sophie said during rehearsal.

"You distract me."

I smiled and moved closer to her. Music had that heartening effect on me. She gave me a pop on the head with her script.

"Help! My true love is abusing me!"

She rolled her eyes and glanced over at Hans who was busy with some children.

"Please, Max, be professional, get serious!"

"I am, Sophie, I hate rejection," I said, straightening my top hat.

She leaned in and gave me a kiss. *Just one kiss is all I need for a lifetime,* I thought. I savored this sweet, exquisite, perfect moment.

Surveying the grounds with me, Freidle clearly had something on his mind. He finally commented, "The inspection should be documented."

"Why don't you make a film?"

The thought came easily to me—the whole place was a film set after all.

Freidle was startled and stared at me curiously. "A movie?"

"A documentary film."

"Could you help, Max?"

"No, but I bet Kurt Gerron can. Starred in *The Blue Angel.* Directed productions at Filmtek Berlin."

"Maybe he can do something for us. Ask him over to the office."

Gerron was in his barracks, and after I filled him in on the situation, we walked over to meet with Freidle.

The commandant offered Gerron tea as we sat on his newly slip-covered couch.

"Quite frankly, Mr. Gerron," Freidle said, leaning forward across his desk, "I want to know what is required to make a documentary film. Have you that kind of experience?"

"What do you want to accomplish?" Gerron asked, showing little interest.

I hoped Freidle could convince him.

"What do you want to say?"

"I want to make a film for everyone to see," Freidle said, "*A Day in the Life of Terezín.*"

"Is this an order or a request?" asked Gerron.

There was a moment of tension as Freidle paused. "A request, of course."

"In that case, you have my attention. Do you want to shoot in sixteen or thirty-five millimeters?"

"I don't know. What is the most efficient way?"

"Shooting sixteen millimeter is lighter and more portable. I need two cameras. Arriflex in Munich makes the best. Carl Zeiss in Berlin crafts the sharpest lenses. Sound effects, narration, and music can be dropped in during postproduction."

"If you can make me such a film, Herr Director," Freidle said, "I'll give you a medal."

"I'd rather have three meals a day, thank you very much," said Gerron, with bitter humor. "I'll need a crew—three men—to help with equipment, lights, and setups. I'll shoot and direct, but it's necessary to have two cameras, for different angles."

"We'll do it!" Freidle said, a smile expanding into a huge grin.

"Can I help, Commandant? It was my idea."

"Can you use Max?"

"Of course," Gerron said, with a wink of confidence. At last we heard his explosive laugh.

"This doesn't mean you're relieved of your duties at the post office, Max," Freidle said. "No dancing Busby numbers. No skipping classes with Mrs. Branka."

I gave my most sincere look. "Double duty. Overtime. No worries."

"I'll need lots of film," Gerron said to Freidle. "Fine grain for quality and high speed for shooting in poor light. Have the film processed in Prague. Luxe Labs are the best."

"We will make the arrangements, Director Gerron."

I met David at his *Vedem* office.

"You mean you're going to make a movie?"

"We've recruited Kurt Gerron."

"That's great, Max! He's not only a big star, but one of the most noted directors in Europe!—and, there'll be a documented history of the remaking of the place. I bet food, clothes, and medicine will surely be arriving soon."

I nodded my head in agreement.

Sophie beamed: "Amazing. You won't mind if I tag along. I want a close-up view."

"As long you won't be stepping in and out of the shots."

"Hard to resist. I'll do my best."

Frau Schmidt didn't waste any time ordering two sixteen-millimeter Arriflex cameras from Berlin and cans of hundred-foot rolls of film from a list Gerron provided.

"Black and white or color?" she asked.

"Color!" Gerron insisted.

Gerron explained that color stock was in short supply because Minister Goebbels, in charge of Berlin film production, was using thirty-five-millimeter stock for his propaganda productions; but sixteen millimeter was easier to get.

Frau Schmidt mumbled under her breath, "For God's sake, here we are becoming Village Hollywood."

The director had friends in Terezín who had worked in film production. Bernie Steine was the best cameraman in Germany before the war, much in demand thanks to his steady hand and a keen eye. Gerron told me that Steine "could feel light in the dark."

On the first day of shooting, I lugged all the equipment outside before the sun was in the sky.

"Best light is in the early morning and late afternoon," I said, nodding.

"Quite right; it has a softer quality. How do you know that, Max?" Gerron asked.

"Troller told me."

"You're a fast learner. You like film?"

"Everybody likes film."

"You're smart. There's nothing like making a picture."

Everyone on Gerron's team—Bernie, a two-hundred-pound gorilla named Herman, and I—wore black cotton sweaters and pants. We scouted the camp for locations, designing shots, preparing a script. Gerron was a perfectionist. He wouldn't make a shot unless it was exactly right, careful not to waste film. Every scene had to be set up from a storyboard, and Gerron held to a shooting schedule. He knew what he was doing.

When Sophie first saw us, she stifled a laugh.

"What's so funny?" I asked.

"Nothing, you appear very, um, professional. Like a team of cat burglars."

"For your information, Sophie Mahler, Hollywood sets the fashion."

I lifted my nose into the air and strolled away as her laugh followed me.

I learned a lot about directing from Gerron, who carefully framed scenes from various angles. "Always useful for cutaways when editing," he said. He wanted an establishing shot from the church so we climbed to the top for a view, past the gates to the hills beyond. Herman, the "gorilla," was so strong that he could have easily carried all the equipment and an overweight Gerron to the top landing. When we reached the top, out of breath, we were rewarded.

"Beautiful picture!" Gerron said.

"Breathtaking," David chimed in.

It was worth every step. Gerron framed a shot of a pink sunset over Terezín with the sun's last rays falling on the river.

The view made our world seem beautiful.

After a "wrap," the crew disbanded and grabbed what sleep they could before gathering once more at sunrise the following morning. Exterior shots followed Terezín's makeover program. As each project was completed, Gerron filmed the scene. He took the camera inside the hospital ward, where the set was already dressed with patients in clean linen and new hospital beds which had arrived a few days before. Gerron got the scene he wanted with panning shots of the wards.

Just as he set up an exterior shot, Sophie appeared wearing a fresh white apron.

"There you are, Mr. Hollywood," Sophie flirted. She smiled and took my hand in hers.

"I've been working, Sophie. I'm sorry."

"She's got star quality," Gerron said.

Sophie fluttered her eyes.

"I think everything is going to be all right," I said.

"I'm glad you didn't give up on Poppy."

"And don't give up on me."

"You are being slushy, Max Mueller."

"How're you doing without me at rehearsals?"

"Oh, don't be so smug. Just because you know the play

inside out, it might be helpful if you came over every so often, Mr. Leading Man."

"I know my lines, except I forget them when I'm distracted by you. Otherwise, I'm a natural."

"Oh, Mr. Confidence now!"

"I'll come over this evening. I want to hear you sing!"

"Anything else?"

I kissed her until Gerron said, "Cut."

"Would Miss Garbo and Mr. Gilbert like another take?" he asked.

"I should get back," Sophie said.

"Good luck!"

Gerron continued filming: residents reading in the library, strolling in the park, picking flowers, dining in the café; football games, children at school, a gardener mowing a lawn, ladies chatting on park benches, a group of men doing calisthenics; a dance recital, concerts, rehearsals. He filmed numerous takes to capture the right mood, at times on a tripod, but mostly handheld. He always carefully explained each setup.

David followed behind, writing down every detail.

During production, Gerron filmed from other perspectives, making sure the action matched in every take. He was doing what he loved most, directing films as a serious and dedicated professional. Each night, the film was sealed in canisters, secured in boxes, and shipped to Prague.

Freidle, resident film buff, was so pleased with the progress that he ordered up a director's megaphone for Gerron from a studio in Berlin.

"I thought you might like one, Herr Director," Freidle said to Gerron one afternoon while we were waiting in Freidle's office to hear reports from Luxe Film Laboratories. Gerron needed to make sure we had the right exposure and a work print for "rushes" to give us an idea of the day's shooting.

Gerron chuckled. "Don't you think my voice is big enough?"

Before we completed the first act of Siegfried Freidle's "For the First Time on the Big Screen with Cast of Thousands" production, I had memorized phrases from the shooting lexicon, like *reverse angle*, *atmosphere*, and *in the can*.

"Will you be filming *Brundibár*?" I asked. "It's cinematic."

"Just a few scenes," he said. "Freidle wants a clip of joyful children in the film." Gerron snorted. "*Joy* . . . right," he added under his breath.

The following afternoon, while shooting a *Brundibár* dress rehearsal, David quietly took me aside. "Do you think Gerron can make a shot, just both of you together?"

"Why not?"

I asked Gerron in the middle of filming.

"Cut! For you, Herr Director, anything."

Gerron had talked about overlapping dissolves to be done in the editing process, in what he called montage. In a shooting sequence, the scenes would convey an effect of one image blending into the next. I thought it would be fitting if I stayed in makeup and costume, with my hurdy-gurdy, and took my mark at center stage.

"Just a clip of me playing, and if you could zoom in close."

"Yes, Herr Director."

David smiled. The camera rolled. I turned the hurdy-gurdy, and he asked to be in the shot with me; to the camera, we gave a wink and an okay sign. It was a reminder to anyone who saw the film that we were not defeated. Because we hadn't been defeated, I thought. Not yet.

David gave a thumbs-up. "It's a wrap." He had mastered the slang.

VILLAGE HOLLYWOOD

Terezín's final touches were the new coach lampposts over the entrances, and then the camp's makeover was almost complete. Gerron filmed some cabaret events and concerts, and finished shooting.

The evening we wrapped, Freidle announced over the public-address system.

"This beautification comes with deepest appreciation for so much individual effort. You have contributed to the welfare of your fellows. In a few weeks, a delegation will be arriving from Switzerland. Thank you."

What he didn't say was that if anyone mentioned former conditions they would be punished. But we knew.

I was walking a tightrope between two worlds—heroes and cowards, life and death, absurdity and reality, who I was and who I wanted to be.

Workers came from Germany for the final polish. Poppy came with them. Trucks of fresh provisions filled the iceboxes in the camp's kitchen. Curiously, no adequate medicine was included in the shipment, only a few bottles of drugs desperately needed for infectious diseases, and a box of basic first-aid materials—aspirin, bandages, and gauze for minor cuts. This bothered me, and I told Poppy.

"You won't forget, Poppy?"

"I won't, Max. I'll take care of it."

Poppy refocused on everything he could do for the place, for me, for Sophie and David, and for Hans. A velvet act-curtain and seats had been lifted from the best theaters in occupied countries. Norbert painted canvases of musical instruments and flowers, and attached the panels to the walls on either side of the stage.

If the Great Viktor Mueller had an unlimited budget, he made sure he exceeded it. With the work completed and the camp refreshed, we were ready for the final dress rehearsal for *Brundibár.* Freidle entered as showman and commandant. "We must make sure of a great performance," he said.

I saw a bit of worry written across his face.

"Don't give it another thought," I reassured Freidle. "You're leading the team, and we're going to have a terrific show."

Sarah Markova was assigned to choreograph; she used the skills she'd learned at the Kirov. Hans could compose music but was hopeless at directing actors, moving them like furniture. It was a running joke—when he was out of range, he was called Mr. Moving Man.

"Care to move a chair, Mr. Krása? Where do you want the bench, Mr. Krása?" the children teased.

Sarah fixed Hans's staging and eased concerns.

During rehearsal, Sophie had trouble sustaining notes. Over and over she failed.

I pulled her aside during a break. “What’s wrong?”

She gave a wan smile. “I’ll be fine.”

“Sophie, what is it?”

“I’ll be okay.”

“Sophie?”

“It’s Mama,” Sophie finally explained, her facing crumbling. “She’s sick again.” She was being brave. “Max, you and Mama and David are all I have. I can’t afford to lose you. And I’m concerned about her. She cares more about her patients in the infirmary than herself.”

I wanted to reassure her and held her close. “Sophie, she’ll be fine. Poppy is bringing medicine.”

She nodded. “I know, I just . . .” She brightened for a moment, trying to find strength. “Her resistance *is* pretty strong.”

She ran back to the stage and carried on. *She’ll always carry on,* I thought.

A few days before the premiere I asked, “How do you think the show will go?”

“We can’t take anything for granted,” Hans replied, trying to project confidence. “We have to be the best we can be. I want the show for the Red Cross Committee to be exceptional, for all of us.”

“Max,” Hans added after a thoughtful pause. “You, the kids, are wonderful! You’ve made a difference.” He nodded and spoke more softly. “Remember that.”

At the first preview, we took our marks, the stage lights came on, we sang:

"Sound your trumpets,
Beat your drum.
We won a victory.
It's getting late,
And our fate,
We won a victory
Hand in hand
We love our land
To the very end
You have a friend,
We are your friends.
Wir haben einen Sieg errungen!"

The final curtain came down and the theater burst into applause. Freidle led the audience to their feet.

They demanded an encore and sang along with the cast.

Sophie's mother came backstage. Dr. Frankl had allowed her to attend. "You're all a pretty good tonic. I wanted to see but I mustn't overdo it. I love you both. I'm so proud of you, of all of you."

The little makeup she had kept hidden in her purse for special occasions now hid the many lines that had come with worry. Underneath all the fractured powder, I had always seen something else, a lovely and appealing face, and once again I understood why Sophie was so perfect in the world.

We watched her leave, her shawl wrapped tightly around her narrow shoulders.

"We've made her happy," I said, smiling broadly.

"It's really something," Sophie said. "When we march

victorious in the finale, the Jews celebrate a victory, the Germans think it is theirs."

"Amazing."

"Max, it's not so amazing," Sophie said. "We see what we want to see."

Rabbi Baeck had said many times, it was just a matter of perception.

Several hundred well-dressed residents assembled outside their barracks, lined up for inspection by Freidle and Frau Schmidt. Everything was perfect, except for one detail.

Pulling at Freidle's jacket, I reached up and whispered in his ear about something he was quite familiar with: "Shoes!"

Freidle glanced at his own, with their high military polish, and at the squads of residents in front of him. He turned to Frau Schmidt and repeated, "Shoes."

She scanned the rows of broken laces, dirty slippers, shoes without soles, evidence of how they'd all lived for so long, and sighed deeply, frowning at her oversight.

"Thank you, Max," she said. We went back to Freidle's office where he called Thomas Bata, a company who made shoes for the military. The ones he could requisition were from an army and navy warehouse.

"What do you mean you only have 44 EE wide?" he asked. "All sizes; top priority from Berlin. Do I have to call Major Mueller or the Führer? Be sure you include small sizes. There are children here!"

He put down the phone and smiled. Not a day had passed before trucks laden with shoes arrived. Most were black, some brown. Many were too big for the children, and they began walking in them, clumping and clopping, turning it into a game. Everyone was amused by the smaller kids walking around, one plop after another.

The camp was stepping out, compliments of the German infantry.

I'LL BE SEEING YOU

There was little left standing in the heart of London after the relentless bombing by Göring's Luftwaffe. Major buildings had been destroyed, St. Paul's Cathedral with its Christopher Wren cupola set flaming. After all the whistling, falling bombs, a pause, then an explosion, air raid shelters crowded to capacity. Londoners had been terrified night after night, wondering if their homes would be there after the raids. Wondering if they would survive. Even though Churchill had a remarkable breakthrough with radar as an early warning detection system, and the RAF fought courageously, protecting British skies, they suffered heavy losses, the deaths becoming statistics with countless individual tragedies. Each evening was filled with criss-crossing searchlight beams that were interrupted by platoons of giant, high-flying helium balloons with suspended steel cables dropping downward to intercept and tangle enemy aircraft. London had braved it out and still sang songs like "I'll Be Seeing You," "The White Cliffs of Dover," and "When the Lights Go on Again (All Over the World)." Vera Lynn sang Hits of the Blitz, filling the airwaves that fed into every home across the nation. The Battle of Britain had been fought and won, but the war in the skies raged on.

Anna had worked herself to a state of exhaustion by

candlelight, ignoring the blaring sirens. At dinner with Madeline, her mood was as dark as the blackened windows of every flat and house across the city, hiding the light from the home fires that might be detected by the enemy.

"The war is so bleak, Nana. The Germans look set to destroy all of us. What do the planets predict now?" Anna was being caustic.

"We'll come through, Anna, we always have. We did in the first World War, and we will again."

Anna thought that their spirit did not keep Jews from being murdered. Hans could have come home with her to London!

Madeline wasn't at all surprised by Anna's feelings. "You are thinking about your man, and the boy."

"Of course, Nana. It's hard not to."

"Hope, faith, stars, it's all nonsense. Words and ideas don't replace people. If they only had a place to go, to return to, a homeland, Palestine."

"I suspect the Germans would bomb that too."

"Weren't you in Palestine once?"

"I was there a few years back, and I met Raoul Wallenberg when he partnered with a bank in Haifa."

"What's he like?"

"I knew you were getting to that."

"How did you know?"

"In the stars, my dear, it's all in the stars. And sometimes in more earthly ways. He's a very good man. Just like his father."

"You know the family, then."

"Yes, I knew Oscar. Your grandfather and the Wallenbergs formed the Scandinavian Trust, which turned out to be a banking enterprise that was indeed successful. I suppose you want to meet him?"

Raoul Wallenberg was an essential contact with the Resistance and was known to be carrying out missions saving Jews, but the information she had was classified. "Yes, I'd like to meet him."

"Why?"

"Nana, I think he can be helpful in many ways, and you know the family."

"Winston knows them all very well."

"I might have to go outside diplomatic protocol on this."

"I know what you are thinking."

"I shouldn't discuss it."

Anna had received word of an inspection by the International Red Cross. She had to go and see for herself. There were other reasons to go of course. There could be a way that she could become part of the delegation. Every report she had received, every word she had written had softened her feelings, but they had also hardened her determination. Had she been no more than a bystander, an observer? Journalists were supposed to make a difference. They were not supposed to get involved, just report the news objectively. But she was well beyond that now. Nothing would stop her from what she was destined to do and who she was destined to be. It was in the stars.

Churchill had indeed roared back into greater power. His residence was still in a bunker, a suite of bomb-proof Cabinet War Rooms under Whitehall, where he spent most of his time during the Blitz and the devastation it wrought upon his city. Sitting in a modest room, adjacent to the oversized map in the planning operations area, Anna made her appeal.

"I'm part Danish; I could easily fit in as a member of the team. And think how useful what I might report firsthand could be. I'll be on the front lines of the Resistance."

"I can't stop you now, Anna. Even if I wanted to."

"It's more than a case of not stopping me—it's taking my assignment to a new level. I need your help, Mr. Prime Minster."

"You're serious, and there's merit to the plan, but do I suspect something more, a personal matter?"

"I think everything is personal for all of us now, isn't it?"

She didn't want to go into detail about her feelings, especially with Churchill.

He pondered for a while and then spoke slowly, but with assurance: "I think Wallenberg can fix it."

This was exactly what Anna was aiming for.

"He's part of my team, very active in saving Danish Jews, and he has close contacts with the Danish Red Cross." Churchill continued, "It is hard, perhaps impossible to imagine the atrocities in the killing fields, but I am getting reports every day. And now this sorry bastard wants to present some mendacious compensation for his brutality by promoting his model concentration camp to the world? Yes, we need to do whatever it takes. You must go, with my blessing and the country's faith in our cause."

STOCKHOLM

With Sweden declaring neutrality, it had become a refuge for many Norwegian and Danish Jews. Instrumental and influential, the House of Wallenberg had become a unique if secretive institution, establishing a tradition of humanitarian good deeds. They were European bankers, and Raoul Wallenberg, who had studied in the United States to be an architect and held diplomatic posts around the world, championed a very personal cause of saving Jews. He was someone Anna could turn to.

She secured passage on a fishing vessel leaving from the Shetland Isles, crossing the heavily patrolled waters to Gothenburg, and traveling across the country to Stockholm, where she met with Wallenberg. She had the credentials he respected, her documents bearing the clear imprimatur of her friend and colleague the prime minister. Anna didn't have to fully explain her mission. Raoul Wallenberg understood at once and agreed to intervene with the Danish Red Cross.

"You've come a long way, and I'd ask how your voyage was, but I know your trip may have been uneasy over the North Sea," he said, welcoming Anna to Drottningholm, the ancestral home of the Swedish royal family. They met in the small theater, which had been constructed in the seventeenth century and was now a well-appointed guesthouse on magnificent grounds. The king had gifted him an office there.

Anna liked him immediately. He had stood with noted physicist Niels Bohr to save over seven thousand Norwegian and Danish Jews from being deported. Wallenberg, part of the Resistance, had personally financed their safe entry into Sweden.

He had the kindest brown eyes she'd ever seen.

"I need to get to Terezín," she confided. "Can you help?"

The warm, confident smile was all the answer she needed.

A POTEMKIN VILLAGE

On June 23, 1944, Major Viktor Mueller arrived at Terezín along with the Red Cross delegation and strode into the post office in full dress. I glimpsed Freidle behind him, ushering in a group of representatives.

When Poppy saw me, he beamed and, as he always did, ruffled my hair. "Come, Max," said Poppy. "Join us."

"What you will see here is a normal provincial village," Freidle announced to his guests. The representatives heading the delegation were Frants Hvass, of the Danish Foreign Office Political Section; Dr. Juel-Henningsen, a director from the Department of Health; Maurice Rossel, head and director-general of the International Red Cross; his deputy, a modest and unassuming observer named Dunant; and a woman representing the Danish Ministry.

Much to my amazement, among the delegation was Anna. But I shouldn't have been surprised. Isn't that what angels do, just appear? Before I could run up to her, she discreetly put a finger to her lips. I could hardly contain myself, but knew it was best to keep quiet. She was introduced as Anna Simonsen. She had not changed at all, wearing a crisp, white ruffled blouse, as beautiful as I remembered her. Poppy gave me a wink.

The visitors, eighteen in all, set out to see for themselves what Terezín was all about. Another limousine was added, moving along a predetermined route. The cars stopped by the park and at the shopping street, the group continued on foot. They visited the bank—Terezín now had its own banknotes with a picture of Moses engraved upon the currency.

It was a clear day, perfect for sightseeing, the landscape interrupted only by signs reading, TO THE SCHOOL, TO THE CAFÉ, TO THE THEATER, TO THE BATHS. The newly constructed bandstand had a uniformed brass ensemble softly playing German army marching songs. The leader turned and bowed. Leading the inspection, Viktor Mueller nodded to Anna. "Our camp band. They play very well."

Women in clean coveralls with rakes over their shoulders, looking as if they had stepped out of a poster, marched past on cue. Then they went to the farm that had been cultivated just outside the village; it had taken a few months for the freshly arranged "harvest" of lettuce, tomatoes, and cucumbers to ripen. Viktor listened as Freidle remarked, "We grow most of our own vegetables here." To produce enough vegetables to feed the village population would have taken miles of cultivated fields, but it appeared reasonable enough.

The smell of freshly baked pumpernickel invited the delegation to meet a line of cheery bakers in white hats and gloves, dispensing slices from loaves just out of the oven. Hvass and Juel-Henningsen, concerned about their fellow Danes among the residents, dropped into their refurbished quarters, bringing greetings from King Christian and the bishop of Copenhagen, spending enough time with them to observe their well-being so they could report back to church and state.

The group walked past chess players studiously plotting their next moves. In a converted park square, spectators joined soccer fans and cheered as a goal was scored. Hearing the voices rehearsing Verdi's *Requiem,* for which world-famous Raphael Schächter had recruited soloists and a fifty-member choir, they stopped and listened to the last refrain, a rising crescendo of "Libera Me," which was well understood. Viktor Mueller walked with the guests through the remodeled living quarters facing replanted gardens, and a newly supplied pharmacy. I wondered if the delegation was buying any of it.

When the delegation entered the post office, Freidle introduced me. "This is the son of Major Mueller with us, whom I am pleased to care for while the major serves the Fatherland." They murmured to themselves about meeting the son of a celebrity. A precursor of favorable conditions, if he was living in Terezín.

I apologized to the group, "I'm afraid I've not received mail for any of you this afternoon. The postal truck has been detained because of a small battle at the border. The afternoon delivery truck was obliged to take a detour, but, ladies and gentlemen, if you leave me a forwarding address, I'll make sure you receive your mail on time."

That brought a tentative laugh from the guests and from Poppy.

We walked through the camp, following Freidle.

At the hospital, a nurse, trusting a kind-looking woman in the delegation, pressed a folded piece of paper into Anna's hand: *Was Sie sehen hier ist nicht wahr. Bitte helfen Sie uns. What you see here is not true. Please help us.* She hid the paper in her pocket and broke away from the guests.

Leaving the delegation with Poppy, Anna carefully and finally reached the man she had traveled so far to see. When she saw Hans, she was deeply moved. For years, she had been keeping her spirit and hope alive for the man she had come to care about so deeply. He was the same, a little thinner, giving Anna a smile of smiles.

"For some reason, I thought you might come," Hans said gracefully, folding Anna into his embrace.

Every part of her soul reached out to Hans. "Oh, Hans," was all she could say before nearly collapsing. She found what little composure she could gather. "Well, I came to Prague, and now Terezín. I guess I'm starstruck. And how could I miss *Brundibár*?"

Hans sat at the piano, and played a few bars in a ragtime tempo. It was "Anna's Song."

"Apologies for the sentimentality."

"You are incurable!"

"Now, why would you think that?"

"I've got to get you out of here."

"Not so easy these days. When does the next train leave for London?"

"Hans, stop. I can't stand it."

"Anna, I'm no patriot, nor am I a partisan. The war will be over, and I'll be coming to you."

"Is that a promise?"

"A most emphatic yes."

"I don't believe you. This time, I'm not leaving you here."

"Headline: BRITISH WOMAN DETAINED IN NAZI SPA! I don't think so, Anna. All the king's men and Humpty Dumpty himself can't put us together again just now."

"I'm staying."

"Anna, the Nazis would hang you in a minute. Do your work, Anna, and if I know you, I suspect you are doing a lot to end this madness. You are reaching for a better world."

"What makes you think that?"

"You wouldn't be here if you weren't."

"I'll carry on, Hans. I promise. I must see this war end before I lose everything I love. I promise to do all I can."

At Himmler House, Freidle arranged a lavish dinner, a well-dressed table, plenty of fresh flowers for the banquet, and a squadron of waiters behind each chair. Noticeably absent was the ominous presence of the SS. I was seated next to Anna. She wanted to know all about me, how I was, and about the opera, and I wanted to know how Hans had seemed to her. We talked between the lines, so to speak, because it was essential that we appear not to know each other. It was a night of pretending—and a night that I would remember forever.

"I've borrowed the chef from the kitchens at the camp," Freidle casually mentioned to the guests, folding his napkin, "Albrecht Steiner, formally of the Adlon." Steiner was dressed in dapper white, holding a silver-plated ladle, as if he had just tasted soup on his stove. "He has brought some of his best recipes with him. Terezín is lucky to have him as chef de cuisine. Ladies and gentlemen, Albrecht Steiner." I had never seen Albrecht Steiner before in my life. Frau Schmidt was not particularly pleased either and murmured that Freidle must have found him at central casting. "This is extraordinary," Frau Schmidt whispered under her breath.

"Sautéed sole, not from Dover but from Calais." Steiner's remark made them all chuckle. "Fresh asparagus from the farm and roasted potatoes," which delighted the Swiss director sitting stiffly in his pin-striped suit. "For dessert, a soufflé made from Lindt & Sprüngli Swiss chocolate." It was an over-the-top and outrageous menu. Suddenly I didn't care if Steiner was an imposter or not; it sounded like a pretty good meal. In fact, it was a culinary miracle; the dinner was delicious, far more palatable than the revolting swill we had been fed much of the time. After a round of applause, Chef Steiner, still wearing his white hat and apron, went back to the kitchen. One guest suggested the food was probably better in Terezín than in Berlin or Prague.

Frau Schmidt was in awe. The provisions had arrived directly from Berlin.

I excused myself as the banquet was finishing, and ten minutes later, I was in costume. The entire delegation soon followed to see a performance of *Brundibár*.

At the side of the stage, I whispered to Sophie, "I'm not exactly sure what's going on. It's either a very good thing indeed or . . ."

The houselights started to blink for the audience to be seated.

She gave me a quick hug. "I've got to warm up. See you onstage. Break a leg!"

Just before the overture began, I had the usual butterflies but reassured myself that this was normal. No wonder I was nervous, not least because I felt that this might be the most important performance of my life. The words I would sing had such resonance, such potent meaning, and the evening could be a turning point in the lives of everyone there. It was a symbol of how things might be from now on. Just as I began the breathing exercises that Poppy had taught me to control my nerves, I felt a tap on my right shoulder. I turned and Fritz was staring at me. He was breathless, had a look of terror in his eyes, and was clutching the dreaded red packet under his arm.

"Max, p-please, I must s-speak to you." He was stammering

and sweating. "I just got word, I mean . . . I know that . . . there's an order."

A train whistle blew, and he turned white.

"Fritz, what's wrong?"

I had never seen him so obviously distressed.

"As soon as the performance ends, there'll be a train to transport the cast to Auschwitz."

"They can't. They wouldn't dare. An entire delegation is here, and Anna. Who told you?"

Fritz pointed to the red packet. "It hasn't been delivered, you need to speak to the major."

I felt that everything had suddenly changed. Had we really been lured into a trap? Had we simply given Terezín a fleeting moment of hope and then, afterward . . .?

Fritz slipped away.

Poppy said he wouldn't allow transports ever again. Never. I had to believe him.

Sophie stood in the wings, and just before curtain, the kids went out front to distribute programs. They had cut out yellow paper stars and were pinning them on each member of the delegation sitting in the first row.

The cast took their places onstage before the curtain rose. "Are you okay?"

I had to be. I had no choice.

"Take a look," Sophie urged. I peeked at the audience from the wings and saw the entire delegation and a row of yellow stars.

The house was full, although Edith was absent. Dr. Frankl thought it would be best for her to rest. Ava was in the front row with Fritz, whose jacket hid the fateful packet. He gave me an okay sign, as if to say, *Safe . . . at least for the moment*, and I heaved a sigh of relief—a temporary respite. I knew I had to do something, I had to speak to Poppy. But first I had to perform.

I'm okay, I said to myself, over and over again. *I'm . . .*

I sighed. "Just so many important people out there."

Sophie and I locked arms, and she smiled: "You've done this before."

I nodded. "Let's knock 'em out, Sophie! Let's show them exactly what we can do."

She squeezed my hand.

The overture began.

Once you heard a Krása melody, it hummed inside you for a long, long time. It helped me remember, in an instant, that I would get through this. I knew what I was doing and I had a powerful feeling that I belonged there at that moment. I was ready. We were all ready. We had come a long way to tell this story.

The performance went like a dream, everyone there feeding off a collective confidence that we understood what we were doing and all of us fully recognizing the importance of the occasion. It was an evening freighted with such significance for everyone on the stage and off. Between scenes, the kids scuttled off to change costumes, and were back on their marks ready to reach their audience. The finale inspired a standing ovation.

The horror of impending doom stunned me when a line of Czech guards presented flowers to Sophie and Hans. I joined Sophie with the cast center-stage, and we held hands during the curtain call. If only for this one shining moment, we had each other. Then she left for the infirmary.

A train whistle blew again, louder, and I heard a steam engine chugging closer. I had to get to Poppy. He had to know that at any moment a truck would back up and take us away. At the conductor's podium, Hans had turned over his slender baton to the Great Viktor Mueller. I couldn't reach him. For one last time, one last encore, the Great Viktor Mueller, with a shaking hand at his side, conducted the ensemble in a song from the production. For Poppy and Hans, it was an overture to a new beginning. I dared not interrupt. I made my way over to him when the applause subsided.

Just when I was about to grab Poppy, I felt a hand clap me on the back. "We did it, Max!" said Freidle.

I had to get Poppy alone.

"Wonderful show, indeed," he said to Poppy.

David ran toward me, his scarf trailing behind him.

Taking me aside, and out of breath, he said urgently, "Fritz gave me the packet. We can't keep this quiet any longer. Everyone needs to know." He looked at me. "You know what this means, Max. You know we have all been sentenced to die." He shook me hard.

"I know. We must tell Poppy!" Seeing him, we rushed him to a spot near a lighting booth, motioning Anna to join us too.

"I left twenty boxes of medicine at the infirmary," Poppy whispered.

"Yes, Poppy. It means a lot to Sophie, to everyone."

I shoved the packet into his hands. "Read this."

Poppy scanned the documents with growing fury.

"It won't happen, Max. I told you, not on my watch. Count on it! You too, David. That train will leave empty. I'll take care of this now."

"But, Poppy, it will come back, you can't believe them."

"No transports, Max! Everything we've done will be in vain. I have a promise from Berlin. We have powerful people here, reporting to the world's press and diplomats."

David quietly shook his head. He needed proof.

"Walk with me over to Himmler House," Poppy said.

Anna was beside me. "I'm sorry I didn't have a chance to meet Sophie. Please congratulate her for me, and you, too, Max. And give my love to Hans."

"But . . ."

"Don't worry, Max. Trust Poppy. You must. I must get back to the delegation. I hate to go."

It was a bittersweet moment. It was heartbreaking.

Poppy wasted no time. We took his car instead of walking. "Wait here, Max." He got out and rushed into headquarters. In a few minutes, he returned, calmer. "I've spoken to Berlin."

Holding me close, he said, "I love you, Max. Don't worry. I wouldn't leave if I didn't know you were okay, son. Just hold on for a little longer. As soon as I return, I'll come for you. You have my word."

"A few weeks?"

My heart was about to beat its way out of my chest. I lost confidence and my fear returned. "No! We can't wait a few weeks! I don't feel safe here anymore, Poppy. Please . . . don't leave me!" I clutched Poppy's jacket and whispered, "I worry about the camps and the gas and—"

"Max, easy now," Poppy said glancing over his shoulder. "I need a few weeks. Wait for me."

"And Sophie? David? Hans?"

David stared at him. "Where are you going, Poppy?"

It was the first time he had ever referred to my father as Poppy.

"I have to get to Berlin."

"Why?"

"I have an agreement that must be kept. I'm coming back for the whole lot of you. We're going home. I'll bring a large car."

"I can't be this brave," I said. "I'm not the Great Viktor Mueller. I'm just a kid."

"You're a young man," Poppy said. "You're a great young man."

I was having trouble catching my breath. I heard a train departing in the distance, releasing bellowing steam.

Poppy took me in his arms again. "You are everything to

me, Max," he said, smoothing my hair. "Your mother would be proud of you."

"Will Anna be all right?"

"She's with the group. She had to leave. She'll be fine."

He waved goodbye.

David buried his head in his hands. I wept.

That night Huck Finn was waiting for me. I read page after page; the book was coming to a close. Deep down I was upset about a scam that I had been part of, helping make Terezín what it was not, what it had never been.

> It don't make no difference how foolish it is, it's the *right* way—and it's the regular way. And there ain't no *other* way, that ever I heard of, and I've read all the books that gives any information about these things.

After the Red Cross visit, Freidle rewarded everyone for their cooperation, granting a holiday from work, and the camp had a new vibrancy.

Gardens were tended, comfortable beds remained in the barracks, weekly band concerts were held in the park pavilion, food and medicine were in better supply, and the stage lighting and theatrical equipment stayed in place for future productions. For a while we allowed ourselves to think that the war was almost over.

Karel Švenk staged a new sketch about the Red Cross visit. As the settings of each scene changed, the same furniture was dragged in again and again, satirizing the previous week's grand scale deception. The nightly curfew was extended until nine o'clock, and the camp's cultural life flourished.

It didn't last.

AN ASSAULT

Visiting David beyond curfew was always a risk. I sat at a table by the window and was distracted by some commotion in the distance. I peered out, taking care not to be seen. My eyes scanned the scene, much of which was bathed in darkness, save for an inquisitive spotlight, its beam sweeping slowly back and forth. After a few seconds, the light settled on a bizarre tableau beside a neighboring barracks perhaps fifty meters away. Two uniformed men were holding a civilian, his head bowed, against the barracks wall, while a third, whom, even at this distance, I identified as the overcoat man, was swinging a heavy wrench repeatedly against the man's hands, first one and then the other, again and again, each sickening thud accompanied by a howl of pain. I cried out: "David, quick, come!"

Seconds later, David was at my side. I whispered, "Look over there," but as we turned to look out of the window, all was dark again.

David said, "What am I supposed to be looking at?"

"Well, listen then, over there." I nodded toward the barracks. "A man was being attacked."

Opening the window a crack, we could hear muffled but unmistakable whimpering sounds. Nothing else.

I turned to David. "We have to help him somehow. That poor man was being attacked by . . ."

I ducked instinctively as the beam from a torch flashed through the window, passing over David's face.

The familiar voice of one of the more sympathetic night guards barked: "That you, Grunewald? You know the rules. Window shut, blackout blinds down. Go to bed now."

"Of course, sir," David called out. "Right away."

We talked long into the night, wondering what we could do, how we could possibly cover the story in *Vedem*? It would be suicide to write about it. But how could we not?

As early as I could the following morning, I set off to speak to Hans, to seek his advice. I knocked quietly but urgently on the door and was shocked to see it opened by Sophie. She looked exhausted and scared. "Max, come in quickly."

I was horrified by the sight that confronted me. Hans was slumped in a chair, his hands heavily bandaged. He was struggling to conceal the pain he was obviously in, and he barely managed a weak smile. Sophie said, "I've done what I can, cleaned and bandaged them, but it's just not enough. We have no morphine."

I fought back tears: "I . . . I saw what happened, that man in the overcoat and his thugs. They did this to you. Why, would they . . . why would anyone . . .?"

Hans didn't shift his gaze from mine. "Yes, well, it's no big surprise. There's nothing that would shock me anymore, Max. I wish that I could say this in a different way, but I can't. Reasons? Why worry about reasons when being Jewish is crime enough to these people? As it happened, the reason they found was that they wanted me to perform at Himmler House. They asked, then they commanded, and finally they threatened. In a way, I suppose it would have been easy just to say yes, except it wasn't. It was impossible. I can't just give them the one thing that they haven't taken from me already and pretend that it doesn't matter, that it's the smart or expedient thing to do. If they take our music, then we are giving them everything, our souls, whatever we have left of our dignity, our hope. You know, Max, I've heard it said that to lose dignity is to lose a great deal, but to lose hope is to lose everything. I simply can't give that away. I said no, and . . . here I am."

The three of us remained silent for some time. At last, I asked, barely above a whisper, "So, what do we do now?"

Hans reflected for a while, staring out of the window, and then turned back to me. "We do what we can. We sleep, we wake up, we eat, and we drink, we put one foot in front of the other, we look out for and after one another. We survive."

A BATHHOUSE FOR THE MAJOR

I sized Major Karl Rahm up.

He parted his hair with the few remaining greasy strands on his scalp reaching from ear to ear.

"Major Rahm," Freidle said with a nod, greeting the man who had just arrived.

Artless and instantly contemptible, Rahm carried a tattered brown briefcase, a portfolio fitted with two matching straps, and when the brass buckles opened, they released an accordion file. There were photographs of his wife, Dorothea, whom he called Der Dot, and he thought he was clever when he referred to his three obese daughters as Ein, Zwei, and Drei.

He blew his nose without a tissue, wiping the residue on his sleeve.

Before Rahm's arrival, Freidle had confided to me that the SS thought he'd been too easy in terms of bending rules. Rahm and the SS were now fully in charge of the camp.

"I've briefed the major about your privileges, Max. Perhaps an article in *Vedem* would be a cordial welcome."

The last thing I wanted to do was be cordial to any of them, but I had to function in this world, to remain in the background, and not be too conspicuous.

"What is this *Vedem*?" Rahm asked, raising an eyebrow, making a dismissive gesture.

"We have a paper here, Major, with news and a diary of events," Freidle answered before I could reply.

"I like taking a sauna, a very hot one. It refreshes me," he commanded with a trenchant grin.

Then, stumbling for the right word, he drummed his fingertips onto the table. "Cleanses me, yes, helps me think. After all, I'm just an insignificant German officer, and aren't we supposed to have a spa here? That's what I've read," he added with a sarcastic sneer.

"Of course, Major," Freidle replied. "We'll see what we can do."

"See that you do."

"Max, please bring Troller to my office."

Finding Norbert, I warned him about the major's request.

Norbert shook his head. "This could be a bit of a challenge."

Back at the office, Rahm sized Norbert up.

"I hear you can build things, Troller. That's all I need from you, so don't think you'll be getting any special treatment."

Norbert nodded. "Of course, Major. I am here to assist you."

Rahm poured on the oil. "Yes, Himmler House is only equipped with showers, but I would love to have a bath. Do you think you could make one of Finnish cedar?"

"Major, it will be difficult to construct one inside," Norbert said. "It would be better to build a bathhouse in the enclosed garden next to the building."

Rahm placed his meaty hands together. "Yes, that's what I'd like. Build me a bathhouse. How long will it take?"

"If I have my crew, we can build it in a week or so. But I'll need two-hundred-thirty-volt, fifty-cycle wiring for the gas heater."

"The specifics mean nothing to me. Make it happen, Freidle."

Freidle nodded, but from the expression on his face, it was obvious that the commandant didn't like Rahm any more than I did.

Frau Schmidt ordered the necessary supplies from Berlin, and a shipment of special cedar was sent from Oslo. Norbert was too smart, too professional to let his resentment inconvenience him. He was a consummate pragmatist in such dealings, but in his work he was a perfectionist. He designed a wooden cabin with a sauna, shower, and a large Roman bathtub on a platform, and—adding the Troller touch—he trimmed the bathhouse with fancy gingerbread molding.

Staring at the completed structure, Frau Schmidt commented with a sharp bite of disdain, "Norbert should install a Bavarian cuckoo clock."

Troller could build anything, and even Rahm had to admit that it was an exceptionally well-crafted structure. It even had a flower box at the window. It was finished off with fresh towels and a bathrobe monogrammed with an *R,* which had been sewn by one of the camp seamstresses.

There was a special opening to show off his bathhouse. I invited Sophie and David along. Surely the event would make news for *Vedem.* We had to present a front, a veneer of respect for these people.

"Perhaps Rahm can invite his colleagues to take a 'public bath,'" David said. "Mustn't include any photos of Rahm naked though, Max. Life is already too full of horrors." He gave a short laugh.

"That would be something to see," Sophie added.

Every day thereafter, at exactly four o'clock, following a regimented schedule, Rahm took his bath and sauna.

A few weeks later, Freidle handed me a package from Poppy. He'd included a pair of sturdy shoes, a new wool blazer, a few pairs of thick socks, and other odds and ends.

"Be glad you have me in your corner, Max," said Freidle. "Rahm would've confiscated everything."

"Thank you, Major," I said, and in my room, I tried on the specially made shoes, one with a built-up sole. As I slipped my right foot into it, expecting a comfortable fit, I felt something odd under the insole. Removing the shoe, I examined the offending area. After feeling around for a moment, I managed to peel back the insole to reveal a folded, single page of newspaper. A newspaper column! My special shoe had come in handy. *Thank you, Poppy.*

I locked the door, sat down on my bed, smoothed out the piece of paper, and began to read.

THE OBSERVER

July 1, 1944

A POTEMKIN VILLAGE

To quash rumors about the killing centers, the Nazis permitted an International Red Cross visit to Terezín, the model concentration camp, a few weeks ago.

According to *The Observer*'s underground reports, the Nazis launched a *stadverschoenerung,* a stunning theatrical production, but a failure by any ethical standard. It became a Potemkin village, much like the fake settlements that were specially constructed at the direction of Russian minister Grigory Potemkin to deceive Empress Catherine II during her visit to Crimea in 1787.

This week in Geneva, Dr. Maurice Rossel, head of the International Red Cross, issued his report: "Living conditions are a little crowded, but the food is terrific." He concluded, "After our inspection and tour of Terezín, we report an extraordinarily high standard of care, outstanding medical facilities attended by European doctors in residence, and that the number of Jews sent to labor camps is exaggerated."

Rossel and his delegation did not know that the men playing chess studiously in the park had never played chess in their lives or that the patients in the hospital were under clean white sheets that had just arrived a few weeks before. They didn't know that the pharmacy rarely dispensed medicine or that the school marked CLOSED FOR SUMMER VACATION had never been a real school. And they certainly did not know that sentries had preceded their every step giving signals, so that the young women with rakes over their shoulders would be marching past the visitors, or that the finale of the Verdi *Requiem* would be sung on cue just at the right time.

The only genuine thing the delegates were treated to was a children's opera by Hans Krása. It was as brilliant as any performance in the West End.

A fifteen-page document, *Hitler's Gift to the Jews,* along with a documentary by noted director Kurt Gerron, edited by Leni Riefenstahl, are works

> of propaganda whose production values are matched only by the Nazis' Nuremberg rallies.
>
> Director Rossel must be the most misinformed man in Europe today, or the most near-sighted.

I crumpled up the article. A strike of a match and nothing remained.

Terezín returned to miserable conditions, and I needed to reach Poppy. I appealed to Frau Schmidt: "Can you get a letter to Poppy for me?"

"I'll try. Leave it to me."

Rahm wasted no time enforcing his authority. Less than a month after the Red Cross visit, the transports resumed.

As part of the regimen, he ordered my classes over, and instructed Frau Schmidt to escort me to and from the camp each time I went in.

"I wouldn't want anything to happen to my little German boy," he said, sneering at me.

In the meantime, what to do?

A PERFECT NEW ALLIANCE

"It has been a long time. I haven't seen you since we lost Heydrich. Word has it you were very close to Reinhard," Goebbels casually remarked as Viktor arrived at his Berlin offices in the Chancellery. "We must always remember his contribution. Now more than ever."

"He was my friend, of course, a great friend, not only to me, but also to the Reich."

"You must continue your work carrying Germany's message to our occupied countries."

"You made a promise, to me, General. The word of the Führer is a bond. No more transports."

"You have my word, Viktor. You have my assurance. We're slowing the operation down. We only need workers in the east."

"If you can't stop the transports, you'll lose me."

"Is that an order, Viktor?"

"No, that would be presumptuous, but it is a promise, and I am a man of my word. I have a new plan to present to the Führer. It's very secret, but you'll be pleased."

Viktor was confident. He knew he could get to Hitler. He had called him from Terezín.

"The Thingplatz program and the concerts with the Berlin Philharmonic have been very effective," Goebbels said. "You and the orchestra will be welcomed in Budapest; you and Furtwängler are necessary to the cause. An evening of Hungarian rhapsodies for the audience will be much appreciated."

Hungary. Wallenberg was there.

"You know, I have created little music productions of my own, Major Mueller."

"What would that be?"

"We all very much love music, and my little groups have been so nicely received at Mauthausen that we will do the same at Auschwitz-Birkenau. When the workers arrive on the transports, there will be quartets playing soothing music, to put them at ease. I've selected Mendelssohn of course, to welcome them."

Viktor said nothing but stared across at Goebbels and wondered if the contempt he felt for this man in every fiber of his being was evident on his face.

Since 1938, Hungarian politics and foreign policy had become increasingly pro-Nazi and pro-German. Most Jews were protected from the Holocaust in the first few years, but after the beginning of the German Occupation, few Jews could escape, and thousands were shot by mobile Nazi killing squads. Viktor's orchestra included some fine musicians from Hungary, and several still had family in Budapest. Eichmann went to Hungary to oversee the large-scale deportation to Auschwitz-Birkenau, which offended all that Viktor stood for. Pink Tulip had a Hungarian Jew in its ranks who had, along with Raoul Wallenberg, set up the Central European Trading Company, allowing Wallenberg frequent visits to Budapest. Churchill had authorized a rescue program with the American War Refugee Board, and Wallenberg needed help to save Hungarian Jews from being transported to Auschwitz.

For Goebbels, low public morale was a serious problem; the German High Command needed to Germanize their newly acquired lands.

Viktor Mueller and Wilhelm Furtwängler had been booked at Hotel Kulturinnov in Budapest's Old Town by the Reich. When Viktor and Wallenberg finally met, they realized they were much the same in sentiment and character. Wallenberg was tall and fair. Viktor much the same. They shared a certain panache, some inexpressible charisma, a theatrical flair.

"You deserve a medal," Wallenberg said as he embraced Viktor.

"You flatter me, and you're the one who deserves a chest full of ribbons," Viktor replied. "Pierre has told me much about your work: banker, Resistance fighter, a man of countless good deeds. I simply see what mischief I can make when not waving my arms around in front of an orchestra."

With Wallenberg, Viktor saw that he had met another consummate performer, the soft-spoken aristocrat who could transform himself from a gently insistent diplomat in one moment into a belligerent freedom fighter the next.

At the end of their first, brief encounter Wallenberg grinned at his newly discovered comrade. "Let's get to work and see how much havoc we can create."

Wallenberg was the kind of man that commanded respect, the kind of man Viktor loved. The Nazis dared not violate his orders. He was sophisticated, self-assured, well-traveled, fluent in German and Russian. He had studied in America, and once held a post at the Dutch bank in Haifa. In Palestine he'd met Jews who had fled Germany, and their stories about Nazi persecution affected him immeasurably. Both he and Viktor knew about the Nazi death camps, and together they moved ahead with full force. The Germans had already deported more than four hundred thousand Jewish men, women, and children from Budapest. While visiting Eichmann's vacated home, Viktor wondered how Wallenberg had done so much damage with a staff of only thirteen men. But then he had help from a notorious group of Hungarian militants called the Arrow Cross who were known for accepting bribes and for their willingness to change sides whenever necessary.

Against the advice of his colleagues and diplomats in the Swedish Legation, Raoul Wallenberg didn't use traditional diplomacy. With Viktor's gift for creativity, they applied bribery and blackmail effectively.

"We'll need safe houses, Viktor. I've already rented buildings in the name of the Swedish Red Cross, and if we can just save a few lives, it will be worth it."

Viktor found a shop that made signs, and he had official ones painted reading SWEDISH LIBRARY and SWEDISH RESEARCH INSTITUTE, and placed them on their doors. Admiring his work, Wallenberg patted him on the shoulder. "A very nice touch, Viktor." The major felt better than he had in long time. Even though at risk, he was finally doing work that yielded measurable results, results that could be seen.

Wallenberg had gotten a message from his Arrow Cross (now joined with the Hungarian secret police, many of whom were on his payroll) that five hundred Budapest Jews were scheduled for transport by train from Keleti Pályaudvar to Germany in just a few days.

"Why don't we issue them passports?" Viktor suggested. "Swedish passports, Swedish papers."

"Why not indeed? We have an international publishing

house in Budapest, a family interest. Atelier Atlantik, maybe you have heard of it."

Fully aware that their respective bureaucracies had a weakness for symbolism, they designed fake papers attractively printed in Sweden's national colors of blue and yellow, emblazoned with the three crowns coat of arms, appropriate stamps, and signatures. In just a few hours, they met with a book designer, plates were engraved, presses were set, and overnight hundreds of passports were coming off the production lines.

When they first saw the hastily produced results of this fanciful idea Wallenberg grinned at his new friend. "I love the personality of fresh ink. It is a kind of genius, Viktor. A banknote is either a meaningless piece of paper or, in the right hands, worth precisely what the figures printed upon it proclaim the value to be. These papers should mean nothing, but right here, right now, we imbue them with significance, and so for anyone who can get hold of one, for anyone that we can give them to, they will mean one thing and one thing only: survival. That is some printing press we have, my friend."

Traveling by limousine, flying both the German and Swedish flags on the front fenders, Wallenberg and Mueller went to train stations in Budapest where transports were leaving for Auschwitz and Bergen-Belsen. Wallenberg distributed passports placing Jewish families under his custody right at the station. He went as far as climbing up on the roof of the train and handing out the protective passes through the doors, which were not yet sealed. They ignored commands from a few German guards for them to stop. Then orders were given for the secret security police and Arrow Cross to begin shooting. Wallenberg ignored them too and calmly continued passing passports to reaching hands. Somehow the men deliberately aimed over his head, and observers would argue for years to come as to whether this was down to some display of courage, or because they'd been bribed by the mysterious German major accompanying Wallenberg. Whatever the reason not one shot hit him. Viktor watched in awe.

Hundreds of lives were saved that day, and thousands more in the days and weeks that followed. Viktor danced effectively, just one step ahead of the Nazis, who he knew would become increasingly aware of his duplicity, until he left the city and disappeared, knowing he had work to do, that he had to save Max. Despite Viktor's pleas for him to come along to save himself while he still had the chance, Raoul Wallenberg remained in Budapest, and in time he, too, disappeared.

A HERO RETURNS

A terrific explosion shook every building, waking up the entire camp in a chaos of deafening shouts and muffled murmurs. I stumbled, putting my hands behind my ears. Others scurried to shelter. In the distance, plumes of smoke, discharged debris, and clouds of ash. Had bombs fallen? There was a burning stench in the air, and screaming sirens sounded throughout the camp.

All around was confusion, with guards running in every direction. I listened for rumbling tanks but the sound and fury fell silent. I raced to Freidle's office to find out what had happened.

"It's a tragedy," Freidle was saying to Rahm and a platoon of SS troops when I reached the commandant's office. I decided it would be smart to make myself as invisible as possible, so I stood motionless by the commandant's coat rack to avoid Rahm's wrath.

Sweat poured down his face onto his collar as he pounded on Freidle's desk. "Forty SS replacements on their way to Terezín were killed, blown up by some idiot!" he screamed, spittle flying from his mouth.

"You'll rebuild the track with work details around the clock," Rahm demanded in a steady growl, glaring at Freidle.

"There *will* be transports," Rahm said, his face bright red.

Turning around, he discovered me standing alone and gave me an ice-cold stare.

"Print *that* in your little paper."

He kicked the front door open and left, his men marching out with him.

"Who do you think did it, Commandant?" I asked.

"I think the Czech Resistance. One of the doctors has been called to the Little Fortress to treat a man wounded in the explosion."

At first, I wondered if it was Pavel, whose family Norbert had painted, but he didn't seem the type.

I discussed the matter with David. He lit up when I told him about the injured prisoner. "Max, that man is a hero! Do you think we could interview him? We can find out a lot."

"Rahm won't permit it. Maybe if I speak to Freidle."

"Use the Mueller powers of persuasion. What can you lose?"

"Honestly, David, I'm not sure I want to know."

"If you could get to the prisoner, we can find out more. A firsthand account, Max. Think of it. Someone blew up the tracks!"

I took a minute to think. Maybe David had a point. I could indeed find out more, and then maybe figure out a new way to get word to Sam Raggle, if he was still around. I wasn't sure.

"Keep your eyes open while you're there, Max. Scope it out. Maybe we can even free him?"

In Freidle's office, I noticed something new: a large framed map over his desk. I examined it carefully; all of Germany's occupied territories were in green. England was in red. I allowed my finger to follow the map to Czechoslovakia. I studied the terrain and was pinpointing mountains and rivers around Prague when Freidle appeared.

"You wanted to see me, Max?"

"I think this is an important story, Commandant," I said boldly.

"Story?"

"The prisoner at the Little Fortress. We've never had an opportunity to interview a traitor before, if he is a traitor. How can we know unless we speak to him? I'm sure Berlin would like to know more, don't you think? You built a station with tracks and did something helpful, and some dumb Czech blows it all away. Maybe he'll talk to me. If I take some medicine and food, I bet I can soften him up and find out more."

"You have a lot of confidence. Rahm's men will make him talk."

"I don't trust Rahm. My loyalty is to you. I'm a kid and prisoners talk to kids, not bullies."

Freidle gave a nervous chuckle. "And how do you know that?"

"I don't, but how could it do any harm? I'll tell you everything I find out. It's important to Berlin. I know how much my father respects you. This has always been your camp. I'd like to prove who really blew up the train, who's behind it. Rahm will use any excuse to discredit your work."

Freidle thought deeply. "Max, I like what you do. You have my appreciation. I think there is some wisdom in what you say." He sat back in his chair. "I'll arrange a permit for you to visit him. Oh, and let's not discuss this with Major Rahm."

I smiled. "Never, Commandant."

I now knew the Little Fortress was a notorious and mysterious brick garrison, holding political prisoners ever since its construction over a century before. I would finally get to enter.

I arrived alone at the heavy gate in front of the building. Inside, conditions were miserable. The place was dirty and dark, a moldy damp jail. Cement floors, little ventilation, and the whole place smelled of decay.

I carried with me, along with the permit, a packet of sandwiches, fresh bread, fruit, and water. With just a nod, a guard led me down to a musty, cold cell. In the shadows, I saw the man, bruised and bandaged, wearing old, shredded, and bloodstained clothing.

"Hello, Max."

I froze. I couldn't scream with the German guards waiting outside the cell. The man's face was so wounded that it was almost impossible to recognize him. But I did in an instant.

"Poppy, what happened to you?" I whispered. My father was broken, his body cut and torn apart. I took a step toward him, but Poppy put his finger to his lips.

"My God, what happened to you, Poppy?" I whispered. "I've got to get you out of here."

Finally a smile emerged from Poppy. "*I blew up the tracks.*"

But he had been seriously wounded. I was beginning to panic. Poppy was my rock. I couldn't stand to see him hurt . . .

"I can't hug you, Max. I love you." Quietly he said, "I promised you I would stop the transports and I did. You don't have too much time, Max. Get out of Terezín, Max. Do whatever it takes. Get out and get to Prague."

I whispered, "We'll go together, Poppy. Here's some food and water."

"You're the best son a man could have. Everything was for you. You need to know that," he said, smiling sadly. "You'll be okay, Max. Remember, whatever it takes."

After what seemed like only a few minutes, the guard

entered. I pretended to finish the interview, closing my notebook, and thinking quickly. "So you were just walking to the station?"

"I'm Czech," Poppy said, for the benefit of anyone listening. "I was attacked by some soldiers, they were drunk. They took everything from me."

"Your time is up," the guard said.

"I'll come tomorrow."

He stared straight into my eyes. "Max, you must carry on your work." These were the last words that escaped from his lips.

Returning to Freidle's office, I was barely able to hold back my tears. I organized my thoughts, knowing that I had to save my father, and play the most convincing role of my life.

"Max, how did it go?" Freidle asked.

"I only had ten minutes, but I'm sure the man is innocent and we should help him. He was just in the wrong place at the wrong time. He's Czech and I believe he was knocked out of his wits, if not by the explosion, then probably by Rahm's men, who beat him to a pulp. He's an honest man, I know he is, and he needs medical attention. He said he has something to tell me. Tomorrow I'll find out."

Freidle frowned. "You really don't believe he's the man?"

"I know it. I'd stake my life on it. I'm good at reading people, you know that, and I want to be sure. He seems like a good person, cooperative, and maybe he knows something, something important. He was right there, we have an eyewitness, so maybe he saw someone."

"Right. Let's get to the truth. Maybe Major Mueller can help in Berlin. It's the best thing to do. I'll try to get word to him."

"Can David come with me tomorrow?"

"Be careful, and get Frankl to give you some medicine to take with you," he said, turning to his paperwork. "We've got to keep the prisoner alive."

Reaching Hanover Barracks, David was waiting for me outside; there were just a few people around. I was still trembling.

"What did you find out, Max? Are you all right?"

"It's Poppy."

David stood there, openmouthed.

I stared at him, scarcely believing what I was saying: "He blew up that train, David. He blew it up!"

"No!"

"Freidle said you can come with me when I go back tomorrow. We've got to save him."

I thought long about my father, and his bruised and battered face. Poppy was invincible and could improvise a way out of any situation, but I was ashamed that I had doubted him for so long. I longed for the Distant and Mysterious Man and White Dog.

Early the following morning, I asked over at the infirmary, hoping against hope that there might still be some medicine from the little supply that Poppy had brought.

Taking a shortcut to the fortress, passing a few camp workers on our way to a farm, David and I climbed up the steep hill and were out of breath when we reached the top. There was a commotion below.

"Max, wait, get down," David called.

We dropped to the ground and, studying the scene at the bottom of the hill, we saw a long, black line of guards lined up as a firing squad. Not thirty feet away from them was a man against a brick wall, blindfolded, his hands tied behind his back. The black overcoat was a witness.

"Oh, God, David, that's—"

A volley of shots rang out in a fusillade of hot bullets, and the man crumpled to the ground.

No, no, no. I shook. I tried to stand, to run to my father, I had to help him, but David held me back.

"Max, stay down!" David said, his voice breaking.

David held me, his scarf muffling my scream. Over and over again, I heard the volley, then the echo of the final shot to my father's beautiful head.

Where was God? I thought.

"I don't . . . I can't. He was everything, David. I . . ."

Wiping my tears with his maroon scarf, David held me as my whole body shook. I couldn't breathe, as if a thick, heavy blanket had been thrown over me.

"Max," David said quietly, over and over, "dear Max."

I tried again to break free and run to my father, just to stroke his hair, to feel his face with my hands, to comfort him, but David wouldn't let go.

Then I had a glimpse of Poppy making fresh fruit juice in our kitchen in Prague, my father toasting, to me and "To life!" What life? There was nothing left.

"You've got to be brave; you have got to be strong, Max." David's face was tear-streaked and he threw his yellow notepad to the ground.

"What's the point, David?"

"Max, your father was trying to save us . . . to help us. That's the point."

I saw a small piece of paper on Poppy's chest. I wouldn't have noticed if I didn't know what it was. It was a yellow star, the same one the kids had pinned to his jacket before the performance of *Brundibár*. That morning he had worn it like a medal. Then a breeze came along, and like a butterfly, that yellow piece of paper floated upward, and turned, then sailed skyward until it was no more.

MOURNING

David found out that it was Rahm who had ordered the prisoner shot.

In the days that followed, a black fog descended on me. Every step I took felt like a superhuman effort. I couldn't sleep, and would just lie awake, my eyes dry, staring into the nothingness. David tried to shake me out of my depression. Devastated, I felt alone, as if in a dark closet, unable to move, unable to think, in a place where no one could reach me. I realized that Poppy had been there all along. No words, no songs, no prayers—nothing, nothing, nothing. Sorrow shredded everything I believed in, everything I had hoped for.

Sophie came. The Brankas managed to convince Freidle that I had the flu, and the best medicine was Sophie. She hadn't seen my room before, and I hoped she wouldn't comment on the wallpaper with the roses and my sweet surroundings. But she did.

She seemed frail from too many days of worry. She was tired..

"Max, I like your room, I feel quite at home," trying to lighten the evening, with a sensitive touch. I had become accustomed to the place over the years, and I blushed at her comment.

She sat by my side, holding my hand, caressing my head.

"Max, Poppy was incredibly brave."

I pulled the quilted blanket around me.

I just want him back. My colors are washing away.

"We've got to carry on, Max," Sophie said. "We must hold on. I'm here, and I won't leave you."

She stayed with me until I fell asleep.

It was a night of voices clamoring for attention. They came and went; it was Poppy in a drowsy flow of dreams. "Go gently, Max, and always be strong. You're my son."

After dark, I awoke, turned on the lamp, stared at the open pages of my notebook. Once I began writing I couldn't stop. My feelings filled page after page. Poppy was my father, doing all he could do. But no words, even a thousand pages, could measure my feelings for him.

I wrote all night before going to visit Rabbi Leo Baeck in his study.

"They killed my father, Rabbi. And they pretended they didn't know who he was. They murdered him."

With deep sadness, he placed his hands on my shoulders. "David told me."

With the pressure of his hands, he seemed to be saying, *Don't give up, Max. Just don't give up.*

"Please say a prayer," I asked. The rabbi had a permanent look of world-weariness.

He recited:

"דעו םלועל ותוכלמ דובכ םש ךורב."

"That is the holiest of all prayers, the Kaddish. It means, 'Blessed be His name, whose glorious kingdom is forever.'"

"Thank you, Rabbi. I know Poppy wasn't Jewish—"

"He's one of us, Max."

The rabbi placed his hand on my head, leaving it there

for a long time, as if to give me strength, some blessing, some wisdom, hoping to release me from my sorrow.

Leaving the study with the hope that Poppy had found peace, I met up with Sophie and David. We walked over to the concert hall. Sitting at a piano at a corner of the stage, Hans stared at the keys and forced his broken and bandaged fingers to play. Slowly, with great effort, willing his hands to move, he managed to create a tune. David took up his violin, and so the four of us shared a moment, united in grief, knowing, all of us, that music had a perspective, a conscience, and knew right from wrong. It had the ability to heal and the ability to take us all to another place. I wasn't alone at Terezín. I heard the song of it all. It was proof of my existence.

With every bit of will he could summon up, Hans played the opening melody from one of Poppy's favorite pieces, "Theme and Variations," written before the war. His shoulders were slumped over, his musical eulogy was vibrant, its faraway sounds joining my immeasurable sense of love and loss, serving up a tribute to my father.

Later, Hans managed to hold a cup of tea. "I'd offer you a cup, Max, but it's really only a little hot water with lemon and a tea bag from Prague that has seen better days."

I felt a wave of despair all around me. I couldn't stop thinking about the wretchedness, of Poppy, of everything.

Hans tried to change the subject, to a happier time.

"We've always loved him, haven't we?"

"Tell me more about Poppy, Hans. Tell me things I never knew. Tell me what you remember. Anything."

"There were so many good times. Viktor made hard times

good and good times better. We met at the Conservatory. We were very different people then, maybe always, yet with so much in common. Music. In those days, your Poppy had a flamboyant lifestyle, so glamorous, conducting an orchestra, heading off to Paris, directing a play, inventing and always reinventing himself, playing roles like an actor. He was an actor, Max, a wonderful actor. I don't have to tell you that he was remarkably clever. I wanted to compose; Viktor wanted to conduct. We balanced each other, complemented each other. Your father was restless and imaginative. Me, not so much. He was driving the tram, and I was sitting in the back."

I had always wondered about my mother, what she was like. She existed almost only in my imagination, re-created from snatches of stories that Poppy told me and the few photographs of her. Maybe it was time to ask Hans more.

Taking a breath, I asked, "How did Poppy meet my mother?"

"One rainy afternoon in Municipal House. Maria knew who he was, the Great Viktor Mueller. I'm surprised he didn't have it printed on his business card. She wasn't going to fall for his practiced lines and saw right through him. But I suppose she saw something else, maybe the real man behind all those characters, all that surface charm. To begin with, she wouldn't go out with him unless I came along. Imagine that—I was Viktor's chaperone! We went to concerts and plays, had picnics, took trips. Your mama . . . well, it's hard to find the words, Max. You're much better at words than I am. I could compose some beautiful and graceful piece of music to capture who she was. It wouldn't do her justice. We loved her. She was so like your Sophie, Max."

That night as I fell asleep, I thought of where I'd been and where we were going. I had often asked myself this question as I struggled to understand it all: Are we all going to die? And I almost laughed a bitter laugh as I saw then with a horrible clarity that of course we were. But death is not something that you wait for. It is happening all the time everywhere—even coming for my mother before the war. I still had a vivid memory of her. I couldn't avoid it, and I couldn't sit back and blame God. I came to the realization that it was up to me and me alone to sort through the sadness, to try somehow to make things better, brighter if only for a moment, to make things right. I was in a world in which the walls were closing in all the time, and I needed to see what was still possible. Those who were dead were dead. But I was still here and so were many that I loved, and, more than ever, I had to muster up every bit of strength. One thing I knew for sure was what Poppy would want. I would never forget this, just as I would never forget Poppy. He would want me to have music. He would want me to have all that music meant in the world. I had to learn to hear the music again. After all, music can't be kept in a box, otherwise it ceases to flow. I had to carry on. I had to fight. I had to take over for my father.

I made a silent vow to the Great Viktor Mueller. "I promise I will look to the day when I can feel the sunlight on my face and smile. I promise I will hear the music, Poppy. I promise to fight. I promise I'll make a plan. I promise."

A black Mercedes stopped in front of the SS headquarters and two SS men got out. They were from Berlin. I could tell by the plates. It was enough. A word formed on one of the officer's lips: *transport*. Within a few minutes, everyone would know the trains had been replaced. Poppy's heroism had given me a little more time. I ran back over to Hans's studio.

"We have to get out of this place," I said. "It was Poppy's last wish."

"Someone has to run the music program," Hans said with conscious irony. "I'm a piano man, as you say. I wouldn't be very good at making an escape. I'm too old. That's a plan for a younger man. And look at my hands. I'd only hold you back. How are you going to do it?"

"I'll figure it out."

"I believe you will. But you know I can't go with you, Max."

"Dammit, Hans."

"Be careful, they must know by now that you're Jewish."

I looked at him in bewilderment. "What are you talking about? I'm Catholic, Hans. You know that."

Hans sighed. "I thought Viktor would tell you. Your mother, Maria, was Jewish, although she was brought up in a convent by nuns."

I stared at him, openmouthed.

"There's a bit more," Hans said. "I suspect that Heydrich knew this all the time, and he used it to blackmail Viktor, with the promise you would be safe, under his personal guarantee. He needed Viktor to serve his own cause. Viktor was exceptional, and you were the exception."

I was lost for words. I was Jewish. All this time. I didn't need to try to feel Jewish. I simply was. It was as though suddenly everything made sense. I belonged.

Hans looked at me silently. I found myself amused. I managed a smile. "I hope you won't hold it against me, Hans."

He smiled back. "Congratulations and bless you."

Sophie was right again. *When you least expect it, something happens.*

"I'll be all right, Max. Whatever happens."

Could I believe that he would really be all right? Could I make myself believe? Hans didn't allow anything or anyone to diminish his faith or his unfailing optimism. I had a clear glimpse of a man who suffered alone, of a graceful poet.

"You financed Mrs. Blomberg."

"Why do you say that?"

"You eventually gave up all your property, your house, everything."

"How do you know?"

"Because you never mentioned it. Oh, and I did see you handing over that envelope to her that time of course. I'm pretty certain that it was a bundle of cash and the deed to your house."

"You know how to keep a secret, don't you. I did what I could."

I noticed a shedding cabbage rose Hans had picked from his garden. It was in a vase and had not lost its bloom. Its color was fading, but its petals were still alive.

Transports KR 431, 432, and 433 took away some of Terezín's most gifted artists and musicians. Even the great Steinway Boys had gone. I had formed a close attachment with them, and it broke my heart. But every departure did.

The lists came through before anyone knew. There might be three or four transports waiting, one after another. It happened quickly.

That night, I picked up *Huckleberry Finn* again. I began skipping pages and then read how Jim sought freedom, rafting over the Mississippi River through rain, strong currents, floods, and shipwrecks. Resting for a moment, random thoughts from the book began to cobble together in my head, leaving me with a torrent of inspiration.

We said there warn't no home like a raft, after all...You feel mighty free and easy and comfortable on a raft . . . So I took my paddle and slid out from shore just a step or two, and then let the raft drop along down amongst the shadows. The moon was shining, and outside of the shadows it made it most as light as day. I poked along well onto an hour, everything still as rocks and sound asleep...A little riply cool breeze begun to blow, and that was as good as saying the night was about done.

And just like that, I had my great idea.

A MEASURE OF COURAGE

Norbert Troller's architectural skills were in demand after he built the "great bathhouse," and he'd been working in SS quarters.

He pulled me by my blazer lapels into a side street. "Max, I overheard the SS saying that the Russians are advancing and Germany is in ruins."

"It seems like fantastic news, Norbert."

"No, Max. There's something else. I saw the transport lists on Rahm's desk." He spoke quietly. "You and David . . . I suspect you've been marked."

No surprise. We were on the list. And with my father dead, I realized that they had known my mother was Jewish all along. There was no more time.

My father's words, *Get out of Terezín, Max. Do whatever it takes. Get out, and get to Prague,* rang in my head.

"I heard that Rahm plans to close down *Vedem,*" Troller said.

"How do you know?"

"You overhear a lot when you're working at Himmler House. Freidle has lost his authority."

I had to leave. Now was the time. "Norbert, have you ever read *Huckleberry Finn*? It's an American book by Mark Twain."

"I have, yes. I loved the adventure, the lyricism, the

freedom . . . *lights out for the territory*." He seemed briefly lost in reverie.

"About the Mississippi River."

"The great Mississippi! It's a mighty river."

"You're a genius, Norbert. You don't need me to tell you that, but in case you do, that's just what you are. You can do anything. You're an architect, designer, artist, master carpenter. Can you do it, Norbert?"

"Calm down, Max. Do what?"

"Build me a raft."

Norbert wrinkled his brow. "Why?"

"I'm leaving."

He waved his hand in the air. "I don't want to know anything about this."

"You already know, Norbert. I just told you."

After a moment's pause, he smiled. "I can do it. It's not so difficult."

"You're a saint, Norbert." I smiled. "And guess what? I've discovered I'm Jewish!"

"Mazel tov!" Then with a glint in his eye, "You know, you might be the only person around here who would celebrate that. Max, you're one of a kind."

Norbert was busier than ever working at Himmler House. Rahm was demanding improvements, frustrating Norbert, who only wanted to paint the countryside. For the SS headquarters, he had been ordered to fabricate a door separating the anteroom from the offices. He made it unusually large, figuring that a space twelve feet high and nine across only needed a double door. By making two, he would have extra for a raft. He reinforced it with balsa wood and three coats of marine varnish that would dry in a matter of days.

Always a student of design, he confided to me that at night, he had been studying naval architecture in the library at SS headquarters. He was reading a book about boat construction, by Vice-Admiral Wilhelm Kronowitz, a noted naval architect. Learning that airtight oil drums could make a flotation device, he found several empty ones near the Little Fortress. Lashing one to each corner of the raft would ensure it would float.

"What's in the drums?"

"Highly flammable kerosene," came the answer.

"We'll need to clean them."

"How much time do we have?"

"I don't know. It took God seven days to create the world. Maybe I can do it in six."

"You're a good man, Norbert Troller."

"I know."

Norbert took every safety precaution. He had a crew of loyal carpenters.

"You might have a slim chance of getting away with this, Max," he said.

If I could get to Prague, I knew I could manage.

Moving the raft out of the carpentry shop wasn't a problem. Norbert's workforce had been enlisted to carry waterproofed wooden doors over to the Hotel SS. A supervisor thought they were just remodeling materials. Troller ordered up some lightweight canvas from the army to cover the roof of the headquarters while reinforcing it. He laminated the bottom of the raft, sealing it with water-resistant materials. Four plastic drums were attached and hidden in an equipment shed. His craftsmanship and attention to detail were remarkable.

"Would you like blue canvas or dark gray, Max?"

"I have a choice?"

"You have a choice."

"I think dark gray."

"Custom-built; give the client what he wants."

Extra canvas was used to construct a tent, attached to an eight-foot mast. The craft was beautiful. It was functional, made right in plain sight of the German authorities! Norbert had been brilliant in his deception. They had no idea what he was up to.

There was one more thing I had to do. Taking my cue from Troller, I did some research and scoured the library for chemistry books. In class demonstrations at school, I'd learned how magnesium and sulfuric acid could cause combustible reactions. I found a case with some old journals. Page after page had diagrams about fire, gas, and kerosene. I found a simple and explosive way to say goodbye.

From our "shipyard" I thought about my imminent escape. I knew my plan was the only way out—it would be far too difficult to travel by foot. I copied diagrams of the rivers from the map on Freidle's wall whenever I was alone. If I could navigate the Ohře down to the Elbe tributary and join up with the Vltava, I'd be okay. I didn't know about currents or weather, but the rivers were high, and the tide was running downstream. With any luck, there would be no obstacles. Huck and Tom had managed. So could I.

Little by little, in the late afternoons, with Pavel's help, we carted supplies down to the shores of the river. We hid them, along with the raft, under the dock, between wooden pilings.

At any time, we knew we could be betrayed by the farmer. But as long as Norbert was painting portraits of Pavel's entire family—currently his mother-in-law, much to the pleasure of his wife—we would be safe and furnished with modest provisions. After all, Pavel had never liked Germans.

With a final touch, Norbert presented me with a round life-saving buoy. He really had thought of everything. He had cut and fitted a circle from some cork that was to have been used for kitchen flooring in the officers' quarters. After rounding the edges, he wrapped it with white waterproof tape and secured it with navy-blue-and-red bands. The center read SS *Max*. It was an impressive achievement.

I recalled the best word I could think to describe him. Only extra special people had my admiration, only a few really counted, and, like David, Norbert Troller was a *topper*!

"I'll need a box, Norbert, for my hurdy-gurdy. It's not so big, and I need to take it with me."

Norbert frowned. "It's extra weight. With provisions, the raft will only hold three people as it is."

"I hate to leave it behind. I'm attached to it, just like you to your velvet coat. We can make it work."

"I'll make a waterproof box." Norbert shook his head. "You're quite mad, you know. A hurdy-gurdy on a river raft escape. Even Huckleberry Finn wouldn't dare to try it."

Finally, he presented a blue linen bag—he had had one of his workers sew pillows and wool scraps between two sheets. "Sleeping bags, compliments of Hotel Himmler. Max, you can now say you're sleeping with the enemy!"

I couldn't suppress a smile.

"You know there's space for you, Norbert. Come with me?"

"No, Max, this is your adventure. Take your friends. If I'm busy working for the SS, and they need my services, I should be secure. And anyway, Max," he said with a shrug and a small smile, "I'm too old to travel."

Suddenly, we heard guns booming far away, and seconds later, more gunfire edging closer. Formations of planes flew overhead. Clouds of smoke darkened the sky in the distance. Were they Russian or German? We couldn't see through the fire and smoke. Cannons and shells exploded, sounds which could only mean a fierce battle. The conflict was getting ever closer.

Freidle later told us that British and American troops were crossing the Rhine and planes were bombing an industrial plant near us, sending layers of dust over the camp.

The end of the war was near. It had to be. The Germans were getting desperate.

Heading back to the Hotel SS, I turned and went to David's barracks.

When I stumbled into David's room, I found him sitting on his bunk, his face ashen.

"David, what is it?"

"We're on the list." Rahm had ordered additional transports, taking whole blocks of people indiscriminately, with no exemptions. We had watched people leave in despair, walking with a shambling gait, helpless, disoriented, while only a few kept an ever-dimming spark of hope alive. One father entered a transport holding a heavy woolen jacket that belonged to his son who had left a few weeks earlier; a few women wanted to rejoin their husbands and friends at any cost.

"The war may be almost over, but we're leaving," I said, sitting down beside David.

He shook his head. "I'm assigned car DK 413. It's over for me. I know where I'm going and what will happen to me there. It's done!"

He slammed his fist on his cot. I grabbed him by the shoulders. "You're not going to be on DK 413."

David was scared and impatient. "Max, I'm not exempted. Do you understand? I'm a Jew, and we're all going to be murdered!"

"I know, I know. Rahm's a ruthless bastard. We're both going to be called up next. That's why we're getting the hell out of here. We're going to Prague."

"What are you talking about, Max?"

"We have two options. We can go to Auschwitz and die, or we can try to escape. You can be my first mate."

I grinned and saw a glint in David's eye.

"In a boat?" he asked.

I nodded.

"On a raft. Hundreds of people are next. I don't think we'll be missed at the station. It's chaos down there. You'll be sailing on the SS *Max* by the time they even notice we're gone. I have charts and provisions."

"You have this all planned out?"

"The operative word, David, is *out*! We have an appointment to keep. I must do this, I promised Poppy."

"I had no idea what you were up to . . ."

"I didn't know if I could pull it off—we may not yet—and I wasn't sure if you would have supported my plan, because it's crazy." I laughed, and knew I sounded a little crazy. "I think I may actually be nuts. Norbert wouldn't disagree. David, I'm thinking of us. We might not succeed, but this is your only chance of getting to Palestine and reuniting with your folks. What could be better?"

David couldn't believe my plan.

"Did you know that Rahm is shutting down *Vedem?* Doesn't that tell you something?"

"It tells me a lot."

David stood up and began to pace the room. "What are we going to do for money?"

"I have a stash that Poppy gave me. I've been saving it. I'll come for you tomorrow in the afternoon; Freidle thinks we're working on the last edition. And don't bring more than ten suitcases. I know you like to travel light."

David stopped in front of me. "Max, you're actually going to do it! Why are you taking me?"

Before I replied, I thought that, like Huck, I was planning to repay David for his troubles and send him home a hero, giving him a reception with a marching band.

"To always be your friend," I said. "We need each other."

"What do you mean?"

"Hans told me that my mother was Jewish."

"Welcome to the tribe."

"I thought you'd be surprised."

"I've always liked you for who you are."

"I know that, David."

"What about Sophie?" David asked, throwing clothing into a small suitcase.

"She's coming too."

"You've told her?"

"Not yet. I'm going to tell her now and convince her to come."

"Do you think she will?"

"Yes, I think so. She has to."

"How do you know that?"

"I guess because we love each other. I know we belong together."

A LAST GOODBYE

I had to get word to Sophie so I sent a note with Sarah Markova. *Please tell her it's important!*

"Did you know Edith had a relapse?" Sarah asked, shaking her head. "I think she's been moved to a different ward."

"Damn, why am I the last to know?" I had been so preoccupied with my escape plan that I'd failed Sophie. Clasping Sarah's hands, I urged, "Please get word to her. I must see her."

Then to Hans. I was desperate, ready to do anything to get him out of Terezín.

"We'll make room for you on the raft. You've got to come with me."

Regardless of every argument I could muster, I couldn't persuade him to leave—he had been set in his ways for too long. He was too committed to the children. He could never leave them. He was resigned to be who he wanted to be. Even when I told Hans how much he counted, I couldn't shake him out of his stubbornness. And I was sure and told myself over and over that the Germans would never kill children, that no one would do that, and that Hans would take care of them. That was his assignment. I could only say goodbye.

"The war will be over," Hans said. "There will be a new beginning. Things will get better . . ."

"Until we're together again."

There didn't seem to be much more to say.

Walking over to me, Hans grabbed me in a long embrace. "I love you, Max. I loved Poppy too."

He clutched me even tighter. "You've always meant everything to me."

Stepping back, he said, "We'll make it, I know we will. The Great Viktor Mueller is depending on it."

I left and didn't look back. It was too painful. I wondered when I would see him again.

Sarah got word to Sophie and she came to Ava's house that night. I pulled myself together.

When she appeared at the door to my room, I began speaking faster than I could think. "Sophie, this is the most important decision of our lives."

"All right, Max. Tell me."

She sat on my bed, her hands in her lap.

"We're leaving." I went to the window, collecting my thoughts. I could hear the river running not far away.

"I want you to come with me. I built a raft and we're sailing down the river to Prague. David is coming too."

"Max, you're crazy. But I'm not surprised."

"So I've been told. But I want to be sure you're safe and, with me, I think you will be."

Sophie took my hand. "You're very brave, Max."

My heart beat quickly. "I'm not so brave. But, come with me, Sophie, please."

"I want to, Max, more than anything. But Mama is ill. She needs me. I can't leave her."

"I know. Sarah told me. And I feel terrible."

"I don't want to worry you. The medicine Poppy brought is helping. It's a new drug. What worries me is that she won't take it. She says there are other patients who need it."

"But it's got to be in short supply. Is there any left?"

Tears welled in her eyes. "I can't leave her, Max, I just can't."

"Oh, God . . . Sophie."

I didn't know what to say.

"Maybe she can come too, and we'll look after her, keep her warm."

"She's in quarantine, Max. I could never . . . we thought it was just a bad cold at first, but it got worse. Typhoid."

"Oh, God."

I summoned my final plea. "You've got to come with me, Sophie. I think Edith would want you to."

My voice was raised, panic creeping in.

"Max!" Sophie cried, grabbing my shoulders and shaking me. "Max! I can't! Listen to me. Don't make me choose. Don't hurt me like that."

"Okay," I said, throwing my shoulders back. "Then, I'm staying here. I'm not going to leave you."

Softening, she took me in her arms. "Max, you must go. Do it for me. For Poppy."

"You've always been my . . . I love you."

"I know. You always have," she said, brushing a strand of hair from my brow.

"There are rumors the war is almost over. It can't be long now."

Sophie brightened slightly. "I think so too. We'll hold on. And someone has to take care of Hans."

I held her, kissed her.

"I'll come back for you, Sophie."

"I'll be waiting." She gave a shaky smile. "I can just picture you and David, rafting down the Mississippi."

"Did you know?"

"Yes, I knew."

"There's a secret I want to tell you before you hear it from anyone else."

"Tell me."

I took a deep breath. "I'm Jewish. Hans told me my mother was Jewish."

Sophie smiled again. "I always knew there was something about you that I liked."

"I haven't had time to even think about what that means or how I feel about it, but I know that I like it. I feel I belong. At last."

"You've always belonged, Max," said Sophie. I looked at her face, so thin, yet still so beautiful to me.

"I have a few words to say, and I don't have to think about them because they're what I feel and have always known." I never had the ability to compose a poem on the spot, but now I was going to do it.

Her eyes were shining. "Well, go ahead."

I cleared my throat.

"I hurt because I love,
I say goodbye so I can say hello.
I cry so I can smile
I go out so I can come in."

Sophie led me out into the hall, where she had found a Victrola left over from the Red Cross inspection. Taking a record, she turned the handle and placed the needle on a groove. It was one of her favorite songs, "The Way You Look Tonight."

She took my arms and wrapped them around her shoulders.

"But, Sophie, you know I can't."

"But, Max, you can. I've always wanted to dance with you."

As the music played, I was awkward at first, but with Sophie's encouragement, I moved gracefully with the song and in this Fred and Ginger moment it was Max and Sophie. I would never forget that lyric. Maybe just sentimental slosh, but it touched me. I guess like Poppy, I'd always been hopelessly romantic.

Someday, when I'm awfully low
When the world is cold
I will feel a glow just thinking of you.

She tearfully snuggled into bed with me and laid her head on my chest. I stroked her hair and she kissed me. I whispered in her ear: "I guess being happy is not necessarily having what you want, but always truly knowing what you have."

She smiled weakly. "Why, you are a poet, Max. I knew that all along too. You know, I was always afraid of loving you so much. This isn't the end, Max. I can't—I can't even think—"

"I *will* come back for you."

Sophie gave me a small envelope, wrapped in blue paper. "I've been carrying this close to my heart for weeks, and I want you to take it with you. You can't open it now, only when you are safe, Max. Promise me."

I drew her closer, never wanting to let her go, kissing her cheeks, wet with tears. We held each other for hours, lost in our own thoughts. I drifted asleep with her in my arms, but when I woke in the darkness she was gone.

I was leaving Sophie and Hans. Maybe they were right to stay. If Poppy had been ill, still a prisoner, I couldn't think of leaving either. They would be all right. They had to be, I had to believe it.

In the distance, near a forest that loomed close by, a train whistle blew, wailing up through the valley toward the station, then the chugging became quiet, with only the intermittent sounds of puffing steam.

My wristwatch ticked 2:00 a.m. Getting up and dressing quietly, I went down the stairs, into the night air, passing through darkness, and made a final check. I had to be sure everything was in place and ready. Norbert had found an old navigation chart in the library, and he didn't think that the river's path had changed much in the last twenty years. Pavel and I had stashed my hurdy-gurdy on the raft, but still there remained one detail to take care of—for Poppy. I stole over to the Little Fortress, where a stack of drums were stored in a field. Then, over to Rahm's bathhouse. I took every precaution not to be seen, just like on my scouting trips with David. I moved easily and silently, my legs cooperating like a military ranger undercover. The operation took less than two hours and wasn't as difficult as I'd imagined.

Returning to my room, Twain was still on my bed with favorite passages marked in the margins:

> I was pretty tired, and the first thing I knowed I was asleep. When I woke up I didn't know where I was for a minute. I set up and looked around, a little scared. Then I remembered. The river looked miles and miles across. The moon was so bright . . . Everything was dead quiet . . . The stars were shining, and the leaves rustled in the woods ever so mournful; and I heard an owl, away off, who-whooing . . . and a whippowill . . .

Early in the morning I popped in to see Fritz. I wanted to say goodbye but no one was around. After the war was over, I thought I would send a postcard to him every day just to keep his mailbox full. After all, what is a post office for?

Right after lunch, prompt and correct, Frau Schmidt walked me to Hanover Barracks, where David was waiting with lanky hair and a shuffling gait. Passing a few guards, we were a familiar sight, ever since Rahm had demanded Frau Schmidt accompany me to visit my "little Jewish friend."

She gave her usual greetings, barking at the guards, "Straighten up, wake up, Valter. Attention, Bernhard!" They didn't seem to mind having a few orders thrown at them in a way no one else dared every time she passed. Was she their conscience? Or, strutting plump and proud, did she simply remind them of their mothers?

When Frau Schmidt paraded past the guards, she leaned over and whispered to me, "I know about your plan, and the raft." She glanced around the empty square.

"How?"

"I know your every move. Be careful."

"And Freidle?"

"Not so much. And he wouldn't want to know. For all his faults, he's fond of you," she said, marching straight ahead.

"I thought it was a secret. How did you find out?"

"Max, quit asking questions. Do as you're told."

"I'm going to miss you," I said, taking her hand.

She almost smiled, shooing the thought away. "Get serious, Max."

Then she paused and whispered, "I'll miss you too."

"I'll see the lists as soon as they come over from the SS," she said in a raspy tone, speaking out of the corner of her mouth.

"You must make sure Sophie and Hans are not numbered."

She nodded when she heard the desperation in my voice. "I'm good at making up rooms and rearranging books. Part of what I do. Of course, I'll be arrested if Rahm finds out. But it couldn't happen to a nicer person."

I laughed. "Frau Schmidt, I never—"

"Knew that I had a sense of humor? Well, just don't tell anyone. Here's the address of Pension Burger in Prague, don't lose it. Pierre worked for me in Berlin before he opened his own place, in better days. He knows you're coming, and he'll be expecting you boys, so don't let me down. I'm never pleased when someone cancels a reservation without twenty-four hours' notice. He'll be waiting for you at Judith Landing just before the tower at Charles Bridge in two days' time, Tuesday at four o'clock. He'll wait as long as he can. I'll give you some money."

"I have some that Poppy gave me. Having a contact in Prague will make all the difference."

"Your father knew Pierre as well. You'll be safe there."

We kept walking, and Frau Schmidt kept barking. "Straighten up, Leopold, pay attention! You're on duty."

The guards tried to hide their smiles. After we passed, she dropped her voice back to a whisper: "Max, when you and David are no longer around, Rahm will think you have both been transported."

"Thanks for helping me."

"That's what I'm here for," she said, never losing her disapproving demeanor. "And I owe a lot to your father. He was a hero to the cause."

The cause?

"And you'll watch over Sophie?" I asked. "Promise me that."

"You can be sure."

We had arrived at David's barracks and he joined us outside. He was surprised by Frau Schmidt, and raised his brow at me. I gave an innocent shrug.

"Okay, boys, we're twenty minutes from the river. Follow me."

David was quiet, looking neither to the left nor right. I kept my head down and tried to calm my racing heart. Walking through the gate, Frau Schmidt carried on straight ahead, not blinking an eye.

"I've been watching you and Norbert for days," she said. "You always amaze me. Let me just say, without getting too sweet, that I have liked knowing you."

Her words filled me up inside. "Frau Schmidt, I feel the same, I always have. I think I have a crush on you."

"Crush? Crush? What kind of crush?"

She blushed and even David was tickled.

"You're a formidable woman, Frau Schmidt!"

"I'd come with you, but I'm afraid this formidable woman would sink your bloody boat," she said, keeping her composure. "Now, Max, there are reports that the Russians are near. I'll let you and David know what happens through Pierre. It'll satisfy your reporting needs."

"Please drop in on Hans when you can, Frau Schmidt, he means a lot to me."

"I know. He means a lot to us all."

"It's very nice of you to see us off."

"I'll wish you *bon voyage*."

Passing the utility door of Rahm's bathhouse, "Excuse me," I said. "I have to go to the bathroom. I'll meet you at the raft in a few minutes."

I had my supplies ready, hidden the night before, having scouted out the location of the large propane gas tanks used for heating. I didn't have enough explosive materials to blow up Himmler House, but there was an ample supply of kerosene for what I needed to do. By the time I'd finished, Major Karl Rahm was going to have the bath of a lifetime. As soon as Rahm turned on the sauna, the heater would ignite a slow-burning fuse, giving him just enough time to get into the tub before he was blown to high heaven.

I stopped and thought about what Poppy would have wanted me to do to the man who'd ordered his death. I hadn't lost my courage. I just couldn't kill anyone.

Pulling away the fueled cord leading to the propane tanks, I turned around and ran outside until the asphalt became a muddy path, leading through the pine woods. I eventually arrived, out of breath, at the riverbank where Norbert, David, and Frau Schmidt were waiting for me.

Pavel had given Norbert six large loaves of freshly baked black bread, some cheese, fruit, and bottles of water.

"Max, I'll see you after the war," Norbert said, choking up as he waved to us. "Godspeed, boys!"

Frau Schmidt, with a softness I had not heard in her before, said, "I'll just say a few words, and leave it at that. *Auf wiedersehen,* Max . . . You too, David. Goodbye, old friend."

I embraced her and she tensed up, but I held tight. I didn't have a mother or a father, but I still had family. I felt her relax and return my affection. "Thank you. For everything."

Then she gave David a big, long hug.

We didn't linger—we couldn't—and quickly launched the raft into the water. David and I were carried from the shore.

ON BOARD THE SS *MAX*

Willow trees formed corridors, and curtains of oaks and lindens along the river hid the landscape beyond. We were an hour downstream, with the sun shining down in all its glorious radiance and the wind whispering its March sadness across the pines, when I clenched my fist by my side and prayed to my Jewish God for forgiveness for even thinking about taking another life. At that very moment, I heard an explosion in the distance, and a blue plume of smoke floated upward over the treetops. David raised his eyebrows and I shrugged. I was sure that I'd defused everything.

After a moment's hesitation, I told David about my explosive device and how I'd wanted to surprise Major Rahm with the hottest bath of his life, to leave a personal thank-you from the son of Viktor Mueller.

"With my help, he was going to blow himself to smithereens, David! But I couldn't go through with it. I removed the fuse."

"Well, you're learning that there might just be a higher power after all, working in strange and mysterious ways. You did the right thing, Max." He almost managed a grin. "If you had, though, it would have been a hell of a story for *Vedem*!"

A rippling current caught the raft, following the banks of the

Ohře, a narrow stretch of water. I had memorized the route: even against swirling unpredictable currents, the river gave way and cooperated, taking the raft twenty kilometers toward the Elbe, which joined the Vltava, sometimes called the Moldau, leading to Prague, where it would become a stretch of riptides with treacherous waters forming when the two rivers came together.

Scoping my surroundings, ready for anything, my pulse was racing, and David was almost jumping out of his skin. But we were moving, every second taking us farther from the camp and closer to Prague. We were heading for safety. We were heading home.

There was a patch of thick fog, but I kept my confidence, not allowing myself to think that I might not be able to find my way.

Norbert had provided essential tools for navigation: plenty of rope, two lanterns, a rudder that could be removed and refitted to the stern at will, paddles fashioned from broomsticks, and a clever platform with wheels, should we need to lift the raft to get around the locks.

Early afternoon had passed, and we were now well on our way. The air was warm, the spring rains had come and gone, the ice on the river had melted, and the countryside was lush and green.

We allowed ourselves to relax a little after securing the canvas tent to protect us from rain and the evening chill. The river made light swishing sounds as I checked the construction of the raft. Everything was in order. The sun broke through as the craft slipped into a part of the river that was quiet, its path following wide, gentle curves. David improvised a pole, a smart bit of deception, giving the appearance that he was fishing.

Villagers waved from the shore and returned our greetings as we continued rippling through a rural countryside spaced with farmhouses. We were occasionally interrupted by a squadron of planes humming overhead. So far up in the sky, we could see a formation of eagles migrating to Germany to drop bombs. About an hour later, the planes were once more overhead, returning to their home base in formation.

"This war will be over soon, David. We had to leave. I know that in my heart. God, it was hard, but I'm going to go back to get Sophie and Hans."

"I'll go with you, Max."

"We've been together a long time. I can't imagine it being any other way."

"We'll always be looking back."

"I know we've done something, and that counts in the great scheme."

"We've been through so much together. A lot has happened."

"What has happened to us? We grew up."

LEAVING AND RETURNING

After folding our straw-filled sleeping bags into makeshift chairs, I took out my chart and confirmed we were on course. Falling just off his shoulders, David's maroon scarf flapped in the late afternoon breeze like a windsock indicating our direction.

Floating swiftly, making good time, we saw no soldiers. Familiar landscapes seemed to reappear every few kilometers, the same scenes, something Norbert would have appreciated. Red and yellow houses, carpets of lawn with grazing livestock searching for fresh spring grass. Occasionally, a swan or a trail of dabbling ducks crossed our wake.

"If I had known this was going to be so pleasant, I would have set sail with you a long time ago," David said lightly.

"Then who would have played Brundibár?"

David yawned and pulled a straw hat down over his face, catching the last few rays of sun bouncing off the water.

"Where did you get the Panama?" I asked.

"I helped stimulate the camp's economy and bought it during the Red Cross visit at the shop on Potemkin Day."

"It's pretty snappy. Poppy would've loved it."

Thinking about him triggered a sudden bottomless feeling, but I tried to push it aside. I was a sailor heading home, making good progress, fulfilling my father's last wishes. I was on another assignment, doing what I should be doing, my best friend at my side. We were Tom and Huck, the wind and tide were with us, and all was set fair.

In the spring, light lasted late into the day, so I decided we would sail until dark, till almost nine o'clock. We found a mooring on a riverbank. Landing near a patch of grass, David and I went ashore, pulling the raft behind. We removed our sleeping bags, provisions, and lantern, and lit a small campfire with some twigs and dry driftwood.

After a supper of black bread, cheese, and fruit, we were full and content. All the stress and sadness left me for a moment, and overhead there was a sky full of stars shining down on me. The air was sweet, life was good, and the night welcoming. I took out my notebook and wrote.

Leaving and returning. I wondered, since I'd been away for so long, would everything be the same when I returned? Would there be any familiar faces to open the door? I wrote of hellos and goodbyes, and how soon I'd be back to those familiar things that I might never have left at all.

"What are you doing, Max?"

"Just scribbling a few thoughts."

"You really are a reporter, Max. That's what we do. Write. We do it all the time. We can't stop."

They were more than a few notes. I was a Chinese poet, with no verses memorized. I could make up my own and simply recite that the rains were lighter, the music softer, the river stronger, the days brighter, the nights shorter, and my dreams nearer. Under distant stars I would give each a name: Poppy, Sophie, and Hans. That was all I had to write. It was not scribbling at all. They were my names too. They were my identity.

"How did you think of this plan, Max. How did you get the idea?"

David waited for an answer as I washed my face in a cool stream leading into the river. "I think you'll appreciate this," I said, taking out my treasured Twain.

David smiled when he saw the cover. "Good ol' Huck!"

I turned a few more pages until I found the right passage.

"We catched fish and talked . . . it was kind of solemn, drifting down the big, still river, laying on our backs looking up at the stars, and we didn't ever feel like talking loud."

I smiled at David. "It's smart to be well-read."

"Do you think we'll get to America someday?" David asked, sounding melancholy. "A free world? A safe world?"

"We're on the Mississippi now. Don't you feel like Huck and Tom, sitting around a campfire?"

David paused. "I think I do." He settled into his sleeping bag. "Well, good night, Huck."

I finally had a moment to open the blue envelope Sophie had given me. Inside was a drawing one of the kids had sketched in Sarah Markova's improvised classroom. It was a watercolor of Sophie and me under an umbrella.

What could I say? Sophie, my wonderful Sophie. The longing for her was overwhelming and the image blurred in front of my eyes. It was if I had left part of myself behind. I wondered if I would ever get it back. I put the sketch away, carefully securing it in a safe place in my jacket. I turned onto my back. Starring at the constellations far away, I thought of everyone that I had ever loved. A million stars crowded the sky, arching over some tall pine trees and sheltering me. The last thing I remembered were fireflies, like luminous raindrops, flickering in the darkness.

I wasn't sure if it was the morning light or the voice that woke me.

"Hello, you," she said. I saw a girl with braided blond hair; she must have been about twelve or so, wearing a white apron embroidered with multicolored flowers. Was I dreaming or was this Becky Thatcher out of the pages of Mark Twain?

"Where are you from?"

David sat up, rubbed his eyes, and said, "Hello to you too."

"Do you live around here?" she asked.

"We're just camping out, fishing," I replied.

"Catch any?"

"Not yet. My name is Max. Meet Peter the fisherman."

David glared at me.

"Hello, Peter the fisherman. My name is Julia," she said brightly, "and if you both would like to wash and get something to eat, I live just up the hill."

"Uh, no," we both said quickly.

She gave a small pout. "But thanks," I said.

We began packing up our stuff while Julia watched, sitting cross-legged in the grass. From behind her, someone in a white tunic appeared, a tall man with long, flowing, gray hair. He was a vision, sunlight silhouetting him.

"You boys fishing?" he asked in a soft, melodious voice.

"Yes, well, trying to catch something," David said, hurrying to get everything back onto the raft.

"If you head farther downstream, you'll have better luck."

We need plenty of that.

"Father, can we invite Max and Peter up to the house? They might enjoy a good meal . . ."

"Yes, boys, please come with us. You can't disappoint my daughter. We get so few young fishermen here."

He had a glint in his eye.

"Father!" Julia blushed, jumped up, and ran off along a path.

"Sure, we could, um, have a cup of tea."

Together, David and I gave a small shrug. It could easily be a trap, but what were we supposed to do?

We followed the path Julia had taken and soon reached a house. Beyond it was a church—a small, simple, white-wooden structure with large, polished oak doors and a golden steeple.

"We should first give thanks," said the man, who had introduced himself on the walk as Alexandr. "We're happy to welcome you," he said, "just in time for our morning service."

Then it occurred to me it was Sunday morning. And that our new friend was dressed in white. I smacked my forehead. Alexandr was a preacher. He certainly had his hands full with our escape to the Promised Land.

David and I followed him into the church where a small congregation was waiting for him, singing vigorously. I wasn't sure if it was Anglican or Catholic, and out of respect, I made the sign of the cross, touching my head, and then my heart. David, watching me closely, followed my lead.

"The other way, David," I whispered. "Left side first."

We were introduced as fishermen. Then Pastor Alexandr, robust and imposing, delivered his sermon. David and I listened respectfully.

"When Jesus first began to call his disciples, two of them were fishermen. Jesus knew the hearts of everyone; he knew fishermen spread the gospel. Let's turn to Luke 5:4–6. When Jesus first met Peter, he had been out all night fishing, but had caught nothing. Jesus tested his faith. He wanted to show Peter that all things are possible with God. As God's children, we are called to become fishermen of faith. God uses us to spread the Gospel, spread the good news."

"Just like *Vedem,* David," I whispered, "spread the news."

"If we make it, promise me, Max, we'll write about this benison someday."

Benison. Great word. I liked it.

Alexandr took the fitting stance in prayer, lifting his hands upward, and implored, "Cast the net upon the waters and ye shall find."

The congregation murmured, "Praise God."

I suspected David had never been in a church, and I didn't know whether to laugh or cry at our predicament. Did the congregation really believe we were fishermen? I didn't think so. But we were treated with kindness, and if blessings existed, this was one.

After the service, we went to Julia's home.

"Father has to say goodbye to the congregation, but he'll join us later," Julia said, showing us around the house. "If you want to freshen up, there's a bathroom upstairs."

I took advantage of the opportunity, taking a long shower; as I washed, I saw pine treetops out the window.

I had not felt so fresh in a while, and after drying off with a fluffy towel, dressed and went down to Sunday lunch. David had already done the same, and was talking to Julia's grandmother, Marta.

I joined in the conversation and learned that Grandma Marta was from Budapest. She had prepared an old family recipe of paprika-laced roasted chicken, vegetable goulash with peas and potatoes, and for dessert, something I had never had before, a delicious sponge cake called *dobos torta*. They were farmers, raising livestock, growing vegetables. "Eat, child, eat!" Grandma Marta urged. And we did.

David noticed a violin case on a table and admired it.

"Do you play?" Julia asked.

"I haven't for a time."

"He plays quite well," I happily announced.

"Would you please play something for us?" Julia asked.

"Yes, play for us, Peter," I said.

I didn't mind putting David on the spot; after all, it was a way to return their hospitality in some small measure.

To my delight, David picked up the violin with a self-conscious flourish. He tuned the instrument, and, after placing a white napkin under his chin, vigorously played Brahms's "Hungarian Dance no. 6." Julia did a folk dance and Grandma Marta gleefully clapped her hands. David played so well that Marta urged him to continue, so he surpassed himself with Brahms's "Hungarian Dance no. 7."

"Where did you learn those compositions?" I asked when he finished with a dramatic bow.

"My teacher must have been a gypsy. 'Number 6' was his most popular piece."

Gravel crunched outside. I glanced out the window and saw a German staff car had pulled into the driveway in front of the church. I couldn't see them clearly, but could make out a few officers talking among themselves. I didn't think they'd come to pray. When the pounding on the door of the chapel became louder, Aleksandr stepped outside.

I couldn't hear what they were saying, but I wasn't going to stay around to find out. Grabbing David's hand, I jerked him up from his chair.

"Thank you all so much, but we really have to go. You know, this time of the day is the best for fishing."

David nodded and grabbed another piece of sponge cake from the table as I pulled him out the back door. Julia ran after us.

"Wait!" she cried.

"Thank you for everything, Julia," I called back over my shoulder. "Goodbye!"

We arrived at the raft, jumped aboard, and pushed off onto the water.

"Hope you catch a lot of fish!" Julia called to us as we floated from the shore and sailed away, still waving as we negotiated the next turn on the river.

"That was close," David remarked quietly. "But we were lucky. We meet people along the way and there must be reasons. I wonder if they were sent by God."

"Maybe Poppy is upstairs conducting the show."

David started to enter the makeshift cabin, but abruptly stopped.

We were just a few hundred yards down the river, as David quietly sidled up to me and whispered, "Be careful."

"What's going on?"

"We have a passenger, there's someone or something inside the canvas. I saw it moving."

I caught my breath? *A stowaway.* It couldn't be possible.

"It moved again." David pointed.

He was right. "Who is it?"

"I don't feel good about this."

The cover of the tent was thrown open, and the man in the black overcoat loomed over me pointing a gun. When had he gotten on the raft?

It should have come as no surprise. The overcoat man had been patient, finding just the right time and place to strike. And now it was convenient to make sure we would never reach our destination. I hadn't thought about inspecting the raft—too intent on running from the German staff car.

"You bastard. What do you want?" I shouted.

"Care for a glass of milk from the green box, you little prick? I've caught you. You're a spy, an enemy of the Reich, just like your father."

Had he been responsible for Poppy's death? I was consumed with rage.

I diverted his attention, yelling, as David slid to the side of the raft.

"I know who you are and what you do."

I lunged toward him. But in that instant, David picked up a paddle and slammed it across the man's back. *Craaaaack!*

It was stunning.

Then a crashing blow to his head, rendering him senseless.

Blood gushed from his head and with a spilling moan he fell overboard, trying to hold on.

It happened quickly.

David stamped on his hands and kicked him in the face. The man was lost in the water.

"You don't waste time with the enemy," David said without looking up. "If you have a weapon, you use it." I stared at David. He acted fast, so decisively. I never knew he had such strength in him.

The current carried the overcoat man away, floating unconscious some distance behind us.

"We can't just leave him to drown, David."

"Oh, I think we can, Max."

He watched the man drift farther away.

"The Gestapo all carry guns, Max. He was going to kill us."

"Self-defense?"

"Of course, but more than that, Max, a statement to make up for everyone he murdered. It was the right thing to do, Max. It is tough, but the right thing. I don't regret it."

The wind calmed, the raft paused, and a black ledger floated past us. It was as if time were dancing in slow motion. David reached in and retrieved it.

There were hundreds of entries that had been recorded, but

they were no longer legible. The river had washed away names that now belonged to the past.

The raft continued along the Ohře another ten kilometers. The skies turned a dark gray, with a flash of lightning signaling a storm. The SS *Max* rocked as the river became choppy. Steadying the rudder in the rapids, it picked up speed just before the rain came.

"The calm before the storm, Max. I thought we might run into some heavy weather."

"David, we'll be all right."

The water lashed the raft, and soon we were flying downstream with tremendous speed in the pouring rain, the tent catching the wind, propelling us even faster.

"I'll protect everything," David said, as he secured our belongings to keep them dry.

"Stay inside!" I shouted to him when he poked his head out for a weather update.

"Do you swim, Max?" His voice was muffled inside the tent.

"Yes, a little."

"I don't!"

"Hold on!"

We sped over a whirling, zigzagging current, turning back and forth toward shore, and I hoped David wouldn't get seasick.

Following the path of a streaming current, I held the rudder and straightened the craft. A cloud opened up and another torrent of rain drenched me. But the raft held up.

"Whoopeeeee!" I yelled, as lashings of rain fell from the sky.

David stuck his head out again; the water was whipping me with pellets. "You're crazy, Max!"

"So I've heard!"

The storm lasted a few hours before the sun finally broke through. The rain subsided, and, reaching calmer waters, the craft approached a lock. The keeper opened the gates, with no hint of concern about an unconventional craft passing through. For a few minutes, the raft was placed between two watertight doors. The lock filled and, when the water level was higher, the steel enclosure opened to a wider expanse of the river. Reaching the Elbe, we stretched out on the small deck, which still smelled like varnish. Dining on bread and cheese, we celebrated the completion of another leg of our journey. The sun warmed us. David turned to me. "That was close, Max, we could have drowned. But I'm impressed with your seamanship. You might want to pursue a career in the navy when all this is over."

But then, as if on cue, we heard a boat speeding toward us, and as it approached, I saw the colors of the German flag.

"Start paddling, David! They've found us!"

"Maybe we should've built a submarine!" David tried to settle down.

The powerful gray boat, leaving a rolling wake behind, came slowly alongside the raft. I cringed when I saw the three-man crew on the German gunboat.

Taking a deep breath, I called to the captain in perfect German, "*Guten Tag!* It's a nice day and I'd welcome you aboard, but we don't have much room!"

The captain was puzzled, but in a flash, burst out laughing. "What are you doing out here?"

"On our way to Prague for a spring holiday. How is it down there?"

I knew that the Elbe flowed through Czechoslovakia and Germany. "My uncle is in the navy, Captain Ernst Donitz; do you know him?"

They didn't, of course; I had made up the most seaworthy name I could think of. "He helped us build the raft."

"*Ach,* German ingenuity," the captain called back.

"What are you doing out here?" I asked.

"Patrolling the waters."

"For fish?"

That, too, brought a measure of good cheer. "Not for little fishes," the captain said. "Be safe, boys."

And with that, they sped away.

David shook his head and stared at the receding boat. "That was the finest bit of acting I've ever seen you do. Award-winning. I don't know how you get away with it, Max."

I stood tall and lowered my voice. "Trust me, David," I said, and with a familiar gesture, I imitated the confidence of the Great Viktor Mueller. David recognized it immediately, clapped and called, "Bravo!"

"Did you notice how they kept looking at your shoes?"

David was wearing the official military issue ones acquired for the Red Cross visit. They were probably made for the German navy.

"You must be our lucky charm, Max, you jumped over the cracks on that one."

"We don't need luck. We're the Czech All Stars, David!"

David laughed.

The river was unpredictable, always changing. One moment, the tidal current ran fast. In another, we floundered and flopped around a bend, decorous and stately. The afternoon brought calmer waters and we had to paddle, which was more strenuous than I had anticipated. Soon we were caught in the current once again, and sailed easily, skimming along in our craft. We cut through fast-moving water, bouncing over the whitecaps.

"We should announce Norbert Troller as the best naval

architect in the world," David said. "He's an admiral! Give that man a gold star! I don't think even the German navy could sink us."

Along a deserted pier, we lit our lanterns, setting up camp for the night.

Early the next morning, flat barges were chugging down the Elbe.

"Give me a few loaves of bread and a wedge of cheese," said David.

I wasn't sure what he was up to. "Do you need a few crowns?"

I had my secret supply stashed away in a can of baby powder that had been with me for years now.

"Not a problem. But I'll need plenty of rope."

One of the smaller barges was nearby and David flagged it down. I wondered what he was up to. I watched as he negotiated with the captain, gesturing with his hands. A few minutes later, we were following in the wake of the *Maria Victory,* a small postal boat headed toward Prague and calmer waters. We were secured by a rope that stretched fifty feet or so, pulling us along.

"Traditionally, we Jews are not very good sailors, Max; we're better traders. What's that biblical saying?" In his best German, David proudly quoted, "*Wirf dein Brot hin auf die Fläche der Wasser.* Cast thy bread upon the waters." He stretched out his full frame and sunbathed for the rest of the morning.

The Elbe suddenly calmed into the Vltava and I heard Smetana's classic melody echoing in my mind. The same melody that would someday become the anthem of Israel. It was soft at first, then slowly it became louder and bolder, as the river opened to Prague. It was such a haunting tune. I hummed it for the next few miles.

Reaching the sunlit distance, the raft rounded another turn, and there was the Charles Bridge and the red roofs of Malá Strana. Clustered carriage houses sloped down the hills nearby, their images stirring colors on the river. They were landscapes of sorrowful beauty, nowhere lovelier. Off the river's edge, a few small boats with white hulls and flapping pastel-tinted sails caught the afternoon wind. With the singing spirit of the Vltava, we were home.

JUDITH LANDING

There we were, in familiar surroundings. But David and I didn't need to exchange a look, let alone a word, to express what we both understood at once. We were passing through and this was no longer home. The Prague that we had known was gone forever, in the same way that our childhood, so much of it shared, was gone. And with it, our innocence. I recognized so much of the place, but it was changed in ways I couldn't quite understand and perhaps never would. What I knew almost at once was that it was no longer the city of my parents. It was no longer my Prague. And I knew that it could never again be home.

But we were there for a time and we owed so much then and always would, to our host, our friend. Pierre Burger's name was really Petr, but he had worked for Frau Schmidt, and liked his job so much, he decided to study at a school in France to be a hotelier. Like a tenor learning a new part, he adapted to his role so well that he now appeared authentically French. He affected a slight accent and, just as Frau Schmidt promised, he was waiting for us in an old broken-down car at Judith Landing.

"This is some raft," he said and whistled, admiring the detail and craftsmanship. He greeted us with joy, surprise, and the warmest of welcomes. "Viktor would have enjoyed this adventure, Max." Just being close to someone else who knew my father—who could say his name to me—gave me a sense of peace.

"Let's go, boys," he said, and began to dismantle the craft. I had formed a sentimental attachment to it, but Pierre said it was necessary, just in case, not to leave evidence. As we took it apart I saw stenciled on the side of each flotation drum, a black swastika. I'd bet the officers on the patrol boat had also noticed them. Ironic that the hated symbol would have protected us.

We transferred our clothing and removed the box containing my hurdy-gurdy to Pierre's old automobile, one of the few private cars left in Prague. It wasn't in great shape, but it was able to carry us across the bridge, coughing puffs of white smoke all the way. Driving up the hills, it was clear that Prague hadn't changed, except that it was mostly populated by German uniforms. Every building was waving multiple red-and-black German flags. But for how much longer?

Pierre's pension was a small bed-and-breakfast inn on a cobblestone street just above an area called the Castle Steps. It was an attractive three-story house, with dark green flower boxes under the windows planted with tulips in a flow of pink.

Was it a symbol, a sign, a statement? David said he was sure that the pink tulips were flowers to celebrate every member of the Resistance.

A large living room had light cream walls and a pale green molding bordering the ceiling. An antique, petite-point rug with a quiet flower pattern gave warmth, along with a few nicely placed botanical prints on the walls.

There were certain formalities after we arrived. I opened my secret can of powder, giving all my banknotes to Pierre. After counting the large bills, Pierre said, "Max, you have given me enough for six months' stay." I had no idea of the amount Poppy had deposited but I was sure it was a hefty portion of his savings.

"You don't owe me anything. But I'll hold this for you," Pierre told me, removing the rug and hiding the currency in a little safe under the flooring. Then Pierre showed us to a small room on the top floor.

"We only have fourteen rooms, but we're rarely full, not like the old days," Pierre explained. "Mostly people from Berlin. And please, not too much conversation with the guests. You never know who they are. Right now, we just have a Mr. Hoff, who appears to be a businessman.

"You and David will live in these servants' quarters; they're comfortable, quite suitable, and I will ask you to wear blue aprons. You'll be expected to change linen, sweep the floors, and do light cleaning. If you have time, straighten the drawing room. Be earnest and occupied as you work. If you want to clean the brass from time to time, fine, but not essential. It should take you no more than a few hours a day, but it's a good cover. The rest of the time, you are on your own; but be careful, stay in the neighborhood, and don't do anything suspicious. If anyone should inquire who you are, I'll mention we're related—my sister is working in a porcelain factory near Prague, and you're helping me out with the family business.

"You will be safe here. But you mustn't be noticed, Max. I cannot emphasize that enough. You'll not find the Prague you knew. Do you have papers?"

"My passport won't be much good."

"And David?"

David shook his head.

"Not to worry. We'll get papers for you. You'll need them, not for long, but just until the war is over, and a new identity too."

Pierre had a well-thought-out plan, and David and I would do everything to handle our end expertly.

I had been quiet for almost the entire afternoon, but now I had to ask: "Pierre, have you heard from Frau Schmidt?"

"Max, she and your friend Hans were on transports with the children after you left. I'm just learning the details, but I know they've been sent to the family camp next to Auschwitz."

David gasped, and I felt the room spinning around me.

Sophie. I pushed the terror down. Fear was not an option. Sophie was alive. Sophie had to be alive. I must have looked like I was about to faint because I felt Pierre's hand on my shoulder. "Steady, Max. Trust me, if anyone knows how to deal with the Germans, it's Frau Schmidt. And the children will be all right. The Germans are fleeing; the war is almost over. It's only a matter of a few weeks."

David put his arm around my shoulders, as if to say he understood my anguish. I knew he was feeling the same thing.

I held my breath, hoping he was right.

"She's a formidable woman, indeed," Pierre continued. "And by the way, she gave Rahm the biggest bath of his life."

"She didn't!"

I thought back to the explosion we'd heard after our launch.

"I suspect there was some unfinished business to attend to, and she took care of it."

It confirmed my suspicion that Frau Schmidt kept tabs on everything.

"She blew him up?"

"To the moon!"

I couldn't find the words to express my admiration.

"Don't worry, she'll be back running a boarding house one of these days."

"When you least expect it, something happens," David said, trying to sound lighthearted.

"Please, come sit down," Pierre said, pointing to a small wooden bench in the alcove.

"There's much you need to know. Things that your father couldn't tell you."

Finally, some answers.

"Frau Schmidt is one of us," said Pierre.

"One of who?" I asked.

"A member of Pink Tulip, the underground Resistance. We're determined to wipe out the Nazis using any means necessary. Your father and Frau Schmidt . . ."

Everything began to fall into place.

"Poppy was working undercover? With you?"

"I recruited him through Sam Raggle. Max, your father was—a great man. We were going to blow up the State Opera House at a Remembrance Day Concert in Berlin when he conducted Brahms's *Ein Deutsches Requiem*. Fate intervened."

David didn't bat an eye.

"You do know that Viktor was Hitler's favorite conductor, right?"

I nodded. *Poppy was everyone's favorite conductor.*

Pierre continued, "This killing business was part of the job. A necessary part of the job, do you understand?"

"Wasn't Poppy with Heydrich when he was killed?" I asked. "He wasn't involved?"

"Winston Churchill was running that operation and he gave direct orders to keep Viktor in the dark about that plan, especially considering he was the only one who could lead us to Heydrich. And after that failed bombing at the opera house, Churchill didn't think Viktor had what it took to kill."

Churchill?

I had another burning question.

"What happened after the Red Cross visit?"

"Viktor went to Hungary. We had work to do there with Raoul Wallenberg. You'll learn the details in time, but the simple fact is that by our estimates, Raoul Wallenberg and Viktor saved over one hundred thousand Jews in Hungary.

"You have to know that there was one decision that Viktor struggled with every single day. If he had removed you from the camp, it would have aroused suspicion. And he was engaged in such a delicate game with Heydrich and others. You understand this, Max? Keeping you at Terezín would reinforce his dedication to the regime. It was a charade that had to be maintained for the success of the operation. After Budapest, he finally faced what he had to do and blew up those Nazi bastards on the train and destroyed the tracks—the transports leading in and out of Terezín. He was coming to get you, Max, and he was a good man, and he loved you more than anything. He was part of the Resistance, and what he did took courage and strength. That was your father."

I felt my heart cracking in my chest. But I still had so many questions.

"Can you tell me more about Frau Schmidt?" I asked. "Why did she really come to Terezín?"

"You remember her guesthouse in Berlin?" I nodded, recalling it as though it were yesterday. "The Nazis accused her of protecting enemies of the state. We huddled with Viktor and found a place where she was needed, and lucky for us, it was Terezín. I'm sure with her experience, she managed quite well."

"So you know Sam Raggle?"

After taking a moment, Pierre admitted, "Quite well. He's a colleague. He was very much a part of our team. Max, when you were delivering papers, you were not just delivering news, but information we had placed inside each paper to get to our network. We had Anna Kingsley, our operative in London, working for *The Observer,* who published our reports. While you were at Terezín, everything you sent to Sam, along with all of Viktor's information, got to us."

David and I stared at each other, without a word.

"Everyone was suspect," Pierre said.

"Including me?"

"Including you. It's complex, Max, we work in strange ways. Viktor was our inside source in the Chancellery. He sent strategic information in newspapers from Berlin to the stand, intelligence that we needed, and reports that went to London. That's the way we distributed the news. That's the way we got the word out."

Pierre chose his moment carefully. "I'm deeply sorry about what happened to Viktor, Max. I know it's too painful to talk about when it hurts so much. I lost my family too. And I wish I had news about your parents, David. I don't, except my sources tell me they are safe."

I barely knew Pierre, but I knew his every word was accurate.

How about Hans and Sophie? Surely, he would know if they were alive? But he said nothing. David was white-faced, his hands gripped in fists.

I looked across at him, and then back at Pierre: "I have to go back and get Sophie."

Pierre shook his head slowly, closed his eyes for a while, and finally spoke: "Let things settle a bit, Max."

He was trying to tell me something that I wasn't ready to hear.

I wept quietly, and Pierre said, "Viktor was a heroic man, but in the end, what you need to know is that, more than anything, he loved you."

We wore customary blue housekeeping aprons. In fact, David had all the brass in the pension gleaming in no time, and I took to polishing Mr. Hoff's shoes, leaving them outside his room in the morning. We were free in the afternoons. Once more the city was ours.

We were anxious to visit all the places we had known, but for the first week, Pierre thought it was a bad idea. "It's better to hold some things in your mind as they were," he said. "The places you lived are different. The Nazis have seen to that. Some Germans are still here, the Russians will be coming soon, the Americans are nearby. You might be safer in Český Krumlov. It's an agreeable thirteenth-century town, situated where the Vltava begins, near the border, not far from here. I have friends if you want to go there."

"We'll take our chances here. Prague is our home."

But even as I said the words, another plan was taking shape in my head.

"It's time we went out and walked the streets."

I decided that, risky or not, we had to get out into the city. We had identification papers. We packed up my hurdy-gurdy, boarded a trolley, and with the familiar *clang-clang,* David and I were on our way to the Companie Musik. I hoped that Mr. Mannheim, the blind music master who used to give me my piano-tuning jobs remembered me.

When we passed the park, Mr. Raggle's newsstand was gone. Out of respect, I stood and saluted.

So many of the places I had known had disappeared. I was relieved when we arrived at Mr. Mannheim's Companie Musik.

Nothing had changed in the shop except perhaps a little more dust had collected.

"I didn't forget you, Mr. Brundibár," Mr. Mannheim said,

when we arrived at his shop. "I've missed my partner." He had a wide smile on his face. "How was your performance?"

"It took me to Berlin, and Terezín."

"Terezín. You're Jewish then?"

I smiled at David. "It's a long story, but yes, we're both Jewish."

"And you escaped, you've survived?"

"A lot happened, and along the way, you were with us."

"You're music makers."

"Yes, that's just what we are."

"Then, I want to know, how was the hurdy-gurdy?"

I carefully unpacked it and passed it to him after all those years. "She sure is a beauty," I said.

Mannheim smoothed his hand over the wooden box.

"Working well?"

"Like a charm, but it might need a tune-up."

The instrument was designed to play eight tunes on a single cylinder.

"Do you have any other rolls?"

"I have another hurdy-gurdy that takes twelve, nice condition, nice melodies."

"I'd like to keep the one I have, I'm used to it, but I need a few new tunes."

Inspecting the box, he mumbled to himself, "Standard size. I have about forty. What do you require?"

"I could use three rolls—Czech, Russian, and German tunes."

Entering a room that had several dozen violins and bows on consignment, Mr. Mannheim unwrapped three wooden rolls that were already pinned.

"David, pick out a violin."

David frowned and pulled me aside. "How are you going to pay for it, Max?"

"I have enough for the down payment with some of the money Poppy gave me. I didn't give all of it to Pierre."

"Max, I can't let you do that. Who knows when you'll need that cash?"

"David, you know as well as I do that Poppy would be happy if we were spending funds like this."

David smiled. "I'll do it for the Great Viktor Mueller!"

"I have recently acquired a D. Soriot you might like," Mr. Mannheim said, gently removing the polished instrument from its case as if it were a masterpiece.

David soared up and down several scales; the violin was responsive, the tone resonant. "Max, why are you buying me such an expensive gift?"

"You deserve it, and besides, I'm booking us on every street corner in Prague."

"What?"

"I'm going to play for my father."

Mr. Mannheim knew exactly what I had in mind, and what we would need. He referred us to his son, who managed a shop that carried formal wear.

"Max, you both have to be very careful. Don't assume anything."

"After what we've been though, nothing can be so dangerous. Music will protect us."

He nodded. "I suspect it will."

"We need to dress for our assignment. Would he have anything in our size?"

"Everything for gentlemen of your stature. Mannheim II has a warehouse full of the stuff. I'll take you there; it's just around the corner."

A few minutes later we were each fitted out in black tails,

white shirt and vest, white tie, and wing collars. And on a makeup table, I found a fake mustache like I'd worn in *Brundibár.*

"Pretty dapper," I said, selecting a new top hat. "I might even dance with Ginger Rogers."

David decided a black fedora would go well with his scarf. The hat was one size too big, but it didn't matter; he liked wearing one.

"David," I announced, "we're going to perform as if we were playing with the Berlin Philharmonic."

The way I figured it, even with the danger from German troops still occupying the city and Czech Resistance fighters on the streets, music was international; everyone loved music. No guns would harm us.

Our first performance was in front of Hradčany Castle, where the German high command still had offices. It was not far from Pension Burger.

We attracted a small crowd of officers as we played "*Denn heute da hört uns Deutschland, Und morgen die ganze Welt*"—"For today, Germany hears us, and tomorrow, the world." Before we finished, the Germans had formed a patriotic circle. David had his violin case open, and it was filled with deutschmarks and crowns. I took part of the collection to Mr. Mannheim's shop at the end of the day.

The hurdy-gurdy roll swept into Strauss's nostalgic "Radetzky March" and the group clapped along with the music. I cranked the barrel organ; David played his new violin like a virtuoso. Our next stop was in Old Town, where we wasted no time changing rolls to some *trampská hudba,* romantic Czech folk songs. If a unit of Germans came along, we could quickly switch rolls. It would be a while before Soviet forces would enter Prague and we would have the opportunity to play Russian songs.

We aimed to fill every street corner we could with music. When Pierre found out, he asked us to report any unusual activity coming from different quarters. Like Poppy, we too could be part of the underground movement. We were part of the Resistance.

I asked Mr. Mannheim for a music roll of Yiddish songs so we could play them in Josefov. What we should have known before we went there was that none of the Jewish population had survived.

"Everything Jewish has been destroyed, Max. Where are the houses and shops and libraries?" David couldn't control his rage. "Utter madness, Max. Look, even the monuments in the graveyard have been overturned."

David picked up his violin case.

We went to another part of the city to play. We never accepted another coin.

The end of the war was near and this had a powerful effect on Czechs all over the country; their bitter hatred strengthened by Nazi uprisings from the last of Hitler's soldiers. Pierre led what he called the "battle of the rails," disrupting German troop trains and damaging tracks and bridges. When Radio Prague announced that the Allies were at the outskirts, the city's remaining residents began streaming into the streets to welcome the victors, tearing down German traffic signs, flags, and store inscriptions, attacking any Nazi in sight, seizing their weapons. But it wasn't over yet. Armed Resistance fighters overwhelmed the Waffen-SS defending Gestapo headquarters.

There was still the daily briefing Pierre received not only from Radio Prague, but by shortwave. We knew that partisans had managed to reoccupy half the city before the Germans reacted in force. The Germans again responded by cutting off electricity, water supplies, and telephone wires. Pierre left for hours at a time and when he returned, David and I received the latest information and updates—we could feel that this was an important moment in history. The remaining German forces outside of Prague were moving toward the city center. As their advance ran into significant resistance, Luftwaffe planes dropped bombs, and David and I took cover. We listened as Czech Radio, the national station, broadcast an appeal to the United States' General George Patton, whose Third Army was just twenty kilometers away; but there was no response because of an agreement the Allies had made. The Russians would be permitted to claim victory and occupy the capital.

Pierre was back in the streets again until morning. David and I stayed at the pension; we dared not go back out just now. Frustrated by the lack of decisive progress, the German infantry had launched several furious tank attacks. The situation was grave. Germany's air force raided Prague out of pure spite, destroying many historic landmarks. Then the Germans began to scatter. Mr. Hoff, our only guest, left in a hurry. Pierre and many partisans barricaded the block; there would be no more German guests at Pension Burger. German civilians residing in Prague—administrators, officials, and family members of the military—were all targets of Czech anger. They fled by any means, even stealing vehicles when they could find no other way. Their army was trapped both inside and outside Prague. On May 9, 1945, Radio Prague announced that the Red Army had entered the city, and the conflict ended. Along with everyone, David and I welcomed the Russians, playing "Kalinka" on a street corner to waving commanders passing by in their tanks.

Music always took me back in time. Just hearing the tinny

tunes from the barrel-organ, I thought about the six long years we had lived under Nazi tyranny. Pierre told me that General Patton's Third Army had overpowered the Sudetenland. Then he told me the most important news of all.

Anna Kingsley was traveling with Patton.

One of Prague's newspapers was back to printing a daily edition and reported that the German army was literally melting away; thousands of its soldiers deserted daily. Finally, American and Soviet forces linked up and the rebuilding of the country began. Then one day, there was a new guest arriving at Pension Burger.

With a knock at the front door, there she was. It was Anna. When Anna walked into a room, the room came to her. I cannot describe the joy I felt. She had appeared so many times that it was just too wondrous, too magical to account for it. Except to say, in the great scheme of things, it was meant to be.

"Friends are treasures that come our way," David said. "They walk in when the world seems to have walked away."

Anna never walked away.

"You built a raft!" she cried as I ran into her waiting arms. "Max Mueller, Horatio Nelson himself, First Lord of the Admiralty!"

David and I shrugged our shoulders and stood there in a casual modest pose as if we had just made an ordinary outing, a few days on the river.

"I'm here, Max. I'm here to take you home."

Anna was dressed in shades of khaki, a British correspondent's kit, but her face was the same as I remembered. Memory had not played tricks. Her hair was swept back, not much makeup, but she never needed any. I couldn't say a word, and then David took out his violin and began to play. Pierre and Anna and I held hands and danced and shouted, and laughter brimmed the room.

"I want to go back and get Sophie," I said to Anna. "I made a promise. She's expecting me."

She said nothing. For what seemed like a lifetime, she stared out the window, apparently hoping for sunlight. There was none. The day was as overcast as her ashen face. Then she was holding a copy of *The Observer* dated April 22, 1945. I could see tears forming in her eyes. "I never wanted to give this to you." She put her arm around me. Then I knew.

WHILE THE MUSIC PLAYED

Six hundred British troops liberated a concentration camp on April 15, 1945. I flew into Poland, carrying a war correspondent's passport with diplomatic credentials. I hitched a ride with Sgt. Ernie Jacoby from Charleston, South Carolina. He was shuttling supplies back and forth between the newly liberated camp and Krakow. In his Southern drawl he said, "Lady, it's not pretty." Arriving at the camp at dusk, I entered Auschwitz with the Black Watch Regiment. Captain William McDowell said, "If hell is on earth, this must be it." Walking through the gates with his men, I saw human beings who had been beaten, starved, and tortured, many standing hopelessly in their striped pajamas, with hollow, deep-set eyes, reaching toward the soldiers in a desperate effort to hand over their suffering. Then I learned the tragedy of what had happened while the music played, something that will forever be embedded in my memory. Sitting around a dying, flickering bonfire at dusk, I stumbled at last upon three men and a woman who told me that they were the musicians, the welcoming group at the station in Auschwitz. To survive the horror, they played to their own people who were coming there to die. They were part of a quartet. When the last doors of the transports were thrown open to a breath of fresh air, the bleary-eyed and tired, barely clinging to life, moved forward in single-file lines to barking orders. Brahms and Strauss and Mendelssohn gave them just enough hope to live for a few more minutes. A violinist, a soft-spoken lady from Prague, told me about a composer she had recognized.

Hans Krása had arrived from Terezín with a group of children. As he strode past her, a teenage girl was holding his hand. She looked up at him and said, "They're playing Mendelssohn. Isn't it beautiful?"

A member of the quartet told me that they stopped for a moment. The German officers had little patience for stragglers, but they allowed the composer and the girl to stand for a few moments with the rest of the children, listening to the music. I wrote down the woman's words exactly.

"The world needs to remember. You need to know."

The children were told to follow a line on the right, not for the labor force, but for the showers. The young girl was with them. The men were grouped with the men assigned to the left side to work, but Krása refused. "To the left, you belong left, left!" a guard shouted, pointing to him. But he insisted on staying with the children. He joined the line on the right never letting go of the girl's hand. The SS officers led everyone to Block no. 11, a concrete room disguised as a shower facility. The gas was turned on, and they were dead.

These words that should never have existed, never been spoken, never written. I couldn't breathe, couldn't speak for a full minute, maybe longer, falling into a chair, my head in my hands.

Sophie died at Auschwitz.

In my mind's eye, I saw children together, holding hands in a single wave, short pants, swirling skirts, sweeping hair, until they disappeared over a field of wild poppies. The pages in my memory became unglued.

"Sit next to me," Anna said, patting the couch. I looked across at her, my eyes making a desperate appeal. "I should have never left. Everyone's gone. Sophie, Hans. So many of them. They're all dead. All of them. How many did they murder? How many? Millions?"

Anna stroked my head. She lowered her voice. "I lost someone too, Max. Someone who meant so much to me, meant so much to us, someone who gave everything he had, someone who gave us the gift of music."

David was nearby. He had seen it all. A newsman to the end. But his heart was hurting beyond all comprehension too.

I put my head in Anna's lap and sobbed.

For all my life, I had been focusing on each day as it happened, on what each day, each moment needed, struggling to stay alive, to love my friends, to do whatever I could. Now the true horror of it all was hitting me, and I felt unmoored, lost, broken. I wondered what it had all been for. I wondered if I still had a life in front of me. I wondered if there was still a purpose, a reason to carry on.

That night, I saw the Milky Way; it was like a river of stars. I desperately looked for Sophie among them. Sophie, whose gentle presence gave me enough reason to know that providence had decided that such light could fill darkness. She was the brightest of them all. When dawn breaks, and each day begins, in the province of my imagination, I see myself at the end of a long road, and on each side there are tall green pines and sycamores swaying in a summer wind, and walking toward me is Sophie wearing a smile of smiles, walking step by step, leaving footfalls from a thousand yesterdays.

There were countless numbers of displaced Jews all over Europe at the end; they all carried a strong wish to rebuild their lives, hoping to immigrate anywhere. As before the war, their efforts were limited by quotas put in place by the British, but many managed to make their way over mountains to Europe's coasts, and some gained passage to Palestine on clandestine boats.

Jewish families crowded onto rickety ships attempting to make it through the British blockade. Discovery meant arrest. Despite the risks, sixty-four ships delivered more than seventy thousand people to Palestinian waters. Another fifty thousand were stopped and taken to British refugee camps on Cyprus, in the Mediterranean. But the brightest moment came for those who managed to get a visa, and Anna had secured one for David, knowing he might soon see his parents, and sent word to them.

I was going to miss him with all my heart. *The Topper!*

"I guess this is it. I'm finally going to make it to Palestine," he said, standing in the front hall of the pension surrounded by his few bags. "I wouldn't have made it without you, Max. I'd be gone and you know it."

I had tears in my eyes. "Tom and Huck to the end."

David patted me on the shoulder. "Now I'm not sure how

I'm going to manage without you. We've been through so much together."

I felt an emptiness in my heart. "I miss you already, David." I tried to smile.

"Not as much as I'll miss you, Max."

"We'll be pen pals until I join you. Someday soon."

Perhaps if I believed this enough, it would come true. David looked at me, eyes bright, and nodded his head.

"We thought we'd run out of tomorrows, but look at us. We made it, and here we are, tomorrow is here."

He pulled me close and hugged me. "You're my best friend, the best friend I could ever have."

I nodded. "You too."

I could barely stand it. Who was left? What was left of my past, my whole life?

"When you come visit, I'll have a paper up and running. The *Palestinian Post.*" He smiled.

"You're a great reporter, David. You taught me everything I know."

"Keep your notebooks, Max. Never let them go."

"Maybe I should censor any passages I've written about you!"

"All right, enough of this mutual admiration stuff," David said, tying his scarf around his neck. I escorted him to the relocation center.

In his pocket, David had a copy of Yeats. He always had a book nearby. Turning to me, he recited, "*Think where man's glory most begins and ends, and say my glory was I had such friends.* Put that in your book!"

"Well spoken by my editor!"

"You'll come and see me?"

I smiled. "Of course. I'll be there."

"Promise?"

"Promise."

David saluted. The last thing I saw of him was his maroon scarf flying behind him as he walked through the entrance.

I knew he would become a journalist of distinction, grounded in curiosity and truth, fighting with determination—a teacher, a witness. The heads of the Royal Typewriter Company would certainly be inspired to name their most advanced model after him, a fine piece of work named the Royal Topper, which would without exception produce words and narratives that would be remembered for all time by a congregation of editors, so fortunate to be sitting at the same desk, all with green eyeshades, all tapping, each confident that the Topper was destined to be the finest among them, a journalist's journalist.

As the door closed behind him, I felt more alone than ever.

PASSAGE TO LONDON

A British officer arrived and invited Anna and me to come with him to the station. I was going to London. My trip had been postponed for too long. While we were standing in line for my papers to be reviewed and stamped for Great Britain, there was a man in front of us. "I see you are going to America," the customs official said to him. "That's a pretty long trip."

In an instant, the man responded, "Not so long."

"Where are you coming from?"

"You don't want to know."

A lot had happened in the world. Ships went to the bottom of the sea, soldiers died on blood-swept battlefields, families were lost, a war was fought, music was almost silenced.

He couldn't begin to describe his camp and years of suffering. He carried a lot of baggage, and I knew how heavy it was.

I was easily accommodated in my own berth as the night train took us to London. I snuggled under my blanket, looking out the window, and calling out to Anna every so often, just to hear her voice, to see if it was all real. My emotions must have been very like those of someone who had been forgotten and locked away, only to find himself suddenly outside. I had savored the sweet taste of freedom, yet I returned in my mind, again and again, to a place inside those dark gates. I was exhausted and gripped with such foreboding about my future that my mind retreated from any notion of what the next years might bring. My thoughts rummaged through and fiddled with the past. I looked over to the night table near my bed and saw the one companion that had never left me: my red notebook. I had not revisited it for a time and turned to one of the last entries before the raft. It was about *The Adventures of Huckleberry Finn.*

> It was an extravagant voyage of freedom, giving relief to Jim's tormented slavery, confused by incalculable feeling underneath his essential humanity. It was not merely freedom for Jim, but for good people like Tom and Huck.

I read a few passages and then I fell asleep.

I had a dream about Mark Twain. I was sitting on the porch of a plantation house along the Mississippi River, sipping a cool, minted iced tea with the great author. Twain wore the same white linen as the table before me and a coral-colored camellia in his lapel. There was no hesitancy when he turned his deep blue eyes upon me, no embarrassment in the sudden, light touch of friendship by his hand on the back of mine, nor was there anything unusual in his Midwestern manner of speaking as he uttered, "Max Mueller, your diary has been an inspiration to me! Without it, I could not have finished my story."

But in the end, as I worked through the riddle of conflict, it was Tom and Huck and Jim who had inspired me.

"I'm happy you're here, Max. You've had a long journey. Let's go home," Anna said.

Pierre had arranged for me to stay until I reacclimated to life after Terezín. Now London. He'd given me a sealed letter, with these goodbye words: "Open it when you're ready, Max."

Anna's home was an eighteenth-century terrace house that had been in her family for generations and had been given to her by her grandmother. It reminded me that somewhere things had remained as they had always been, that some families had bonds that held. Each generation had something unbroken. Something that had been passed on to them. *What has been passed down to me?* I wondered.

The house felt oddly familiar to me, reminding me of homes in Prague before the war, with the polished grand piano in the drawing room and the large windows with their miles of silk, roped to each side. Perhaps there were places in the world where you were meant to be. There were flowers and formal green hedges in the park outside, and inside, beige walls hung with paintings. It was a world of riches, one that I had thought belonged to the distant past. It was a crack of new light between my two worlds—the world of my childhood and the years at Terezín. I imagined Poppy hovering above me with a magic lantern. Poppy would have been at home here right away.

It took some time, but eventually I called on every bit of strength in me to go on. Terezín haunted my dreams, and I wondered whether I would ever get through a night without these dark dreams, without returning there time and again.

In a few weeks after my arrival, news from David arrived, forwarded by Pierre, news that brightened my spirit.

Dear Max,

The voyage was a little smoother than the SS Max. *It was early in the morning when our ship approached Haifa, and from the deck, I watched the sun rise over Mount Carmel. It was one of the most beautiful sights I have ever seen. Most everyone on the boat had survived a camp, and we all stood up and sang "Hatikvah." It means "the Hope." Can you imagine? A tune from the Vltava followed me. Then we all hugged each other. I feel I have come home. Hopefully it will lead to a homeland for all Jews.*

When we arrived and I walked onto the gangplank, I saw my father. He was crying, "My child, my child!" He had grown much older, and he was there with my mother. I will never forget that Poppy saved them. They had waited so long, and they took me into their arms and kissed me. They hadn't wanted to leave me, but Viktor convinced them he could keep me safe. He did, didn't he, Max? The Great Viktor Mueller helped keep me alive. But it was the son of the Great Viktor Mueller who saved me. You saved me, Max. I know Sophie and Hans are gone. I never had any hope that they wouldn't die at Auschwitz. But you did, Max. And your hope helped me want to live.

All the friends, families, and officials cheered. We all had something in common. We had survived. I think our hearts seem to die a little before we can grow. Let me know how you are, and maybe one of these days, on a street corner somewhere, we'll play together again. I'll always remember you, Max. You were, and will always be, my dearest friend. I miss you, Huck.

David

Sitting in Anna's summer-filled garden in Eaton Square with David's letter in my hand, I suddenly felt a new sense of calm. Something shifted within me and I was sure that Sophie's spirit had landed on my shoulder. I sat in the middle of a green patch of lawn at a round table with biscuits arranged on a silver tray and a frosted pitcher of fresh lemonade. I poured a glass.

At the end of the war, there were no marching bands, no fifes, no pipers, no gallant trumpet calls—only a dirge of muffled drums in a gray downpour of memory. Then the rain stopped. Life moves forward, and you can't will it any other way. I didn't know where the strength I summoned came from, but I found it. I began listening to music on the radio. One evening I realized that I had not thought about Terezín for an entire day.

I blinked awake on a sun-splashed bed, listening to a bird chirping in the garden outside my window. Only months before, I had been surrounded by death. It was hard to make a bridge, forge any real connection between then and now. Still, I needed to bring the story to an end. I needed to hear it.

I began by tuning the Bechstein in Anna's drawing room. Out came my tool kit and red ribbons, and slowly, I brought that piano back to life—and in some way recovered a measure of courage.

Later, I used that courage. "Anna, can you tell me about Poppy's work? Pierre told me about Pink Tulip, but . . ."

"Viktor worked for us. You probably thought he had lost

all reason when he was conscripted into the German army. Heydrich blackmailed him because he knew you were Jewish, and under the Nuremberg Purity Laws, you were marked. They always knew, those bastards. They knew who was Jewish, who had 'pure' German blood, who read what newspaper. That is just how it was. Your father made deals, but it was a double one. 'Protect Max, and I'll work for you.' A deal. 'Send David's parents to Palestine.' A deal. He was prominent enough to do it. In his way, he had something they wanted. It was his way of blackmailing them.

"When you were in Berlin, Viktor received an invitation to go to the Berghof. He sent you home, back to Prague. I think it was intentional. We had plans to assassinate Hitler but, in the end, it was too dangerous. We could never lose you or him. We pulled the plug.

"He was a good man. They all were. We were in the company of heroes."

"And Kurt Gerron?" I asked.

"We all believed his film was a preview of coming attractions."

All that was left were the closing credits.

Anna, with a deep sigh of resignation, said a single word, "Transport." That word had enough meaning on its own. It told its own story.

I had no words. Anna was silent. She knew my feelings and hugged me. Perhaps because of all the dispatches she had written, she understood where I had been, all that had happened. It seemed we had a bond that would hold us together.

Every day, I watched her walk down the steps of the terrace on the way to join her colleagues at *The Observer*. One morning she asked, "Would you like to come with me, Max? After all, you're a journalist."

In no time, I was in a room smelling of polished tables and typewriter ribbons, punching one typewriter key while trying to keep up with the precision of her *clickety-clack* on another. I wandered around the floor, peering into offices. Gooseneck lamps with green shades were arranged on the wooden tables weathered by work and time. David would have loved it. Outside the windows, I saw a city landscape of proud buildings that had been reduced to rubble. Immense yellow cranes were shoving and lifting splintered bricks, shattered windows, and broken doors high into the air. The piles of concrete rubble were the calling cards left by German bombers during the Blitz. London was going to rebuild, piece by piece.

Feeling aimless one day, I returned to *The Observer* offices. Anna's job was just as heroic as those cranes, rebuilding the world—the future—word by word, brick by brick. There had been so much destruction: of cities, of the human spirit. Anna filled in all the spaces, telling me so many things I had never known. The world had been transformed, so much had been destroyed, so many people lost. Now was a time of renewal, a time of rebirth, a time for the music to play again.

I was sure I could help that process. I was going to tune pianos in every pub, concert, and music hall in London. No matter how old or new, I would find my ladies, and we'd become friends again.

At St. Paul's Cathedral, there were flowers around a few marble steps under the charred dome. On the side, a workman had carved 1939–1945 as a reminder of the war. Gentlemen took off their hats when they passed, even if they were on the top deck of a bus. Music-hall songs played over the radio. The famous singer Vera Lynn took to the stage singing "When the Lights Go On Again (All Over the World)." Soldiers returned from battle, still in uniform, and hanging on their arms were "khaki-whacki girls." And even though I had not worn a uniform, Sophie had been my khaki-whacki girl too. The lights in London were on, and the rebuilding process had begun.

I carried memories that would stay with me for the rest of my life. They were part of me, all that I had known. One day I borrowed Anna's bicycle, a black one with a straw basket she used when going to market. I felt a need to push my legs and ride until I exhausted myself. I peddled toward St. James's Park, leaning forward over the handlebars nonstop until I came to a green bench near a fountain. I looked up as I rested and was astonished to see, silhouetted against the blue sky, a flying piano gliding in the distance, ivory keys rippling over a string of chords. I was sure it belonged to Hans. My imagination was being tested. A piano flying over London. I heard the strains of *Brundibár* echoing from far away. I thought of all that had passed, everything. I understood then that I was a part of everyone that I had met, and that I was the sum of everything that I had done and seen, every decision that I had made, all the times I had lived through, all the people that I had known and loved. They were all there, still alive, within me. No one is truly gone who lives on in the memories of others and they lived on through me as I would live on through them. Sophie, Poppy, Hans—all of them were gone but all of them had survived because I was still here. We had survived. We were the music makers.

I rode over to the Thames, a winding historical waterway of

rippling currents passing beneath a place of history and memory. Leaving my bicycle, I walked and reflected on many things, almost forgiving myself for cutting a path through St. James's Park, whose gardens were planted by the great landscape master Capability Brown, with streams of yellow daffodils surrounded by endless green lawns. London was under my feet. I passed beneath the shadows of great trees. Crossing a meadow, I came to a pond with children launching miniature boats, in the same place that England's most inspired child, the poet Percy Shelley, folded banknotes to make his own little rafts and set them sailing. Had I not done the same thing in my own way?

Ahead of me was a pavilion called the Orangery that I had heard of so many times from Anna, and inside were orange trees. I remembered the endless walks that Poppy and I took together in Prague, before the war came. And here I was at the end of the war, walking away from youth and into adulthood.

It was late one night, several days later, and I knew it was time to open the letter Pierre had given me. I reached into my bag and retrieved a battered manila envelope.

My hands shook as I recognized the handwriting and realized that I was reading the last words I would ever receive from my father.

Dear Max,

I wanted you to have the letter you are holding should anything happen to me during these terrible times. Max, forgive me for not being with you every day that you needed me, every day that we needed each other. But, ah, the times we had! Sitting on riverbanks, our marching band, what shining days they were. You and me and Hans. We put on quite a show, didn't we?

Should you come to read this, you must know that you were the most important person in my life. I wanted you safe until we could be together. How I wish I could watch you grow into the stunning man that I know you will become. Your mama would be so proud of you, Max, and I admire your courage and curiosity, your decency and spirit, everything you are. You must believe in who you are and think of who you can become, and how you can make a difference.

After the rage, after the battle, after the struggle, after the heartbreak, after the sun sets over Prague, after a thousand notes are played, listen to the music, and, Max, never forget your friends. They are part of us, who we are, all we have known, and have come to love and remember. Remember the Music Makers. They are your guardian angels.

Your Poppy
(The Great Viktor Mueller)

Memory dissolved into overlapping, overwhelming emotions, almost flickering through the lens of a motion picture camera, projecting moments to remember. My movie recalled his slender arms waving over deep-throated chords progressing and finding softer melodic keys in all their glory and resonance with notes that transcended time and space, enriching every moment. I saw his ivory baton resting in his hands, easily positioned to receive and control and attain perfect harmony with his orchestra. It always moved as if it were alive, dancing with a perfect, uplifting precision as if each stroke were reaching toward the infinite, toward the inexpressible, toward love, toward God, offering unimpeachable proof that music provides unforgettable recollections of love, and an interconnecting emotion of immeasurable beauty that was nothing short of inexplicable wonder.

My thoughts were compressed in this appreciable moment in time, yet opening into something we all aim to do, making a difference. Had I made a difference too?

I rode back to *The Observer* offices. Anna was standing over her typewriter, and she looked up at me. I put Poppy's letter on her desk.

"I guess it's just you and me now," Anna said.

I took her hand as we watched evening pass from her window.

It was twelve o'clock. The hands had come together. A new morning was about to begin.

AFTERWORD

After Israel was awarded statehood by the United Nations in 1948, the Six Day War broke out in 1967 and the country was heavily outnumbered by her neighbors.

After studying at Oxford, Max became a journalist. But his hands never left a piano.

I remember how concerned I was the day he received a letter from David, inviting him to come to Israel. He thought they should cover the war together. It would be like old times. By then Max was an editor at *The Observer.* He had become the man he wanted to be.

Max traveled to Tel Aviv to join David. Two best friends, two correspondents. Had they not always fought for freedom in their own way?

Reunited, they traveled to the Negev, where General Moshe Dayan, leader of the Israeli forces, gave them press credentials to go to the front lines.

They traveled with an Israeli tank division over the dusty desert, strong in spirit, dedicated to their shared mission. It had always been that way. They had come full circle. To fight, to report, to document, and now to defend their homeland from an attack from Egypt, Jordan, and Syria.

On the second day of that war, Max was killed while riding

in a half-track with members of the Israeli army, during a desert battle. David was following on foot with an infantry platoon a hundred yards away and saw the explosion. There are no words to describe David's devastation.

He brought Max's body home to Jerusalem, where he rests on the Avenue of the Righteous. It's a touchstone of honor for heroes. Today a steady breeze blows through the leaves of six hundred trees.

When I first learned that Max had been killed, I went to the room that was his when he came to live with me, arriving on what he had called the shores of friendship. I was surprised to find four red notebooks in a closet, stored long ago, long overlooked. I recalled when he had first mentioned them to me, on his way to becoming a journalist. They were his first writings.

Reading them, I was overwhelmed by his terrifying experiences. Yet he wrote with grace. In the box was a well-thumbed and water-marked copy of *The Adventures of Huckleberry Finn*. I wondered if he had indeed, as it seemed, left them for me to read.

I attended the memorial wearing a lovely hat that Max had given me. On a note of poignant tribute, David Grunewald asked the conductor of the Israel Philharmonic if he might join the orchestra that night.

The audience rose as the evening began with the Jewish National Anthem, the same sweeping stirring melody from the Vlatava, now known as the Moldau, and I was moved with memory.

Then David played for his friend one last time. Onstage there was a polished Steinway, alone in an oval pool of light. Draped over the piano were three red felt ribbons.

The orchestra performed a work by Mahler. Afterward, I happened to notice an elderly woman staring at me. She introduced herself as Frau Schmidt. Things do happen, I have learned, when you least expect them.

After telling me that she was the proprietor of a boardinghouse nearby, she just said, "Thank you." There was no more she needed to say. I was touched by her sentiment, knowing that she was thanking me for my friendship with Max rather than any dispatch I had ever written.

For several years, I wanted to understand the real consequences and circumstances of the war I covered.

As a journalist, I've tried all my life to understand the nature of evil. And like many of us, I cannot reason the source of the terrifying logic by which the Nazis inflicted so much pain. In six years, a heritage, religion, culture, and tradition were almost annihilated, and it is difficult to imagine the scale of the outrage against humanity.

All over Europe, physicians, teachers, artists, and children were on lists. They had no power or privilege, but what they did have was hope. They also had a love of music. The transports were a collective struggle. At every sunrise, we can remember those who saw life not always as it was but heard it as they wanted it to be.

I still treasure Max's notebooks, including the first one I gave him so many years ago with the blue-scored lines.

Rabbi Leo Baeck said that there must be three witnesses for every battle. Two were Max Mueller and David Grunewald. Now I'm the third. And this was my assignment.

Anna Kingsley

ACKNOWLEDGMENTS

There are many people who craft a book, to whose appreciation transcends lyrical boundaries. The one you hold in your hand happened because of those who played its song—and indeed, they were the music makers. Deepest admiration and affection to my supportive agent Beth Davey, who championed this novel—making sure this author never forgot the song of it all. And in harmony, great editors—Karl French, Madeline Hopkins, Professor Mary Posses. They all fine-tuned and underscored every line. My thanks to those who contributed in so many ways; Tara Baiman, Richard Steinberg, Aki Schilz representing The Literary Consultancy in London, and Kveta Pacovska, the loved artist of the Czech Republic. My love and appreciation to Zdena and Václav Flegle in Prague, who introduced me to Hans Krása's magnificent score—the children's opera that was sung with courage in a concentration camp, and whose spirit overcame direst conditions. His music and their voices were my inspiration. It has been my privilege to publish with Blackstone, whose unwavering dedication was conducted with amazing contribution. Deepest appreciation to the remarkables—Addi Black, Josie Woodbridge, Megan Wahrenbrock, Jeffrey Yamaguchi, Lauren Maturo, Deirdre Curley, and book designer, Sean Thomas—for who you are—for what you do. And for Natalya and Andrew Lande, who make me better than I am. With the writing of this book, I have been in the company of heroes whose stories I can never forget. Thank you.

Nathaniel Lande
Santa Barbara, California

AUTHOR'S NOTES

While Max Mueller and many of the characters in this novel are my own invention, real people and events are threaded through the narrative—although I have taken some liberties with details and dates to accommodate a Terezín timeline. Also, for example, the Elbe and Ohře tributaries make their way into the Vltava River, which runs through Prague. Yet I have taken artistic license with the flow of unpredictable currents.

Today, an exceptionally large number of performances of *Brundibár* are seen around the world, mainly in Europe and the USA, but also in Israel, Canada, South America, Australia, and Japan, and they are staged by both professional and amateur companies. When *Brundibár* is performed, the opera is received with heartfelt appreciation. In the Czech Republic, the most renowned *Brundibár* production is performed by the Disman

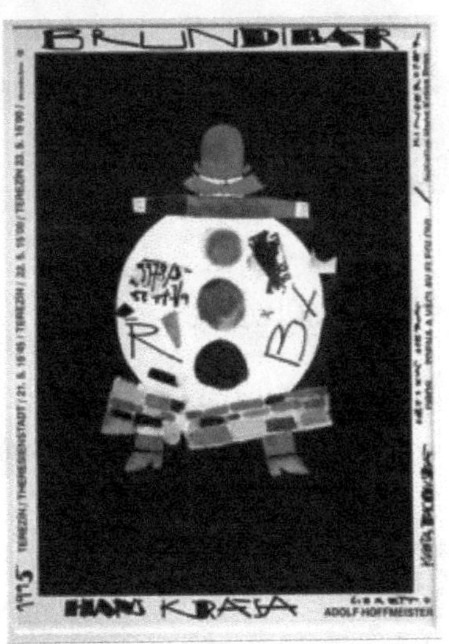

Artwork by Květa Pacovská

Ensemble of Prague under the direction of Václav and Zdena Flegl. This production is also "officially" recognized as the closest to the original. In contemporary *Brundibár* productions, such as Tony Kushner's adaptation, there is an attempt to create a link between the opera and its background to understand the special circumstances at Terezín, but the original Theresienstadt production seems to be much more authentic and powerful, one that was used as a metaphor of personal and collective resistance. Selections from the score can be heard on Amazon.com and the album is available to purchase.

Brundibár expressed with music and image what could not be easily said in the spoken word. Terezín audiences were given courage and hope for the future. The moral of the opera was close to the children's hearts; it reflected their perception of the world, their need for justice and right.

There are over eighty texts of the opera in German schools, and it is studied in many other languages and presented in major concert halls around the world: London, Essen, Trieste, Leipzig, Utrecht, Antwerp, Washington, New York, Geneva, Montreal, Vienna, Paris, Berlin, Frankfurt, Oslo, Stockholm, Brussels, Barcelona.

HANS KRÁSA

Hans Krása was a Czech composer. He studied both the piano and violin as a child and went on to study composition at the German Music Academy in Prague. *Brundibár* was based on a play by Aristophanes and was the last work Krása completed before he was arrested by the Nazis in World War II. He was deported to the Terezín concentration camp, where a remarkable musical community flourished among its Jewish prisoners. The children's opera was performed fifty-five times in the camp and for a visit by the International Red Cross before Krása and most of the cast were transported to Auschwitz, where they perished. The opera's final scene was later captured in the Nazi propaganda film *Theresienstadt,* under the deceptive title *Der Führer Schenkt den Juden eine Stadt,* "The Führer Gives the Jews a City." Ironically, the scene included in the film where *Brundibár* is defeated never made it to the German screens during the war. The opera was a moral triumph over the horror in this time and place. While he was interned, Krása was at his most productive, composing a number of chamber works although, due to the circumstances, some of these have not survived. He was killed at Auschwitz.

KURT GERRON

The famed actor and director made a film of the Red Cross visit at Terezín. It is currently held in the United States Holocaust Memorial Museum archives in Washington, DC. Gerron died in Auschwitz in 1944.

RABBI LEO BAECK

A twentieth-century German rabbi, author, scholar, and theologian who survived Terezín. The Leo Baeck Institute for the study of the history and culture of German-speaking Jewry was established in 1955 in New York and London.

VIKTOR FRANKL

The noted psychologist and physician was the author of *Man's Search for Meaning.* A Terezín survivor, he had held a position as professor of neurology and psychiatry at the University of Vienna Medical School before World War II.

RAFAEL SCHÄCHTER

A Czechoslovak composer, pianist, and conductor of Jewish origin, and an organizer of cultural life in Terezín. He led approximately sixteen performances of Verdi's *Requiem,* the first in January 1942 with a chorus of one hundred and fifty and a piano for accompaniment. Over the following months, even as his choir shrank, the *Requiem* was performed approximately fifteen additional times. The final performance, however, served as propaganda, as Schächter was forced to perform excerpts of the oratorio before the visiting members of the International Red Cross. A few months after this final performance, on October 16, 1944, under transport serial number 943, Schächter was loaded into a railroad cattle car with the entire cast. They were taken on a three-day journey to the Auschwitz death camp where they were murdered.

RAOUL WALLENBERG

Raoul Wallenberg was a Swedish diplomat who worked for the British Resistance. In Nazi-occupied Hungary, he led an extensive and successful mission to save the lives of nearly one hundred thousand Hungarian Jews. Though his efforts to save Jews from the Holocaust is among one of the most treasured achievements of the Resistance, his ultimate fate remains unknown still to this day. On January 17, 1945, on his way out of the capital with a Russian escort, Wallenberg and his driver planned to stop at "Swedish Houses" to say goodbye to his friends. He never arrived there, nor was he ever heard of again.

REINHARD HEYDRICH

Reinhard Heydrich a high-ranking German Nazi official during World War II, and the main architect of the Holocaust. He chaired the January 1942 Wannsee Conference, which formalized plans for the final solution to the Jewish question—the deportation and genocide of all Jews in German-occupied Europe. He helped organize Kristallnacht, a series of coordinated attacks against Jews throughout Nazi Germany. Upon his arrival in Prague, Heydrich sought to eliminate opposition to the Nazi occupation by suppressing Czech culture and deporting and executing members of the Czech Resistance. He was directly responsible for the Einsatzgruppen, the special task forces which traveled in the wake of the German armies and murdered over two million people, including 1.3 million Jews, by mass shooting and gassing. Heydrich was critically wounded in Prague on May 27, 1942, as a result of Operation Anthropoid. He was ambushed by a team of Czech agents trained by the British Special Operations Executive. Heydrich died from his injuries a week later.

PHOTOGRAPHS AND ILLUSTRATIONS FROM TEREZÍN

Children at Terezín

Original photograph at Terezín

Work Makes You Free,
(Arbeit Macht Frei)

Original cast of *Brundibár*

MAJOR CONCENTRATION CAMPS AND JEWISH DEATHS AT EACH

Auschwitz: 1.6 million
Bergen-Belsen: 50,000
Buchenwald: 65,000
Dachau: 35,000
Dora-Nordhausen: 20,000
Flossenburg: 27,000
Gross-Rosen: 105,000
Janowska: 40,000
Kaiserwald: 10,000
Klooga: 2,400
Mauthausen: 120,000
Natzweiler-Struthof: 17,000
Neuengamme: 55,000
Ninth Fort: 10,000
Pawiak Prison: 37,000
Płaszów: 8,000
Poniatowa: 15,000
Ravensbrück: 92,000
Sachsenhausen-Oranienburg: 105,000
Sajmište-Semlin: 50,000
Sered': 13,500
Stutthof: 85,000
Terezín: 48,930
Trawniki: 10,000

TOTAL DEATHS FROM NAZI GENOCIDAL POLICIES

European Jews: 6,250,000
Soviet Prisoners of War: 3,000,000
Polish Catholics: 3,000,000
Serbians: 700,000
Roma, Sinti, and Lalleri: 250,000
Germans: Political, Religious, and Resistance: 80,000
Germans: Handicapped: 70,000
Homosexuals: 12,000
Jehovah's Witnesses: 2,500

The author appreciates and acknowledges the research and dispatches adapted from the Holocaust Chronicles Publications International, Ltd., and the support of the Holocaust museum in Washington, DC.